T0359501

MEDICAL
Pulse-racing passion

Paramedic's Fling To Forever
Sue MacKay

Her Summer With
The Brooding Vet
Scarlet Wilson

MILLS & BOON

PARAMEDIC'S FLING TO FOREVER
© 2024 by Sue MacKay
Philippine Copyright 2024
Australian Copyright 2024
New Zealand Copyright 2024

First Published 2024
First Australian Paperback Edition 2024
ISBN 978 1 038 91740 9

HER SUMMER WITH THE BROODING VET
© 2024 by Scarlet Wilson
Philippine Copyright 2024
Australian Copyright 2024
New Zealand Copyright 2024

First Published 2024
First Australian Paperback Edition 2024
ISBN 978 1 038 91740 9

MIX
Paper | Supporting
responsible forestry
FSC® C001695

Published by
Harlequin Mills & Boon
An imprint of Harlequin Enterprises (Australia) Pty Limited
(ABN 47 001 180 918), a subsidiary of HarperCollins
Publishers Australia Pty Limited
(ABN 36 009 913 517)
Level 19, 201 Elizabeth Street
SYDNEY NSW 2000 AUSTRALIA

Cover art used by arrangement with Harlequin Books S.A.. All rights reserved.

Printed and bound in Australia by McPherson's Printing Group

Paramedic's Fling To Forever

Sue MacKay

MILLS & BOON

Sue MacKay lives with her husband in New Zealand's beautiful Marlborough Sounds, with the water on her doorstep and the birds and the trees at her back door. It is the perfect setting to indulge her passions of entertaining friends by cooking them sumptuous meals, drinking fabulous wine, going for hill walks or kayaking around the bay—and, of course, writing stories.

Visit the Author Profile page
at millsandboon.com.au for more titles.

Dear Reader,

Nick has lost everyone special to him, so believing he's lovable and able to risk his heart yet again is nigh on impossible. Yet when he meets Leesa, everything changes—except the caution wrapped around his heart.

For Leesa, who's been bullied by her ex-husband and a boss, it's all about being strong for herself and not letting another man try to take over her life. But when she falls for Nick, it's hard and deep, and she's willing to take another chance on love—if only Nick was, too.

Enjoy reading how these two resolve their differences to find their HEA.

All the best,

Sue MacKay

DEDICATION

To Auntie Joc. Thank you for all the
wonderful memories. Love, Susan.

PROLOGUE

'Hi. Mind if I sit here?'

Leesa Bennett looked up at the guy standing in front of her with a beer in his hand and nodded. 'Sure.'

She was hardly going to say no when this was a communal party, in the park next to the apartment block where she lived. Though only for one more week before she was on the road heading north, home to Cairns. Back to her family and the world she'd missed ever since coming to Brisbane with her ex. If only she had known what awaited her here, she'd never have packed one bag, let alone all her belongings, to move south.

'Thanks.' The newcomer's voice was deep and husky, and a dark beard covered his lower face. A sexy combination, if ever she'd seen one.

Gasping, she swallowed a large mouthful of gin from her can and promptly coughed. Sexy? Definitely. But she didn't usually get in a twist about a hot-looking man. Didn't get in a twist at all these days, especially about men. One too many had made her life hell to be letting any others close.

'Easy.' A steady hand patted her back.

'Thanks.'

She sat up straighter and took a smaller sip. The guy wasn't familiar to her, but then she didn't know everyone living in the block or attending the barbecue, which had been organised by the apartment tenants' committee. He hadn't been helping the other men cooking the steaks and sausages, but not all the men had. There wouldn't have been room.

'Did you have some food?' she asked.

'No.'

Not a great talker then. Suited her. She was feeling low and not in the mood for idle chatter, especially with a stranger. Even a sexy one.

There she went again. Sexy. Showed how long it was since she'd let her hair down and had some fun with a guy. Was it time to do so?

Now that she was finally leaving Brisbane it was dawning on her how she was closing a chapter of her life. A chapter that had been tough and full of hurt and that she was ready to leave behind. Still, she felt sad. The earlier dreams she'd had, of a wonderful marriage and a new life in an exciting city, had all turned into a nightmare.

She'd left her husband after accepting that he would never stop bullying her, even when she stood up to him. After being bullied at school, she knew there was only one way to go with Connor and that was to leave him. He'd get worse as time went on, not better. He'd tried to deny her a divorce, saying they had too much to lose and that he loved her to the end of the earth and back. So why demand she make the bed with hospital folds like his mother used to, and expect roast lamb for dinner every Tuesday, and make her wash the car on Saturday mornings even if she had to go to work? The list went on, but she'd put it behind her when she left him.

Only to end up working with another bully who thought he could tell all the female staff at the ambulance base what to do and when. Not the men. Oh, no, they were free to sit back and let the women clean the ambulances and restock everything. Not that any of them did, but that wasn't the point. That prat hadn't counted on her having already learned how to deal with someone like him. When he'd sacked her for standing up to him, she'd fought her dismissal with management and won, because they'd heard rumours about the man's attitude. After that she went on to stick up for the others he bullied and, in the end, he was the one to leave with his tail firmly between his legs.

Despite everything that had gone down over the last two years, in some ways she was sorry to be moving away. Brisbane was a great place to live, despite the feeling something was missing for her. She did have a great job lined up with the Flying Health Care service in Cairns, and spending more time with her family was high on her priority list, especially now her mother had been diagnosed with early-stage Parkinson's. Her grandmother's house was waiting for her, as Gran had moved into a retirement village and didn't want the house sold yet.

'You live in one of the apartments?' her companion asked.

'I do. A one-bedroom unit. It's great.' She watched some of the women dancing on the lawn to the music belting out from speakers hanging from trees. 'But I'm moving on in a few days, going back home to Cairns where my family are.'

'I've just moved up here.'

'So, you're not on holiday then?' She didn't really need to know, but might as well keep the conversation ticking over and put her glum thoughts behind her.

He shook his head. 'No, I'm spending a couple of nights with a mate while I find somewhere permanent.' He drained his beer. 'I'm starting a new job in a couple of weeks.'

So, he could do talking when he chose. 'Doing what?'

'I'm a doctor. Going to work with the emergency service.'

'Right.' Small world. She decided not to mention she'd finished working in the same area one day ago. Her reputation went before her and, while most people thought she was great for helping her work mates face up to that prat, there were a few who thought she was nothing more than a troublemaker. 'Think I'll get another drink. Can I get you something?'

He stood up. 'I'll come with you.'

Not the answer she'd expected. He seemed reticent about talking too much, but he had sat with her so it could be he knew no one and wanted some company. She understood that. After all that had gone down over the last two years, she was cautious about who she talked to. People always took sides even when they didn't know the whole story.

That had been a major lesson she'd learned in all the turmoil. She used to be a slow learner, too willing to trust people even after being bullied at school. She hadn't recognised the signs when she married Connor. But she knew better now and was not going to hand over her heart so readily ever again, if at all.

'Grab some food while we're at it,' Leesa suggested.

'No, thanks.'

'Not into barbecues?'

Who wasn't? They were an Ozzie tradition.

His sigh hung between them. 'I had a big lunch.'

Okay, she'd shut up now. She might be feeling flat, but this was a party, and keeping quiet wasn't really her thing—not for long periods anyway. Digging into her chilly bin she grabbed another gin and popped the top.

'Who's your friend that lives here?' So she didn't know when to shut up after all. No surprise there.

At least he replied with a small smile, giving her a name she didn't recognise. 'Logan Brand. We met in med school.'

'I don't know if my apartment has been rented out yet, if you're interested. I'm on the tenth floor,' she added.

'I'll think about it.'

Taking a mouthful of her drink, she watched those who were dancing on the lawn and decided to join them. 'Into dancing by any chance?'

His eyes widened and he actually laughed. 'Yes, I am. Let's give it a whirl.' Without waiting for a reply, he took her arm and led her over to where people were shaking and wiggling, laughing uproariously about who knew what.

Leesa struggled to ignore the hot sensations his hand caused on her arm. Not only did he look sexy, he had a touch that sent her off balance. Blimey. So much for a quiet night. She was about to wiggle her ass in front of this guy. Best she went and sat down again.

Except they were already in the midst of the crowd and being jostled left and right. Her new friend's hand was now on her waist, making sure she didn't get nudged too far away from him. Moving in time to the music, she drank in the sight before her. Her companion might be quiet, but did he have the moves or what? Those firm hips swung all over the place, keeping a perfect rhythm to the music, while his feet were light on the ground and his upper body was a sight she couldn't ignore. She did try, but, hey, some things weren't meant to happen.

Settle, girl. You're leaving town in five days.

Yes, so why not have some no-strings fun with a sexy man?

Because she didn't usually hook up for one-night stands. That was why. Would it hurt to stretch the boundaries for once? Taking in the sight before her, it was hard to come up with an answer to that. Other than, 'Yes, go for it.'

'Why are you smiling so much?' he asked.

'Because I'm happy.' It was true. She really was. Gone was the sadness over this being the end of another phase of her life. Suddenly she felt there were opportunities out there she hadn't considered. Like letting go of her hang up over trusting a man not to demand her utmost attention all the time. She was probably overreacting because this man was hot, but did it matter? Tomorrow was another day. Tonight was to be enjoyed now. 'Nothing better than dancing.'

Nothing she was mentioning at any rate. He'd probably run away faster than a greyhound on the track. Even if he didn't, the last thing she wanted was him knowing what was going on in her mind, and other parts of her body.

He took her hand and whirled them around. 'Couldn't agree more.'

Thankfully he'd be thinking about the dancing and would have no idea of the thoughts racing through her head. Fingers crossed.

Suddenly the music stopped mid-song. 'That's it, folks. It's midnight and as you know the council forbids music to be played in their parks after that.'

Leesa blinked. 'Where'd the time go?' She'd have sworn they had at least another hour to go. Went to show how much fun she'd been having dancing with Dr Sexy. What was his name? Did it matter? Dr Sexy suited him better than any other name she could come up with.

'Feel like another drink before you head upstairs?' he asked.

'Sounds good to me.' She had nothing important on in the morning so it didn't matter if she slept in.

'I'll get your chilly bin.' He sauntered across the grass, looking more at ease than when he'd first sat down beside her a couple of hours back.

Had she made him feel comfortable? Or had he just got over whatever had been keeping him quiet? Whatever. She liked him. She knew nothing about him, but that didn't matter. She was out of here on Wednesday and wouldn't be looking back, no matter what.

'Here you go.' He handed over a can and sat down beside her on the park bench, a beer in hand.

'Thanks.' She popped the can. 'Is your mate still here?'

'He and his girlfriend headed away to his apartment a little while go. I'm giving them some time alone.'

'You can come and checkout the apartment I'm in if you like.' *This late at night? Why not?*

He studied her intently. 'You sure? You don't know me.'

'You dance okay.' After dancing with him she really wanted to have some more fun.

A grin appeared. 'Then yes, I'll take a look at your place. I like the location and I know from my mate's apartment the place's kept in good shape.' So far, he was keeping to the script.

She could do that too. 'I've had no complaints in the time I've been here.'

'Which is how long?' He'd got a whole lot chattier. Must've liked her dance moves too.

When I left Connor.

'Over a year, give or take.' She stood up, suddenly restless. She wasn't into talking about her past. Plus, this man was attractive beyond reason, making it hard not to reach out and tuck herself into that amazing chest. Which would really have him thinking she was a fruit loop. Or a loose woman. Something she most definitely was not, but for some reason tonight she was ready to make the most of whatever this man had to offer. 'Let's go.'

'Give me your chilly bin.' He took it without waiting for an answer.

'Thank you.' Not that she'd have turned down his offer, even if the bin weighed less than a banana. It was nice being treated so well for a change. She had let her barriers down a little. Dr Sexy had been nothing but decent all evening. Throw in the growing need to have some me-time and he was getting more attractive by the minute.

In the crowded elevator Leesa found herself pressed firmly against his hard muscular body, liking every moment. His long body was a good fit. It wasn't often she felt comfortable with her height, but for once she did. Being taller than all the other girls at school had been another reason kids teased her. Apparently, girls were supposed to be slim and medium height. It had got better out in the adult world, but the sense of being different hadn't quite left her, especially when her ex had told her that she should be grateful he found her attractive.

As the lift became less packed at each floor Dr Sexy didn't move away, instead he stayed right beside her with his hand touching hers without actually holding it.

'Level ten,' intoned the metallic speaker.

They stepped out into the corridor. Without thinking she took her companion's hand, and didn't let go. His warmth felt so good she didn't care if this was a suggestive move. Which, come to think of it, it was. The realisation didn't change a thing. She couldn't remember ever feeling so relaxed but so fired up, her body melting on the inside for the first time in for ever. 'This way. My apartment's on the front of the building.'

He didn't drop her hand until they reached her door. Delving into her pocket for the key, she shivered. What was she doing? Showing this guy the apartment, or looking for that fun she wanted? Leesa's breathing stalled. He was watching her with the same need reflected in his deep blue eyes. Did she let him in? Or was this the opportunity to come to her senses and say goodnight?

'I can go if you'd prefer.'

His face was open and honest. The light beard covering his chin made her palms itch. Desire spiralled throughout her. Elbowing the door open she stepped inside. 'Come in.'

He followed her inside and closed the door quietly. Turning to face her, he said with a crooked smile that added to his sexiness, 'We haven't introduced ourselves. My name is Nick.'

Funny how they hadn't got around to mentioning names before. 'Leesa.' A lot of thumping was going on in her chest as she fell into those eyes. Beautiful. They stirred up her desire so it was now an eddy whirling from her mouth to her toes.

The chilly bin hit the floor with a soft thump as Nick reached for her, his hands on her shoulders pulling her close to that sensational body.

Slipping her arms around his neck she pressed into him, her breasts hard against his expansive chest, making her nipples tight as she lifted her mouth to his.

His sex was hard against her lower abdomen, telling her there was no doubt why he'd come up to her apartment. He wanted a first-hand view of the bedroom.

A view she was all too happy to share. But only when she'd had her fill of his kisses. He kissed like there was no tomorrow, devouring her while at the same time tender and teasing. She held him tighter, pushed closer and kissed him in return, giving way to the need taking over, going with him all the way until finally she had to have more.

Pulling back, she grabbed his hand. 'Come on.' Heading to her bedroom, she rued the fact she had to wait even seconds to get down and naked, but the condoms were in her bathroom cabinet in the ensuite. 'I need to get protection.'

'I've got some,' Nick told her.

'Cool.' A prepared man. She lifted her t-shirt over her head and dropped it on the floor. 'Then there's nothing to wait for.'

'You are in a hurry.'

She blinked. Did she sound too eager, when she rarely did something like this? 'Sorry.' Hello? Sounding like the girl who tried to placate people to keep them onside.

'Don't be.' Perfect answer. Nick touched her face so softly her eyes moistened. He really was special.

Better not let him get to her more than he already had. 'I'm not usually so fast to get this close to someone,' she whispered.

'Relax, Leesa. I'm not either. If you want to change your mind that's okay.'

'Hell no.' She was grinning like crazy. He really was awesome. She wasn't talking any more. His lips were soft as she kissed him. But not for long. Within moments he was returning her kiss with a depth that would've turned her on if she wasn't already wound up so tight—she was about to spring apart.

Somehow, they ended up naked on the bed, unable to keep their hands to themselves. Drinking in the sight of Nick's body she spread her fingers over his chest, his hips, his thighs and onto the throbbing erection teasing her, begging her to let him in.

All the while Nick's fingers were working magic on her heavy breasts, tormenting her with soft caresses, heating her already overheated skin, making her head spin. She wanted him. Now. But she didn't want him to stop touching her breasts.

Then his fingers walked lightly down her body to where her pulse was throbbing so hard the whole street could probably hear. He touched, ran his finger over her sex. Almost immediately she was coming. Her whole body quivered with the explosion of desire. 'Nick, now. Please,' she begged.

When he slid inside, tears spilt down the sides of her face. This was awesome. More than awesome. There was no word to explain the out-of-this-world sensations filling her from scalp to toes. Wrapping her legs around him she hung on for the ride, loving when he pushed into her, holding her breath when he pulled back. Then she rocked as she shattered.

Nick stood looking down at the woman who'd shared her bed and herself with him. Leesa. A lovely name to suit a lovely lady. She was special.

Sure, it had been one of those nights where a few drinks and sensational dancing had played a part in them getting together. But there'd been something more about her that attracted him. She was nothing like his usual one-night stands. She hadn't pushed him for any info, she'd taken what he'd said in reply to her questions and let him be. She was friendly without going over the top— until they fell into her bed and then there was no holding back.

He smiled widely. Then stopped. Unbelievable how a few hours with Leesa made him wonder if it was time to stop and question what he was doing with his life, why he was driven to keep moving on from job to job, city to city, every couple of years.

The fact his wife had waited until she'd had an abortion to tell him she'd been pregnant, and been having affairs for a while, had had him up and leaving and filing for divorce as soon as possible. But he'd always moved on from city to city, looking for something he wasn't sure he'd find.

'*What about you, Leesa? When you love some-*

one, is it with all you've got?' he asked silently. Because she had stirred him up, made him think about the impossible, even long for the life he'd always dreamed of again. Did that mean she could be the one to turn him around and help him settle down?

Of course, he knew the answer to that. Nothing was going to change because of an exceptional one-night stand. After his grandfather died, he'd spent most of his life alone, living with people in the welfare system who hadn't opened their hearts to him, who couldn't love him. Nothing about tonight changed that.

And yet his heart felt lighter and brought a flare of hope for something, someone, in his future. Something that hadn't happened since his marriage went west. The passion he'd known during the night could be a game changer if he was prepared to listen to his heart and not his head for once—as his mentor, Patrick Crombie, kept saying. The judge had saved his butt, and he'd always respect him for that, as well as the in-depth conversations they'd had over the years since.

But the night had been about Leesa. He would love more than one hot night with her. Might find more with her than only amazing sex. He shivered. What? Lower the barriers in place around his heart? Let Leesa in and risk being hurt yet again? Not likely.

But really, what was there to lose? She was heading away in a few days. They could have some fun and say goodbye at the end. Nothing unusual for him, but for once he wanted more.

Because of Leesa? Because he'd shared her bed once?

She'd been so refreshingly open, saying what she wanted without getting coy, he'd taken a second look at her. Different, for sure. But his nomadic lifestyle with few close friends hadn't made him out and out happy. If only it was as easy as stepping forward and holding out his hand to get the life he yearned for. But protecting himself had become ingrained as he'd grown up, first losing his parents, then his grandfather. He'd loved his wife, trusted her to reciprocate his love, and got that horribly wrong.

Leesa breathed heavily and rolled over onto her other side, that silky long hair spilling over the pillow.

Yes, his heart definitely felt eager for more. This wonderful woman had had his chest squeezing with something akin to love, had him thinking he might one day change his life around and find happiness. Another shiver as emotions flooded him. He wanted that so much it frightened the pants off him, despite believing he must be unlovable if his parents, grandfather and wife had left him for one reason or another.

Whatever steps he took it wouldn't be Leesa who followed him into whatever came next. She was heading away, while he'd just arrived in Brisbane.

Relief poured through him. He wouldn't be tempted to make a mistake and get hurt again. Then disappointment shoved aside the relief.

He more than liked Leesa. Way more. He had to get out of here before he gave into these warm feelings of longing—the hope of dropping this inability to settle down with someone and make love and happiness happen. He really wanted it all, and suddenly, all because he'd met this wonderful woman, he could see it just might be possible. Every thought came back to Leesa.

Time to go. Not only to reflect on what had happened in the space of a few passionate hours, and make sense of these new emotions, but to try and accept he was ready to make some changes in his life.

Moving quietly so as not to disturb her, he headed for the door, then paused. In the light thrown by the full moon coming through the window he saw a notepad and pen on the kitchen bench. He couldn't help himself. He crossed to the bench, picked up the pen and wrote.

Thank you for a wonderful night. N.

He didn't know if he was saying goodbye or setting himself up for more enjoyment.

* * *

By six o'clock that night he had his answer. Pulling up outside the apartment block he turned off the engine and got out to stare up at level ten. Leesa had run around inside his head all damned day, even when he'd been looking at available rental properties. Laughing, dancing, kissing him, opening up to him. Smiling, sometimes not smiling, just sitting beside him as they watched others dancing.

Oh, man, how she'd got to him. So much so that he had to see her. He'd knock on her door on the pretext he wanted to look around the apartment, properly this time, as a possible option to rent. The location was ideal for his upcoming job, and his mate was on hand, but that had nothing to do with why he was heading up to her floor and not stopping at level four where he was staying with Logan.

He and Leesa hadn't swapped phone numbers so he was taking a punt she'd be at home. If she wasn't he'd come back later, unless he'd managed to talk himself out of it. Which he doubted was possible.

Leesa's face split into a warm smile when she opened her door to his knock. 'Nick. I didn't expect to see you again.'

Ignoring the thumping under his ribs, he asked,

'Is it okay to take a look around the apartment to see if it suits me?'

She stepped back for him to enter, her laughter tickling him on the inside. 'Let's be honest, you never really intended to inspect the place last night.'

He would've if that was all that had been on offer, but, 'You're right.' So did that mean he'd get it right this time?

'I just ordered pizza to be delivered. Want to join me? I can add to the order.'

Just like that he relaxed some more. 'Absolutely. Seafood would be great.'

'Take a look around while I deal with that.' She already had her phone to her ear. 'It won't take you more than a minute. It's kind of small in here.'

Except it did, because he paused in the doorway of her bedroom and stared at the bed where he'd had the time of his life with Leesa. He could picture her long, slight body pressed against his, under his, over his. Her tongue on his heated skin. Her fingers touching, rubbing, making him explode with desire.

'Nick? There a problem?' Leesa called from the lounge.

'Not at all.' Not anything he was mentioning. Stepping away, he turned and poked his head into the bathroom, where everything looked fine for his needs. At the end of the day apartments were apartments, and this one was in good condition and had everything he wanted. But there were still a couple more to look at tomorrow before he made a decision.

Or was he prevaricating? Because Leesa lived here? How that mattered didn't make sense since she'd soon be gone. Yes, but it would be where she'd lived, where they'd made love, where hot memories could tease him.

Once again, she interrupted his errant thoughts. 'Want a beer?'

He should leave while he still could. She was rattling his cage a bit too much. 'Love one.'

'What do you think?' she asked when they were sitting on the narrow deck watching the world go by below.

That I'd like another night in your bed.

He took a swig from his bottle, swallowed hard. 'About what?'

'The apartment, silly. Isn't that why you're here?'

Is it?

'It's fine. I've seen a few today and have agreed to look at more tomorrow, but really, it's a no-brainer. The location is ideal, my mate's handy, and I don't have any lawns to mow.'

Her eyes had widened. 'When I first met you last night, you didn't say as much in an hour.'

Yeah, well, you didn't know me then.

Still didn't, but he was working on it, because

he couldn't walk away. They had a few days to enjoy if she was up to it, and hopefully by then he'd have worked this need out of his system. 'Like I said then, I didn't want to scare you off.'

'As if.' Her grin was wicked and winding him up fast.

'How long before those pizzas arrive?' Because eating was suddenly the last thing he wanted to do.

Her grin just got more wicked. 'Patience, man.'

'Are we on the same page?' He had to know or he'd blow a gasket.

'You mean, do I want to share my salami pizza?' Damn, her eyes were the sexiest he'd ever encountered.

'You got it in one.' The sound of a bell ringing cut through the air. 'Thank goodness,' he muttered. 'Unless you've invited the neighbours in.'

'No, just my mates from work,' she grinned. 'Relax, Nick. I'll go deal to with the delivery and then we can get down and sexy.'

He watched her walk inside, that sassy bottom making him hard just thinking about touching her. Twenty-four hours ago, he hadn't even met Leesa and now—now he wanted to fall into bed with her again and make love like there was no tomorrow. He wanted to leave his mark on her so she'd never forget him. He wanted to make more memories to hold close after she left town.

And yet he knew the old fear of being let down was lurking behind all the happy thoughts. There would be nothing to gain if he didn't take some chances, but that was a huge ask. Could he do it? Could he leave the past behind and get on with the future?

'I'd say by the look that just crossed your face we'd better eat first.' Leesa looked disappointed as she stood in front of him holding two pizzas.

On his feet in an instant, Nick took the boxes from her and placed them on the table. Then he leaned in and kissed her, lightly at first, then deeper and deeper until his head spun and Leesa was gripping him tight. He raised his head. 'Which do you want?'

She took his hand and raced to her bedroom. 'I've spent half the day thinking about this while not really expecting to see you again. I'm not going to waste any more time thinking.' She spun around in front of him, tearing her t-shirt over her head, exposing her lace-clad breasts.

He should've come up hours ago, to hell with looking at apartments. The best one in town was right here. 'Thinking's highly overrated,' he groaned before his mouth found her nipple and she bucked against him.

Wednesday morning and Leesa was up at five thirty to see Nick out the door for the last time.

She had a few last things to pack before the removal company arrived to box up the furniture and transfer it all to her gran's house in Cairns, and then she'd hit the road before the heat became unbearable. 'Thanks for some amazing nights,' she said before giving him one last kiss. A not-so-passionate kiss, since she was leaving town this morning and their fling was over.

They'd shared four incredible nights with little sleep and a lot of mind-blowing sex. How was she going to move on from that? *'Apart from the four days driving that lay ahead,'* she laughed to herself. There'd be plenty of time driving to consider her options about the future.

'Back at you,' Nick said as he returned her kiss. Stepping back, his arms dropped to his side. 'Thanks for everything, Leesa.'

'All the best with your new job.' She was filling in the air between them, wanting him to leave before she grabbed him tight and changed her mind about heading north. At the same time glad she could take in more of that honed body and beautiful face to brood over later.

'Drive safely,' he returned.

'Sure.'

'Good.'

Um… 'Bye, then.'

Nick spun away, took two steps, called over his shoulder, 'Bye, Leesa.' This time he kept walking all the way along the corridor to the lift.

Before he reached it, she was inside the apartment, closing the door and scrubbing her face with her fingers. The nights with Nick had opened her heart to really getting on with finding the life she wanted, once she got home to where her family and friends were. The new life might one day include a man she'd give her heart to and who'd love her to bits in return. Plus, children to love as well. A complete family. Yep, couldn't ask for more than that. If she was ready to try again.

At six thirty she slid into her car, buckled up and then flicked some music on—loud. Pulling out of the underground garage she glanced up at the apartment building one last time. 'See you, Nick. You're an amazing lover. I've had the most wonderful time with you.' Funny thing was they'd not talked about themselves at all. As though they both wanted to have fun without getting deep. Maybe that had been a mistake. And maybe it hadn't.

Indicating left, she turned onto the street and began the long haul home. All the way Nick stayed with her, reminding her there were decent men out there and that she only had to step up and be herself and she'd find one of them.

Sure you haven't already?

Unfortunately, the music couldn't get any louder to block out that annoying voice.

CHAPTER ONE

Fourteen months later

NICK TILTED HIS head and slid the shaver down his neck. Day one of another new job. How many jobs would he have held by the time retirement age came around? His hand pulled the razor down a second time, pausing as he stared at himself in the mirror.

He was tired of always moving on.

His eyes widened as the truth struck. He was? A truth he'd been denying since those wonderful nights in Leesa's bed. No, he hadn't forgotten her, no matter how hard he'd tried.

After rinsing the shaver, he made another clean line on his neck. Yes, he was ready to make some changes. The judge had been right there. It was time to settle in one place, and stay on in a job he enjoyed for more than a couple of years.

Since Patrick, as he now called the judge, had had a serious cancer scare a few months back, he'd become more persistent that Nick should stop wandering the country and follow his dreams of love and family. To see this strong man, who Nick had always thought the world of, looking so lethargic and ill had been such a shock. It'd woken Nick up in a hurry to the fact that no one knew what was around the corner, and that dreams should be followed, not avoided.

But did that include finding a woman he could love? Yeah, well, that requisite had been high on the list of reasons not to settle, because no one ever stayed with him for long, though there were no rules saying he had to fall in love to put down roots. Except he'd love to have a child and raise him or her, giving them all he could to make their life wonderful. Not like the life he'd had growing up in the welfare system after his grandfather died, but a life full of love and understanding, support and care.

The one man who'd understood him enough to give him a second chance, the reason why he was now a doctor and starting work today at Flying Health Care, had been Patrick. Judge Crombie could've sent him to an institution when he'd been caught stealing a car because he wanted to learn to drive, but had instead handed him some strong words of advice. 'Pull your head in, stop being an idiot and start behaving, or you are going to ruin your life for ever.'

Nick had always believed that Patrick had seen

something in him that no one else had. If not for him who knew where he'd be now. Nick shook away the memory of being a hothead to get attention. No point looking back. His appalling behaviour had actually put him on the right path, something he'd be grateful for for ever, but that didn't make him ready to risk his heart by falling in love and believing he'd be loved in return. It didn't happen to him. His previous attempt had proven that, and he wasn't stupid enough to believe he'd get it right next time.

The fire alarm shrieked. And kept on shrieking.

'Great.' Nick dropped his shaver and hauled on his shorts. Probably a false alarm, but he'd better play safe or someone would have to come looking for him. He tugged a t-shirt over his head, snatched his wallet and keys from the bench, ran to the door and swung it open.

The smell of smoke struck him. This was real. Supressing a shudder, he slammed the door shut and joined the crowd racing to the stairwell, including the neighbours he'd met briefly last night—two parents who were tightly gripping their children's hands.

'Can I take your daughter?' he asked his neighbour who had a wee girl clinging to her hand while her husband held the hands of two kids a bit older.

'You'd be a champ.' The woman shoved a child in his direction. 'Cally, this is Nick. Please hold Nick's hand tight and do what he says.'

No one stopped as hands were swapped. 'Cally, is it okay if I carry you?' Nick asked as lightly as he could. Walking down the stairs would be slow for the small girl, nor would it be safe in the panicked crowd.

'Yes.'

'Thanks, Nick,' Cameron looked over his shoulder as Nick swept the tiny five-year-old up and out of the way of people intent on getting down the stairs ASAP. 'Really appreciate it.'

Like anyone wouldn't do the same. 'No problem.' He concentrated on the stairs along with the pushing and shoving going on. It wasn't easy avoiding people. Each step seemed to take for ever, though the ground level was thankfully coming up fast.

Before he knew it, he was outside and handing his precious bundle over to her mother. 'There you go, little one.'

'I owe you a beer,' Cameron said as he looked around. 'What a nightmare. I thought it was a practice run, but that smoke's for real.'

'Move along. Everyone needs to congregate on the footpath on the opposite side of the road.' A policewoman was walking through the groups of shocked people. 'Out of the way so the firemen can get access. You all need to register your name and unit number with the two constables over the road. Do not go anywhere until you have.'

A small crowd had already gathered over there. Nick reached into his pocket. No phone. Damn it. He hadn't given it a thought when he'd grabbed his wallet and keys. How was he meant to inform his new boss, Joy, that he'd be late? Great. First day on the job. Not a good impression. According to Joy, he was meant to be going on a flight to Cook Town to pick up a young boy and bring him down here to the hospital for treatment. He needed to move. Fast.

He aimed for the front of the queue of tenants waiting to register their details. 'I'm sorry to push in, but I'm a doctor at Flying Health Care and need to get to work fast.' He might also be needed here of course. 'Unless I can help you out?'

One of the constables looked up. 'Got ID?'

Fair enough. In his wallet, he found his medical licence as well as the pass for the hangar he'd work from and handed them over. 'Here you go.'

'Thanks for the offer of help but the ambos are almost here.'

Nick realised sirens were approaching. 'That's good as I am supposed to be at work shortly. What is the time?' His watch was on his bedside table. When he was told he gasped. Where had the last thirty minutes gone? 'Right, I'll be on my way.'

'Hope your car's not in the apartment block basement.'

His heart sank. No phone. No car. Getting worse by the minute. 'I'll grab a taxi.'

'That ain't happening. The road's closed to all but emergency vehicles.'

Another officer stepped up. 'I'll take you to the airport.'

'Thanks, mate, but surely you're needed here?'

'They can do without me. So far it doesn't appear that anyone's injured, and plenty of other cops are waiting for the all-clear to go inside and check out the apartments to see what happened. It's important to get you where you're needed most. Come on.'

'Cheers, mate.' The guy seemed determined to give Nick a lift. Had someone close to him been saved by the Flying Health Care service?

'It's going to be noisy till we get past the traffic block,' the cop said as he flicked on the siren.

'Nothing I'm not used to on the ambulances.' Nick settled back for the crazy ride. 'You had much to do with Flying Health Care?' Might as well find out more while dealing with the frustration of the traffic jam.

'They flew our daughter to Brisbane Hospital when we were holidaying south of Townsville. She'd drowned and been resuscitated by the life guards but wasn't really responding to them. Scary time, I can tell you. Those guys are heroes.'

'Yes, they are.' Staring out at the backed-up traffic where kids crossed the road to a school, he wondered what lay ahead for him. That sense of finally wanting to stop and put down roots had returned.

Why now? Why here in Cairns? His apartment was like all the others he'd rented over the years since qualifying. A tidy place to cook a meal and put his head down after a long shift at work. He'd met people he enjoyed socialising with in every place he'd lived and worked. There'd been no pressure to get on and make the most of what he had. Yet less than a week in Cairns and the apartment already felt impersonal, despite the furnishings he took everywhere.

The town interested him. There were lots of beaches to enjoy, rural townships to visit, plenty of walking tracks. Nothing unusual except that, for the first time, he was considering staying around for longer than normal.

Leesa had something to do with that. Though he wasn't sure that was such a good idea. After all, this time the images of her smiles, laughter and sexy body were most likely overrated. She'd turn out to be a disappointment if he bumped into her again.

He laughed to himself. Give that time. A few

weeks on the job and he'd probably be changing his mind. Except work was the one thing that always kept him grounded. Along with making him proud. He'd done well training to become an emergency doctor. He still relished every moment on the job as much as he had the very first time he'd stepped into an emergency department as a house surgeon.

'You're new on the block?' the cop asked. 'Haven't seen you around.'

'Moved up last week from Brisbane where I was on the ambulances.'

'You'll find it's not quite as busy up here. Though we do have our share of problems too. Like any town I guess.'

'There are high tourist numbers here and up the coast, aren't there?'

'Yes, but they cause less trouble than the locals. Mostly anyway.'

A road sign indicated the airport was ahead. Nick heaved a sigh of relief. 'That didn't take long.'

'Helps having the right bells and whistles.'

Now to face the day. Hopefully no one would be too disgruntled with him. More than half an hour late wasn't good, but it could've been a lot worse.

'Morning everyone. I'm Dr Nicolas Springer. Joy told me to come on out and get on board. She's tied up with someone from the hospital at the moment.'

You've got to be kidding me.

At the sound of that gravelly voice Leesa's head spun around. She grabbed the door frame of the pilot's cabin to stay upright as she came face to face with their new colleague. Dr Sexy himself.

What were the odds? It had been over a year since he'd left her bed for the final time after lots of the most amazing sex she'd ever known, and still her gut tightened when he spoke. Wonderful. Now what? She had to work alongside that voice. Unless she gagged him every time they shared a shift. 'Hello, Nick.'

His eyes widened. 'Leesa? I knew you'd moved up here and figured we'd probably bump into each other somewhere on the job, but I didn't realise you worked for this lot.'

She could feel her face redden as memories of his hands on her body swamped her. Not appropriate. They were colleagues now. Yeah, so how to stop this reaction? Carry a bottle of cold water all the time?

'Would that have made any difference?' she snapped in an attempt to get back on track. It wasn't as though she'd been hankering for more time with him. No way. Those nights had been so wonderful it was unlikely they could be repeated. Besides, she still didn't do trusting men when it came to her heart. Though she was moving closer to thinking it was time to try again and to hell with the past. And, if she were honest, she had to admit that her passionate fling with Nick had gone a long way to letting her guard down.

'To me accepting the job?' He shook his head. 'Not at all.' He glanced past her and saw the pilot looking back at him, and repeated, 'Hi, I'm Nick.'

'Darren, your pilot today.'

Leesa stepped back as the men shook hands.

The last thing she wanted was to feel Nick's touch. She'd turn into a blob of jelly.

'Look, I'm very sorry to keep you waiting but there was a fire in the apartment block I've moved into, and I wasn't allowed into the basement to get my ute. Fortunately, one of the cops gave me a lift or who knows when I'd have made it.'

'Guess we can't complain about that.' Leesa sighed. It wasn't as if he'd slept in or stopped at the supermarket to get lunch on the way. She was still aghast to learn he was the newest doctor at Flying Health Care. Of all people, he had to be the one she'd prefer not to bump into again. It had taken some time to put it behind her, and already hot images of Nick were reappearing at the front of her mind. Not to mention the tightness in her gut. That was enough to put her off eating for the rest of the day.

She headed through the plane to confirm with

the groundsman they were ready to have the stairway taken away so she could close the door. 'We'd better get a move along. Jacob gets stressed when he has to wait for us to pick him up.' And she needed to focus on work, ignoring Dr Sexy in every other respect.

'Our patient this morning?' Nick asked as he put his backpack away and buckled himself into the spare seat.

'Yes. Once a fortnight we transport him from Cook Town down here for treatment. He has acute lymphatic leukaemia and has just started his second month of chemotherapy. He stays overnight, sometimes two nights depending how he does, which lately has been tough on him. When he's cleared to go home, we give him a lift back. The road trip is too far for the little guy.'

'How old is he?'

'Eight. He's the cheekiest kid about and we all adore him. Even when he's stressed.' She hated when Jacob got upset. She might be a paramedic and see a lot of distress on the job, but it still hurt to witness anyone, particularly a child, in pain or ill or frightened about what they were going through. How parents coped was beyond her. These scenarios had to be their absolute worst nightmare.

Darren came through the headset. 'All tied in back there?'

'Ready and waiting.' Leesa sank into her seat and stared out at the tarmac beyond. In the distance a passenger plane was beginning take off. It was a superb day with the sun shining and no wind. That wouldn't last. The sea breeze would make itself known later in the day.

Dr Nicolas Springer. Nick, in other words. Dr Sexy. No, she wasn't going there. That was behind them. Anyway, he was good looking and appeared to be a great guy—he probably wasn't on his own any more. Not that she one hundred percent knew if he'd had anyone special in his life back when they got together, but for some reason she'd trusted him. Which was plain dumb, considering how she'd trusted her ex not to be a bully and got that so wrong. Her trust was no longer given so easily under normal circumstances, and her affair with Nick had certainly been a moment out of time. One she hadn't regretted at all.

The propellers began spinning, rapidly gaining speed. Leesa watched as they rolled towards the tarmac, absorbing the thrill this always gave her. Sometimes she thought about getting her private pilot's licence for small planes, but then where would she fly to? Cairns was a long way from anywhere except the many small outlying communities. It was better to let the professionals give her a buzz.

'Is this the job you came to after leaving Brisbane?' Nick asked.

'Yes. It's the best one I've ever had. I especially get a kick out of helping kids and their families.'

'That's one reason I applied to work here. Helping people who want us there for them during difficult times. I've had enough of the abuse we get on the ambulances. Drunks thinking they should get special treatment, or fighting what you're trying to do to help them.' He shook his head. 'Sometimes it makes me wonder why we go to so much trouble to aid people, and then the next patient is wonderful and I have my answer.'

Blimey, he could be talkative. Not how she remembered him. The circumstances couldn't be more different though. They were at work, not having a drink or dancing. Or—yes, well, enough.

'I get what you're saying, and on these flights we mostly get gratitude.' There was the odd exception when someone thought they should be treated like royalty because they'd paid for their flight. Not all trips were provided by the health system. As far as she was concerned, everyone got the best help possible, irrelevant of who was paying and how old the patient was.

'Makes sense.' Nick settled back and studied the interior of the plane. 'I need to familiarise myself with everything. I like to be more than one hundred percent on board with it all. I don't want to waste time looking for equipment in an emergency.'

No one wanted that, and he was only doing what everyone did when they first started flying with this outfit. 'Go for it.'

Her pulse was still racing. All she'd known before he stepped on board minutes ago was that the new doctor was named Nicolas Springer and had been working on ambulances all over the country. Not once, even for a moment, had she thought Nicolas might be the Nick she'd spent those fiery nights with. 'What do you prefer to be called? Nick or Nicolas?'

'No one's ever asked me that before.' His focus was now on her. 'Nick. Nicolas is more formal.'

'What do your family call you?'

His mouth tightened. 'Either, or.' His focus returned to the emergency equipment.

Seemed she'd touched a raw nerve. Which was kind of sad if family was an issue for him. Everyone deserved a great family. In reality that wasn't always the case, but she'd been lucky with hers and still believed most people were, despite what she'd seen over the years, first as a nurse then a paramedic. 'I didn't recognise your name when Joy told us you were joining the gang. But we didn't exactly talk much about ourselves, did we?'

Jeez, Leesa, shut up, will you? Her head needed a slap.

'Sorry, forget I said that.'

'We can't avoid the fact we've spent time together, but it is in the past.'

Sometimes honesty could be a bit too blunt. He either wasn't wasting time remembering their time together or was letting her know how little it had meant, just as she should him.

'Yep, it definitely is,' she muttered and opened Jacob's case notes even though she pretty much knew them off by heart.

'I don't want to go to hospital.' Jacob stood near the steps up to the plane with his arms folded and tears pouring down his face. He stamped his foot and shouted, 'I'm not going.'

Leesa knelt down in front of her favourite little patient, resisting the urge to hug him tight. That wouldn't achieve anything until she knew what the problem was. 'Hey, Jacob, what's up, man? You love flying in the plane.'

'I don't want to.'

'Why not? What's happened to change your mind?'

'I don't like being sick. It's not fair.'

Leesa couldn't agree more. Glancing over to his mother, she noted the worry emanating from Kerry's tired eyes and gave her a smile that hopefully said, 'I've got this,' when she had no idea what was going on.

Even when he was stressed about what lay ahead in Cairns, Jacob was usually compliant when he had to board his ride. She sat down on the ground and reached out a hand. 'Sit with me.' She held her breath as the boy stared at her before slowly sinking down beside her. 'Isn't it cool being allowed on the airport tarmac?'

'It's my friend's birthday today and I want to go to his house and give him my present.'

Now she got it. Her heart broke for Jacob. Being so ill was hard for anyone, but for a child who didn't fully understand everything only made it twice as difficult. Though sometimes she suspected there wasn't much this boy didn't get about his condition. Today's reaction would be fairly normal even for adults.

'I bet you do, but you know what? He'll get lots of presents today so when you come home later in the week and give him yours it will be the only one that day, and that'll make it special.'

Jacob stared at her. 'I want to give it to him today. Everyone else is.' He wanted to be normal like his pals.

'I've got an idea. You could ring him later when you know he's home from school and sing *Happy Birthday*. That'd be special, wouldn't it?'

'Yeah.' A little bit of tension left Jacob's face. 'I s'pose.'

'You can practice singing the song all the way to Cairns.' Hopefully they had a quick flight.

'Will you sing with me?'

A gravelly laugh came from behind them. 'Go, kid.'

She grinned but didn't look over her shoulder at Nick, even though she wanted to see that sexy face with the neatly trimmed beard. What if she started calling him Nicolas? Would that be less sexy? Except it wasn't his name that set her blood racing.

'You'll regret asking me. I sound like a dog under water when I sing.'

'Max's having a party on the weekend. I have to stop being sick by then.'

'Then the sooner we get you to hospital the sooner you will have your treatment and start getting over it.' Of course she was exaggerating, but if it worked then what the heck? This kid had to have his chemo. Along with as normal a life as possible.

Jacob stood up and held out his hand to her. 'Come on then.'

'Cool.' Relief filled her.

'Thank you so much, Leesa,' Kerry said. 'He's been upset all morning and I just didn't know what to do.'

'You were brilliant,' Nick said quietly, sounding a little awe struck.

She'd take that as a compliment, especially from this man. 'Jacob knows the drill and will be fine now.'

And he was, talking excitedly to the new doctor, telling him how the plane worked and where they were going to land and how the pilot had to look out for other planes flying in the sky.

Leesa relaxed, glad that Jacob had moved on from his distress. It was hard enough going through the treatment without being upset over missing out on fun with his friends.

When they disembarked at Cairns he was still yabbering to Nick, pulling him along by the hand and telling him not to be so slow because he had to get his treatment done so he could ring his friend.

'Quite the little charmer, isn't he?' Nick said when the ambulance had left with Jacob and Kerry.

'It breaks my heart to see what he's going through.'

'You're amazing. The way you took your time to persuade him to get on board made all the difference.'

'How else would I deal with it? He's got enough going on without needing a bossy paramedic telling him to do what he's told.'

Nick touched her arm. 'I agree with you whole-heartedly. But it was special, Leesa. I've never seen anyone deal with a distraught young patient quite like that.'

Someone else who was a charmer, huh? She knew all about them. Shrugging, she said, 'Let's grab a coffee while it's quiet.' There was a warmth where his hand had touched her that had nothing to do with the balmy warm winter temperature. It was a familiar sensation from the past. Except then there'd been nothing warm about what went on between them. No, it had been all hot. Searing hot. Something she wasn't meant to remember at all.

'Do we know what our next job is?' Obviously, Nick wasn't affected by her in any way.

'We're taking a teenage girl home to Mackay once she's been discharged from Paediatric Orthopaedics. She was in a serious quad bike accident two and a half weeks ago and has multiple fractures to both legs. Her mother is a solo mum and a GP. She's going to look after her daughter around her job as it's easier than coming back and forth to Cairns every night after work to be with her.'

'Who's going to be with the girl while her mother's at work?'

'I've been told she practises from rooms at home, and she employs a nurse as well who'll also keep an eye on Matilda. It's going to be a difficult couple of months for them.'

'You certainly see a painful side of parenting in this job, don't you?'

'True, we do, but we also see wonderful parents coping with their worst nightmares while supporting and encouraging their children through hell.'

Another touch on her arm. 'You're very empathetic. I like that too.'

Too? What else about her was ticking his boxes? Did she even want that to be happening? As much as she'd liked him, she really wasn't ready to get to know him any better. Apparently, he moved around a lot and that wasn't her style. She preferred to be grounded in one place where she had family and friends.

She'd gone to Brisbane because her then husband had wanted to take up a great career opportunity, and in her book supporting him was part of being together. She should've read Connor's book first, then she'd never have married him, let alone left Cairns.

'You talk more than I remember.' Here she went again, raising the one subject that was taboo because she didn't need to go there. Make that she didn't want to, as it brought back wonderful memories that were unlikely to ever be repeated.

'We were usually too busy to talk.'

She had no idea how to respond to that statement. He definitely had no qualms about mentioning their time together. He'd have to learn that she did, except she wasn't actually doing any better thinking about it.

They reached the hangar where Darren was standing in the kitchen doorway with a full coffee plunger. The tightness in her gut eased a tad.

'You drink coffee or tea?' Darren nodded at the man striding alongside her.

'Coffee's good.'

Joy appeared behind Darren and the conversation turned to work and all things acceptable in Leesa's thinking.

Not that she could drop the mental picture of that long, muscular body wrapped around hers after they'd made love. Nick had been extraordinary, and lifted the bar for her. Which could make things tricky going forward. She'd always be looking out for another Dr Sexy. Had been since she'd moved back here, though cautiously, in case she found another bad one.

'So, you two know each other?' Joy cut through her thoughts.

'Umm, briefly,' Leesa replied uneasily.

'Not really,' Nick said at the same time.

Joy gave them both a studied look. 'As long as nothing gets in the way of you working together then we'll leave the subject alone.'

It seemed Joy suspected there was more to the story than either of them were letting on. So what? It had nothing to do with work, hadn't even happened in Cairns, so there wouldn't be a problem. Apart from the rattled sensation she got when too close to Dr Sexy.

Leesa turned away to stir sugar into her coffee, ignoring the raised eyebrows of her colleagues. Nosey lot. She was hardly going to announce to everyone that she'd had a one-night stand with the new doctor—which had turned into a five-night stand. Dropping the teaspoon in the sink, she got her lunch out of the fridge and took a seat at the tiny table where everyone knocked elbows all the time.

Nick was leaning against the bench, coffee in hand.

Of course. 'You didn't have a chance to get any lunch, did you?'

'I'm good.'

In other words, no. 'There're yoghurts in the fridge and I've got a couple of bananas in my locker.'

'Girl food,' Darren retorted. 'Here, man, have one of my sandwiches. My wife always makes too many.'

'Cheers, Darren. If you're sure?' Nick reached for a sandwich, not looking her way once.

Awkward.

* * *

'Matilda, can you hear me?' Nick asked the teenager lying on the trolley bed.

Apart from the dark shadows beneath her eyes, her face was very pale. 'Yes, Doctor.'

'Good. We're going to get you inside the plane now. We'll be careful not to jar you in any way, but if you feel pain please tell us.'

Matilda did the defiant teen eye-roll thing. 'You think?'

'More pain than you're already feeling.' He knew from the notes she was on strong medication, but it wouldn't take much to inflict more hurt. 'Let's do this, Leesa.'

Leesa, the woman who'd toyed with his mind ever since their short fling in her apartment, which had then become his apartment. Until he'd packed up to come north, only to bump into Leesa so soon. It seemed as if something out there was toying with them, bringing them together at every opportunity. Were they meant to be together?

Try again. Nick shivered as he lifted his end of the trolley. They were stepping around each other, as if afraid to relax in each other's company, when not with a patient to deflect any thoughts they might have about their brief past. It could get tricky when they had to spend quite a bit of time together.

He usually dated women who loved having a bit of fun and then moved on. While getting involved with someone who wanted the whole shooting box was his dream, it was also scary beyond description. He had no idea if Leesa wanted the same. She appeared comfortable with her lifestyle, whatever that was, but that didn't make risking his heart again any easier.

His ex Ellie's revelation about the pregnancy, and that there'd been other men in her bed after they'd married, had taught him not to believe anyone when they said they loved him. Of course, he wanted nothing more than a woman to love for ever and who'd love him equally.

The only person he remembered ever loving him unconditionally was his grandfather, who'd passed away when he was twelve. He didn't remember anything about his parents, as they'd been killed in a car crash when he was barely a year old. Now here he was in Cairns working alongside Leesa, who'd got to him in lots of ways. Was that why he'd moved north? He wasn't sure, but suspected she'd had at least some part to play in it.

'How's that, Matilda?' Leesa asked their patient, more focused on the job than he apparently was. He'd say she was deliberately avoiding him as much as was professionally possible.

If Leesa was going to be such a distraction,

then he'd have to ask Joy to roster him with other staff and never her. Might as well hand in his notice and move on now then, because that would be impossible with the small number of medics working the shifts. 'How's the pain level, Matilda?'

'You did a good job,' the teen retorted. 'No change.'

'Glad I'm good for something,' he grinned, comfortable with the patient if not his work partner. 'Let's get you tied down so we can get out of here.'

'You're making me sound like a wild pig you've just caught.' She giggled.

At last. Nick sighed, pleased to have lifted his patient's spirits, if only a little. He wasn't quite as good as Leesa with difficult patients, but he'd managed to make this one smile. 'One way of looking at it.'

Leesa was attaching monitors. 'Just keeping tabs on your blood pressure during the flight, Matilda.'

'Is that necessary?'

'I like to be cautious.' Leesa smiled. 'It's all part of the package.' Her gaze swept over him, wariness blinking out of those beautiful green eyes.

She hadn't been cautious the night they first met. Heat filled him. Just like that. Too easy.

Yep, he definitely should ask to work with someone else. Except Leesa had been so good with Jacob he wanted to work alongside her. He'd had to blink fast as she talked the boy into calming down and doing what was required. Leesa was special. But then he'd already suspected that. Which still wasn't a reason to spend more time than required on duty with her. Even then, he needed to keep her at arm's length. Like that was going to be possible inside a small plane.

Leesa shut the door and leaned into the cockpit. 'We're good to go, Darren.'

'We've got a five-minute wait. A flight from Sydney's on finals.'

'No prob.' Buckling herself in, she glanced his way. 'What do you think so far?'

About her? Amazing. *Yeah, right. Get a grip.* 'Flying in a plane certainly beats sitting in an ambulance, being held up in traffic mayhem at peak times.'

'Thankfully it doesn't get that busy in the sky.' She looked at the teenager and a frown appeared. 'Matilda, do you like flying?'

The girl was clenching and unclenching her hands. 'I've only been in a chopper and that wasn't nice.'

Nick asked, 'Was that the day of your accident?'

'Yeah.' Her hands tightened.

'You'll find riding in a plane a lot smoother than in a helicopter.' In an attempt to distract her, he asked, 'What happened? I heard you were in a quad bike accident.'

'I hit the accelerator instead of the brake and went over a bank. The bike landed on top of me.'

No wonder her memories of flying in a helicopter weren't wonderful. She'd have been in horrendous pain and shock, along with probably being frightened about what was going to happen to her. The case notes were on the end of the trolley. He picked them up. 'That must've been scary.'

'Try terrifying.'

Leesa stretched across to hold Matilda's nearest hand. 'Today will be a lot better. Darren's a great pilot, there's no wind to make it a bumpy ride, and you're in a lot better place than you were that day.'

'Were you with me?' Matilda asked her.

'I was. You gave that quad bike quite a fight.'

The signature eye roll appeared. 'I wish that were true.'

The notes Nick scanned made hideous reading. Three fractures in the left leg and two in the right. Five broken ribs added to the count. 'You're very lucky not to have sustained more serious injuries.' How Matilda avoided internal damage was beyond him.

'Thanks a lot, Doc. I don't see the luck in that, but if you say so I'll go along with it.'

Outside the windows the props began turning. Matilda's eyes widened and she gripped Leesa so hard it was a wonder bones weren't breaking in Leesa's hand. 'I remember this. It's like the chopper, how the noise gets louder and louder. I thought I was going to be in another accident.'

'Surely you were on strong painkillers?' Nick said.

'They didn't stop me thinking awful things.'

'They probably added to your mental confusion,' he told her. 'Today you can relax and take in what happens as we leave the ground and fly to your home town. You might even like the experience this time. How's that pulse?' he asked Leesa as she finished checking it with her free hand.

'As normal as any fifteen-year-old on an out-of-this-world experience can be.' She smiled at Matilda before turning and giving him one too. 'Up a little,' she mouthed.

Not surprised given Matilda's stress, he nodded. 'Wonder if we'll see any UFOs today.'

Another eye roll. 'You're nuts, Doc.'

'I've been called worse.' The silly talk was working though, as she didn't seem to realise they were already lined up at the end of the runway.

'Argh.' Matilda's cry of pain had him unclipping his belt and jumping out of his seat.

'What's up?'

'I moved my leg. Or I tried. It usually moves with a bit of effort.'

'Which leg?'

'The right one.'

The cast held it straight, so movement shouldn't have affected the fractures. 'Where exactly did you feel pain?'

Leesa was checking the BP monitor. 'All good.'

'Top of my thigh.'

The femur was fractured near the knee, not by the hip. 'Have you felt pain here before?' His fingers worked over the muscles.

Matilda winced. 'Sometimes when I've tried to roll over in my sleep.'

'I'd say it's happening in your muscles. Currently they're not being used, your movement went against what the casts are trying to prevent so they reacted.' He pressed lightly. 'How does it feel here?'

'All right. They told me the same in hospital but sometimes I forget.'

'You might need to have some massages,' Leesa said. 'Or get your mum to do it. I presume doctors have a basic idea?' she asked him.

'Very basic, but that's all Matilda needs.'

Matilda closed her eyes, like she had had enough of the conversation. She didn't appear to have noticed they were airborne and climbing rapidly, or wasn't concerned this time after all.

Nick returned to his seat. 'Where are we landing? I presume there's an airstrip near the town.'

'There's one right on the outskirts, about half a kilometre from Matilda's home. The local ambulance crew will transport her from there to the house.'

'Then we'll be on our way again.' Different to being in the ambulance, not knowing where or when the next call out will come. 'Do we know what's next?'

'Coffee?'

That cheeky glint in her eyes wound him up tight all over again. He knew what he'd like instead of coffee, and it didn't come in a mug. More of a rerun of some certain nights. 'Sounds like a plan.'

'Followed by taking a fifty-one-year-old woman to Townsville. She has early onset dementia, she's been in Cairns for respite care while her husband arranges permanent accommodation for her in the local rest home.'

Flying Health Care catered for all sorts of illnesses and emergencies. It was all about making the most of the staff and aircraft. They also covered emergencies with the Fire and Emergency Service with a helicopter when necessary. 'Every call is different, isn't it?'

'Makes the job exciting.'

At the moment Leesa was doing that. Not a good look for a doctor who needed to be fully focused on the case in hand. The doctor he'd always been until this morning. His phone pinged. Grateful for the interruption he looked at the message and glanced across to Leesa. 'The cop who drove me to the airport says the apartment building's been given the all-clear and everyone's allowed back in.'

'Did he say what caused the smoke? Or fire?'

'Someone on the floor below mine left a pot on the gas ring with oil in it and went out for a run.' *Idiot.* 'I'm glad the smoke detectors came on fast or who knows what the outcome might have been.'

'So you're renting another apartment.'

'Yes.' No ties that way. When he decided to move on, he only had to pack his bags and call in the furniture moving company.

Leesa stared at him for a moment. 'Why not a house?'

His shrug was deliberate. 'Suits me best.'

'Right.' Disappointment blinked out of those thoughtful eyes before she turned away.

What did she expect? A full explanation about how, after his grandfather passed away, he'd grown up in foster homes, where no one cared about giving him a loving environment to enjoy and get used to? It was the driving force behind why he never stayed in one place for too long. The max was a couple of years, not always that long.

But that wasn't something he put out there. He didn't want anyone feeling sorry for him. He'd done enough of that all by himself in years gone by. Now he got on with making life work for him without getting too involved with anyone, though he stayed in regular contact with Logan.

'How're you doing, Matilda? That leg settling down?'

'Kind of.'

'I can't give you any more painkillers. You've had maximum dosage.'

'Whatever.' Typical teen response.

He leaned back and stared out the tiny window at the passing sky. The sense that the time had come to turn his life around had begun on the night he'd met Leesa at that barbecue, the ensuing nights only intensifying the idea.

She'd been the opposite of the women he usually knew, but there'd also been something about her quiet demeanour that had drawn him to her. She hadn't been quiet all the time, but for the first hour, as they'd sat having a drink and watching everyone else enjoying themselves, she had. He'd told himself to get up and leave, because there was a confident yet wary air about her. It had him wondering if he should try for a future that held the promise of the love he craved. But it had proved impossible to walk away. Look at the fun he'd had because of that—and the memories that haunted him.

Over the intervening months he hadn't stopped thinking about her, and what could be out there for him if only he could let go of the fierce need to protect himself. All because of a few nights spent with Leesa.

So was she the reason he'd come to Cairns? Along with the wake-up call after Patrick's cancer scare? Really? It couldn't be. That was too much to believe. Wasn't it?

He'd taken over her Brisbane apartment as a way of keeping her near in a vague kind of way. Though he'd quickly learned Leesa wasn't exactly unknown in the Brisbane emergency services, after all she'd done to help the women being abused by the previous boss of the ambulance station. Most people were in awe of her, but naturally there were a few who thought she should've minded her own business. Personally, he thought she had to have been very gutsy to do what she did, never mind the outcome for herself.

Had he truly moved north to get to know her better? Deeper? His mouth dried as he realised it was very likely why he'd gone online looking for a position up here, instead of reading all the situations vacant in the ambulance field over the whole country as per usual. Though not for one moment had he expected to be working out of the same base as her. He'd thought she'd be on the ambulances, not in the air. 'Idiot.'

'Pardon?' Leesa asked.

'Nothing. Ignore me.' For ever.

CHAPTER TWO

LEESA TOSSED HER car key in the air and caught it again. Offering Nick a ride home since he didn't have his vehicle would be the right thing to do. But then she'd have to cope with him sitting in the car beside her, taking up all the air and space, while setting a new rhythm to her heartbeat.

There were plenty of taxis over at the terminal building. He'd be fine. And she'd be selfish to drive off without offering him a lift. It wasn't an invitation to get close again.

Remember that the next time you get all hot around him.

'Nick,' she called, looking around for that tall, well-honed body that had taken over the interior of the plane like he owned it.

'What's up?' He came up behind her.

Her palms tingled. 'Do you want a lift to your apartment?'

'That'd be great, thanks.'

No hesitation about accepting her offer. More proof she wasn't upsetting him the way he did her. 'Let's go then.' She wanted this over and done, then she could pick up Baxter, head back to the house Gran had lent her and give the dog a walk before relaxing over a cold beer after an unusual day.

The cases had been much the same as usual, except there'd been no emergencies or a patient going bad on them. It was Dr Sexy who'd really upset her equilibrium. Something she needed to get over fast because they would work together a lot. Not every shift was with the same person, but more than enough to worry her. He still had the power to turn her on fast. More than a year had gone by since they'd been so intimate, and yet the moment she'd heard his voice when he boarded the plane she'd been in trouble.

'I'll just grab my bag.'

'I'll be out in the carpark.' She wasn't hanging around inside waiting for him. That'd seem too eager, wouldn't it? Or normal for some people. Not for her. At the moment not a lot felt normal, all because Nick had turned up in her life again, and this time for more than a few nights.

Twenty minutes later Nick strolled out to join her. 'Sorry, Joy cornered me. She wanted to know how the day had gone and had I enjoyed the work.'

'Did you?' Did Joy mention again the fact Nick knew her?

'Absolutely. It's different to what I've done before in that we seem to get closer to the patients and learn more about them because there are repeat visits. If Jacob hadn't already spent time in your care, it might've been harder to calm him down and get him on board without a bigger fuss.' Then he shook his head. 'I take that back. You'd have managed no matter what. You have a way about you that has patients eating out of your hand.'

Nothing awkward about that. Opening her door, she looked at him over the car roof. He really thought that? Yes, he would, because from the little she knew he wasn't a man to say something he didn't believe. *Wow.*

'Let's hope whatever it is, it keeps working,' Leesa replied. 'There're times when patients seriously need to calm down for their own safety, and if they didn't listen to us, we'd have a load of problems on our hands.'

She got into the car before she said too much. Just looking at Nick undid a lot of the determination to keep her distance. Pulling on her straight-face look, she turned on the ignition and music filled the car. One of the songs they'd danced to in the park by her old apartment, to be exact. Heat tore up her face. That was happening a lot today. She flicked the sound off.

'You don't have to turn it off for my sake.'

But she had to for hers. She'd downloaded the music and sung her heart out on the long drive home from Brisbane. She'd tried telling herself it was because she loved the tunes, that it had nothing to do with how she'd felt exhilarated and happy dancing and making out with Nick. 'I have it too loud sometimes.'

'It's the only way to listen to good music.' He grinned.

That damned grin was too sexy for her to be able to switch off the emotions it brought on. Putting the car in drive, she didn't waste any time heading out of the airport perimeter. The sooner her passenger was out of the car the better. She'd be able to breathe freely, for one.

'The apartment block's on George Street.'

'Right.' She hadn't thought to ask where they were headed. Another mistake, all because Nick was so distracting it was becoming embarrassing.

'Know where that is?'

'Yes.' She could do uncommunicative. Safer than saying something she'd instantly regret, which she seemed to do an awful lot around Nick.

He must've got the message because he said no more until she turned into his street and parked outside the apartment building. Looking around, he said, 'Not a sign of what went on this morning.'

'Why would there be?'

He shrugged. 'Don't know really. Want a beer?'

Love one.

'No, thanks. I've got to take my dog for a walk.'

'Okay.' He shoved the door open. 'Where do you go walking?'

'I'll take him along the promenade.' It wasn't far from here and Baxter would be chomping at the bit to get out and about. So much for going home first. Something else to put on Nick?

'Mind if I come with you?'

What? Nick wanted to join her for a walk? Outside of work? After she'd made an idiot of herself with that music.

He was watching her too closely. 'I think we need to clear the air if we're going to get along at work.'

'We got along fine today.' She'd liked working with him. He took his job very seriously. They all did. It was her dream job, and not once had she regretted returning home. But now Nick had landed on her workplace doorstep that might change everything.

Only if I let him.

True. She was in charge of her own destiny, something she'd repeatedly told herself over the years dealing with bullies. While Nick wasn't a bully—as far as she'd seen anyway, but she'd got that wrong in the past so would always be wary—he did seem to hold sway over her emotions. That needed dealing with sooner than later. He was already changing her, in that she did want to get to know him better and to have some fun. Like between the sheets again? It had been incredible before.

He was still watching her.

She sighed. 'You're right. Close the door and we'll go pick up Baxter.'

'I'm not trying to cause trouble, Leesa. I know I've landed on your patch and I don't want you to regret my arrival. We're adults. We can work together without that brief fling causing trouble between us.'

Blunt for sure. Also correct. 'Of course we can.' She went for honesty. 'I enjoyed today. You're a great doctor, and good with our patients. They liked you.'

I was relaxed when I wasn't recalling how your hands felt on my body, which was most of the time.

Feeling her face redden, she indicated to pull out and drove away from the apartment block.

Nick said nothing more until she pulled up outside a building with a high fenced yard, where a few dogs were waiting impatiently for their owners to turn up. 'You put your dog in day care?' He grinned. 'You are such a softie.'

'So what?'

'Just saying. I'm not surprised after seeing how you handled Jacob.'

Relax, Leesa. Give the guy a break.

'Baxter came from a rescue centre. His previous owners used to leave him tied up for days on end with little food or water, so I just can't tie him up and go out for very long. He gets distressed believing I'm going to leave him there for days, so when I've got something to go to other than work, I leave him with Mum and Dad.'

'How can people be so cruel?' Nick shook his head. 'Why have a dog if you're going to treat it like that?'

'The million-dollar question. Won't be a moment.' Out of the car, she strode inside to collect her beloved four-legged boy who was wagging his tail frantically as always. She knew he never expected her to come and pick him up, but at least here he was petted and loved by the staff running the centre while he waited for her to reappear.

'Hey, there, Leesa. Baxter's chomping at the bit to go home,' Karin said as she clipped the dog lead on. 'There you go, fella. Mum's here.'

Leesa dropped to her knees to hug her pet. 'Hello, Gorgeous. Had a good day?'

Baxter pushed into her, his lean body hard up against her.

'That's a yes then. We're off to walk the esplanade.' Standing up, she took the lead. 'See you tomorrow, Karin.'

Outside Baxter bounced up and down to the car, then stopped and stared at Nick through the window.

'It's all right, boy. Nick's a friend.' Sort of.

Nick opened his door and got out, holding his hands out for Baxter to sniff. 'Hey, Baxter.' He kept his voice light and calm.

Baxter sat back and looked up at him.

'Give him a moment,' she said. 'He's cautious around new people.'

'Wise dog.'

'There you go.' Her boy had stood up and was sniffing Nick's hand. 'You're in.' Easy as. But then she'd been much the same when she first met Nick. Would be again if she didn't keep a watch over herself. Sudden laughter bubbled up. She really was mad, and right now she didn't care at all.

'What's funny?' Nick looked as though he'd like something to laugh about too.

Good question. She wasn't really sure. 'Dogs. Men.'

He stared at her, then finally laughed too. 'Add women and we're on the same page.'

'Fair enough.' Opening the back door, she indicated for Baxter to get in so she could put on his safety harness. 'Let's go.'

* * *

Why had he suggested he join Leesa for the walk? Nick wondered as they strolled along the esplanade with Baxter bounding ahead. It was all very well saying they needed to iron out the hitches between them, but he had no idea where to start. Seemed Leesa didn't either, as she was staying very quiet except for an occasional word to the dog. She was probably waiting to see where he was going with this—it was his suggestion in the first place.

'Unreal.'

'What is?' she asked without looking his way.

He could say the stunning outlook across the harbour, but that'd be avoiding her. 'That I started work today at the same place you're employed. What were the odds?'

'Fairly high, I'd have thought. Cairns isn't a huge city and there aren't numerous air or road ambulance services.' Sarcasm dripped off her tongue. 'Did it never occur to you that you might end up at the same place?' It was coming across in spades that she wasn't pleased.

'I wondered if our paths might cross, but I didn't expect to end up at the same service centre.' He had thought about what it would be like to work for the same company, and hadn't really come up with a satisfactory answer. It was feeling more and more like he really had wanted to meet up again. Going by her reactions over the day, Leesa probably hadn't given much thought to their fling, other than maybe she didn't want anything more to do with him. She was blunt at times and friendly at others, but never fully re-laxed.

'Face it, I know very little about you, and for all I know you might be like me and move around a lot.' He winced. He'd said too much about him-self.

'I'm the dead opposite. I grew up here and the only other place I've lived is Brisbane.'

'I've no idea what it's like to live in one area for most of your life.' He could add that made him feel a little bit jealous, but best he didn't. She'd want an explanation he wasn't prepared to give.

Prepared? Or ready? As in he might eventu-ally want to take the risk of exposing his inner demons? He'd already said too much. Coming on this walk with Leesa hadn't been his bright-est idea. She had the ability to make him want to talk about things he never discussed with anyone.

'I'm sorry to hear that.' The tension had gone from her shoulders. There was a quizzical look in her eyes when she glanced across at him.

Don't ask why.

'Baxter's happy.'

'Nick, relax. I'm not going to pummel you with questions. Since we met in Brisbane, I have sometimes wondered what you were up to and if you were happy there. You're an okay guy and I'm happy to be working with you.' There was some heat creeping into her face and she'd begun walking faster. 'I don't see any reason for Joy to worry about us.'

'I agree.' He upped his pace to keep beside her. 'Thank you for making it easy. It can be tricky spending a lot of time with someone after what we enjoyed that week.' At least he hoped she'd enjoyed it. By the ecstatic sounds that came from her mouth at certain moments he was certain she had. He didn't believe she'd faked any of their love making. Sex, man. It was sex, pure and simple. Except never before had he spent so much time thinking about a woman he'd had sex with. Nothing pure and simple about that.

'My job is the most important thing I do and I won't let anything jeopardise it. Not even get offside with you,' she added with a tight smile.

'Good. Shall we start afresh by having a meal at one of the cafes on the other side of the road?'

'Meal? Flip. Sorry, I have to phone Mum. I'm meant to be having dinner with her and Dad.' She tugged her phone from her back pocket and tapped the screen. 'Mum? I'm going to be late. Sorry, but I was caught up in work stuff.' She glanced at him and grimaced. 'Now I'm walking Baxter and the doctor who started on the job today. He was at a loose end.'

'You're walking me?' He laughed.

She started to smile. 'Get in behind.' Then her smile vanished. 'Really? Maybe not.' Her sigh was dramatic. 'Okay, I'll ask him but we'll be late.' She held her phone away from her ear. 'Mum wants to know if you'd like to join us for dinner.'

Obviously, Leesa wasn't too happy with that idea. He wouldn't mind spending more time with her, but not if she wasn't keen for him to join the family.

'Nick?'

He thought she didn't want him joining her. But it would mean he'd be getting to know Leesa better. No, not yet. If ever. 'Thank you but not tonight. I've some chores to do.'

'Did you hear that, Mum? Nick's got other things on.' He couldn't make out if she was happy or not. 'I'll head back to the car now and be on my way ASAP.' The phone slid back into her pocket. 'Come on, Baxter, we're going to Ma and Pa's for dinner.'

'Leesa.' He paused, uncertain what to say without making matters worse.

'It's fine, Nick. Probably for the best.'

Silence hung between them as they walked back to the car and set off for his apartment.

Finally unable to stand it any longer, he asked, 'Where do your parents live?'

'Twenty-five minutes north of the city. Dad grows sugarcane, has done for decades. He thought my brother might want to continue with the farm but Kevin took up commercial fishing. He works out of Port Douglas, about an hour from here.' It was as though she'd grabbed the chance to talk without going over what hung between them.

'Sounds like a busy family.'

'It was drilled into us as kids that you've got to work for what you want. Nothing comes in a Christmas cracker apparently, though I did keep pulling them in the hope Dad was wrong.'

Silence fell between them, making him wish he'd said yes to dinner with her family, but deep down he wasn't ready for that. Maybe when they were fully established as colleagues and not ex-lovers it would work. Or when he had the guts to follow up on the feelings of need and wonder for Leesa he was desperately trying to deny.

Leaning forward he turned the music up to fill the silence. The blasted song they'd danced to that night.

Leesa threw him a quick glance. 'You stirring, by any chance?'

'Not at all. I like that tune. Also, we agreed we needed to lay the past to rest, so turning music off because we heard it that first night isn't going to help.' Not saying he liked the memories it invoked—hot memories of Leesa dancing, kissing, sharing her body. Should never have turned the damned sound up.

'Of course.'

'Leesa, I'm not saying I want to forget the time we had together.' No way in hell could he. He'd tried and tried, and still the memories taunted him. 'Only now we work together things are different.' Get it? There wouldn't be any more time between the sheets for them.

'Right.'

He had no idea what she thought. Fortunately, his street appeared and Leesa turned the corner a little fast. Eager to get rid of him?

When she pulled up, she surprised him. 'Nick.' Her hand was warm on his bare arm. And electric. Like she'd flicked a switch so a powerful current raced through him. 'Your honesty is confronting but I'm grateful. I don't like ducking and diving around a problem, and yet I confess I've been doing exactly that all day.'

It was quite exciting realising he didn't, and wouldn't, always know what would come out of that sexy mouth. He gave her a smile. 'See you tomorrow.'

CHAPTER THREE

ON FRIDAY MORNING Leesa arrived at the hangar early, determined to find out who she was rostered with and sort her day out before Nick arrived. That way she'd feel in control of something at least.

'Morning, Leesa.'

So much for that idea. 'Hi there.'

Who are you working with?

Even on the days they hadn't worked together during the week she'd been aware of him whenever they were at the base at the same time, which had been often. The roster was lighter than usual.

'I'm on with you today.' So, he did mind reading too. Or just got on with the day. That was more likely as he was a practical man. Among other things.

'Have you checked the list for what's up first?'

Be tough, don't give in to the beating going on in your chest. Practise so that if you do apply for and get Joy's job, you'll know how to cope with left-field problems.

Like Nick, except she'd have to keep well away from anything more than a working relationship with him if she got the job. Since Joy had told her yesterday that she was leaving in eight weeks she'd been tossing the idea around about applying for the position.

A part of her wanted to advance her career, but a deeper part understood it was working with people needing medical help that really ticked her boxes, not sitting in an office doing paperwork for hours. There was nothing to lose thinking about what the job involved. She could always withdraw her application if she decided it wasn't for her. Plus, she'd have something other than Nick to think about.

'Should be a straightforward trip.'

'What?' She'd missed everything he said.

He stared at her and enunciated his words clearly. 'We're picking up a fourteen-year-old boy from Cook Town. He's got an infected club foot.'

'Not something they can deal with at the local hospital?' She really wasn't concentrating. The doctors up in Cook Town wouldn't send the boy their way unless there was a problem.

'Apparently it's serious, the lad didn't go to the doctor until he could barely stand on it.'

'Wonderful,' she muttered. Why did people wait until their condition was so far gone before getting help? It only caused more problems.

'You'd think he'd have learned what to do by his age.'

'Could be he gets teased about his foot and doesn't want to make a fuss.'

Air huffed over her bottom lip. 'I should've thought of that. I know all too well how kids love to tease or bully anyone who doesn't fit in.'

'I heard about what you did for those two women at the ambulance base in Brisbane. Pretty impressive. Not many people stand up to bullies the way you did.'

'I have experience of being bullied.'

His eyes widened. 'Why? You're beautiful and kind and not disdainful of anyone that I've seen.'

Her heart melted a little. 'Thanks. I was very tall as a teen, therefore I didn't conform with the others.'

'What a load of twaddle.'

Nick certainly knew how to make her feel good. But then so had her ex, until he'd got what he wanted, then he went into bully mode and never stopped. Not that she was saying Nick was bully material, only that she'd learned to be ultra cautious when it came to getting to know people. Might as well get it all out of the way. 'I was also married to a prize jerk who believed I was there to do as he wished all the time.'

'You left him?'

'Yes. There was only so much of his crap I

could take. I deserved a lot better.' Always would. Be warned. Not that Nick seemed at all interested in her, other than as a colleague, something to be grateful about, but it was hard to raise that emotion. Especially when he was standing only a few feet away, his tall frame making her feel warm and happy. Like they were a match. It would be too easy to reach out and touch him.

She spun away and snatched up the medicine kit to put on board. Time to get to work. To focus on reality, not daydreams. She was not touching Nick.

He was standing beside her, looking impressed. 'You're tough. Go you.'

Tough enough to keep her hands to herself? Tugging her shoulders back, she said, 'I had to be.'

Have to be if I'm going to keep my heart safe.

Heart? That was going too far. Being attracted to Nick did not mean she was falling for him. No way.

But her head would not shut up. Its next question was, *Surely not every man you're attracted to will turn out to be a bully?* Definitely not, but how was she to know who to trust? Men didn't come with referrals.

Joy stood in the doorway. 'You're both here already. That's good because we have a prem birth with complications needing retrieving and taking down to Brisbane ASAP. It was called in by Dr Jones five minutes ago.'

'Matilda's mum, right?' Hopefully someone was with Matilda while her mother was seeing to her patient.

'Yes. The woman's at her clinic, it's been arranged for the ambulance to take her to the airfield when I let her know you're on your way.'

'Let's do it.' Leesa headed out to the plane where Darren was already waiting, ready to go. It was good to have something to think about other than her partner. Work partner. *Gorgeous partner*, added a cheeky part of her mind.

It was true. Nick was awesome. And not for her. The idea of a full-on relationship gave her warm fuzzies—and chilly shivers. Being single had its advantages. She didn't get told what to do all the time, could make her own decisions and stick to them—or dump them, whichever suited.

It could also be lonely not having that special person who was hers, at her side. Family and friends were great. Having a man to share the big and little decisions, the fun and not-so-fun moments, would be even better.

Nick was right beside her, case notes in hand and wearing an expression that said he was mentally running through the equipment they'd need and what was in the drug kit.

She nudged him. 'Everything's on board.'

'I know, but old habits don't go away.'

'They're the best.' She trotted up the stairs. 'Hey, Darren.'

'Morning you two. No rest for the wicked, eh?'

'You think?' Leesa gave a snort. If only she could have a bit of wicked in her life. Her gaze flicked over her shoulder to Nick as he closed them in. It might be better if they got down and dirty and she could get this craving for him out of her system. Yeah, nah. Best not. Disappointment filled her. But she could only laugh at herself. This was out there crazy.

Get over the guy.

Like it had worked last time.

'Can I take a front seat ride?' Nick asked Darren. 'I won't hold you up or get in the way.'

'Help yourself. I've already started take off procedures. Just get buckled in pronto.'

'Thanks, mate.'

Darren spoke to the control tower and the props began turning on one side of the plane, and then the other. 'Here we go. You'll get a clearer idea of the layout of the land from up above,' he told Nick, who was strapping himself in.

Leesa stretched her legs out in front of her. Great. Now she'd have all the air back here to herself.

'Do you want to read the notes?' Nick leaned back to her. 'There's not a lot to see.'

'Sure.' She took the paper he held out and shivered when their fingers collided. The man was a permanent fire sparkler with how he always set her alight. His hands were firm but gentle, hot while sensuous. Another shiver tripped down her back as she recalled them touching her. What she wouldn't do to share her bed with him again.

Biting her lip, she stared at the page in front of her. The words blurred as heat filled her. *Blink, blink. Swallow.* Her lungs filled, emptied.

The page slowly became clearer. Lucy Crosby, thirty-two, thirty-one weeks' gestation, had gone into labour at five that morning. Baby was born at six ten hours, was put into a ventilator and all functions were being monitored continuously. Mother had lost a significant amount of blood, and needed a transfusion on arrival at the designated hospital in Brisbane.

A glance at her watch told her the baby was barely an hour old. 'Come on, get cracking, there's a baby needing to be in the NICU.'

'We're airborne,' Darren replied through the headset.

'Oops, sorry, didn't mean to speak out loud.'

Both men laughed. 'Typical,' added Nick. 'But I know what you mean. These flying machines don't go fast enough sometimes.'

'This one will,' Darren sounded as though he'd been challenged.

Leesa watched the airport grow smaller as they rose quickly and listened to Nick's deep husky voice through her headphones. He could talk about paint drying on walls and she'd still be riveted. How pathetic was that? Definitely time to get out amongst it and find a guy to have some fun with. Not the one sitting in the right-hand seat up front. He'd be a lot of fun, but she feared he might snag her heart when she wasn't looking and that was not up for grabs. Not until she knew him very well anyway, because that was the only way to be safe. Besides, if she got Joy's job, she'd have to keep him at a distance.

'Leesa, can you set up the monitors while I get a needle into Alphie for fluids?' Nick leaned over the incubator. The little guy weighed fourteen hundred and twenty grams. It seemed an impossible number to survive, but he knew Alphie had every chance of putting on weight over the coming days as long as they got him to the intensive care unit ASAP.

'Onto it. His breathing's shallow and a little faster,' she said calmly.

'That's changed since we loaded him. I'll put a mask on him before anything else.'

'What's happening?' demanded the distraught father from the cockpit. He wasn't happy being there. He wanted to be with his son and wife.

Leesa looked up. 'Nick's going to help Alphie's breathing by putting an oxygen mask over his face. It won't hurt him at all.'

'What's wrong with his breathing? It was all right back at Dr Jones's.'

Nick carefully tightened the band around the baby's head just enough to keep it in place and turned to James. 'His breaths are coming a bit quick. I can't see anything else wrong with him.' He glanced at Leesa who nodded.

'BP's normal, heart rate good.'

Even though he expected that, Nick still felt relieved. These cases could go wrong very fast. This was when he was more than glad to have Leesa alongside him. Her competence was awesome.

'Can you check on Lucy?' Nick asked Leesa. The woman had haemorrhaged after giving birth, and while the bleeding had slowed, it hadn't stopped. Dr Jones had sutured the external tears but there was a serious internal wound that would see Lucy on her way to Theatre the moment she got to hospital.

'Onto it.' Leesa's smile warmed him through and through. At the moment they were a team, nothing else mattered other than getting their patients to hospital and giving them both all the care possible on the way. Would it be possible to get along just as well outside the job? It would be wonderful if they did, if he could give in to his feelings with no fear for his heart.

'Lucy, how are you doing?' Leesa asked. 'I'm going to check the bleeding.'

'Don't worry about me. Look after Alphie,' the woman whispered.

'Alphie's in good hands. Nick's watching over him like a hawk.'

His heart expanded at Leesa's words. She knew how to make him feel good. 'Alphie's doing great. He's a tough wee man. You need to be looked after, too.'

'Alphie needs you, Lucy,' James called from the front.

'It doesn't feel right to take your attention away from my baby,' Lucy said.

Leesa nodded. 'I understand, but your boy doesn't need two of us right now, whereas you need some help.' She snapped on fresh gloves. 'Let's get you sorted. You want to be cleaned up before we arrive at the hospital.'

Again, Leesa was being patient. Nick sighed. She was hard to ignore. Impossible, in fact. But he'd keep trying—until he couldn't any more. Which wasn't far off.

Darren raised his beer to everyone round the table, those not on duty who were at the pub down the road from the airport. 'Here's to the end of another week.'

'All right for some.' Leesa tapped her bottle against his and then everyone else's. 'I'm on all weekend.'

'Yes, and we know you love it.' Nick gave her a return tap.

It was true. She loved her job. Had even enjoyed working with the new doctor on the days they'd been rostered together. More than enjoyed. He was great company and just as sexy when he was being serious as he was when he was away from work. 'Most of the time I do.'

Nick looked surprised. 'Most? I'd have said all the time.'

'No job is that perfect.' She'd put her hand up to cover call this weekend because she wanted to be busy. It was the first anniversary of when her best friend was involved in a car versus bus accident that she didn't survive. It had been hard for everyone, especially her husband. John wasn't coping at all, to the point he'd been temporarily stood down from working as an aircraft engineer.

She looked around for him, having seen him with a couple of engineers when she'd arrived. He was leaning on the far end of the bar looking lost. She'd keep an eye on him and probably join him shortly. In the meantime, she'd focus on her workmates. This unwinding time was important for everyone after a week dealing with some heart-wrenching cases. Turning to Nick, she asked. 'What are you up to this weekend?'

Nick shrugged. 'Haven't planned anything really.'

'Sounds dull.'

'Not really.'

Strange how at work he talked more easily, but when they were away from work he seemed to go quiet. Just with her? No, he hadn't been very chatty with anyone. 'Have you ever come up this far north before?'

'No, never. It is a long way from anywhere,' he replied.

Hadn't she heard that before? 'Come on. We've got an airport. An international one to boot.'

'I've mostly spent my time in the large cities. This is a new experience for me.' Finally, a smile came her way. Plus a few more words. 'I do need to get out and see more of Oz, don't I?'

'I reckon.'

I'd make a good tour guide.

So much for keeping her distance. Thankfully she hadn't put that out there. Nick didn't need to know what she'd thought. Not that he'd be likely to take her up on the offer, he seemed as intent on keeping his distance as she was.

'I hear the Daintree's a great place to visit.'

'Watch out for the crocs,' she laughed. 'There

are plenty of warning signs around the area, but still.'

'So, you want me back at work next week?' He grinned, making her head feel light.

Damn him. He did that too easily. 'Maybe.'

His grin remained fixed in place.

And she continued to feel light headed. Time to move away and get her mental feet back on the ground. She'd check on John and come back to the gang shortly.

'I'll be back,' Leesa said before heading over to the bar and hugging a man staring into the depths of his glass.

Nick sipped his beer and listened to the conversation going on around him at the table. They were a great bunch to work with. This past week had highlighted the reason he'd moved yet again. New faces, new challenges as far as the job went. Nothing exciting about the new apartment, but that was normal. Time to buy his own place? Thanks to Patrick he was very lucky not to have a student loan hanging over his head. Buying a house suggested permanence, something he longed for. Here? In Cairns, where Leesa lived? The million-dollar question.

'You hear Joy's handed her notice in?' said Carl, another doctor working for the same outfit as him.

'When did she do that?' Darren asked.

Nick was intrigued. Only a couple of hours ago Joy was telling him how pleased she was with the way he was fitting in. Not a word about her leaving had passed her lips, but he was the new boy on the block.

'A few days ago, apparently. She's not leaving for a couple of months, and then she and her husband are going to tour Europe for an indefinite period.'

'Does that mean her job's up for grabs? Or have management already got someone lined up?' asked Jess, a nurse he'd worked with yesterday.

Carl shrugged. 'Joy only said she was going to talk to the staff about it next week. No idea what that means, but could be they're looking for a replacement amongst you medics.'

Interest flared in Nick. He could apply. If he was going to settle down it would be perfect. It might help him stay grounded as it wouldn't be as easy to walk away.

Leesa.

It would mean no getting away from her. But did he really want to? His gaze strayed across the room to that tall, beautiful woman who had somehow managed to start him thinking of a future he'd believed impossible. Hard to imagine not seeing her every day. But did that fit in with her being the one person who'd find him lovable enough to stay around for ever?

Leesa was holding the man's hand. Her head was close to his. She appeared to be talking quietly.

Nick's stomach dropped. It was one thing to hug a guy, but to hold his hand? No, there was more to this. Those two were acting like they had something going on. Yet she hadn't raced over to him when she arrived.

Just then the man ran his other hand down the side of his face, and Nick's mouth soured. He wore a wedding band. Married, and Leesa was holding his hand. He could not abide by that.

Leesa wasn't his girlfriend, but to see her with a married man like that had the warning bells clanging. Here he'd been thinking she might be the woman who could help him turn his world around. Wrong. His ex hadn't been honest with him, which was why he had to be able to trust whoever he fell in love with, when it happened. *If* it happened, and that had started to look possible—until now. Or was he over reacting? There could be a perfectly sane explanation. This was Leesa, after all.

'Want another beer?' Carl asked.

'No, thanks. I'm heading away.' Sitting here seeing Leesa getting all close and tender with that man was doing his head in. He'd been mistaken about her. All those sensations that heated his body, that had him looking at her, were a joke. She wasn't his type at all. He had to stick to dating women who were honest about their wish to have fun with no expectations about the future. Far safer that way. Except it was hard to believe Leesa would be dishonest about a relationship. But how well did he know her?

'Hey, I'll see you all at work.' Leesa stood at the table.

How had he missed her approaching? She sure didn't look guilty about anything.

She was still talking. 'I'm giving John a lift home. He's had a few too many to drive.'

'He's not looking great,' Darren noted.

'He's not in good shape,' Leesa agreed. 'It's the one-year anniversary.'

'Sure he's going to be all right home alone?' Carl asked.

'His father's staying the night. He was meant to be here but got held up at work and has gone straight to the house.' Leesa glanced Nick's way. 'John's wife passed a year ago tomorrow. She was my best friend.'

Guilt tore through him. How could he have immediately suspected the worst? Why hadn't he waited to find out what was going on before jumping to the wrong conclusion? Went to show how screwed up he was. How much Ellie's betrayal had affected him. Still did, apparently.

He wanted to move on, to create a happy, loving life while denying anyone near his heart. There was a lot to put behind him for that to work. 'Leesa, I'm really sorry to hear that.' In more ways than she could imagine. 'It's not going to be an easy day for you either.' Hence, she'd opted to work. She must be hurting big time. 'Who else is on tomorrow?'

Carl put his hand up. 'Going to miss my wife's first golf competition.' He laughed. 'Might be a blessing in disguise.'

'How about I cover for you?' Nick suggested. He could be with Leesa if she wanted to talk about her friend, or support her silently if that suited.

'You serious? I owe you, Nick. Cheers.'

'No problem.' Unless Leesa wasn't happy with him, but he'd deal with that if it arose.

Darren stood up. 'Leesa, I'll come with you out to the car.'

'Thanks.' Leesa's face was grim. 'I'm hoping John's all right for the ride home.' She headed back to her friend.

'Poor bugger,' Carl said as he drained his bottle. 'Sure you don't want another?'

'No, thanks.' He stood up. Leesa was worried about her passenger. He'd offer to go with them. It was the least he could do for jumping to the wrong conclusion. His medical skills might be useful. Leesa wouldn't be worried without reason.

Leesa and Darren walked past with John between them. Leesa held the man's arm as he staggered.

Following them out to her car, he got a surprised look from Leesa. 'Thought I'd take a ride with you in case your friend needs help.'

'You don't have to do that.' She sounded snappy, but the relief in her eyes suggested she'd be glad of some help. He wasn't in the habit of jumping to conclusions, except when it came to trusting people not to let him down, so it only showed how much Leesa was getting under his skin. She was special, and he couldn't get past that. 'Not really. I'll sit in the back as the front might be best for John in his condition.'

John appeared to be past hearing what was going on. Not a good look.

'It'll be a slow trip but we don't have far to go,' Leesa said as Darren helped John into the car. 'Hopefully his dad will be there by the time we arrive.'

'We can wait with him if not.'

Leesa glanced at him in the rear-view mirror. 'Thank you.'

'Where do you want me to drop you off? At work to pick up your ute or the apartment?' Leesa asked Nick, who was looking very comfortable in the front seat of her car. Despite all the warnings in her head, she couldn't deny how much she enjoyed his company at work and at play. Though there hadn't been any play so far, and might never be if she managed to keep her wits about her, which was proving difficult.

John's father had been waiting for them and, after they'd got John inside and sprawled over the couch, Nick had given him a quick check over. 'Sleep and a bucket at the ready is all I can recommend. Too much to drink and probably little or no food all day,' was his conclusion.

'Happening too often,' his father had muttered. 'He refuses to get help. Apart from tying him to the back of my truck there's nothing I can do.'

She'd hugged John, her own sadness at losing Danielle feeling heavier than usual. She missed her so much, it was almost unreal. No wonder John wasn't coping. Danielle had been the love of his life. Still was.

'The apartment's fine.' Nick brought her back to the here and now. 'Why don't you come up for a bite to eat? I'll order something in. You look done in, Leesa.'

She'd love nothing more than to sit down with him and not talk a lot, just relax in each other's company. 'I can't. I've got to pick up Baxter and take him for his walk. He'll be thinking his throat's cut since dinner hasn't arrived in his bowl.'

'Can I join you? Fresh air would be good for me too. We could stop for some food afterwards and take it back to my apartment. Baxter's welcome to join us.' Nick said.

It was impossible to fight the need to spend time with him right now. It was too hard when she was aching for her best friend. Good company would help ease the pain and, despite her misgivings about getting too involved, Nick was more than good company.

'You're welcome to,' she said.

At the dog care centre Baxter bounced around both of them as though he'd been imprisoned for a week.

'Freedom, eh, mate?' Nick rubbed his ears, making Leesa think she should bounce around too and get a few pats.

Baxter nuzzled in against Nick's leg, his tail wagging so fast Leesa figured it'd was about to fall off.

'He likes you. Let's go to the esplanade again. It's his favourite walk.' Hers too.

Once there, Nick threw a ball for Baxter to race after and bring back.

'I like you doing that. I don't cover half the distance when I throw it and Baxter doesn't get so worn out.'

Baxter dropped the ball in front of Nick and

sat back, waiting impatiently for him to throw it again.

'As long as it doesn't go into the water,' Nick hurled the ball. 'A wet dog in the car would make me unpopular.'

'There're plenty of towels in the boot. Anyway, what's the point of having a dog if I can't deal with the odd mess to clean up?'

'I agree.'

'Have you ever had a dog? Or a pet of any sort?' He was so good with her boy, he seemed to understand what Baxter wanted.

'Never.'

The usual shutdown when she asked about his personal life. 'Ever consider it?'

'Sometimes, but I'm not home enough.'

No family, no pets. Friends? Best avoid that one. 'I mightn't have taken in Baxter if I hadn't known Karin. She's amazing, looking after him out of hours when I'm caught up with work. Mum and Dad take him if I'm really stuck, that's his favourite place to go to.'

'Gets spoiled rotten?'

'Totally. We always had a dog when I was growing up, but now Mum's got Parkinson's she's unwilling to get another as the day will come when she can't look after it. Dad disagrees but she won't budge on her decision, says having Baxter some days is enough. I think it's part of her way of coping with the Parkinson's.'

'I bet that's hard for both your parents.'

'A complete game changer. Mum mostly tries to carry on as she always has, but she did a lot of work on the farm driving tractors, fixing fences, you name it, and now she's had to give all that up. She was also a crack amateur golfer. I know there are days she can't deal with things, but she never lets Kevin, my brother, or I see it. Sometimes Dad talks to us about how he feels, but mostly he keeps it to himself.'

Not always the way to go, as things got bottled up, but Dad had taken up golf himself in the last year. While nowhere near as good as Mum, he said hitting the ball for as far as possible was a great way to let the frustrations go.

'How long has she had the disease?'

'About eighteen months. It was the main reason I came home. Not to hang around being a pest, but to support Ma and Pa as and when they need it. Besides, I can't imagine not being here. They're my family and that means everything to me.'

Nick took her hand and swung it between them as they walked along. 'I'm glad for you.'

Glancing sideways she saw a wistful look in his eyes. She wanted to tell him he could have that too if he really wanted it, but she suspected he already knew. From the little she'd learned she wondered what held him back from putting himself out there to find the special person to go through life with. 'Your family life wasn't so wonderful?' Her fingers tightened around his.

'No.' He dropped her hand, looking shocked he'd taken it in the first place.

'I'm sorry to hear that.' She took his hand back, and held him lightly.

The relaxed feeling when he'd first taken her hand had gone, replaced by a stiffness that told her to leave the subject alone. And him. If only he would talk, then he might get some of the angst off his chest and feel a little freer. Of course, she'd possibly misinterpreted his reaction to her question, but she didn't think so.

They were a right mixed-up pair: she wanting to settle down with a great guy while still nervous about him turning out to be all wrong for her, and Nick shutting down every time family was mentioned. How would he react if she asked him to join her for dinner tomorrow? He'd probably laugh at her and remind her he'd already turned her down once this week. Best not ask. She called Baxter and turned around to head back to the car, Nick quiet beside her.

Baxter seemed to sense something wasn't quite right, trotting beside Nick all the way, totally ignoring her. It'd be funny if it didn't make her a little peeved. He was her boy, but truly she was happy he was looking out for her friend. If only she knew which buttons to press that'd make Nick relax as much with her. 'What do you feel like for dinner?' she asked. Then laughed. 'Not you, Baxter. You'll have the dried food that's in the car.'

'I don't get to share that?' Nick asked with a wry smile.

Leesa relaxed. They were back to normal, for now at least. 'Maybe.'

'I'm covering for Carl tomorrow,' Nick said quietly.

Forget normal. Her stomach knotted at the thought of more time together. It *would* be a diversion from thinking too much about Danielle. Sure thing. Funny how she could hear her friend laughing at her.

Go, girlfriend.

CHAPTER FOUR

FAMILY. IT WAS a big deal with Leesa. It was a big deal for him too, but from a completely different perspective, Nick acknowledged as he set the Thai takeout containers on the outdoor table. She had what he'd only dreamed of since his grandfather had passed. What he'd been looking for, yet afraid to give it all he had after Ellie did her number on him. Ellie had been the final straw.

He might've jumped into their marriage too fast, all because he wanted love and family so much that he hadn't stopped and really listened to Ellie and what she wanted. But he had learned a lesson. Listen to his head and heart. They had to be in agreement and, looking back, he saw that might not have been the case with Ellie.

Seemed the time had come to let go of the past and move on. If only he knew how do it safely. The idea of being hurt again made him shiver, while thinking it might all be worth the risk if it meant he could be happy. As Patrick said, 'Life's too short to waste it.'

'Want a glass for your beer?' the woman making him rethink a lot of things asked.

Shaking his head, he reached for the bottle she held out. 'It's fine as it is.' Then, before he could change his mind, he said, 'I was married once. It was a complete failure.'

Leesa studied him briefly. 'I know what that's like.'

'Yes, you do. My wife was unfaithful.' Among a few other things. But he'd said more than enough for now. 'Baxter doesn't seem fazed being five storeys off the ground.' The dog was peering between the balustrades at the street below, his tail wagging hard as he spied two dogs.

Leesa stared at him, then nodded. 'He's usually okay with any situation as long as I'm around.' Leesa rubbed her pet's ears. 'Aren't you, boy?'

'Can you give me the details of where you got him from? I think I'd like to get a dog, after all.' It was a sudden decision and yet it felt right. Another step towards settling down.

Another? Try the first. So far everything had been ideas, nothing fixed in reality. Warmth spread through him at the thought of having a pet. He'd never had one before. What the hell was going on? Swigging a mouthful of beer, he glanced at Leesa, and knew she was changing him, whether he liked it or not. Truly, he did like it. Even when he was coming up with reasons not to.

'I'll text you the website address.' She had her phone out and was tapping away. 'I'll recommend you to Karin as she's very protective of the rescue dogs, she usually wants so much background that it can take for ever, unless she knows the person giving a reference.'

'Cheers. It'll have to be a dog that can handle living without a backyard to play in. In the beginning anyway.'

'Lots of walks make up for that. There's also the dog care centre Karin runs for when you're at work.'

He'd seen the big yard there and the dogs running around pretty much nonstop. 'I'd be happy to use that service. I do not want to leave any dog of mine locked inside the apartment alone all day while I'm out.' This was getting serious. None of the usual back-off feelings were in sight. Exciting really.

Leesa opened the containers and sniffed the air like she hadn't eaten for a week. 'Everything smells delicious.'

'Dive in.'

She didn't need a second invitation. Rice and stir-fried vegetables were piling up on her plate, followed by chicken red curry. 'Thanks for this.'

'Anytime.' He meant it. Despite his resistance

she was becoming a part of his outside work life. He couldn't imagine not sharing a meal or going for a walk with her and Baxter—and the dog he would get. Quite an ordinary lifestyle by all accounts, and one he had little experience of. One he would like almost more than anything else. Love would be the deal breaker to being beyond wonderful.

'It's nice just sitting and relaxing. I worry about John a lot. He needs help with his grief but won't listen to anyone about doing something about it.'

'He's not alone with that. People don't like admitting they're not coping. How long were they married?'

'Two and a half years. They were so happy it was unbelievable. I admit to occasionally having been a bit jealous. Then Danielle died and it seemed they'd been cramming in as much as possible before tragedy struck.' She looked at him with a wonky smile. 'Sounds crazy I know but...'

'Hardly crazy. No one knows what's around the corner. They say we should grab everything we can while it's possible.'

Listen to yourself. You haven't exactly been following that advice.

'Danielle was always a bit that way, getting involved with sports, theatre and her career as a pilot. Sometimes I wondered how she fitted in her marriage, but they always seemed happy and there wasn't a moment they weren't doing something they enjoyed.' Leesa was staring out over the railing, sadness filling her face. 'I miss her so much.'

Nick couldn't help himself. He got up and crossed to her, lifting her up and wrapping her in his arms to hug her tight. His chin rested on her head as she snuggled closer. The scent of antiseptic and roses tickled his nostrils. He smiled. Reality was never quite as romantic as it was made out to be, but he liked that about being with Leesa. Reality was key to what he wanted in the future and, if it came packaged in this amazing woman, he could be ready to leap forward with her.

If she'd have him. But he was getting ahead of himself. This moment was about Leesa and her grief, not his heart. Though that was definitely getting more involved every day. 'One day at a time, eh?' He wasn't sure what he was referring to—Leesa's grief or his optimism.

'Only way to go.' She leaned back in his arms and looked at him. 'Thank you for being here for me. I don't usually let anyone see how I'm feeling.'

Everything inside him softened. Leesa was sharing herself with *him*. It meant a lot. 'I'm glad I was able to help.'

Her eyes brightened, tugging at his heart in an unfamiliar way, which was becoming too familiar. 'Funny how we seem to understand each other so easily.'

'Like that night we met in the park when we seemed to click.' Did she understand he wanted to kiss her? Leaning in, his lips touched hers.

Her answer was to open her mouth under his and push her tongue inside, tasting him, winding him up so tight, so fast he felt as if his body would explode. 'Leesa,' he groaned into her.

She pressed her full length hard up against him. Those amazing breasts he still remembered flattened against his chest, her hips rocked against his, as she continued to kiss him with a passion that was mind-blowing.

He'd missed this, missed Leesa as he'd known her those few nights. Her buttocks were under his palms and turned him on even more. Hot, soft, sexy as. He was so hard he ached. 'Leesa?'

'Yes, Nick.' Her fingers were working at his trouser zip, making a job of what should be easy.

'Let me.' He wouldn't last if she didn't hurry.

'Uh, uh.' A couple of fingers slid under his trousers, hot on his abdomen.

Too hot. He pulled back. 'Slow down or I won't be there for you.'

'Can't have that.' She removed her hand so damned slowly those hot fingertips worked magic on his skin, sending his blood racing downward.

He had to bite down hard to hold himself together. 'Stop.'

'Can't do that either.' Her tongue ran over her lips.

'Come on. Inside.' He wouldn't make it to his bed, but there was a large sofa in the lounge.

She must've had the same thought because she headed directly for it, pulling him with her.

Not that he needed any encouragement.

Then she dropped his hand to pull her shirt over her head.

His mouth dried. His memory had failed him. She was so beautiful it hurt to breathe. Her breasts filled their lace cups perfectly. Her skin was creamy and soft, just as his dreams kept reminding him. He had to have her. Now.

No. That's not how this played out. Leesa came first.

'Nick.'

His name whispered against his mouth felt so sexy he nearly exploded.

'Condom,' she whispered.

'What?'

'Condom.'

Yikes. Showed how far gone he was. 'Be right back.' So much for the bedroom being too far away. They had to be careful, no matter how they were feeling.

He pulled the drawer so hard it hit the floor. At least the packet he needed was at the top.

Back to Leesa, who was sprawled over the sofa watching him as he raced towards her, his erection leading the way.

'Give me that.' She tugged the packet from his lifeless fingers and tore it open with her teeth. Then she reached for him, slid her hand down his length, squeezed softly, slid up again.

A breath stalled in the back of his throat. Lowering onto the sofa beside her exquisite body he found her wet heat. Ran a finger over her, and when she bucked under his touch, he did it again. And again. And again. He kept stroking her, drowning in her cries of ecstasy until she cried out and fell back, her eyes wide and her chest rising and falling fast. 'Nick,' she croaked.

Then she was up on an elbow, reaching for him, sliding the condom over his shaft so slowly he couldn't breathe for the heat and tension gripping him. 'Leesa, stop or I'll come.'

Her smile undid him. He tensed and then she was under him, guiding him inside, and he was joining her as she arched up into him. They were together. Completely.

Leesa stretched her whole body. She felt tender all over, and so relaxed and happy. Making out with Dr Sexy had been just what she needed. Hearing a rumbling sound coming from the man himself, she laughed. 'Hungry by any chance?'

'That was quite a work out,' he grinned and kissed her forehead. 'Seriously, thank you. I enjoyed every moment.' He'd said thank you in a note after the first time. Pretty amazing that a man could openly thank her for being so intimate.

'I did too.' She hadn't had sex since their fling in Cairns, hadn't wanted to. Every time she thought that she should put some effort into finding a special man to start the life she longed for, memories of Nick and their lovemaking would stop her in her tracks. He had been wonderful and would be a hard, if not impossible, act to follow. Those few nights had meant so much. There'd been a depth to being with Nick—she knew she'd never settle for less again.

He was getting up. 'I'll get us some food.'

'It'll need heating up. Can I grab a quick shower while you're doing that?' She hadn't had one before leaving work and was more than ready for one now.

'Go for it. Towels are in the large drawer beneath the basin.'

She hadn't even stepped under the water when Nick came through the bathroom door, roaring with laughter. 'Forget the Thai. Seems Baxter's into rice and stir fry. There's curry but it's on the deck, so guess he wasn't keen on that. He's got a very round stomach at the moment.'

'The little brat. I was looking forward to more. It's been ages since I had Thai.' She laughed. 'That'll teach me for being so easily side-tracked.'

'Can't blame him. We kind of neglected him.' Nick had his phone out. 'I'll order some more. Handy that they're only a few doors along the road.'

'I'll have my shower.'

'I'll join you in a moment.'

No food, but having Nick wash her back was going to be just as good. And the food wouldn't be too long. Quite the night.

And it only got better.

Just after midnight Leesa crawled out of Nick's bed and dragged on her clothes. 'I'm on duty at seven, and I need to take Baxter home so Mum can pick him up later in the morning.'

'We both probably need some shut eye. I'll see you down to your car.'

It was cool that he wanted to make certain she was safe. Not that she had any concerns, but still, Nick was a gentleman through and through. What's more, she really liked that about him. It was a first. Not even in the first months of their relationship had Connor been so kind. Nick was nothing like him, hadn't shown any tendency towards bullying, and by now she did have experience to fall back on. She could start to trust her instincts.

After getting Baxter settled on the back seat, she turned to Nick and gave him a quick kiss. 'I've had a great time.'

'Me too.'

She was free tomorrow night to do it again. And the next one.

Don't rush things.

Good idea. Let the excitement and thrill of earlier settle a bit before making rash decisions.

On a sorry indrawn breath, she said, 'See you at work. Unless you want me to come by and pick you up, since your ute's still at the airport?'

'I'll grab a taxi.' Withdrawing already? Or saving her the hassle of having to go across town?

She'd run with that. It felt better. She had to stop looking for trouble and get on with having fun with a decent man. Nick was more than decent. He was sexy as all be it. He was so good looking she wanted to keep prodding him to make sure he was for real. His love making was beyond reality. She lost herself completely when he touched her. Maybe she did need to back off fast until her head was clear, so she could think carefully about where to go from here. 'No problem.' Clambering into the car, she headed for home, and time to dream about the hours she'd spent with Nick.

* * *

Leesa spent most of the rest of the night reflecting on Nick and their relationship. Whenever she closed her eyes, he was there behind her eyelids, smiling, laughing, being kind, gentle. And not giving much away.

Winding her up tight all over again, only this time it was all about her feelings and what to do about them. He was growing on her fast. Too fast, when she wanted to take one slow step at a time. She'd fallen for Connor quickly and look where that led. Part of her, a big part, wanted to let all that go so she could trust Nick. He really was nothing like her ex. Not in any way.

She was getting ahead of herself. There'd been nothing in their hours together to say that he might be interested in her, other than for a good time in the sack.

Now she was heading into work just as she had been a year ago when she got the call to say Danielle was gone. Her fingers whitened on the steering wheel. 'Miss you something terrible, girlfriend.' Would she ever get over losing Danielle? In some ways she probably would, but in others never. 'Damn it, Danielle, I need to talk to you, to hear you give me a speech about how, because I was a moron over Connor, it doesn't mean it'll happen again.'

Had Nick taken Carl's shift to be with her on

the day she was mourning her friend? She suspected so. It would be second nature for him. Turning into the airport, she drove slowly towards the Flying Health Care hangar. She should be buzzing after last night, but now she suddenly felt nothing but trepidation. What if she was making a fool of herself with Nick? Everyone here seemed to think he was a great guy, but that wasn't a reason to fall in love with him. For her that had to be all about trust. The thing was, she did trust him. So why the hesitation?

'Morning, Leesa,' Nick called when she walked into the hangar. He was at the cupboard checking the drug kit they took on board. He didn't stop what he was doing to give her a smile or acknowledge the night before. Having similar doubts as her? Quite likely, considering he had some family issues.

'Hi, there,' she replied. 'How's things?'

'All good.'

Not super chatty. But when was he? When they were sitting on his deck eating Thai and getting hot and bothered. That's when. She shook her head and headed to the locker room, walking away from the temptation of wrapping her arms around him, along with a quick kiss. It wouldn't be professional to do that here. She probably shouldn't follow up on last night either, not when he seemed to have gone quiet on her.

Instead, she went to see if they had any flights arranged. Saturdays were usually quieter but she hoped today would be an exception.

'We're giving Jacob a lift home at eleven.'

She nearly leapt out of her skin at the sound of Nick's voice right behind her. So much for thinking he was keeping to himself. 'I didn't know he was still down here. He'll be fretting about his friend's birthday present.'

'Apparently, he had a rough time after his chemo and was kept in PICU for two days. He's doing all right now, but it's likely to happen again as the chemo takes its toll.'

'It will.' The build-up of the treatment always had a long-term effect, which she hated seeing with her patients. Especially the little ones. Being a parent was on her wish list, and it seemed nothing but exciting from where she stood, but she knew all too well that wasn't always the case. She did know, if she was lucky enough to become a mother, she'd love her kid to bits and be super strong for him or her no matter what.

'At the moment there's nothing else on our schedule,' Nick informed her. 'I'm putting the jug on. Feel like a tea or coffee?'

'Tea, thanks. Is Darren here?'

'Doing his aircraft checks. He'll be in shortly.' Nick turned towards the kitchen.

Definitely not overly friendly. But she hadn't

put herself out to be chirpy either. It was still hard not to rush over and hug him, to feel his long strong body against her.

The main phone rang sharply. Racing to answer it, she silently begged for a job so she didn't have to sit around in the kitchen for hours. 'Flying Health Care. Leesa speaking.'

'Hey, Leesa, it's Michael. We've got a call from Weipa to pick up a man who's been in a truck versus car accident. Internal injuries, fractures to both legs and pelvis.' Michael worked the phones for emergency services. 'I'll adjust the flight time for Jacob to early afternoon.'

Poor Jacob. Things weren't panning out for him this week. 'Right. On our way.' She hung up, feeling guilty. A seriously injured patient wasn't quite what she meant as a distraction. 'Forget the tea and coffee, Nick. We're on.'

'What've we got?'

Moving quickly to the plane, she filled him in on the scant facts. Once they were on the way more would come through on the laptop they took with them. 'Jacob's flight will be delayed until we're back.'

'He won't be happy about that. He so wanted to see his friend and give him his present. I imagine every hour is going to seem like another day to him.' Nick gave her a brief smile.

A smile that touched her, and loosened some

of her worries about them, despite it disappearing almost as soon as he'd produced it. 'You're not wrong there.'

'Why doesn't he go by car? It's only about three hours, isn't it?'

'Jacob gets car sick, and add in the chemo effects and it wouldn't be pleasant for anyone,' Leesa told him as she waved bye to the ground crew pulling the stairs away from the plane.

'Yet he's fine in the plane.' Nick buckled into his seat. 'But that's how it is for some.'

'Ready back here,' she told Darren through the headset she'd pulled on.

'It's going to be a bit bumpy over the hills,' the pilot warned them.

'No problem.' She didn't mind minor turbulence. It was a different story when they had a patient on board, as it added to the stress and pain for that person, and made helping them difficult as they had to remain strapped in their seats.

Nick had the laptop open and was reading the information about the patient they were flying to Weipa to pick up. 'Not looking good.'

'Fill me in.'

'Fractured ribs, both femurs, and right upper arm. Suspected perforated lung. Swelling in the abdomen so there must be more injuries in that area. We're going to be pushing it to get him to Cairns without a major problem occurring.'

'Going as fast as allowed,' Darren came through the headset.

'I figured you might be,' Nick responded. Then he looked her way. 'You good to go with whatever happens?'

'Always.' As if he had to ask. It was the nature of the job to be prepared for worst-case scenarios. They happened often enough for her to know wishful thinking didn't prevent them.

'You won't get a better paramedic than Leesa,' Darren said a little sharply.

'Thanks, Darren.' Turning to Nick, she removed the mouthpiece so Darren didn't hear. 'Do not question my ability. I am well versed in the medical requirements of our work.'

'I'm sorry. It was a reflex question. I don't doubt your medical skills.'

'Thank you.' They had moved on from their intimate night to being tense with each other. Not a good look for the future. Better to know now than later.

She turned to face out the window for the rest of the flight.

Nick knew he'd stuffed up big time. The anger in Leesa's expression told him she wasn't going to forgive him any time soon for questioning her ability to deal with the death of a patient. It had been a mistake. He hadn't deliberately set out to check she was comfortable with what might lie ahead, he'd been speaking aloud in an attempt to discuss what they might face. Except it came out as a question, and she was not happy with him.

Talk about going from a high to a low. Last night had been beyond fantastic. Making love with Leesa couldn't be better. She was so giving. And accepting. Almost loving. Almost. They were not falling in love. They couldn't. He wasn't ready, despite his feelings for her growing stronger by the day. After last night, it was going to be even harder to stay away from her.

Other than at work, and then they were professionals, looking after patients, keeping each other at arm's length. He was also about to apply for Joy's position, which meant he might have to take a step back to remain professional.

But right now, he wanted to reach out and touch Leesa, to tell her how much he believed in her medical skills. Other skills too. When it came to sticking up for herself, she was strong. She'd proved that by helping those women at the Brisbane base. There'd be no walking all over her, and he'd never want to. Leesa was his dream woman. His mind went back to last night when he was inside her and she was crying out as she came. More than a dream. She was real and near perfect, and he was still hesitant.

A while later she turned to look at him. 'Weipa's to our left. Darren must've had his foot to the pedal all the way.'

'No such thing as a pedal up here,' Darren retorted.

'Thank goodness for that or who knows how fast this plane might've gone.' Nick stretched his legs to loosen the kinks in his muscles. 'I've never been this far north and all I'm going to see is the airport.'

'Somewhere to come when you have leave to use up. Lots of people go through using four-wheel drive vehicles. I haven't done it, but know there's certain times of the year when it's safer. The rainy season's not one as the mud builds up and vehicles get bogged down. Not easy to get out when you're in the middle of nowhere.'

'Surely people go in groups?'

'Mostly, but there're always the exceptions. I remember one chopper flight we had to pick up a woman who'd had her leg broken when her husband revved the truck, it ran over her because it wasn't as stuck as he'd believed.'

Idiot. How could a man do that when his wife was in line with the vehicle? 'Lack of experience in the outback then.'

'Definitely.'

'Have you heard that Joy's leaving?' he asked. 'I'm thinking of applying for the position.'

'Me too.'

'That I didn't expect.'

'Why ever not? I'm as capable as anyone to do it justice,' she snapped, taken aback by the shock in his face.

'I know you are. It just never occurred to me you might want to run the outfit. You're so happy doing what you do.'

'I am, but there's nothing wrong with wanting to advance my career. Same as you want.'

'True.'

'It could prove interesting,' Leesa retorted as the wheels touched down on the tarmac and the plane slowed.

Unsure how she felt about his revelation, he moved on. 'There's an ambulance waiting by the shed. No, the driver's started backing towards where I presume Darren's going to park. A woman's already pushing the stairs this way.'

'They're obviously in a hurry. Not a good sign.' Unbuckling her belt, Leesa waited impatiently at the door for the plane to come to a halt, as near to the ambulance as possible without jeopardising anyone's safety.

'I agree.' Internal bleeding could lead to cardiac arrest. Or the man might've gone into a deep coma from a head wound. Worse, his lung might be compromised by a broken rib gouging a hole in it.

Stop. Wait for the facts before starting to work

out how to get this man to Cairns safely. 'I'd say we'll be back in the air in minutes, Darren.'

'Gotcha.'

'Here we go.' Leesa slid the door open as the plane stopped. The stairs were getting close.

They both grabbed a handle as the woman reached them and applied the brakes.

Nick leapt down the steps two at a time and strode to the ambulance as its back doors opened. 'Hi, I'm Nick, a doctor.'

'Hey, Nick. Heard we had someone new.' A woman began moving the trolley with their patient onto the tarmac. 'This is Maxwell O'Neill, forty-seven. Severe trauma to head, lungs, abdomen and legs. He suffered cardiac arrest fifteen minutes ago. We resuscitated him, but his heart rate's slow. Given the injuries blood loss is probably high.'

'Right, no hanging around then.'

Within minutes the stretcher was on the mini lift with Leesa at the man's side, pressing the button that made them rise up to the plane door. Nick shot up the stairs to help unload the stretcher onto the bed. He was barely aware of the plane lifting off as he read the monitors displaying Maxwell's heart reading, blood pressure and his breathing. 'This is going to be one long trip.' Every minute would feel like an hour as they worked to keep Maxwell alive.

Leesa looked up from where she was preparing the defibrillator in case Maxwell's heart stopped again. The chances were high. 'We can do it.' Her smile was small but warm, easing some of his tension.

It felt good to have her with him for this. She fed his confidence so that he did believe in himself. Not that he didn't usually, but there were some cases when he knew the odds were stacked against saving a patient—this was one of them. Having Leesa here took away some of that pressure. 'Thanks.'

Her reply was another smile.

So he was back in the good books—for now at least.

Thirty minutes later the line on the heart monitor flat-lined.

Leesa immediately placed the defib pads on Maxwell's bare chest and stepped back.

Nick pushed the button and waited, heart in his throat, for the electric current to get up to peek.

Maxwell's body lifted from the stretcher as the shock struck. Dropped back.

The air filled with a steady beeping sound.

Nick exhaled heavily. 'Phew. Thank goodness.'

Leesa wiped her brow. 'I can't believe his heart restarted at the first attempt.' There was a wobble in her voice.

'Hey, we were ready for it and wasted no time giving him a shock.'

'I know, but still.'

'Yeah, I get it.'

Twenty minutes out of Cairns it happened again. This time it took two shocks to get Maxwell's heart beating and the rhythm was all over the place.

Darren came through the headset. 'There's a helicopter on standby to take your patient to the hospital. There's been a crash on the main road and traffic's built up for kilometres either side.'

The last thing this man needed was a hold up. He probably wouldn't survive much longer without all the high-tech equipment only available in hospital. 'We'll go with him.'

'That's the plan,' Darren came back.

A thought came out of nowhere. 'Jacob's not going to be happy.'

Leesa glanced at him. 'I know. But we can pick him up in the chopper for the short hop back to the airport and the plane.'

Of course she'd think of that. 'Get onto whoever deals with these things and arrange it when you've got a free moment.'

'Tomorrow?' she laughed.

'Not if you want Jacob to still talk to you.'

'Good point.' Leesa grabbed a moment to call Michael and get Jacob and his mother's flight sorted.

Again, transferring their patient was fast and they were back in the air in no time, this time the thumping sound of rotors filling the cabin, and Maxwell was still oblivious to what was going on.

Nick knew he wouldn't relax until the man was off the chopper and being rolled into ED. Only then would he feel safe to breathe properly. They'd done all they could to keep Maxwell alive. It wasn't always enough, but there were limitations even for doctors. The down side to the job.

'Hey.' A light tap on his shoulder. 'Cheer up. We've done well so far.'

Dang, she read him so easily. And made him feel good when she did, not so alone. 'You're right. We have.'

Had the drama diverted her from thinking about her friend and what today meant? She'd been distracted in bed last night, but had thoughts of her friend's demise returned the moment she was back in her own place? Chances were, they had. Leesa didn't hide from pain, instead she seemed to confront it and work through it. He should take a leaf out of her book and do much the same.

CHAPTER FIVE

'SEE YOU NEXT TIME, Jacob,' Leesa waved at her favourite patient before heading out to the plane.

'Promise you will be here?' Jacob gave her a cheeky grin. He was happier than he'd been when he boarded the plane. Then he'd been sad and tearful, afraid his friend wouldn't talk to him because he was going to be so late home. His mother had managed to get a message through and the friend sent Jacob a text on *his* mother's phone saying he'd saved some cake to share with Jacob as soon as he got there. The lad hadn't stopped smiling since.

'You know I meant next time I'm rostered on to be your paramedic, you ratbag.' Which should be the next visit he had to make for treatment. Joy knew how much she liked being with Jacob and always tried to put them on the same flight. If she did get Joy's job, she wouldn't get to do those special flights with her favourite patients as often. Something else to consider.

Her application was in and still she wondered

if it was the right thing to do. Did she really want to sit behind a desk for hours on end when she could be in the air caring for someone in pain or who was very unwell? Joy did her share of flights when she wasn't tied up with paperwork, as well as discussions with hospital management and other health units, but nothing like the number the rest of the medical crew members did.

There was a bigger question. Did she want to be Nick's boss? It would get in the way of being close friends, something they were rapidly becoming when they weren't being cautious around one another. Worse, it would mean they couldn't be intimate any more. Not when she had to treat all the staff equally. That was essential for good relations, and even if she and Nick continued their fling, she'd follow through on maintaining a level field with everyone. But it would only take one mistake or a perceived error where it appeared Nick was being favoured and she'd be out on her backside.

The other side of this was that Nick had applied too and could end up being her boss. Same issues arose. Plus, she might feel uncomfortable if he was in charge. So far, he came across as eager to work with people, not wanting to be in charge all the time. But she knew how that could be a farce. Hard to imagine that of Nick though. Talk about complicated.

As Darren took off, she leaned her head back and closed her eyes. So many things to consider since Nick had turned up in Cairns. Since returning home she'd been cruising through life, loving her work, enjoying time on the farm with the family and visiting Gran, spending hours with her friends when they were all free at the same time. Giving Baxter all he needed, not necessarily all he wanted. Life had been pretty good.

It still was. Except she'd been living in a vacuum. Taking each day as it came, not looking for more. Not thinking too seriously about her future and the dreams she'd always had about falling in love and raising kids and owning a piece of land with a lovely family home on it.

All very well to think she had years ahead to achieve those dreams, but look what had happened to Danielle. The babies she'd wanted, the trip to Norway to meet her nieces, the career she was building—gone in an instant. Thankfully Danielle hadn't waited to get started on fulfilling her dreams, or she'd not have achieved anything.

'Get a wiggle on, girlfriend. Make the most of today, not tomorrow.'

Leesa's eyes shot open and she looked around. She'd swear Danielle was right here, sitting opposite, locking her formidable gaze on her.

Instead, Nick asked, 'What's up?'

'Nothing. I was daydreaming.'

'What about?'

'Nothing important.' Not half.

'Really?' He sounded disappointed she wasn't sharing.

Something she understood. 'Really.' Some things weren't for imparting to a man she was still getting to know. She closed her eyes again. Hopefully she'd sleep till they reached Cairns. She was tired. Last night had been awesome. Making love with Nick was beyond amazing. She'd also been upset about Danielle. John had added to that with his despair. Yeah, sleep would be good. She sank deeper into the uncomfortable seat and tried to stop thinking about anything.

'Hey, wake up sleepy head. We've landed.' Nick was already out of his seat, looking eager to get going.

After knuckling her eyes, she straightened up and checked the time. Eighteen hundred had been and gone. 'With a bit of luck, we're done for the day.'

Darren poked his head around the cabin doorway. 'I haven't had any notification of another flight.'

'Nothing on the laptop either,' Nick confirmed.

Relief filled her. It had been stressful dealing with Maxwell's cardiac arrests and those horrendous injuries. She'd head out to the farm and have a shower there. Mum was cooking her favourite pasta for dinner as a cheer-her-up treat. Just the thought of diving into the bowl of sea-food and spaghetti made her feel a load better. The sleep might've helped too. 'What are you up to tonight?' she asked Nick as he slung the drug kit over his shoulder.

He shrugged. 'A quiet night in.' No smile was forthcoming. He looked tired. It had been as stressful for him working with Maxwell. Probably more so as the doctor on the job. Nick would've taken it hard if their patient hadn't made it as far as the hospital and into emergency care.

'It's been a long day.'

'It has.' He stood back for her to go down the stairs first, barely looking at her. Now that they'd finished work, he appeared to be taking a step back from her. Like her, he might want to think about where they were headed before he got in too deep. She didn't believe he regretted spending time with her. Nick was too genuine for that. He wouldn't have made love and then turned up at work as though they were merely colleagues if something wasn't bugging him. Like her.

Walking into the hangar, she thought about the warmth of being with her family. Something Nick clearly longed for. She sighed. To hell with all this toing and froing about how she felt. They both deserved to relax over a meal with a beer or wine and easy company.

Turning around, she crossed to the supply room. 'Nick, how about joining me and the family for dinner?' If he turned her down it would be the last time she asked.

Slowly he looked across to her. 'Thanks, but think I'll give it a miss. I'm shattered.'

Fair enough. But studying him, her heart tightened at the despondency she saw. He wasn't being entirely truthful. But he also didn't do the feel sorry for me thing. 'Seafood spaghetti marinara is on the menu.'

'How did you know that's one of my favourite meals?' His smile was strained, but it was a smile.

'Something else we have in common. Mum makes it when she thinks I need cheering up.'

'Today you do because of Danielle.'

'Yes.'

'Have I got time to have a shower and throw on some decent clothes that don't smell of antiseptic?'

That was a yes then. Progress. She'd grab the moment and to heck with everything else. 'Go for it. Don't rush. I'll pop down to the supermarket to grab a couple of things Mum needs.'

'Can you add a bottle of wine to the list and I'll fix you up later?'

She shook her head. 'No. Tonight I've invited you out. Your role is to relax and enjoy yourself.'

Along with my company.

No holding back tonight. Danielle was right. Why wait for life to start? It was already here.

'Hey, Mum. I'm at the supermarket. Have you thought of anything else you need?'

'No, Leesa, just the Pinot Noir and tomato paste.' She laughed. 'Not to go together.'

'I'm bringing Nick, the new doctor, with me. Hope that's all right?' Her parents never made a fuss about her turning up with someone extra for a meal but, since it was Nick, she felt she had to say something so that her mum didn't get all gushy when they arrived. Since her Parkinson's diagnosis she'd been keen for Leesa to settle down with someone special.

Her mother laughed again. 'Not even answering.'

There was a bounce in Leesa's step as she made her way along the supermarket aisles. She added a second bottle of wine to the basket before grabbing a couple of items she needed at home, including biscuits for Baxter.

Nick smelt of pine soap when he slipped into the car beside her. His shorts moulded his tight butt, and the blue and white shirt, with two buttons open at the top, made her mouth salivate. Her fingers tightened on the steering wheel to prevent her from leaning over and rubbing his tanned skin. How did she possibly think she could remain aloof around him? He was stunning.

'I'm glad you persisted about me coming. I feel better already.' Nick glanced her way. 'Your family know I'm on the way?'

'Yep. I think Kevin's bringing a couple of mates too. Dad's got some chores to be done in the morning.'

'Count me in. Beats doing the housework.'

'From what I saw your apartment is immaculate.' Almost OTT in her book. 'You might get to drive a tractor tomorrow. There's early cane to be harvested.'

'Could prove interesting. Probably best I stick to the mundane chores.'

'It's no different to driving any other vehicle as long as you keep an eye out where you're going.'

'Could be a new skill to add to my CV.' He laughed for the first time all day, making her pleased she'd suggested he come with her.

She'd asked him as though it was a date, even if he didn't get that. Last night had been wonderful, today a lot less so, and she wanted to find a balance so they could get along—without watching every single thing they said or did for fear of tripping up. 'Being able to do things on a farm beats living in the middle of a large city.'

'I'm starting to see the benefits.'

'What did you used to do in your spare time?'

'In Brisbane I'd go to the Gold Coast to surf and kayak. I'd done some of that in Adelaide but prefer the Coast. In Sydney it wasn't so easy. It takes so long to get to anywhere when you live close to the Central Business District it's a drag.'

'Why the CBD?'

'I was working at the central ambulance station and the rules were that you had to live within sixty minutes of the station, so you could be called in for emergencies. It's a bit extreme really, as everyone on call stayed over at the station anyway, but the advantage for me was not having to take long, tedious train rides to get to work or home at the end of an arduous shift.'

When he relaxed, he could talk a lot. Showed how often he wasn't at ease with people. 'Central Sydney is fabulous,' Leesa said, 'but I could never live there. I prefer the outdoors being handy so I can get out and about any time I like.'

'You've got the farm for that, and all the beaches up the coastline.' He nodded. 'This is a great place. I could see myself staying here longer than my usual stints.'

'You what?' Had he really admitted that? To her?

'Surprised you, have I?' he asked with a serious look. 'Surprised myself, actually. It would be good to stop moving around.'

'Why do you?'

'Habit?' He hesitated. 'I'm looking for somewhere I feel comfortable.'

'Cairns is doing that?'

'Might be.' His uncertainty spoke volumes.

'Give yourself some time before making a major decision. You haven't been here very long.' He mightn't be either, but hope flared.

'True, but I already prefer the work. Flying all over the place to help people with ongoing issues, not having to sit in peak hour traffic when I'm coping with a touch-and-go case. There're a lot of pluses.'

'True.' What about his private life? Any pluses there?

'It's great being invited to dinner with you and your parents.'

She went with his change of subject. Pushing further might lead to him shutting down completely. 'Baxter will be happy to see you.'

He smacked his forehead lightly. 'How could I forget him? He's a big plus to living here.'

'Still thinking you might get a dog?'

'Yes, but if I do, I seriously have to consider moving into a place with a bit of a yard.'

She couldn't imagine Baxter being in an apartment. He loved bounding around the lawn too much. Indicating to turn left, she said, 'Here we go.'

Nick gave her a quizzical glance. 'You sound like you're uncertain about something.'

What about how her mother was going to act around Nick? 'Think the day's catching up.' Her energy level had fallen again, but not as low as when they'd finished work.

'I'm sure a wine and a bowl of spaghetti will have you bouncing around in no time.'

'Fingers crossed you're right.'

And that Mum keeps quiet about certain topics.

Nick would certainly head for another city if he heard a hint of what her mother hoped for.

'That was superb,' Nick told Jodi, Leesa's mother, as he pushed his plate aside. 'Seriously good.'

'Compliments will get you a third helping any day,' Kevin laughed.

He grinned. 'Except someone beat me to the last spoonful.'

'Only the fast win around here,' Kevin said.

'Relax, boys,' Jodi said. 'There's apple crumble and custard to follow.'

Nick shook his head. 'I can't believe this. Amazing.'

Family dinners had never been a part of his life. Not even when growing up with Grandad, who thought meals were to feed the body and not the mind with dreams of delectable offerings. As for what was doled out in foster care, forget it.

One dollop of something that could've been anything the pigs didn't want, and smelt even worse, did nothing for meal times except make them something that had to be got through as fast as possible. One home had been better, he conceded. Mrs Cole had cooked up decent solid meals that everyone had ate in a hurry, before leaving the table to get back to whatever they'd been doing before the plates were put down.

'Tomorrow it's a barbecue after we've finished in the paddocks,' Kevin told him.

'If you're trying to convince me to stay and help out, I'm in.' It was the least he could do for these kind people. Better than out and out admitting he wanted to spend more time with them.

'Might as well stay the night then,' Jodi said with a little smile. 'We've got extra rooms out the back.'

'I haven't come prepared for work. I'll need to pop home and get some rough clothes and boots.'

'Plenty here,' Leesa told him. 'All sizes.'

'Bathroom supplies available too,' Jodi told him.

With everything he needed on hand, he really couldn't insist on returning to town for the night. 'It's a done deal then.' Sipping his beer, he decided it wasn't such a bad thing either. He could get used to this easy way the Bennetts had about them, though no doubt there'd be nothing relaxed about harvest tomorrow. Standing up, he began clearing the dishes from the table.

Yes, he was comfortable beyond description, and for once he couldn't dredge up any enthusiasm over keeping his distance—especially from Leesa. She'd brought him into her circle without any concerns. Inviting him here tonight had come naturally, despite the tension lying between them throughout the day.

Leesa trusted him. Kapow. Just like that, she trusted him.

Talk about a first. Make that the first time he'd trusted in return so readily. Because, yes, he trusted her not to make a fool of him.

He could be making a fool of himself and she'd prove him wrong, but he couldn't find it within himself to believe so. Didn't mean he was going to leap into a relationship with her. They worked together and he didn't want to leave the job he was enjoying so much, especially if he did get the promotion. Also, he'd once fallen in love only to have it thrown back in his face. It had been the final blow to an already fearful heart. He'd lost enough people who mattered. Losing another would be impossible to cope with.

'Take that crumble through to the dining room,' Jodi told him.

'Yes, ma'am.' Leesa often sounded just like her mother, he realised. No arguing with either of them.

'Don't you "yes, ma'am" me.' She playfully

flicked a tea towel at him. 'Pour my daughter another drink so she'll have to stay the night and
not rush back to that empty house she lives in.'

'Trying to get me into trouble?' he grinned. He
liked this woman. She pulled no punches, again
like Leesa. And the rest of the family. 'Tell me,
was it tough growing up here when Leesa and
Kevin were young?'

'You'd have to ask Leesa. I will say we had no
spare money, the kids didn't have fancy clothes
or toys, but they both learned to work hard and
be proud of what they achieved.'

Though in very different circumstances, he'd
had much the same lessons. 'Sounds ideal.' For
them, not him. He headed away with the pud-
ding before he got hit with a load of questions he
wasn't ready to answer, kind as Jodi was.

Kevin had moved away to talk on his phone
and Leesa's father, Brent, was nowhere in sight.

'Would you like another wine?' He knew he
was supposed to pour one without giving her the
chance to say no, but he preferred to be more onside with Leesa than her mother if it came down
to it.

Leesa looked from her empty glass to him, and
nodded. 'Why not?' Her eyes shone with laughter. 'You seem comfortable.'

'You know what? I am. I'm even looking forward to going out in the sugar cane fields and getting down and dirty.'

'You might regret that tomorrow night when you've had too much sun, and muscles you aren't aware of ache like stink.'

'You suggesting I'm a townie?'

'Would you expect any different?' she asked and picked up the glass he'd filled. 'Joining me? Or saving yourself for tractor driving?'

A challenge was not to be ignored. He flipped the cap off another beer. Despite being momentarily alone with Leesa he leaned close to say quietly, 'Depends what you mean by joining you.' He could hand out challenges too.

Her smile was so sexy he nearly spilt his beer. 'You're sleeping in the staff quarters.'

'Who else will be there?' Kevin would have his own room in the house, surely? His mates weren't arriving till first thing in the morning as something had come up to keep them in town.

'I might,' Leesa teased.

'Better than me sneaking inside like a horny teen.' What with the noise Leesa made when she came, the whole house would know what was going on.

'I don't know. It could be fun.'

He shivered. He might be comfortable with this family, but there were limitations to how far he took it. 'I'd be too worried we'd be heard to actually let go.'

Leesa's laughter was loud and naughty, and brought everyone back to the table for dessert.

But later when she slipped in beside him on the narrow bed in the staff quarters, he had no hand-brake on his feelings. Nor did Leesa.

The only downside was when she left him to go back to her room around three o'clock. 'I'm acting like that teenager you mentioned, but I can't bear to see a knowing look in my parents' eyes when my alarm goes off and I'm not there to stop it.'

After she'd gone, he slept the sleep of the dead. That was so abnormal he was stunned when Leesa's banging on the door woke him.

'What time is it?' The sun was streaming in the window he'd forgotten to cover with the blind.

'Six. I'm heading away. Mum's got breakfast going and the others are already downing mugs of tea.'

He'd been so deeply asleep he hadn't heard their vehicle arriving? 'Great. Now they'll all call me Townie.' He clambered out of bed.

'Take a fast shower before you head over to the house,' Leesa grinned. 'I'll see you tonight.'

He thought she was grinning because he smelt of their night together, but when the water remained cold he had to wonder if she'd been having him on. He wouldn't put it past her.

'Dang, forgot to turn the hot water cylinder on last night,' Brent said when he joined the men around the table. 'We don't leave it on when no one's using the quarters.'

'I'll see to it before we get started in the fields,' Nick told him. 'I'll need a shower before heading back to town.' He didn't want to pong of sweat when Leesa drove him home, hopefully to his apartment for some more fun. Or she might decide to take him to the house she lived in, which he had yet to see. Apparently, it belonged to her grandmother who wasn't ready to sell it, despite living in a retirement village.

'Right. Let's get this happening.' Brent stood up. 'Nick, time for a driving lesson.'

'After I turn the water on,' he returned, feeling so good. Rinsing his plate, he stowed it in the dishwasher and followed the men outside with a spring in his step. To be doing something different and helping this family felt great. It showed how little he did beyond work.

After Patrick gave him his second chance, once he'd begun studying hard to get the grades that got him into university, he'd rarely looked sideways for other interests. His focus had been on proving he was as capable as Judge Crombie had suggested, and now it seemed he didn't know any other way to be.

Leesa was slowly changing him, and through her, her family seemed to be too. Another thing to be careful about? Could be, though a voice was nagging him to let it go and make the most of the opportunity to live a full life, not one that was devoted totally to medicine. He realised he really didn't know how to do that. Didn't have a clue.

'Climb up, Nick. We're heading to that field by the road.'

So began his experience of harvesting.

'How'd that go?' Leesa asked fourteen hours later when she sat down beside him on her parents' deck, where everyone was relaxing with a cold beer.

'He's not bad for a townie,' Kevin answered for him. 'His rows were straight and the cane wasn't mangled.'

'I really enjoyed myself.' Who knew he'd get so much pleasure out of driving a tractor up and down fields in the sweltering heat for hours on end? 'So much so I've put my hand up to help out again when I'm free.'

The smile Leesa gave him increased the happiness. 'Nothing like a new experience to give you a lift.'

She really did understand him. She mightn't

know how messed up he was, but she certainly understood he wanted more out of life than what he already had.

'I wasn't down in the first place.'

'No, but you were looking for something to distract you from work.'

Thank goodness Baxter nudged his knee just then, or he might've grabbed Leesa into a hug that he wouldn't be able to pull back from. Instead, he rubbed the dog behind his ears. 'Hey, boy, is it your dinner time?'

'He's already had it. But no harm in trying to con you into a second round.' Leesa patted Baxter, but he wasn't moving away from Nick's hand.

'Fair enough.' Nick kept rubbing the dog. 'How was work? Busy?'

'Two short flights, one to take a man home after he was discharged from the cardiac ward, another to pick up a tourist who fell off a cliff up in the Daintree and sustained a fractured pelvis.'

'You go by chopper for that one?'

'Yes. It was only a short hop, but not near a road for an ambulance to do the job.' She drained her beer and stood up. 'I'd better give Mum a hand. She seems more tired than usual.'

'She had a restless night,' Leesa's dad spoke up. 'There've been a few of those lately.' The man looked worried.

'The specialist did say that would happen, Dad.

I think a lot of it's to do with her overthinking about what lies ahead.' Leesa frowned. 'Maybe she should have some counselling.'

'Good luck telling her that. She bit my head off the one time I mentioned it.'

'I'm not surprised.' Leesa sighed. 'Mum's always been strong and now she thinks she's letting the side down by being sick.'

'From what I've seen, she's still strong,' Nick said. 'She hasn't given up on getting out and doing her chores and having fun with the family.'

The shaking in her hands had been a bit stronger this morning, but that would happen as time went by. Sometimes it would be because Jodi had done too much, and would revert back to where it had been when she rested, and sometimes the intensity would remain, a sign of the Parkinson's strengthening.

Leesa squeezed his shoulder. 'Thanks for that. I think we're all watching too hard to find something.'

'You're not wrong,' Brent said.

'I imagine it's impossible not to,' Nick agreed. 'It's probably also what Jodi's doing.' He'd seen that with patients when he'd been training. Giving someone a prognosis that had no cure cranked up their anxiety level and had them on guard for more problems. 'It's only natural.'

Leesa was still standing beside him and her thigh was pressing against his arm. 'It's hard.'

He hugged her waist. 'Just remember, these days the outlook is good. Parkinson's can be controlled for years.'

'I know, but this is Mum.'

The only answer he had was to hug harder.

When Leesa stepped away to head to the kitchen she wiped her cheeks quickly, something he'd not seen before. Her mother was obviously her Achilles heel.

Nick's heart tightened for her and this family. There was nothing he could do but be there for her, and them. Something he really wanted. Which was a commitment in itself. One he fully intended sticking to. It was a huge step.

What's more, nothing was getting in the way of it. None of those warning bells were ringing in his head. Whether this meant he was committed to getting closer to Leesa he wasn't sure, but he'd go with this for now and let everything else unfold slowly.

And when they later reached his apartment block, he turned to Leesa. 'Want to come up for a while?' Strange how hard his heart was beating as he waited for her reply. 'Baxter can come too.' Not exactly following the 'slowly' part of his earlier thoughts, but it was impossible not to want to kiss her after what they'd shared last night.

'You didn't think you'd get away with leaving him in the car, did you?'

'I guess not.'

'I'm not staying the night, Nick. You're exhausted after working all day and need some sleep before turning up at the hangar tomorrow. But…' She gave him an impish grin that sent his blood racing. 'I do have an hour to spare.'

Better than nothing.

CHAPTER SIX

THE NEXT MORNING Leesa woke at five. It was a habit, no alarm necessary, though she always set it when on a shift. Today was a day off and she'd go spend some time with her mum.

Stretching as far as possible, she languished in the after sensations of amazing sex the night before. When she'd decided to leap in and see where she and Nick were headed she'd done it with all she had. He was everything she was looking for and more. But it had been physical, not getting close about their future or what each expected.

She couldn't share herself completely with a man who wasn't prepared to talk about himself. Obviously he had issues about family yet seemed completely at home with hers.

Being impatient wasn't going to get her anywhere, so she picked up her phone and texted him.

Morning. Haven't slept so well in ages.

Two hours later when Nick would've been at work, she still hadn't received a reply. Busy? Or playing cool again? Two could play that game, she decided. All very well getting together and having a hot night, and then going back to quiet mode, but she wasn't taking it any more. Either they cleared the air and at least remained friends—though how she'd walk away from their fling was beyond her—or the other option was to stick to being colleagues. Which might be best anyway if either of them got Joy's job.

Climbing out of bed, she hauled on shorts, t-shirt and running shoes. 'Come on, Baxter. I need to clear my head.'

At midday Nick still hadn't come back to her. The pleasure from the night before had well and truly faded. Now she was miffed and wondering if she was wrong about him, that he was another mistake. No, she couldn't accept that. He was special, through and through. Her head knew it, her heart felt it. And yet now she was feeling less inclined to carry on regardless.

Nick had the power to hurt her. A fling with him was no longer enough. It had to be all or nothing. Yet that was all that was on offer, and she knew she couldn't walk away.

She pressed his number to call him. 'Hey, busy morning?' she asked when he answered.

'Has been a bit.'

So that's how it was. 'Okay, I'll leave you to it then.'

'Feel up to going out for a meal tonight?' he asked.

Stunned, she decided she knew nothing when it came to reading men. This one in particular. 'I'd love to.'

'Great. I'll pick you up about seven, unless things turn upside down here.'

'Sounds good.'

'Got to go. There's an emergency come up.'

Wow. Where did that come from? Now she was totally confused. A date with Nick. The first one they'd been on. So far everything had been about sex. Other than Saturday night at the farm, she reminded herself, when she'd invited him to dinner.

Doing a little dance on the spot she hugged herself. If she wasn't in love with Nick, she was so damned close it was scary. Because there were no guarantees everything would go as she hoped. So, she'd go back to taking it slowly, one day at a time, enjoying what time they had together and see where it led.

Which is what she did over the next couple of weeks. Nick was no more forthcoming about his past when they talked over dinner, always bringing the conversation around to work or her family and the farm. Leesa bit down on the questions she needed answers for, hoping that giving him space would eventually lead him to relaxing completely with her.

At the end of one long and difficult day she told Nick she had to go and see her mother. 'I won't drop around to your place tonight. Mum needs me to pick up some meds for her. I want to spend some time with her too.'

'Fair enough.' He looked fine with that apart from a slight shrug.

'It's what I do, Nick, okay? This is my family.' Her life didn't revolve entirely around Nick. She was independent and didn't need him in her life twenty-four-seven. It might be an old hang up from her marriage, but if she didn't take heed she'd only get more wound up. Being around Nick had her freeing herself of the past, but there was a way to go.

'I get it. Truly,' he added sharply.

From the little he'd said, her family life wasn't what he'd known as normal. But he had to understand it if he wanted more than a fling. 'I need to catch up on a few jobs too,' she said. Grocery shopping and tidying the house before Gran came to visit in the weekend were top of the list.

'Me, too.' Finally, he relaxed a little. 'See you back here in the morning.'

'Will do.'

'Leesa.'

Spinning around, she found Nick right behind her. 'Have I forgotten something?'

He shook his head. 'No. I want to say sorry for the way I reacted. I don't expect you to spend every hour of your time with me. We both have more to our lives than work and our fling.'

She stared at him. Coming from Nick that was quite an admission. 'Yes, we do have other things needing our individual attention that can't be ignored for ever.'

I will never become yours or anyone else's total life. Connor tried to make me do that and it was as though he was taking over my mind, dictating who and what I was.

Nick would never be like that, but she still had to stand up and be counted, for her own confidence if nothing else.

Then something dawned on her. 'If you get Joy's job you won't be moving away.'

'No. Think it's time I got on with getting a dog, too.'

'You are looking at more permanence in your life, aren't you?'

That had to be good for him. Might be for her too, because there was no way she wanted to get involved with a man who couldn't put down roots somewhere. But, most importantly, she believed Nick really needed to create his own place and start to feel he was home.

'A pet's a good start,' she added. She wasn't so sure she wanted to go up against him for Joy's job. The consequences might make for more problems.

'One step at a time?'

She dipped her head in agreement. 'Absolutely. Now I have to run or the pharmacy will be closed before I get there.' She touched his stubbly chin. 'Sleep tight.'

'Might do that with no distraction between my sheets.' He stepped away. 'See you in the morning.'

She couldn't wait. Nick had got to her in ways she'd never have believed. He accepted her as she was, didn't even hint at wanting to change her. When she'd said she had other plans for tonight he did tense up a bit, but then he apologised for his reaction. Yes, he was a great guy and she was falling deeper and deeper for him.

Her skin tightened. Was this truly good? Nothing dishonest or untrue was ever reflected in his character, whether they were working together or sharing a meal and bed. Going with her gut instincts felt right. If those needed back up it was there in the way her family accepted Nick. Not what they'd done with her ex. No, they'd tried to warn her Connor wasn't good enough but love could be blind. It had been with Connor. It wasn't going to be with Nick.

Next morning when she walked into the staff kitchen her heart melted at the sight of Dr Sexy perched on a stool, stirring sugar into his tea as he read what appeared to be case notes. 'Morning.'

His head flicked up. 'Back at you. Kettle's just boiled.'

'Who's flying us today?'

'Darren. He's giving the plane the once over.'

Mark, a helicopter pilot, strode into the room. 'I'm on the chopper if you need an exciting ride.'

'Not unless an emergency crops up,' Nick told him with a laugh. 'Our list is all about going to places with landing strips, not pocket-sized squares.'

'What time did you get in?' Leesa asked.

'Just after five. I was out of milk and bread so figured I might as well grab some and come in here for breakfast.'

Sounded like he hadn't slept well. Missing the fun they'd been getting up to?

'Thought you were going shopping last night.' She wasn't going to tell him she'd slept like a log. He might think she didn't miss him much, and she had.

She'd also been glad of time to herself to think through everything going on between them. The past fortnight had sped past, all fun and not serious in any way. Which was fine, but nothing had changed. All fun and no depth.

'I went home to shower and change, then couldn't be bothered going out again.'

'Where are we headed for our first job?' she asked, ready to get to work and away from wondering if Nick ever relaxed enough to get out and have a life. He'd helped at the farm but that had been at her instigation. It was as though he didn't know what to do with himself when he wasn't being a doctor.

'Taking a woman down to Brisbane for a heart valve replacement. She's expected here at eight thirty.'

'I'll go check stock levels and everything else.' With a mug of tea in hand, Leesa headed out to the plane, all the time trying not to think about Nick. Impossible when they spent a lot of time together.

'How was Jodi?' Nick asked as they waited on board for their patient to arrive.

'Not as tired as I'd expected. I do wish she'd take things easier though.'

'You might be asking too much.'

She knew that, but she didn't want her mum's condition getting worse before it had to. 'Of course I am. It's to be expected.'

'I get that.'

Did he though? When he'd said he didn't have family to care about? She sucked air over her teeth. Now she was being bitchy for no reason.

It was because he rattled her. They were opposites in so many ways but they still understood each other. Could they have a future? One that was for ever and not just for a few nights having amazing sex?

'You've gone quiet.'

'It happens occasionally,' she put out there.

'Can't say I've noticed.' Nick tapped her shoulder. 'We've got company.'

The ambulance was backing up to the plane. 'Good. Now we can get going.'

'Impatient, aren't we?' He flicked her a puzzled look.

'It's a long haul to Brisbane and back.'

'Part of the job.' The puzzlement remained.

Fair enough. She didn't know why she was being terse other than she needed more time away from Nick to do some serious thinking. She was in a relationship that she wasn't sure was quite what she wanted, or needed. A fling had its upsides, but they weren't really her thing. She was an all or nothing kind of girl. And that didn't seem to be what Nick wanted.

'Hello, Leesa, Nick. This is Maggie Oldsmith.' The ambulance medic was pressing the button to bring the stretcher up to their level. 'She's been given a mild sedative as she's not keen on flying.'

'Hi, Maggie. I'm Leesa, your paramedic for the duration of the trip.'

'And I'm Nick, the doctor keeping an eye on you.'

'Hello. I'm the old bat needing a new heart valve.' Maggie's smile was tired, as were her eyes. It all went with her heart condition.

'You'll be a new woman when we bring you home,' Leesa told her.

'I hope so.'

'Is there anyone coming with us to keep Maggie company in Brisbane?' Nick asked the medic as he looked outside.

'Maggie's son is already down in Brisbane. He'll be at the hospital when the ambulance arrives.'

'Right, let's get this show in the air.' Nick checked the trolley was secure. Leesa watched the medic lower the lift and move away so she could close the door.

'All set,' she told Darren.

Once they were airborne and levelled out, Nick gave Maggie a thorough check over, leaving Leesa redundant as the two of them chattered about any number of things.

She knew Nick was trying to divert Maggie from worrying about flying. It must've worked, or the sedative had had an effect, because she was soon snoring. The monitors were showing no changes in her readings from what they'd been at the start of the flight. 'Well done.'

'Not sure I like the background music,' he

grinned, then pulled up the laptop and began going through Maggie's medical data, the grin gone.

So no chatting to fill in the time. Leesa sighed. They did do this at times, pulled back from one another without reason. It was quite likely Nick required space to think it all through too. That was a wet blanket on her emotions even when she was doing the same. Talk about mixed up, she smiled internally. But then the experts said love wasn't meant to be easy. She wouldn't know other than her experience definitely hadn't been a walk in the park.

Staring out the window she watched the coast-line bend and curve all the way south. It was a beautiful landscape. The beaches, the blue water and the Great Barrier Reef further out attracted visitors from all over the country and around the world. She lived in one of the most amazing places.

Time to check on Maggie. She unclipped her seatbelt at the same moment Nick did.

'I've got this,' he said.

She could get picky and point out she usually did the obs, but what was the point? They were as capable as each other and Maggie was in good hands, be they hers or Nick's.

'No problem.' Pulling her phone from her pocket, she read her emails and answered two.

* * *

On the return flight Nick studied Leesa from under lowered brows. Damn she ripped him up and had his heart speeding without any encouragement. She was beyond wonderful. The nights they spent in bed were amazing. He couldn't get enough of her. So much so he was teetering on the edge of the love cliff. More than anything he wanted to let go and hand his heart over. Yet the buts remained, holding him firmly on the ground. He knew his love would be safe with Leesa if she reciprocated it.

That was the question. Did she? There was so much he hadn't told her, and the longer he left it the harder it became to put everything out there. As though the more he gained from being with her, the more he had to lose when she learned about his past and how he'd raced into his marriage without so much as a backward glance.

He gave a tight grunt. Seemed these days the only way he looked was backwards. Keeping safe. Staying lonely and fed up. Desperate for something most people had. Afraid of being hurt and of hurting someone else.

'Cleared to land,' Darren told them.

'Good, I'm starving.' Leesa slid her phone into her pocket.

'When aren't you?' Nick asked. He wasn't

only referring to food, but sex. Leesa had a huge appetite for that.

They'd barely started lunch when an emergency call came in. It had them heading to Cook Town, to pick up a fisherman who'd got his hand caught in the winch while bringing in a laden net, and had severed two fingers.

'How awful was that?' Leesa commented after they'd loaded the man into an ambulance back in Cairns. She shuddered at the thought of losing some fingers.

'I bet it won't stop him fishing once the stubs have healed,' Nick said. 'He sounded like a tough bugger. Apparently, he once had a large fish hook stuck in his abdomen for two days while the skipper got the boat back to port in the midst of a storm.'

'How did the hook end up in his stomach?' she asked. 'Kevin's told me some crazy stories about what happens on board fishing trawlers.'

'It's not the safest job about.'

Joy was waiting outside the hangar when they arrived back at base. 'You two are needed on the chopper. A six-seater fixed-wing with four people on board has gone down in the forest behind Hartley's Falls. Fire and emergency have one chopper on its way and need another. You're the first crew I've got available.'

'Let's go.' Leesa was already striding towards the chopper where Mark was sitting in the cockpit.

Nick strode out to keep. 'No rest for the wicked, eh?'

'I'm wicked?' she teased.

'Very,' he grinned. The tension had eased.

'Takes one to know one,' she added as she leapt up into the helicopter.

Nick slammed the door closed behind them.

Mark instantly started the rotors spinning. 'Buckle up, guys. I'm going low and fast.'

Which meant they could get knocked about by wind off the hills. But it was totally reasonable to do that. They weren't going too far and Mark wouldn't want to waste time gaining height that he'd soon have to lose.

'What do we know about the passengers?' Nick asked when they were airborne.

'Four men returning from a safari up north,' Mark answered, 'One of them the pilot. The plane lost contact with the tower about an hour ago. A chopper from Port Douglas was in the vicinity and located the plane. There's no movement, no sign of anyone.'

'We're to expect the worst-case scenario and hope we're wrong.' Nick leaned back in his seat, his eyes closed. 'I hate these jobs.'

'Don't we all?' Leesa agreed.

Nick sat up straight. 'Let's run through what we need to take down when we arrive.'

Leesa tapped one finger. 'The medical packs.' Tapped a second finger. 'The drug kit.'

He nodded. 'Stretchers, oxygen.'

They continued with the list, both working on the assumption they'd be retrieving men who were alive. It was the only way to approach the scene, unless they heard differently.

The closer they got to Hartley's Falls the tighter the tension in Leesa's face got. They hadn't heard from the other chopper yet.

Nick touched her thigh. 'Breathe.'

'I'm trying,' she gasped.

'I get that.' He kept rubbing her thigh.

Mark came through the headset. 'All four men are alive. Three with serious injuries. Fire and Rescue are lifting two out soon, the medics have stabilised them and got them onto stretchers.'

'We're going to have to hover further away?' Nick asked.

'If I can't find a safe place to put down nearby, then yes.'

'What if you got the other chopper to move away so we can be lowered to the site to help out?'

'We'll do it only if the guys on the ground give us the all-clear, but chances are they'll be too busy retrieving their two patients.'

'We don't want to delay their operation.'

A low groan came through the headset.

'Mark, what's up?' Leesa asked.

Silence.

'Mark? Talk to us,' Nick demanded.

'Buckle up tight,' Mark shouted. 'I'm going down.' Even before Mark finished speaking the chopper was dropping. Fast. Frighteningly fast.

His heart in his throat, Nick glanced at Leesa as she pulled her seatbelt tighter. 'What's going on?' His stomach was a tight ball. Something was very wrong. 'Hey, Mark, what's up?'

'Don't feel good.'

'How? Where?'

'Head.'

'Not good.' Leesa stared ahead.

Nick reached for her shaking hand, held it between both his. 'We'll be fine.' They had to be. Leesa had to be. Nothing bad could happen to her.

Leesa would've given Nick an eye roll if fear wasn't gripping her so hard no part of her moved—except her mind, and it was in panic mode.

'Yeah, sure.' Her fingers tightened around his, probably about to break them. What was wrong with Mark? Something to do with his head. Pain? Blurriness? She glanced out the window, and immediately looked away.

The forest was barely metres below, rushing at

them. Then trees were all around and the chopper was tipping sideways. A horrendous racket filled her head of tearing metal, rotors ripping into the trees. *Bang! Ka-thump!* Metal screeched, buckled inwards. She was flung sideways, then backwards.

The movement stopped.

Nick's hand had gone.

She blinked once, twice. Stared around, breathed in deep. 'Nick?' she cried. 'Nick. Answer me.'

'I'm here.' His voice came from beyond where he'd been sitting. 'You okay?'

No idea. She tried to stretch her legs but didn't get far because the cockpit had been shoved back. The stretcher in front of her was at an odd angle. Her upper right arm was throbbing. Her neck was stiff and painful. Otherwise, 'Think so. What about you?'

His reply was a deep groan as he tried to shift.

Her heart jerked. 'Nick? What's happened?' *Please be all right.* Unclipping the safety harness, she stood up only to bang her head on metal. The top of the chopper was caved in. Down on her knees, she forced her way over obstacles to reach Nick.

His face was contorted with pain.

Her heart slowed. 'Where are you hurting?' Nothing could be wrong with Nick. Anything but that.

'My chest. Probably my ribs. Check Mark. I'll follow you.'

'No.' She wanted to stay with Nick, check him over thoroughly. Laying her hand on his chest she touched his ribs as gently as possible.

He winced. 'Something slammed into my chest, possibly cracked a rib or two. I don't feel bad otherwise. Mark was having a medical event. He needs your attention.'

Nick was right. Dammit.

'You stay here.' She was already backing out of the small space beside him. It was the hardest thing she'd ever done. Her arms ached with the need to hold him, to confirm what she knew. They were alive.

Leesa grabbed a seat as the chopper lurched and dropped further to thud onto something solid, hopefully the ground. The thought of falling further gave her the heebies.

'Agh…' Nick groaned loudly.

'Nick?' she called, her heart in her throat as she prepared to go back to him.

'Carry on to Mark. He didn't respond to your call.' Then Nick groaned again, followed by a curse.

'Mark, can you hear me?' She pushed and shoved through the crumpled wreck of the helicopter. 'Mark? Where are you?'

Silence. But only from him. Trees were cracking and metal was groaning as the chopper rocked. She closed her eyes and waited for it to fall further.

Nothing happened.

Slowly she exhaled. Phew. A pounding started behind her eyes. She couldn't feel a wound on her skull, didn't remember hitting anything with her head.

Get over it.

Squeezing through the unrecognisable flying machine, nothing appeared to be where it should. A pair of legs stopped her progress.

'Mark.' Leesa knelt and began to run her hands up Mark's legs to his arms and hopefully a pulse. A branch had bust through the windscreen making it impossible to see his head. Her hand touched a hand, and she felt for a pulse. Very weak but there *was* one. Relief filled her. Not that it meant he was going to be all right, but he was alive. Holding the back of her other hand in front of his mouth and nose she felt erratic, short breaths. 'What happened?' she asked no one in particular.

He'd said 'head' when Nick asked where the problem was. Could be an aneurism or a stroke. Impossible to tell.

Unwilling to try moving Mark on her own when she didn't know what other injuries he might have, she began to carefully and methodically check over the parts of his body she could reach.

'What have we got?' Nick asked from behind her.

She nearly leapt out of her skin. 'Jeez, you scared the living daylights out of me. You were supposed to stay where you were.' She wasn't going to admit she was glad he was with her. This whole disaster was freaking her out. Her hands shook and the throbbing behind her eyes was increasing in intensity.

A steady hand touched her shoulder. 'It was getting a bit lonely back there.'

Looking at him, she bit her lip. He was whiter than white. 'It's a tight squeeze in here but I'm glad you're with me.' So much for not telling him. 'You're bleeding from your chin.' She ran a finger over his jaw.

'Took a bit of a whack. Is Mark alive?' Forthright for sure. But sensible—there was no point in trying to move the man if he was gone.

'He's breathing and his pulse is shallow and hard to find. I haven't managed to check him all over. That branch's in the way. Before you even think of trying to move it with those ribs giving you grief, you are staying away.'

Talking like a kid on steroids, Leesa.

'Sorry, I'm a bit shaken up.'

Nick ran a finger down her cheek. 'It's understandable. I'm feeling much the same.'

She leaned closer, drew a slow breath to ease the tension gripping her. It was so good having him here, if only he hadn't been injured. 'Take it easy. You're hurting.'

'I hear you, but let me take a look at Mark. There might be some way we can shift him without causing any more problems. We need to make certain his spine's not damaged first.' Nick was already removing one of Mark's shoes. A hard pinch on the sole got a small twitch. 'Don't think we need worry about the spine at least.'

'Something on his side.' Seemed all she could do was hope for more good news to come.

Worry belied Leesa's words and Nick wanted to haul her into his arms and never let go. The crash had been close to being dreadful for all of them. Holding Leesa would calm his shattered nerves, but Mark needed his attention more than anyone. Scrambling closer, he bit down hard as pain flared in his chest. The odds of fractured ribs were high. He was thankful his breathing was fine or he'd be scared witless that a rib had penetrated a lung.

'I wonder how long before someone realises we're missing.' Leesa had a hand on Mark's wrist, her finger searching for his pulse. She must've found it because relief filtered through her worry.

'They must've heard from Mark that we were closing in.' Quite the day for aircraft crashes. 'Someone will be asking why he hasn't reported in shortly.' The pilot's left arm was at an odd angle. 'Possible shoulder dislocation here.' Nothing he could do about it. Mark needed to be in an open space for the joint to be manipulated into place, and until help arrived that wasn't happening. Not a lot was.

'Can you reach his head to check it over?' Leesa sounded stronger.

Relieved, Nick held his breath as he lay down prone next to Mark, reaching his right arm up to Mark's head. Pain engulfed him. He waited for it to pass, trying not to breathe too deeply, then took his time feeling for contusions. 'Nothing.' But… 'Hang on. Yep, swelling on the left side.' A bleed? Quite possible, though prior to the crash or as a result of that branch whacking was impossible to know yet.

'Should we try to put him into the recovery position?' There was a hitch in Leesa's voice. 'Just in case.'

In case things went pear-shaped. 'Let's give it a go.' It was going to hurt like stink but they had to do everything they could for Mark. 'You'll have to do most of the work, I'm sorry.' His left side was pretty useless.

'I'll try pulling him my way if you want to work at keeping him free of the branch.'

It was an operation in hell, painful for all of them, though Mark knew nothing. Eventually they had him on his side with his head tipped back enough to keep his mouth open.

Nick took a couple of deep breaths and pushed up onto his backside. 'You cried out a couple of times. Are you sure you're not injured somewhere?'

His heart pounded at the thought. He didn't want Leesa hurting at all. The chances of that were nigh on impossible. The severe landing and then the chopper rolling and twisting meant there was no escaping some serious bruising for all of them. They were lucky both of them weren't far worse off. That's if she wasn't downplaying an injury—something that wouldn't surprise him. Leesa was one determined woman when it came to showing how strong she could be.

Her eyes met his. 'I honestly don't think I've got anything more than lots of bruises. We're going to look a funny colour for a few days.'

'A matching pair.' Crash survivors. What if he'd lost her for ever? Strong shivers rocked him. No way. He couldn't face that. She was special, wonderful. She—

His heart stopped. Leesa meant so much to him it was terrifying thinking about what might've happened.

Leesa's delicious lips finally lifted into one of her beautiful, gut-twisting smiles. 'Does purple match the blue of our uniforms?'

He shuffled closer, needing to put his good arm around her. He had to feel her, to know they'd made it. Kissing the top of her head, he whispered, 'We're very lucky.'

'We are. For a moment…'

His arm tightened around her as she shivered. 'Don't go there.' He already had. It was dark and gut wrenching.

'I'll try not to.' Her lips brushed his. 'Hold me close.'

He twisted to bring her in closer, and gasped as pain shot through his chest.

Leesa pulled back carefully. 'Nick. I'm so sorry. I didn't think. Where's it hurting?' Her fingers were slipping under his shirt, going right to the very spot where he thought the ribs were broken.

'How did you know?'

'That that's where it's painful? There's a lot of swelling. Plus, some bleeding from a surface wound.' Her fingers were moving all over his ribcage, checking, feeling, touching. Then she moved lower to check his abdomen, up to his shoulders and around his neck. 'Otherwise, I think you're up to muster. Unless,' her eyes were fierce when she locked them on him. 'Unless there's something *you're* not mentioning?'

He started to laugh and immediately regretted it as his ribs told him they weren't in the mood. On a light inhale he croaked out, 'I'm fairly certain all's good inside.'

'Thank goodness.'

Another gentle kiss came his way, soft on his mouth, yet tormenting—he couldn't follow up by embracing her hard and kissing her like there was no tomorrow, because there nearly hadn't been.

But they did have a tomorrow. They'd survived the crash, were able to move and talk and be together. For now. He pressed his mouth over Leesa's, savouring the moment, her warmth and softness. Who knew when they'd get a chance to do this again? A crowd would soon arrive to help. Far more important, he knew, but he did need to hold Leesa, if only to confirm she had survived.

She pulled back and stared around. 'Where is everyone? Come on, guys. We need you.' Her gaze returned to him. 'I presume the locator beacon still works after a crash like this.'

'They're made to withstand huge impact. The rescue crews already had their hands full, and they're now one chopper down. Literally,' he added quietly.

'I wonder if Kevin's with a crew. He's a volunteer for Port Douglas's Fire and Rescue and wasn't out on the boat today.'

'Do they bring that station in on these events?'

'Yes. We're closer to Port Douglas than Cairns.' Leesa tipped her head to one side. 'Listen. Is that what I think?'

A low *thwup* sound reached him, getting louder by the second. 'Only a chopper makes that racket.' Hopefully those on board were looking for them. 'That hasn't taken too long.'

'They'll do a recce to see what's happened and then assess how badly injured we are.'

The helicopter seemed to be doing a circle above them, creating a sharp wind and causing small objects to flip around the wreckage. Then it moved away a small distance and hovered briefly before retreating further. 'We might be getting some company.'

Leesa had leaned over Mark to shield him from the dust filling the air. 'Hope so.'

'Hey, Mark, you there?' a familiar voice called. 'Leesa, Nick?'

'We're here. Everyone's alive,' Nick called back as Kevin appeared through the trees. 'Leesa's bruised but otherwise seems in good nick.' The guy would've been worried sick once he heard his sister was on board the chopper. 'Mark needs evacuating ASAP.'

'Kevin, am I glad to see you.' The relief in Leesa's face nearly undid Nick.

He knew she'd been holding it together, but now that help had arrived in the form of her brother, she was obviously letting go a little. He wasn't someone she'd feel she had to keep her game face on for. Which she'd been doing with him, he realised. That hurt. Yet it was who she was, and that was the woman he was falling for more and more. He gripped her hand. 'You're doing well, Leesa.'

She blinked at him, then dredged up a smile. 'Sorry, just had a wee lapse of concentration.' Turning back to Kevin, she said, 'Have Mum and Dad heard about this?'

'What do you think, Leesa? It's not a large town when it comes to these scenarios.'

'True.'

Kevin hugged her carefully, obviously not taking his word about her condition for granted. 'Hell, girl, you know how to frighten us all.' Pulling back, he swallowed hard. 'Nick, how are you faring? Any injuries?'

'Think I've got a broken rib or three, otherwise all good. It's Mark who's the worry.'

'Fill me in on the help required.'

Leesa nodded to him. 'You're the doc.'

Kevin listened while sussing out how to get Mark out of the wreckage. 'Got it. I need Tony down here to give me a hand.' He talked into his handset, then told them, 'We'll take Mark to hospital now, but I'm afraid you two will have to wait a while. The two people at the original accident site you were going to need attention.'

'No problem,' Leesa and Nick said at the same time.

Nick managed a smile. They were in sync and it felt good.

'Though there is a seat for one of you on this trip, but I don't like the idea of leaving either of you on your own.'

'Take Leesa.'

'No way. I'm staying,' she snapped. 'We'll be fine. Get Mark sorted. He's in a bad way.'

'On to it. Leesa, I'll let Ma and Pa know you're okay.'

'Tell them Nick's all right too.'

An unfamiliar tenderness struck him in his chest. Leesa included him in what to tell her family like it was nothing unusual. Given how open and friendly they all were to him, he wasn't really surprised. They had no idea how foreign that was for him.

Spending time with Leesa's family didn't make them his. They had treated him how he imagined they treated most people—with open hearts and kindness. All the more reason to step back before he got too involved and hurt Leesa by messing it up somehow. Because he wasn't great at family relationships, if his history was anything to go by.

It was awfully quiet after the helicopter had left with Mark. Nick held Leesa against his good side and laid his chin on top of her head. 'You doing okay?'

'I've had better days.'

She wasn't opening up to him, but that could be her coping mechanism. She hadn't said much to Kevin either after that first comment.

'Haven't we all? I hope Mark's going to come out of this all right. It's amazing how he did his best to get us on the ground while he still could.'

'We owe him our lives.'

A shiver went through him. They certainly did.

Leesa held his hand tight against her thigh, her fingers shaking. 'I—' Tears streaked down her face.

His heart thumped against his ribs, creating even more pain. He needed to take her in his arms and never let go again. What if? It was a question he knew he'd be asking himself for a long time to come. Reaching for her, he held her carefully, knowing he *would* have to let her go eventually. He'd nearly lost her. As he had lost others he'd loved. It was too much.

He wasn't meant to love. He was meant to run solo. Yet how could he leave her?

CHAPTER SEVEN

IT WAS CRAMPED and beyond uncomfortable sitting in the wreckage. Leesa slowly turned in his embrace, being careful of Nick's ribs, and gazed at him before finding a weak smile. 'Still enjoying your job?'

'I'm getting new experiences every day.'

'Glad to hear it. I'd hate for you to think you'd prefer to be on the ambulances instead the planes.' Though that would be a lot safer. Unless some crazed driver drove into the ambulance.

Doing glum again, Leesa. You're alive and so is Nick.

'What made you choose ambulance work over other options when you qualified?' Time to see if she could learn more about this mysterious man. She was done with messing around, deciding what she wanted to do. Today had woken her up. She adored Nick.

'I like the intensity of picking up people from all sorts of places and traumas and working to save them. I have to be at my best all the time.'

'Doesn't any doctor worth their weight?'

'True, but there's often an urgency that doesn't come with sitting in an office talking about symptoms and past medical history. I like being out and about rather than tied into one place all the time.'

'I know what you mean. It's why I swapped from nursing to the ambulances.'

Was that really why he did this kind of emergency medicine? It sounded a bit like how he moved from city to city to town every year or two. He didn't seem to do getting close to people. They were already involved, though for how long she had no idea.

Last night she'd been thinking about slowing down and taking a long hard look at what she was doing. Today she'd come close to not having that choice—and she wanted him. Badly. To prove she had survived. That Nick had survived. To prove she did have a future. Hopefully with Nick. She wasn't going to waste any more time procrastinating. If the crash had shown her anything, it was to get on and make the most of what came her way.

Turning the conversation onto him, she said, 'Tell me more about why you keep moving around the country.'

He tensed.

She waited for him to change the subject. Or not speak at all.

Finally, 'I don't know what it's like to stop in one place. To live in the same town, or home even, permanently.'

Her heart plummeted. She couldn't imagine what that was like. 'Not even when you were growing up?'

'No.' His fingers were rubbing soft circles on her arm. 'My parents died about the time I turned one. My grandfather took me in but he passed when I was twelve.'

'Nick, that's terrible.' Taking his hand in both hers she held tight.

'It sucks all right.'

'No one deserves that. I don't know how you coped.' She'd always had her family beside her. A loving, caring family who looked out for each other no matter what. Even when she went ahead and had married Connor. They'd believed he was wrong for her, but they'd never left her to deal with the aftermath on her own.

'Who says I did?'

'I do. Look at you. A doctor helping others. A kind man who doesn't put himself before everyone else. You work hard, and—' She found a smile for him. 'You love dogs. Baxter anyway.'

Nick stared at her as if she'd gone mad.

'I didn't hit my head in the crash.' At least she didn't think she had. 'I mean every word.'

One corner of his mouth lifted. He flattened his lips but the smile returned, this time with his whole mouth involved. 'No wonder I moved up here. You say the most wonderful things.'

Her heart clapped. Damn he was wonderful. Even when she wasn't looking for a future with him, he was so tempting. Dr Sexy. 'Glad to make you happy.'

'Remind me to buy Baxter a bone next time I see him too. Seems I've made another friend.'

'You've made a few. Everyone at Flying Health Care thinks you're great. As for my family, Mum's always asking when you're next coming to dinner.' She winced. That info should've stayed in her head.

There'd been a few times where Mum had quizzed her about Nick to the point she looked for excuses not to phone. A girl had to look out for herself, sometimes even from interfering mothers.

'You need to buy a whole bag of bones,' she added. Might as well go for light-hearted and keep him onside. It would be mighty lonely in here if he decided to clam up on her.

'I'll do that.'

'Where did you live with your grandfather?'

'Adelaide. Although he was tough, Grandad

was good to me, gave me the basics in life. In some ways he was my father, my only parent, because I don't remember anything about my mum and dad.' Then he'd lost the man replacing his parents.

'Of course you don't remember. Have you got photos of your parents?'

'A box full. But the weird thing is they've never grown up. They were only twenty and twenty-one when they died. I know that probably doesn't make sense, but I can't help it.'

'It makes perfect sense to me. I can see you as a boy looking at those photos and hoping for something to change. You're now older than they were, and that must seem strange.'

'Leesa, you're so understanding it's scary.' He leaned in to kiss her, wincing as he moved. Guess the shock of the crash was causing havoc with the sensible side of his brain.

'Careful, Nick. You can't take that pain for too long. How about I get you a strong opioid? You've got to get through moving out of here and onto a chopper yet.'

'Might be a good idea, though I'm not supposed to prescribe them to myself.'

'I'm qualified to give drugs out, remember?'

'Glad one of us has their wits about them. My doctor head is getting in the way. I'll put that down to the unusual circumstances I find myself in.'

She wasn't so sure she had any wits, but she could pretend. 'I'll find the kit.'

On her hands and knees, she crawled through the wreckage to search for the drug kit. Equipment lay everywhere, bags and packs broken open. One monitor was smashed, the other looked as though nothing was wrong with it. Unbelievable.

Scrabbling around she finally found what she needed. Hopefully everything inside was in good shape, or Nick might miss out on dealing with that pain. He couldn't swallow a handful of powder if he didn't know what it was.

Swallow. Water. Looking around again she spied a pack of six bottles they carried for patients and staff. Two remained whole. Damn, it was almost pitch dark now. Torch. Where were they kept? Top shelf of the cupboard by the bed. She squinted through the dark to see where the cupboard was. There, twisted on the floor. The door was warped. She pulled to open it but it wouldn't budge. Swearing gave her some satisfaction, but did not help get the door to move.

'Damn. No torches.' She needed to get back to Nick while she could still see enough to read the labels on the bottles of tablets.

Back beside Nick, she went through the bottles of drugs. 'Which one do you want?'

'Codeine.'

Holding a bottle right before her eyes, she laughed, although a bit sharply. 'Good choice. Here it is. At least I think that's what it says.' She handed it to Nick. 'What do you see?'

'Codeine.' He handed it back.

Tipping one tablet into the palm of his hand, she opened a water bottle and pushed it into his other.

Nick's head reared. A tight groan ripped out of his mouth.

'Did I hurt you? I'm so sorry.' Her heart was thudding. She'd hurt him. How could she be so thoughtless? Guilt assailed her. 'Nick, I didn't mean to.'

He placed his palm on her cheek. 'It's all right. You didn't do anything wrong. I moved sharply and paid the price.'

Her heart skittered. It hurt her to see him in pain. 'We might have to ban kissing for a few days,' she said.

That would be bloody hard to stick to. Kissing Nick was her favourite pastime these days. As much as making love. Sometimes a kiss from Nick made her feel right, happy and content, and she didn't need the excitement of sex to do that.

'Not if I have a say in the matter.' He sagged

back against the metal upright that had avoided being bent in the hard landing. 'But I will give things a rest for now. We might have a longish wait before help arrives. It's going to take a while to airlift the others to hospital.'

Time alone with Nick. She'd love it, except he was in pain. 'I reckon everyone's working their butts off to get here ASAP.'

They'd better be. She surreptitiously watched Nick's chest rise and fall with each breath he took. Consistent, not deep, but not too shallow, nor out of kilter. Good. If his lung had been punctured by one of those fractured ribs he'd be in a much more serious condition.

'Because we're part of the team?' He nodded. 'Makes sense I suppose. I've seen police go that extra mile for their own when something terrible has happened.'

'It's a natural response. Look after your own first.'

They sat squashed in the confined space as darkness took over completely. Now that she was sitting still with nothing to do, aches all over her body were starting to get ferocious.

'I got lucky as a teen when I stole a car.'

'You what?' She'd never have believed it if she'd heard it from anyone else, but Nick didn't do lying.

'I wanted to learn to drive and no one would

teach me. The judge gave me a second chance and I grabbed it with both hands, never did anything so stupid again.'

Now she was learning what made him tick. 'Tell me more.'

'His son was in my class and cruised through every lesson like he didn't need to put in any effort. I made him my target, to beat him in all subjects.'

That she believed. 'And did you?'

'Not all, about fifty-fifty. It meant he had to knuckle down and work hard for the first time. Patrick—Judge Crombie—credits me for Darian's success, says he'd never have done so well if I hadn't caused him a headache.'

'Patrick. So you're still in touch?'

'He's been my mentor ever since, though we don't catch up often. I flew down to Adelaide to see him before I came up here. He had cancer but is in remission. Who knows for how long? He's been warned to get on with ticking things off his bucket list.'

Leesa grabbed his hand. 'That's hard for you too. But you did get lucky with him.'

'I did.' He removed his hand. 'Tell me about your husband.'

Blindsided by the sudden change, she took a moment to collect her thoughts. This was part of moving forward into a stronger relationship, and yet she felt he was suddenly aware of how much he'd given away about himself and regretted it.

'Connor was amazing,' Leesa began. 'So kind and generous, helpful, keen to be a part of my life. I fell for him fast and we married, against my family's wishes I admit, and we moved to Brisbane for his career. End of the happy days. It was as though he was free to do what he liked being so far from my family. He was clever, changing slowly, not showing his true colours straight up. I wasn't good enough for him. Didn't matter what it was, cooking his favourite meal, parking the car in the garage, mowing the lawns, I couldn't do anything right, and I paid by being snubbed, then access to our bank accounts was closed off to me.'

Leesa shivered. He'd never hit her, but there were days when she half expected it.

'But you left him.'

'I did.' She could hear the pride in her voice. 'I had to or submit for ever, and I wouldn't do that. It wasn't easy, but I did it and stayed on in Brisbane to prove to myself I didn't need to run home.'

'Except you then faced another bully.'

'By then I'd wised up. He didn't stand a chance. Not with me, and he backed off. The other women didn't do so well until I supported them. After dealing with my husband, I knew how hard it can be for some people to leave these situations. I couldn't stand by and not help them.'

With one finger on her chin, Nick turned her face so he was looking directly at her with empathy. 'I imagine trust doesn't come easy for you.'

Like she thought, smart. 'You got it.' She was working on getting over her issues about her ex, but it wasn't as easy as packing up and leaving him had been, and that hadn't been a picnic either, with him refusing to accept that she was never going back. He kept telling her she'd never manage on her own, which only reminded her how she'd coped at school and could do it again, even if it was trickier.

'How's your trust radar after your marriage fell apart?' she asked.

His sigh was long and slow. 'Not great. Makes me wonder if I'm cut out for a relationship, or if I should remain single and get on with being a good doctor instead.'

'Don't think like that. One mistake doesn't make a lifetime's worth.' Said she who'd thought the same for so long.

Not any longer. Danielle had always said she had to move on, and after today that's exactly what she intended doing. With Nick. And if that didn't work out? She'd keep trying. Her chest ached. As a result of the impact, or because she wanted a man to love and kids to raise under

that love, she couldn't be certain. Probably both.
She shuffled her butt, trying to get comfortable,
not doing well. Tipping her head back she closed
her eyes, exhaustion filling her, closing down her
mind.

'Chopper's coming,' Nick nudged her.

She hadn't heard it but now it was very obvious. 'Phew. I've had enough of this place.'

'No food or anything to drink,' Nick smiled.
'The TV screen was useless too.'

'Funny man. Now we can get you checked over
and make sure those ribs haven't done any damage to your lung.'

'My breathing's normal.'

'Yeah, I have been keeping an eye on your
chest movements,' she admitted. Not hard when
his chest was so damned distracting. She still
worried he was hiding another injury from her.

'No surprise there.'

Tenderness filled Nick as Leesa gave him a wob-
bly smile. As though now they were about to be
lifted out of here, she was letting go of whatever
had kept her calm till this moment.

He wanted to kiss her once more before they
were surrounded by their rescuers. It hurt to lean
closer but, hell, he could deal with that to taste
Leesa under his lips.

'I'm glad I had you with me today,' he said. 'It

made all the difference. But I'm sorry you were in the crash. I don't like that one bit.'

'We had no choice over what happened and who we were with. But having you by my side made it easier to cope. You took everything so calmly.'

'Much like you.' She'd have been tough no matter who'd been with her, but he'd take her words to heart and enjoy them. Because he believed her. He believed *in* her. She wasn't lying, or trying to earn points to cash in on something he could provide her with later.

Remorse struck. His old cautions were still in place and, unless he let them go, there wasn't going to be a later. He might have to be careful going ahead if he was to avoid more heartbreak, but he had to learn to trust. It wasn't fair on Leesa, or anyone, if he didn't. That was like expecting her to turn out to be another Ellie.

Yeah, he sighed. He was falling for this amazing woman. Falling harder than the chopper hitting the ground earlier. Hopefully Leesa didn't break anything inside him. Or he didn't do the same to her.

Bright lights shone through the carnage from the hovering chopper. The noise was deafening. Handy since he'd run out of things to say without putting his foot in it and telling Leesa the thoughts tripping through his mind. He wasn't ready to divulge where his feelings were at. Not yet. Slowly was the only way to go. If at all.

So, he went with practical, carefully leaning close to shout, 'We need to start moving out of this wreckage.'

Leesa was getting up on her knees when Kevin appeared, holding out his hands to pull her through the narrow space.

Then she was gone and it was his turn. Holding his breath, in an effort to keep the pain under some form of control, he shuffled through to where Kevin reached out for him.

He shook his head. 'No.' Being hauled upright would be agony. It wasn't so great doing it all by himself either. What he hadn't mentioned to Leesa was his ankle was in a bad way too. Hopefully only sprained and not fractured. Whichever, walking wasn't going to be fun.

Kevin led them through the scrub and up to where their rescue helicopter had landed, helping Leesa through the rough terrain, turning back regularly to make sure Nick was with them.

Nick hobbled along, biting his tongue to keep the groans to himself. When Kevin reached to help him into the chopper he didn't refuse. He knew when he was being stubborn for the sake of it. Within minutes Kevin had settled him in a seat and buckled him in, then the chopper was lifting off the ground.

'How're you doing?' Leesa asked.

Nick opened his eyes and stared straight into hers. 'Glad we're out of there.'

'What's wrong with your left foot?'

'Think I've sprained the ankle.'

'Not likely considering you were sitting down when we hit the ground. Most likely a fracture.' She was unclipping her seatbelt, in paramedic mode.

'Leave it, Leesa,' he snapped. 'I'm fine sitting here. The doctors will sort it out when we get to hospital.'

Her head shot up. 'I'm only trying to help,' she snapped back.

'I know. I don't like the situation, that's all.'

'What situation? I thought we were getting along fine.'

Too well, if the thumping in his chest was an indicator. 'We are. But it has been a bit of a wake-up call.'

As she kept staring at him, her face filled with worry. But finally, she said, 'That's understandable. We've had one hell of a shock. It's all catching up with us now we're on our way to hospital.'

He suddenly felt exhausted. 'Certainly is.'

'Yep.' Her smile was tentative.

He took her hand in his. It was becoming his go-to move when he wanted to be close to Leesa. Which it shouldn't if he was serious about backing off. Dropping her hand, he leaned his head back against the seat and closed his eyes to wait out the time till they landed.

'Wake up.' Leesa was shaking him gently.

He jerked upright, groaning as pain slammed under his ribs. 'Have we landed?' The door was opening and bright lights filled the cabin. Guess that was a yes.

Kevin appeared from forward. 'We have. Let's get you two inside to ED. Ma and Pa are in the waiting room. Pacing the floor to oblivion, I imagine.'

'Did anyone pick up Baxter?' Leesa asked. 'I didn't think to ask you to tell Mum. What sort of doggy mum does that make me?'

'One who had a lot else going on in her head,' Kevin told her. 'Your boy's fine. He's in Dad's truck, chewing on a bone, I'm told.'

'That's good. He's used to me being late, but not to turn up at all will have freaked him out.'

'Hate to tell you this, but Dad says he's fine. Karin was about to take him home with her as she figured you were on a callout. Come on, let's get this over and done with.' Kevin helped Leesa out, then turned to give Nick a hand.

'There's a wheelchair coming for you,' Kevin told him.

'How…' Oh, Leesa. Of course she'd have got Kevin to call ahead. 'Thanks.'

Looking into those beautiful but tired eyes, his head and heart were all over the place. He did want more with her. That much he was not going to deny any longer. What was the point? He knew he was done for. But that didn't mean he was ready to rush in. After what had happened, the caution had grown even bigger and he wasn't totally sure why. So forget backing off, and try going slowly.

'I'm discharging you,' the ED doctor told Leesa. 'You were quite right. Lots of bruising that you'll know about for days to come, but nothing more serious.'

'Thanks, Laurie.' She wasn't going anywhere until she knew if Nick would be kept in overnight. She swung her legs off the bed and gasped when her thighs protested. 'Painful bruises.'

'The result of severe impact,' Laurie nodded. 'Take it easy for the next couple of days. Stay away from work.'

'I'll see that she does,' Joy answered before Leesa could argue. 'The same goes for you, Nick.'

Joy had turned up within minutes of the chopper delivering them to the hospital. She hadn't been allowed to see Mark, who had had a brain bleed and was now in ICU.

'I'm not arguing,' Nick growled as he lay

sprawled on the bed in the next cubicle, looking shattered.

'Is Nick staying overnight?' she asked Laurie.

'I see no reason for that once we've finished with him,' the doctor grinned.

'Just as well or we'd have argued,' Nick told Laurie.

His X-rays had shown four broken ribs and a fracture in his wrist, none in his swollen ankle. He'd been right on that score. Thankfully, as they'd thought, his lung hadn't been punctured. That was the best result. It would've been horrifying if that had happened. There was nothing she'd have been able to do to help him other than keep him on oxygen, and with a hole in his lung that'd have been an exercise in futility.

Her chest tightened. She could've lost Nick. And she wasn't thinking of a work colleague. No, this was the man who had ignored her boundaries and walked right on into her head and heart. Throw in his injuries and she was going to insist he come back to her place.

'Nick, a nurse is going to put your wrist in a soft cast. You'll have it on for a week then, when the swelling's gone down, it will be replaced with a plaster version,' Laurie told him.

He was looking at Laurie as if it was hard to understand what she was saying. 'Then I'm free to go, too?'

'Yes. Nothing we can do about your ribs except prescribe strong analgesics, along with antibiotics for that cut on your chin I stitched. *And*—' she emphasised the word '—I insist you don't get too physical. For the sake of your ribs and that ankle.'

'The pain will keep me in line.'

Leesa blinked. He was admitting that? Showed how everything had got to him, because normally he was averse to revealing his feelings.

A nurse slipped into the cubicle. 'Nick? I'm Enid and I'm here to sort out your left wrist.'

Then Kevin strode into her cubicle. It was getting like a circus in here, but rescue staff were given more leeway than general patients because of what they did for people.

'Hey, sis, how're you doing?'

'All good. I can go home any time I like.'

'That's what I was hoping. I'll take you home when you're ready. What about you, Nick?'

'I'll be on my way as soon as this cast's on.'

Leesa said, 'Come back to my place, Nick. You don't want to be on your own tonight.' She didn't want to be alone. The crash had been horrendous, and now that they were safe and sorted, she was beginning to feel more shaken than when they'd first hit the ground. Her parents would be happy for her to go to their house, but she wanted her own place with her own things around her. And

Nick with her too, because he'd understand how she felt. He'd been through it too.

'Nick?'

He was looking at her as though he wasn't sure what to do. Finally, he nodded. 'Okay. Thank you.'

She couldn't decide if he was happy going home with her or merely agreeing because being on his own wasn't a good option at the moment, but now wasn't the time to delve deeper. They were beyond making sense after all that had happened.

'Good idea, Leesa,' said Kevin. 'What about some clean clothes, Nick? You look like something the butcher chopped up.'

'Tactful. Could we swing by my apartment?' Nick asked.

'Only if I go in and get what you want. I don't think it's a good idea for you to move around any more than necessary,' Kevin told him.

Nick looked from him to her, and Leesa laughed. 'Don't even think about arguing.' She sensed he was on the verge of doing exactly that and it bugged her, though she didn't know why.

'With a Bennett? Not likely.' Then he turned serious. 'Thanks, but—'

She cut him off. 'But nothing. It makes sense for you to be with someone tonight.' Her heart dipped. Was something wrong? She'd have to wait to find out. She was shattered and could barely string a sentence together.

'I don't want to be a nuisance when you're a train wreck too, but you're right, Leesa. I'd feel more comfortable knowing you're there.'

That wasn't so hard, was it? 'Good. Let's get out of here.'

CHAPTER EIGHT

NICK LOOKED AROUND HIM. He'd thought as it was Leesa's grandmother's house it would be small, but it was huge. The lounge he sat in was the size of a football field. Okay, a small one toddlers played on, but it was still large. Light and airy with big bay windows that looked out over what appeared to be an expansive lawn and flower gardens. Someone had forgotten to turn the outside lights off.

'Who does the gardens?' he asked Leesa. 'They're stunning.'

'I do. Gran set them up over many years, and when I moved in I couldn't let them go to ruin.'

'You like gardening?' Of course she did. It was pretty darned obvious. 'You must if you keep them in such good order.' So this was one of her interests outside of work. Probably the most dominant one, given the size of the plots.

'I get a thrill out of planting a shrub or bulb and seeing the result when it blooms.' She was sitting on a leather rocker with her legs stretched out on the foot rest, a plate of the fried chicken and salad her mother had prepared for them on her knees.

'I wouldn't know a bulb from a shrub,' he muttered. Gardens came with homes.

'There's always time to learn.'

'You know what? You're right.' He was thinking about having a garden? Where? If he got a dog, he'd said he'd move, so how about a place with a lawn *and* a garden? 'I might give it a go sometime.'

'Sometime?'

'Okay, if I move from the apartment, I could be tempted to look into buying a house with a small yard.'

'If?'

'Will you stop questioning everything I say?' He'd just told her what he was thinking of doing and she kept at him, wanting to know more. Frustrating to say the least, because he was so unsure of his next step, of how to follow through on the love he held for her.

He snapped. 'It's new for me to be talking about this. I need to get my head around it.' It was huge to even be thinking about stopping his nomadic life to settle in one place, even more so to tell Leesa what he thought. Although he couldn't guarantee how long for. He had a feeling that if he started on this change of lifestyle he might adhere to it—because he might've found what he'd spent most of his life looking for. The only thing wrong there was he was worried about hurting Leesa if he failed. He needed to toughen up and make some decisions, not drag it out because his heart was involved.

'I'm trying to support you in a backward kind of way.' Leesa bit into a drumstick and chewed thoughtfully. 'I can't imagine what it's been like not to have a house to call home, where gardens, decorating, renovations are all part of everyday things to attend to. You've missed out on a hell of a lot.'

She never minced her words.

He should be thankful, but sometimes they came too close to be easily accepted. Tonight, he'd try. He and Leesa had been through a traumatic experience together and needed to put it behind them without arguing. Now he thought about it, his reaction to her questions might be because he'd felt so out of sorts since the crash.

No, there was more to it than that. He was out of sorts because he'd woken up to the fact that he loved Leesa. Which was downright scary. There was a lot at stake.

'You're right, I have, but I do not want you feeling sorry for me.'

'I don't. I admire how you've got on with your life, and seem to be starting to look for what it is you really want.'

She read him well. Too well, if he was honest. No one had ever done that like she did. Except Patrick, and that had turned out good for him. Did that mean Leesa could be good for him if he stayed around? Frightening. It could mean everything, or it could turn to dust because he wasn't sure he understood how to make it work well.

'It's taken years but you're right, I have started thinking of my future and not my past.' If that wasn't huge then what was? Falling in love most definitely was. As would giving his heart freely. Those would be the final winners. And the largest hurdles. He'd nearly lost her today, and that scared the pants off him. Others had left him in the past. For that to happen again—well, he had no idea how he'd get through that. Yet he wanted so much to try to make it work with Leesa.

'I'm pleased for you, Nick. Everyone deserves happiness.'

Says she who'd struggled to put her past behind her. They really were two peas in the proverbial pod. 'Including you.'

'What's more, we shouldn't sit around waiting for happiness to arrive. We should get on and make it happen.' Leesa was watching him closely, no doubt looking for a reaction to that statement.

And he had one he'd love to share. She was his dream woman. He was making inroads into getting on with living life to the full. He opened his mouth to speak, closed it again. One thing to think how he felt, quite another to tell Leesa.

What if he'd misunderstood her and she didn't want anything more than a friendship with him? What if, when she said everyone was entitled to be happy, she only meant he was too, and wasn't saying it would be with her? The mistakes he'd made in the past reared their ugly heads and shut him down.

'I see.' She stood up slowly, wincing with pain all the way.

He got to his feet even more slowly, the throbbing in his ribs diabolical. But the pounding in his heart was more painful. He had to keep Leesa onside, and the only way to go was by being open with her as much as he dared, so they could at least talk more.

'No, Leesa, you don't. I haven't explained myself. I know that. It doesn't come easily for me, but that's not a good excuse. Spending time with you is a priority. I always feel the best I have in a long time, if not for ever, when I'm with you.'

'I can live with that for now.' Her crooked smile showed how exhausted she was. Holding out her hand to him, she added, 'Let's go to bed. I'm shattered, and you look no better.'

'Your mother made up a spare bed for me.'

Leesa blinked. 'You're serious? There's a surprise. I'd have thought she'd have locked the doors to the spare bedrooms so you had to join me.'

So Jodi liked him being with her daughter. His heart swelled. Another good thing to happen. Except if he let Leesa down, in any way, he'd be letting down her family as well. 'Could she be thinking I need to be very careful in bed right now?'

'Definitely.' Taking his hand, she tugged him gently. 'We can share a bed without getting active.' Another blink. 'I'd say that'll be difficult, but right now all I want is to be stretched out and comfortable so I can sleep. Not very sexy, I know.' She shrugged.

He laughed lightly, aware of not moving his chest too much. 'It's about all I'll be able to manage.' As he followed Leesa through the house, he noted three spare bedrooms with perfectly arranged furniture. 'Which bedroom would Jodi have chosen for me?'

'The one on your right. It's the second largest and the one I use for visitors if I have any.'

'Not many then?' He'd have thought with her caring, friendly manner she'd always have someone dropping by for a night or two.

'Most of my friends live around here.' She didn't sound sad.

'Where does Baxter usually sleep?'

'Where do you think?'

'Your bedroom.' Where else would she have him? This was Leesa, the soft-hearted dog mum. Baxter was with Leesa's parents, as everyone thought it would give Leesa a chance to sleep and not be nudged in those painful places.

'I'm going to have a shower. If you want one, there's a bathroom further along the hall. Towels are in the drawer beneath the basin.'

'Sounds idyllic. Hot water to soak away the grime and loosen my muscles.'

Leesa spun around to face him and gritted her teeth. 'Ow.' Her chest rose as she drew in a deep breath. 'Silly girl. Do you want a hand getting your shirt off? I can't imagine it'll be a picnic.'

'Yes, please.' It'd be the first time she'd removed his clothes without him getting hard.

Her grin told him she'd read his mind. 'Who'd have thought?'

'Not me.'

'Now that you're in my room you can use the ensuite. You can fall out of the shower and into bed with only a few steps. I'll use the main bathroom.' She was already turning the sheets back.

He hated that she was taking so much care of him, but right now he didn't have the energy to argue. After being settled in that comfortable chair in the lounge, walking down the hallway had taken a lot of effort, with pain ricocheting around his body in all directions. 'You're a gem.'

'And you hate being in this situation. I get that.' Heading into the ensuite, she took a towel off a shelf and laid it on the counter. 'There you go. See you in bed shortly.'

Still no reaction from his body. He really was a mess. Hopefully he'd be able to cuddle into her long, warm frame and fall asleep holding her with the arm on his good side.

Leesa stood under the hot water and let the heat soak into her bruised and battered body. It was wonderful. Never mind she'd be too hot and probably sweat some when she got out. Right now, she needed this to relax her muscles, which were tight and damned sore. That crash landing had been horrific, jarring every part of her body. But she was grateful that's all she'd suffered.

Nick hadn't been so lucky.

As for Mark, he was gravely ill and would be for a while to come, by the sound of it. Brain bleeds were no picnic.

It all went to show you didn't have a clue what a day would bring when you got up in the morning.

She shampooed and conditioned her hair, then realised she'd have to waste time drying it before she could crawl in beside Nick. But she couldn't have left it as it was when she felt dirty from top to toe. Now she was deliciously clean. Finally flicking the water off, she grabbed her towel and dried off, feeling so much better.

She was spending the night in *her* bed with Nick. It was the first time he'd come to the house, and it was another step forward in their relationship. He'd seemed concerned he'd given too much away earlier, but for her it was progress. It meant he trusted her, and she felt special that he had talked about how he was changing, because she wasn't holding back any longer.

Nick was lying on his back when she returned to her room. 'How's that working?' she asked.

'Not bad.' There was a familiar twinkle in his eyes.

'Oh, no. We are behaving tonight.' No way would she have Nick in pain from anything they got up to.

'Hate to say it but you're right. I can lie on my right side though. You can back in so we can cuddle.'

'Sounds perfect. I think I'll be asleep in thirty seconds flat.' Which meant missing out on feeling his arm around her. 'I'll do my best to stay awake for a while.'

'Don't even try. We both need sleep more than anything.' He rolled carefully onto his good side.

Leesa slipped under the sheet and leaned over to kiss him. 'What a day. Good night.' Moving carefully, she turned onto her side, back towards him and smiled as their bodies came together. His skin was warm and his breath tickled the back of her neck. Sheer bliss.

'Leesa. Wake up.' A hand was shaking her. 'Wake up, Leesa.' It was Nick's voice.

Dragging her eyes open, she stared around the dark room, feeling cold and shaky. 'Where am I?'

'In your bed. I think you were having a nightmare.'

It came rushing back. 'The chopper crashing. The trees hitting us. You unable to move. Me hurting.' She gulped air. 'It was awful.'

Nick wound an arm around her, beneath her breasts, tucking her close. 'Going through it once was bad enough.'

'That's put me off wanting to sleep.' She couldn't keep reliving the nightmare. It was awful. 'At least we're no worse off than we were the first time.' Her mouth tasted of bile. 'Have you slept?'

'A little. I wake every time I move.'

'Time for some more analgesics.' Except she didn't want to leave the safety of Nick's arms. Shaking her head, she admonished herself. Not safety, comfort. She *was* safe. It was her head causing problems now. 'I'll get them in a moment.'

'I can get them.'

She sat up immediately. 'No, Nick. That'd

mean more pain for you. I'll get some for myself too.' They'd ease the aches and might drag her under to sleep, even if she fought it.

After they'd taken the tablets, Nick lay on his back and Leesa stretched out beside him, holding his hand. She felt her heart melting for Nick. He'd opened up some more during their wait in the chopper. Could the crash have been something good in disguise?

Staring upward, the tension that started from the moment Mark shouted they were in trouble slipped away at last, leaving her languid and comfortable. Nick was her dream man. She trusted him completely. He'd never deliberately hurt her. Was he falling for her? More than anything she hoped so. For now, she'd go with the flow. She was too tired for anything else.

It had been the strangest day of her life, yet she was happy. Yes, happy to have found this man. All she had to do now was make him understand they could have a future together. But not tonight. Tonight was for unwinding and being comfortable together without firing up the lust and getting hot. They needed to be able to share time that didn't involve sex, only love. And if Nick wasn't into loving her then she'd deal with that another day. Right now, she was happy to roll with her own feelings.

Shuffling closer to him, she laid a hand on his

chest and closed her eyes. This was near perfect. If she didn't move too much and set off the aches.

'Time I got back to work,' Joy said as she stood up the next day after dropping by to see how they were doing. 'Glad you're both feeling a bit better.'

'I'll be back on the job tomorrow,' Leesa told her. 'Thanks for the filled bread rolls. They were delicious.'

'You're welcome.' Joy paused, looked from her to Nick. 'Does the accident change either of your minds re my job? Last week's interviews went well I hear.'

'The job's the last thing on my mind at the moment,' Leesa told her.

'I'm in,' Nick told Joy.

'If one of you gets the job is the other going to throw their toys out of the cot?' Joy asked.

'Not at all.'

'No way.' Leesa glanced at Nick, then back to Joy. 'My concern is how the rest of the staff will see it. They might read too much into situations where say I give Nick a job to do that someone else wanted, and vice versa.'

Nick was watching her closely. Looking for what? She was only putting the truth out there.

'We're a small crew compared to ambulance stations you've worked in previously, Leesa. We're close. I've never had any problem with any member thinking they should've been given a job over someone else. I can't see it happening if either of you take my place.' Joy was focused completely on her. 'I know you well, and I can't see you giving Nick, or anyone else, more than their fair share of the good jobs. It's not like you.'

Her heart softened at the compliment. 'Thank you. I should've talked to you sooner, then I could've stopped worrying.'

'So your application remains in place?'

'Yes. I don't know if I'll be comfortable flying in choppers any more. Spending time in the office seems far safer.'

Nick watched Leesa as she made a plunger of coffee. She looked thoughtful, as though he'd done something wrong applying for Joy's position. 'You still okay with us competing for the same job? First time we've come up against each other.'

'Interesting area to be doing so.' Her finger was scratching at the hem of her shorts, where a huge bruise covered most of her thigh. It had to be painful but she never mentioned it, or any of the others he'd noticed during the night.

'Look, Leesa, if you're really worried about being my boss—' he paused and gave her a smile '—I promise to behave.'

His smile hadn't worked. She looked unsettled. 'I am nervous about flying now.'

He tried another smile. 'That's natural but you'll get over it.'

'You don't know that.'

'I know you. You're tough.'

'Is this you trying to talk me out of trying for the job?' The spoon she'd been holding slammed onto the bench.

Nick came straight back. 'Not at all. I don't need you to do that to make me feel more optimistic.' Why were they even talking about this? It hadn't been an issue before, as far as he knew.

Her head shot up. 'I know that. You'd be brilliant as chief of operations.'

Knock him down. Now he was confused. 'Thank you, but so would you.'

Her mouth twitched. 'We're doing well so far. Everything feels like a big deal at the moment, probably as a result of what happened yesterday.'

Just like that the angst left him. 'Good idea. Who gets the job's not up to us anyway.'

'We won't be the only applicants.'

'True.' If he got the position it would be a step forward in changing his life. He'd be stopping in one place. The place where Leesa lived. Could he do it?

'What are you thinking now?' she asked. 'I can't read you.'

Leesa never let him away with a thing. 'I'm wondering what it would be like to live in one place for more than a year or two. To settle down permanently.' If yesterday had taught him anything it was that he loved Leesa to bits. The ramifications were huge after he'd lost others he'd loved. What if he lost Leesa? He'd lost too many people who were important to him already.

'Nick, before you go any further, hear me out.'

His chest was tightening. What was coming next? He should leave before his heart was shattered. Or before she showed how much she expected of him. But it wasn't that easy. He cared too much. He wanted to believe they could make this happen, he just didn't trust life to give him a chance.

'Meeting you has been the best thing to happen to me in a long time.' Her gaze was steady.

His heart wrenched at her words. But there was something in her voice that said there was more to come. 'Carry on.'

'Like you, I have problems from my past.'

He gasped. 'You think I'd bully you? No damned way. How can you even begin to think that?'

'The same way you feel about settling down and trying to make a life for yourself. I want to follow my instincts but they've got me into trouble before.'

The anger disappeared. 'I get that. Believe me,

I would never pressure you to do something for me that you didn't want to.'

'I know that. Truly. It's just that—' She stopped, hauled in a huge breath. 'I'm scared. I've fallen for you, Nick.'

This time it felt as though his heart had stopped. 'Leesa—'

Her hand went up in a stop sign. 'Wait. I've spent years not believing I could find a man who'd treat me well and accept me for who I am. A man to love for ever and have children with, to establish a loving environment for a family. I have finally found him—you. Despite what I've just said it is you.' Her breasts rose on a deep breath. There was more to come.

He waited, heart in his throat.

'I know you still struggle with trust, or admitting you might be there now. I'm taking a huge leap here, but this is my heart speaking, so if you're not interested then please tell me.'

His mouth dried. His head spun with what she'd told him. She loved him. He loved her, but how to tell her when he couldn't put the past completely behind him? Ellie had said she loved him and look what she'd done.

Leesa's not Ellie.

She'd never play around behind his back. She'd tell him outright if she'd stopped loving him. He'd had a lifetime of learning not to trust people, which led to him not trusting himself, hence wanting to step back from Leesa before he hurt her. 'I don't know what to say.'

After the crash he'd thought he could walk away to save them both from more hurt. Now it seemed he was wrong. He couldn't turn his back on her for any reason.

So talk to her—speak from your heart.

Therein lay the problem. He didn't know how to. The last time he'd done that it had come back to wreck his heart.

Silence fell between them.

Finally Leesa stood up and crossed to look out the window at the garden beyond. After a few minutes she turned, and the sadness in her face shocked him. 'You don't believe you're ready. I get that. If I'm putting pressure on you, it's because I think you are ready to make the changes you've been looking for.'

She paused, fidgeting with her hair. 'It's obvious you need some space, and I'm pushing you. I've told you my feelings. I don't want to hear anything you don't one hundred per cent believe.' She shoved a hand through her hair and sighed. 'Or I've just made a complete fool of myself.'

'Leesa, it's not that.' Her family had stood by him last night, and brought home the fact that if he was involved with Leesa he was also involved with them. They'd share their lives with him. They'd also have him for dog tucker if he hurt her. And he couldn't trust himself not to. He had no experience of true loving family. Messing up would not be hard.

She waited, her foot tapping the cork tiles.

What to say? What to say?

Finally Leesa shook her head at him and said, 'Go away, Nick, and think long and hard about what you're really looking for. You can't go to work at the moment, so use the time to sort yourself out. If I'm not going to be in the picture then let me know sooner rather than later.'

His heart was breaking as he watched her walk out of the room, her head high and back ramrod straight. His heart tightened for this amazing woman, who he was already hurting. She was strong, and not afraid to show him.

'Goodbye, Leesa.'

For now. She was right about one thing. He had to sort himself out, starting now. When he did tell her he loved her there couldn't be any hesitation. No looking back. It would be an all or nothing decision. He wanted all.

He pulled his phone from his pocket to call a taxi. Leesa was right about one thing—he had decisions to make, and the sooner the better for both of them.

She'd told him she loved him. Hope was flapping around inside his chest like a stranded fish.

He'd followed her here on a whim, which he hadn't been able to admit to himself until recently. They'd happily reconnected and had been getting along well. Now he had to find the courage to follow his heart.

The taxi pulled up and he got in, taking a long look at Leesa's home with him.

CHAPTER NINE

'WELCOME BACK, LEESA,' Jess said and got up from the table to give her a careful hug. 'Love the colours on your face.'

'I'm going to scare my patients, for sure.' Leesa filled a mug from the coffee plunger. Everyone was here, as if they'd been waiting for her.

'How are you feeling?' Darren asked. 'Apart from sore all over.'

Heartbroken. I haven't heard from Nick for nearly two days.

'Wary of helicopters, but otherwise ready to get back in the seat.' Planes seemed a whole lot safer at the moment.

'Here's the thing,' Darren said. 'The helicopter didn't fail. Mark did, and I'm not being nasty about that. The poor blighter had a serious medical issue.'

'He did an amazing job getting us so close to the ground before he lost consciousness. That's what Nick and I think happened anyway. We owe him, for sure. But I still think I might find my first ride in a chopper a little scary.'

'I don't doubt that for a moment,' Darren agreed.

'How's Nick doing?' Jess asked. 'Joy says he's not coming back to work for ten days or so. Lifting trolleys or boards with patients on will be a no-no for quite a while.'

Ten days? Her heart sank. That was longer than Laurie had said was necessary. So he wasn't in a rush to see her and become a part of her life. He could've done other less physical jobs. 'Broken ribs are nasty by all accounts.'

'They hurt like hell with every little move you make,' one of the paramedics said. 'Speaking from experience after a particularly rough rugby game years back.'

'He could do the paperwork and let Joy have some air time,' Darren noted, unaware he was on the same track as Leesa.

'Hey, good to see you.' Joy walked in carrying a plate with a large chocolate cake. 'Here's to you, Leesa, and having you back on board.'

She stared at Joy. 'A cake? Chocolate too.' She wiped a hand over her eyes. 'You're spoiling me.'

Placing the plate on the table, Joy gave her a gentle hug. 'You gave us a huge fright, you three.'

Leesa swallowed down the lump in her throat. She hadn't given much thought to how everyone else would've felt when they heard the chopper had gone down. Just knew they'd have been in a hurry to help them. 'Thanks, guys.' She reached for a tissue and blew her nose. So unlike her to get emotional in front of people. 'We'd better put some aside for Nick and Mark.'

Joy handed her a knife and some plates. 'Nope. They get their own cakes when they return.'

Nick might miss out altogether, she thought as she cut into the layered cake, if he chose to move on yet again. He had said goodbye to her, not see you at work. Should she call him and ask how he was doing?

No. She'd said she'd give him space and she had to stick to that. The last thing she needed to do was upset him all over again. But she missed him more than she could believe. Every minute of the day and night. Listening out for him, looking for his ute in the driveway, holding the pillow he'd used, burying her face into it and breathing in his scent. Pure male with a hint of spice. The best smell in the universe. Her universe anyway.

'Here, get your teeth into this.' Joy had taken over cutting slices of cake and plating up. 'When we've finished here, I'd like a moment of your time, unless a call out comes in.'

Her stomach sank. Time to face reality. 'No problem.' *Liar.*

The cake sat heavily in her stomach when she went into Joy's office. Had Joy heard from Nick? Had he handed in his notice and was in the throes of leaving town?

'Wipe that grim expression off your face, Leesa. I'm not here to make things difficult for you.' Joy took a seat opposite her. 'I want to re-iterate that I believe you and Nick can work together if one of you has my role.'

If Nick comes back to me. Or comes back at all.

'You haven't heard from him?'

'Only to say he wanted a few more days off than originally agreed on when we discussed his injuries.' Joy was watching her closely. 'Is there something more to this?'

'Not really. Nick has some sorting out to do.' She'd spent a lot of time since he'd gone considering her future with or without him in it, and had realised changing roles at work wasn't what would make her happy. Even if Nick didn't want to be a part of her life, she now knew she wanted to make more of her life outside work. Clenching her hands in her lap, she returned Joy's steady gaze. 'I'm withdrawing my application as of now.'

'Can I ask why?'

'I've been too focused on work and it's time I had some other interests. Apart from Gran's gardens,' she added with a small smile.

'What if I told you the board members are going to offer you the job?'

Her eyes widened. 'Seriously?' Pride filled her. She was thrilled, but it didn't change a thing. 'That's amazing, but sorry, I won't be changing my mind again.' She wasn't tempted at all. 'Sorry to muck you all around.'

'You haven't. We've a firm second contender.' Joy stood up. Conversation over. 'But I admit I'd have loved seeing you in my role. You'd have been great at it. Maybe at a later date.'

Somehow, she doubted that. Her pride grew though. It was good to hear she was appreciated. 'I'd better get to work. And Joy, thanks for being so patient.'

Walking out to the plane she couldn't help thinking about what lay ahead. The fact was she didn't have a clue, and for once that didn't worry her. Except when it came to Nick, and that was out of her hands. He'd come back to her or he wouldn't. It was beyond hard waiting to find out, and for every hour she did her heart cracked open a little wider. It was going to be decimating if he didn't, but better now than further on. Damn it, it was already bad enough that she struggled with getting on with all her jobs.

But she would. She was strong. She'd made a decision to show Nick her love for him. If it back-fired, she could still feel relieved she'd done all she could.

But was it enough? That was the burning question.

Nick's finger hovered over the 'pay now' icon. The air ticket to Adelaide was a mere tap away.

Did he really need to visit Patrick and talk about his feelings for Leesa, to explain why he was in such a quandary? He already knew what the judge would say. *'Get on with following your dream and stop wasting your life.'* Patrick wouldn't come up with any new answers to the questions filling his head.

Leaning back in his chair, Nick looked around the apartment and sighed. The same old same old. No different to every apartment he'd lived in over the years since graduating. The views altered, as did the room sizes, wall colours, floor levels. In other words, unexciting, uninteresting. A place to sleep at the end of a shift, no more, no less. He was over it, and ready to move somewhere permanent. In Cairns. With Leesa. She meant everything to him.

'See, I don't need to talk to Patrick. I know what to do.'

There would be no avoiding the truth any longer.

He was ready to settle down and try to make a go of having a home life. A full life, not one focused entirely on being a doctor.

There. The truth. And he wanted to do it all with Leesa. He wanted to love her freely, with no fear of letting her down or hurting her. He understood life didn't run that smoothly all the time though. People had to take chances. Including him.

His phone played the tune to the dance he and Leesa had got up close and personal to in Brisbane. The caller ID was unknown.

'Hello?'

'Nick, mate, it's Kevin. How're you doing?'

Why was Leesa's brother calling him? 'I'm good.'

'Those ribs still giving you grief?'

'Unfortunately, yes. What've you been up to?' What was this about? Who gave Kevin his number? Leesa? He doubted it. She'd been adamant about no contact until he'd made up his mind about their future. She wouldn't involve her brother in this.

'I'm heading out on the boat for a few days to catch a load of prawn tomorrow and thought I'd check in on you before I go. Is there anything I can do for you?'

Knock him down. This wasn't a seek and tell call. Kevin was being as decent as the rest of his family. Not really surprising. 'No, all good here. But thanks for the offer. We should catch up for a beer when you get back.' See? Small steps.

'There's a plan. Once those ribs are up to scratch I'm taking you out on the boat for a couple of days, show you how we catch your favourite food.'

Staying here was sounding better and better. 'I'd enjoy that. How's Leesa doing?' he asked without thought. Because she was constantly on his mind. Because she just never went away.

'You should ask her yourself,' Kevin told him. Then relented. 'She's back at work and seems to be recovering from the battering she took.'

That was a relief. 'I'm glad to hear that.'

'Talk to her, man. She's missing you.'

So Kevin knew they weren't in touch, which probably meant so did Jodi and Brent. 'I have to get a few things in order first. I don't want to hurt her by rushing it.'

'Don't take too long. I'll give you a buzz about that drink when I get back at the beginning of next week. See ya.' The guy was gone.

On the laptop the 'pay now' icon had disappeared, replaced with 'time's up'.

Time's up. How appropriate. The decision was made. He was staying. He loved Leesa beyond measure. It was what he was going to do about it that needed fixing. And he knew the answer to that too.

For the first time since the crash a cold beer beckoned. Getting a bottle from the fridge he headed out onto his balcony. He leaned on the balustrade and stared out at central Cairns and the airport beyond. His new home town. The feeling of achievement over reaching his decision filled him with contentment.

Kevin calling to see how he was doing made him feel good. Like he belonged somehow. And while that had worried him, now he grabbed it, accepted it. All because of one amazing woman he'd sat down beside at a party in Brisbane over a year ago, he'd found what he'd wanted for so long. Leesa and love, things he could not walk away from. Ever.

Kevin had raised the subject of Leesa. It sounded as though he knew more than he was letting on. He couldn't imagine Leesa talking about him to the family, but then they knew her well and would have figured out something was up.

The dance tune rang again. He never got this many calls.

This time it was Joy. 'What's up, boss?'

'You have a new job. Congratulations.'

His heart stopped. Did he want this? 'What about Leesa?'

'She pulled out.'

'When?' *Why?*

'Yesterday. I'll leave it to Leesa to explain why.'

Had he said 'why' out loud? She'd better not have done it for his sake. He didn't want that and it would make him very uncomfortable.

'I'm—' What was he? Only a couple of days ago he was going to retract his application. But now that he had made up his mind to stay in Cairns, climbing the career ladder was a start to settling in and making that life with Leesa he so desperately wanted. 'Do you want me to come in and go through everything?'

'You're on sick leave. We'll talk when you're back on duty. And Nick?'

'Yes?'

'I won't tell the rest of the crew until you've had a couple of days to think about it.'

Joy got that he had concerns. But he didn't. He was ready. 'I don't need to think about it, but I'd appreciate you keeping quiet for now. I'd like to talk to Leesa first.'

'Fair enough.'

'Thanks again. Have you got someone covering for me?'

'We're managing. Everyone's pulling their weight and making sure Leesa doesn't overdo it. She might say she's fine, but she struggles with lifting bags, let alone patients.'

Of course Leesa would be downplaying her pain. There was no arguing with her—ever. 'Right, I'll see you on Monday. I don't need those extra days I asked for any more.' He didn't need Patrick to tell him what he already knew.

After finishing the call he stared at the laptop as ideas of what to do next bounced into his mind. He got another beer and sat down to study the real estate options for the area.

Rural or beach? Definitely not in the city. That wouldn't suit Leesa, nor him, now he was coming to understand how much he wanted this. As different to boring apartments as possible for starters. Space for Baxter and the dog he intended getting.

He was getting ahead of himself. Leesa liked living in her grandmother's house and might not want to shift. Only one way to find out, and in the meantime he'd do all he could to get this happening. She'd said she had fallen for him. He could not let her down—ever. He trusted her with his heart. He really did. So he was going to do everything imaginable to make her happy. And more.

There was a buzz in his veins. This was the most exciting thing he'd ever done. He was finally coming home.

Leesa dragged herself through the front door, glad to be home and that the week was over. First stop—the fridge, and a glass of pinot blanc to unwind. The days at work since the accident had been tiring and her heart hadn't been in it.

It had been tied up with Nick, as she wondered if he was still in town or if he'd already packed his bags, headed away to the next city on his radar.

Baxter raced through the house, headed for the kitchen and his food bowl.

Okay, the wine came second to dog roll and biscuits. 'Give me a minute, boy.'

Wag, wag. His tail swished back and forth on the floor.

Her heart expanded at the sight of his face full of hope and love. Dogs were so easy to please. She adored him.

The door chime sounded.

Baxter was off in a blur, tail still wagging, no hackles up.

Who would be calling in now? Not any of her family. They walked in like it was home to them, which in a way it was.

'Hey, boy, how are you?'

Her heart leapt. Nick. Baxter had known. Was this good or bad?

'Leesa? Are you there?'

'Coming.' Slowly.

Suddenly she was afraid. She'd been kidding herself if she thought she'd cope with Nick saying he wanted nothing more to do with her. Her skin tightened and bumps lifted on her arms. Rubbing them hard she made her way back to the door. And Nick.

'Hey, Leesa.' Nick stood tall and confident, a bunch of tulips in his hand. Not a clue to what he was going to tell her. The flowers could be a closing gift. His confidence might be because he'd made some decisions he was happy with that didn't include her. 'I've missed you.' His eyes were full of love, or so she wanted to believe.

Her heart was pounding like a drummer, like it knew that was love streaming her way. Locking her eyes with Nick's, she whispered. 'I've missed you too.'

He didn't move. 'Leesa, I love you with all my heart.' His voice was firm. But his hand shook as he held out the tulips. 'For you, my darling.'

Nick loved her? Nick loved her. Yes. As she took them, she said, 'My favourite blooms.' Had he known that?

'Jodi told me.'

'You've been talking to Mum?' That had to be good, didn't it? As were the flowers. She couldn't quite take in everything, was still waiting for a catch. 'Come in.' Nick was right behind her as she headed to the kitchen. 'I'm about to pour a wine. Want one?'

'I'd love one. But first there is something else I want to tell you.'

Her heart slowed. Damn it. She was done with guessing. 'What?'

'I'm not moving away. I'm going to be a permanent fixture in Cairns, or around the area anyway. And I want to share that with you.'

'You're staying?' She had to check.

'Yes, I am. I meant it, Leesa. I love you.'

'Oh, wow.'

The tulips got a little crushed in the ensuing hug and kiss.

'Easy,' Nick gasped.

Hell. His ribs. Placing her palm on his cheek, she leaned in to brush a light kiss on his lips. 'I'm sorry. In the heat of the moment, I forgot.'

'So did I.' His laughter sent a thrill of desire pulsing through her.

But they had to restrain themselves. Broken ribs didn't make for active lovemaking. 'Damn.'

'We'll find a way round the problem, I'm sure. But let's start with that wine you mentioned. I built up a thirst coming here, stressing over whether you'd be happy to see me or not.'

'Why wouldn't I? I told you I love you.' Oh, not in quite those words. Placing the flowers on the bench she faced him. 'Nick Springer, I love you with everything I've got. I love you,' she repeated, because she loved saying it.

He reached for her again, held her with a small gap between them and leaned in to kiss her senseless. 'Love you too, Leesa.'

It was Baxter head-knocking her knee that drew her back. 'Okay, boy, I guess you've been patient enough. Nick, you pour the wine while I feed hungry guts here.'

'Sure.' He found the glasses and got the bottle

from the fridge, while watching her feed Baxter then find a vase for the tulips.

'Simply beautiful,' she said as she placed them on the sideboard. 'Let's sit out on the deck.'

'I've been offered Joy's job and I'm taking it,' Nick told her as he sat down beside her on the cane couch. 'I know you withdrew your application.'

'If Mark hadn't been so ill, I'd thank him for the crash and waking me up to a few things.' She sipped the wine and continued. 'I don't want to be in charge of operations. I just want to do an honest day's work helping people and then come home to do other things I enjoy.'

'Like gardening and walking Baxter.'

She nodded. 'And establishing a home that's mine, not keeping Gran's going as hers. She's not coming back here, and I'm ready to be creative with the house and grounds.'

'You want to stay in this house?'

'I haven't got that far with future plans. I was waiting till I heard what you were going to say about us being together.' Loving each other meant living together. It had to or any relationship was off the agenda.

Damn but she loved it when he brushed his lips over her cheek.

'Here's what I've been doing these past few days.' He sat back with a smug look on his face.

'I've been looking at properties for sale north of the city, mostly on the coast and one inland with five acres and the potential to buy the neighbour's.'

'You have?' Her head spun with amazement. 'When you make up your mind you certainly get on with things.'

'About time, don't you think?'

She answered with a kiss. 'So is there a property you prefer above all the others?'

'I'm tossing up between the inland one and a stunning house near Trinity Beach. But I'd like you to see them first. You mightn't like either of them.'

'You're asking for my opinion? Does that mean what I think it does?'

'Of course.' His smile was devastating. 'But here's the big question. Will you go on dates with me? Give us time to get to know each other really well? As in looking forward and seeing what we both want individually and together?'

Her knees weakened as she looked into those beautiful blue eyes. 'Yes, Nick Springer, I will date you. But be warned, I already know what I want and you're a part of it all.'

'Afraid I'll get away?' he grinned before kissing her again.

'Too right,' she managed between kisses. 'Let me warn you, you won't get a chance. I love you too much.'

'Good, because I love you back. And, just so you know, one of the two houses I preferred had five bedrooms, while the other had three.'

'Let's go for five.'

'That means we'll be living by Trinity Beach.'

'Bring it on. Dogs love the seaside.'

Their next kiss sealed the deal.

EPILOGUE

LEESA SPRINGER'S HEART was singing as she gazed into her daughter's eyes. 'You are so beautiful, Courtney.' Tears welled up, and she brushed them away impatiently. She'd become a right old softie the night Courtney arrived in the world.

'Just like her mother,' Nick sprawled out in the lounger beside them. He never stopped telling her how much he loved her and that he thought she was beautiful. They'd been married eighteen months and everything was wonderful. More than she'd ever hoped for.

Handing her the tissue box, he said to Courtney, 'I'd never have believed my wife had so many tears stored up until you came along, poppet.' He ran a finger lightly over his daughter's arm.

Leesa grinned and gazed around at the front lawn she'd spent the last year working to turn into a spectacular sight, even if she said so herself. The last two months of her pregnancy had seen a halt in progress as she struggled to get down on her knees or to wield a spade. But it was a work in progress, and being a garden, one that would never stop. 'I need to plant those tulip bulbs or I won't have any flowers in the spring.'

'There's a carton of bulbs waiting in the shed.'

'You bought some?'

'They're your favourites. Besides, we've filled the first spare bedroom, so I figured you'd want to get back to the garden before we start on the next room.'

She laughed. 'You hear that, Courtney? You're going to get a brother or sister but not for a while yet.' Courtney was barely three months old and they wanted to enjoy her before adding to the family again.

'We probably do need to slow down a bit. It's been a whirlwind since the night I proposed, hasn't it?'

'I like whirlwinds when you're in them.'

They'd bought the house by the beach within weeks of Nick coming to Gran's house to tell her he loved her. Then they had a beautiful wedding at her family's farm a few months later.

And out of the blue, Leesa found herself pregnant with Courtney days after they returned from their honeymoon in Fiji.

Life didn't get any better.

'Kevin phoned. He's bringing prawns and his

girlfriend for dinner. In that order,' Nick laughed. 'He mentioned Jodi and Brent might join us too.'

Okay, life could get better. Her heart swelled with love for all the people she cared about, and especially for these two, who she loved more than anything or anyone. Along the way she made the right choices and this was the reward. 'Love you two.'

Nick took his little girl and cradled her in one arm. Then he wrapped his other arm around the love of his life. 'Love you both back.'

He couldn't believe how happy he was. Every morning he got out of bed with a spring in his step. Every night he returned to their super king-sized bed with excitement in his veins to hold his wife against him.

Life was perfect. It wasn't glamorous or OTT, just idyllic and happy.

He'd come a long way from Adelaide, and he wasn't measuring that in kilometres. No, he'd found a life that involved family and a real home right here. All because of Leesa. She was the best thing to ever happen to him.

To think he'd only gone to that barbecue in Brisbane to give his mate and his mate's girl-friend some time to themselves. He might never have found love if not for that night.

He gazed around their property and love tugged

at him. Leesa had done a magnificent job of turning what had been a bald, dry area into stunning, colourful gardens and lots of green lawn for Baxter and Levi, another rescue dog, to play on. One day Courtney and any siblings that came along would play there too.

Yes, his heart was light and full of love. Life couldn't get any better.

* * * * *

Her Summer
With The Brooding Vet
Scarlet Wilson

MILLS & BOON

Scarlet Wilson wrote her first story aged eight and has never stopped. She's worked in the health service for more than thirty years, having trained as a nurse and a health visitor. Scarlet now works in public health and lives on the west coast of Scotland with her fiancé and their two sons. Writing medical romances and contemporary romances is a dream come true for her.

Dear Reader,

Even though I've been writing for Harlequin Medical Romance since 2011, this is my first vet book! It was so nice to jump into something a little unusual for myself, and I had great fun researching all the different animal conditions you will find in this story.

My grumpy vet is Elijah Ferguson, who is not too happy to take over his father's old practice when there's really no alternative. My vet nurse is Aurora Hendricks and she has an unusual job history that comes back to haunt her. Besides my two main characters, there are some other stars in this book, and for once, they are not children! I hope you love the puppies Bert and Hank just as much as I do, as they help my hero and heroine to their happy-ever-after.

I love hearing from readers, so please feel free to get in touch via my website, www.scarlet-wilson.com.

Best wishes,

Scarlet Wilson

DEDICATION

To all the dog lovers in the world. For my own
red Lab, Max, and his partner in crime, our beagle,
Murphy. Best dogs in the world.

PROLOGUE

ELI TRIED TO hold his anger at bay. 'Is that it, then?' he asked his advisers in the room.

His accountant licked his lips, and his solicitor took a breath.

'You have to declare bankruptcy. There's no other option at this point.'

Eli let out the air that had built in his lungs. If it were possible, every cell in his body was exploding right now with pent-up frustration, despair, rage, and part sorrow. All his hard work. All his devotion to opening his own practice and making it a success had now all come to nothing. The countless hours he'd spent doing bone-aching work, concentrating, serving his community, had all been for nothing. All because of a woman.

All because he was a fool.

His solicitor cleared his throat. Eli knew what was coming, and he cringed. 'Your father's practice,' he started slowly. 'The last vet has put in his notice. There are two veterinary nurses. One has worked there for seventeen years. The other has been there eighteen months. The remaining vet is currently undergoing cancer treatment. As of next week, there will be no veterinary cover for the practice, unless you make a new arrangement with other existing practices.'

Eli sighed. He'd never wanted this. Never. His whole life, people had expected him to follow in his father's footsteps and take over once he retired. But that had never been in Eli's plans. No one had been more surprised than he was that he'd actually been bitten by the vet bug. Yes, he'd followed in his father's footsteps and trained as a vet. But from the second he'd started his training he'd made it clear he didn't want to join his father in the family practice.

It had caused many a cross word. But Eli had been determined. He'd served in some larger veterinary practices, gaining experience in small and large animals, taking jobs in the UK, the US, France and Spain. He didn't want to be indebted to his father. He wanted to build his own practice. Eli had always been fiercely independent, even as a child. And now, as a thirty-one-year-old adult, he was back in the situation he'd always sworn wasn't for him.

Would his stubbornness allow his father's practice to fold?

No. It wouldn't.

Being responsible for the demise of two practices would make him unemployable. The vet world wasn't as big as most people thought. Reputation was everything.

'Can you arrange an advert for the practice again?' he asked.

His lawyer nodded, but pulled a face. 'The last advert was out for four weeks. Only newly qualified vets applied. None that have the experience the practice needs.'

'Then maybe I'll need to have a rethink. I could have someone work alongside me for a few months. Get them up to speed. Then, by the time Matt is ready to come back he will be able to take over the supervision.' He pointed to his chest. 'This—me—is only a temporary solution. If we can't find a vet of the calibre we need, then I'll stay as long as it takes to supervise someone new. Get the advert back up.'

His lawyer nodded as Eli stood, staring out across the city. He did *so* not want to do this. But he wasn't too stubborn to see that if he chose to walk away his father's practice would fail, and the people in the surrounding area wouldn't have any care for their animals.

Animals. They always did better for him than people did.

And that was the simple reason he would do this—for the animals.

CHAPTER ONE

AURORA HENDRICKS TUGGED at the edge of her uniform as she juggled the puppy in one hand and her keys in the other. The little guy had wriggled so much her uniform had started to creep upwards, revealing a sliver of skin at her waist. Not exactly how she wanted to meet any potential new clients.

She gave the puppy a rub at the top of his head. 'Hold on, little guy. We'll get you in here and I'll check if you've got a chip. I'm sure someone is missing you very much.'

As she'd driven to work this morning, the car in front of her had swerved and screeched its horn. Aurora had caught sight of the terrified puppy darting across the road and had immediately pulled over.

Ten minutes of tramping through muddy woods, leaving a trail of treats and keeping very quiet, had allowed her to coax the very frightened little guy into her arms.

He didn't look quite so frightened now, and

the mud on his paws, and her shoes, were leaving both a trail on her uniform and on the floor.

'Are you always late? And in such a state?' came the sharp voice to her side.

She turned her head sharply. Standing inside one of the rooms was a tall, lean-looking man, with light brown tousled hair, longer on top, that unshaven but trendy look, and an angry expression on his face.

'And who might you be?' she asked, equally sharply. All her senses had gone on alert. She was supposed to be opening up this morning. There shouldn't be anyone else here—and certainly not someone who was a complete stranger.

'I was about to ask you the same thing,' he responded.

She blinked and took a breath, trying to still her racing heart and stave off her fight or flight response. In her head, she was calculating how quickly she could put the puppy somewhere safely and find something to whack this guy around the head with. There was a broom in the corner. That would do.

'Since I'm the one with the keys,' she said sharply, 'and the uniform—' she looked down at her smudged pale pink tunic '—I guess I'm the one to ask questions. Since when did you think it was a good idea to break into my practice?'

She said the words, but she didn't get the vibe

from the guy. He didn't look like some random thief. In fact, the more she looked at him, the more she was inclined to stare.

He was kind of handsome. In an annoying kind of way.

The one thing she definitely wasn't getting was a fear factor—which she could only presume was good. Because—due to past experience—Aurora Hendricks had developed a spider-sense when it came to danger, and men.

She placed the bedraggled puppy on the table near her and kept one hand on him as she shrugged off her wet jacket.

'So, this is *your* practice, is it?' Her head shot back up as she contemplated letting the puppy go for a second to grab the microchip scanner in the nearby drawer. There was an amused tone in his words. It raised her hackles and irritated her.

She held the puppy with one hand and put a few treats in front of him as her other hand grabbed the scanner. 'Well, until someone else shows up it is,' she muttered. Then paused. 'What? You're not some other random locum, are you?'

A furrow creased his brow. 'What do you mean—another random locum?'

She ignored him, concentrating on scanning the puppy. She checked all the usual spots where microchips with the owner's details were usually inserted on puppies, with no success.

'Oh, dear,' she sighed, picking up the puppy and holding him close to her chest as she stroked him. 'You must be an escapee.'

The man moved forward. It was as if she'd captured his attention. 'An escapee from where?'

She gave a sorry shrug. 'One of the puppy farms. There's a few about here. If he's not chipped, they hadn't managed to sell him yet.' She held the puppy up and squinted at him. 'Or maybe he's not from the puppy farm. He doesn't look like a pure breed.'

The man gave a nod as he looked appraisingly at the puppy. 'Maybe some kind of collie cross?'

She blinked. 'You *are* a new locum, aren't you?' Then she wrinkled her nose. 'But how did you get a set of keys?'

'They're mine.'

Her nose remained wrinkled. He reached over and took the puppy from her hands. 'Let me check him over.'

She'd been too slow to keep a hold of the puppy, but her instincts around animals were strong. She put her hand over his. 'No, you don't. Not till I see some proof of who you are, and your credentials.'

He looked at her in surprise. 'So, you're not bothered about being in here with a perfect stranger, but I tell you I'm checking a stray and you want to see my credentials?'

She couldn't tell if he was angry, annoyed or a mixture of both. But she didn't care.

She looked him up and down. 'I think I could take you,' she said frankly. 'I've learned how to take care of myself over the years. But I'll fight you to the death before I let you near that puppy without checking out who you are.'

They stood in silence for a few seconds, looking at each other, like some kind of stand-off.

Then he gave a nod and gestured for her to follow him. He walked slowly out to the hall and stopped in front of a picture on the wall.

She turned to face it, even though she'd seen it and walked past it a million times. It was of the original owner, David Ferguson, with his fellow vet partner, and his son.

The man raised his eyebrows at her.

And the penny dropped.

She squinted at the picture and moved right up close to it. 'That's you?' she asked incredulously.

She didn't mean it quite the way that it came out. But the skinny-looking kid in a T-shirt and ill-fitting jeans was a million miles away from this over six-foot lean guy with light tousled hair, pretty sexy stubble and blue eyes. She looked even closer at the picture, and then back to his face again.

'You might have the same hairline,' she said finally.

He made a noise that sounded like an indignant guffaw. 'Elijah Ferguson,' he said. 'Son of the late David. I'm only here until Matt is well enough to come back to work, and we can recruit a new vet to take over.'

Aurora was still thinking things through. 'Matt mentioned that you were a vet.'

She'd actually felt instantly relieved when he'd said the name Matt. Because that meant that he knew who usually worked here. This wasn't just some elaborate ploy to break into a vet's and steal some drugs, or an abandoned puppy.

'Where are you staying?' she asked.

'In the adjoining house,' he said quickly. 'But I plan on including that in the advert for the new recruit.' He nodded upstairs. 'I can sleep in one of the rooms upstairs while I train him.'

'Or her,' she said automatically.

'Or her,' he agreed with a smile, before holding up the puppy and looking him in the eye. 'Now, do I have your permission to check this little guy over?'

'I suppose,' she said, unsurprised when he walked straight through to one of the consulting rooms behind him. It was clear he knew the layout of this place. He'd obviously spent a large part of his life here.

She accepted that he was who he claimed to be. But it still didn't explain him just turning up like this. She was an employee. Didn't she have a right to know what was going on? It seemed rude.

She watched him cautiously. Aurora might not have been a vet nurse for too long—only four years so far. But she was wise enough to know if someone was competent or not.

He sounded the puppy's chest. Checked its mouth, eyes and ears. He had a little feel of the tummy and ribs, standing the puppy upright to check its gait. Then he got out the scales and weighed the little guy.

Her hands were itching to take the puppy from him. She wanted to check it over herself. It wasn't that she didn't trust him to do his job, it was just that she didn't *know* him.

Why didn't he work here? Wouldn't it have made more sense to work alongside his father, then take over from him? Maybe he wasn't that good a vet—and his father, from what she'd heard, had exacting standards, hadn't wanted to work alongside him.

Or maybe this guy was one of those fly-by-night vets who locumed everywhere before it was discovered they just weren't that good.

All of this flew through her head as she

watched him examine the puppy, as she filled the deep sink with warm water.

'He's scrawny,' came the deep voice.

'Well, that's obvious.' She could tell that from first sight, and from forty metres away.

'Heart murmur,' he added, and her heart gave a little pang.

'Severe?' Her skin had already prickled.

His eyes were still on the puppy. He shook his head. 'No. I'd want to recheck on a regular basis, but I suspect it might just disappear as he grows.'

She walked over and held out her arms. 'My turn. Let me clean him up, and then give him some food.'

'What've we got?'

She lifted the puppy, who didn't object as she gently submerged him in the few inches of warm water, lifting a soft cloth to remove the dirt and stones from his coat and paws. She named the two brands of food they currently had in the cupboard, and Grumpy vet scowled. 'Is there a deal with them?'

She was trying not to smile. 'Grumpy' vet had just automatically come into her head, rather than his actual name. She let out a sigh. 'I don't know. It's been stocked here since I arrived last year. We sell some over the counter.'

He picked up his keys, and it struck her that she hadn't seen a car out front. 'I don't like it.

I'm going into the city to pick up some other supplies. I won't be long. Don't feed him until I'm back.'

Aurora gave a nod. Dog food could be an endless debate. Some practices had deals with brands to stock their food, and usually received some sort of incentive to do so. She hadn't been involved in any of this. There were websites and chat forums that dedicated hours to the nutritious content of every food on the market and the benefits of raw, dry or wet dog food. What she did know was the practice also had a freezer stocked with chicken and plain white fish—which they frequently used for sick dogs, alongside some rice, or sweet potato. If Mr Grumpy didn't get back in time, she would happily make something up for the little guy.

A few moments later she heard a car engine, and looked out to see a low bright red sports car emerge from the garage next to the house. The same car was in one of the other photographs on the wall. It must have belonged to Elijah's dad.

She finished cleaning off the puppy, before giving him a few more treats and settling him in a basket with a blanket in one of the secure stations in the main observation room. He was already half asleep; clearly his escapee adventure had been too much for him.

Aurora went upstairs and changed into a spare

uniform, before coming back down, turning the sign on the door to open and checking the answering machine.

There were a few routine appointments this morning. Weight checks, nail clipping, eye drops and a skin treatment for a West Highland terrier. She also had a few test results to check from samples that Matt had taken last week before he'd had to stop working. Elijah Ferguson hadn't told her what exactly he was doing here, so she didn't want to make any assumptions.

As the first patient came in, she settled into her normal routine. Finding this practice on the outskirts of Edinburgh had been a blessing in disguise. At twenty-eight, vet nursing hadn't been Aurora's first job. She'd had stars in her eyes as a kid and gone to stage school, getting a few small TV roles, then a lead as a daughter in a new series about a family that had gone to Africa. Funnily enough, the main character in the series had been a vet, and her whole time in Africa had been spent among staff who had great respect for animals.

The series had catapulted her into stardom and onto social media, with pictures of her in clubs with friends, or shopping in London, regularly appearing in the tabloids. Soon after that, the stalking had started. It had taken her a little while to realise at first that the letters delivered to her agent, then the gifts that had mysteriously appeared at her rental, were actually a bit more sinister. As they'd moved into the second TV series, where staff changes made her uncomfortable, and had led to a member of the crew sexually assaulting her, Aurora had quickly realised she wasn't going to continue. Her colleagues had been supportive and leapt to her defence, particularly when the press called the incident a publicity stunt around #MeToo. Her return to London had coincided with the arrest of her stalker after an apparent kidnapping attempt and Aurora was all out of showbusiness.

Her saving grace had been the friends she'd made first time around in Africa, and one of the show's vet advisors had encouraged her to look at vet nurse courses. It had been exactly what she needed. Her course in Hertfordshire, along with some hair dye and returning to her own name, had given her the time and space she'd needed to escape the demons that had chased her. A few of her colleagues had eventually recognised her along the way, but she'd always managed to shy away from talking about her experience, or why she'd left.

Her first year after her degree had been spent at a practice on the edges of London. But when she'd seen this job advertised on the outskirts of Edinburgh, and realised the practice worked with both domestic and farm animals, it had seemed a perfect match for her.

Her old-style cottage was tiny, but she'd bought it outright with her earnings from the TV series. The bills were reasonable, and she was able to keep saving. Life, for the most part, was good now, as long as she could continue to keep out of the spotlight.

She finished checking the weight of a cat whose owner had been told to put the cat on a diet for strict health reasons. It seemed it was an uphill battle. 'Ms Bancroft?' Aurora asked. 'Have you been sticking to the food we talked about?'

The older woman nodded solemnly while not quite meeting Aurora's eyes.

'And no treats?'

The woman's face screwed up and she gave a minimal shrug of her shoulders. 'She only gets a few.'

The cat glared at Aurora—actually glared at her, as if she knew exactly what they were talking about and didn't approve in the least.

'Well, Trudie's weight is still the same. She really needs to lose some. Her bones and joints are under so much strain while she's this heavy, and her heart too.'

The elderly woman lifted her indignant cat back into her arms. 'Well, I'll try my best.'

Aurora gave an inward sigh. 'The good news is that she's not put any more weight on. So, that's at least a step in the right direction. How about you bring her back in two weeks and we'll check her again?'

Aurora could almost sense that Trudie had Ms Bancroft exactly where she wanted her, and likely annoyed her most of the day for treats.

'Two weeks.' Ms Bancroft nodded, before allowing Aurora to put Trudie back into her cat carrier as she hissed in annoyance.

Next, Aurora trimmed a Pekingese's nails, clipped a hamster's teeth, gave eye drops to a young kitten with a nasty infection, and finally treated a white Highland terrier with atopic dermatitis. She gave careful instructions to the young owner. 'Around twenty-five per cent of West Highland terriers develop atopic dermatitis at some point in their life. We need to keep on top of it, as it can cause skin damage, infection and general discomfort. It's really hard to get them to stop scratching. If you treat the skin like this every day, it should reduce the itch, and help keep the symptoms at bay.'

The young girl nodded seriously. Aurora knew that she loved her dog, and would do her best to treat the condition.

By the time she'd finished with the fourth patient, Elijah Ferguson still hadn't returned. She quickly made some chicken and white rice for the puppy, cutting the chicken into tiny pieces before taking him outside to let him relieve himself. 'We need to give you a name,' she said, taking a snap on her phone and uploading it to the vet website page, asking if anyone knew the owner.

She held the puppy up. He'd cleaned up well, his black and white coat almost fluffy at this stage. She studied him for a few seconds. 'Bert,' she said with a smile. Her favourite cast member back on the show. Old enough to be her grandfather, and the person who'd stepped in when needed. It had made a big difference for her, and she'd always be grateful. 'You look like a Bert,' she said to the little guy before sitting him back on her lap whilst she checked some of the test results from samples taken last week. The first result made her close her eyes for a second and take a few breaths.

Cancer. In an older dog. And fairly advanced. The dog had recently developed a limp and the owner had brought him in to be checked. Matt, the vet she'd been working with, had been fairly sure what the diagnosis might be, and had already prepared the owner.

But Matt wasn't here. His own treatment for cancer had taken its toll, and he'd needed some rest and recuperation. Frankie, the French vet who'd worked here up until last week, had put in his notice and gone to work in Dubai.

Aurora knew the owner of this dog. He'd lost his wife a few years ago, and she wanted to make sure she dealt with this sensitively. From first meet, she wasn't entirely sure that Elijah Ferguson was the person to do that.

She picked up the phone, and kept a hold of Bert, as she made the call. It was the one part of her job that she didn't enjoy, but she knew it was one of the most important. So she ignored her heart thumping in her chest and took a deep breath as the phone was answered.

Eli was mad. And there was no real reason for it. He was mad about puppy farms around the vet practice. He was mad about the fact his own car had broken down last night and he'd been forced to use one of his father's. Just driving it now brought back a whole host of memories. He was mad about not contacting the practice staff before he'd arrived. A novice mistake. He'd startled that woman this morning and it was hardly a good start.

He was even mad about the brand of food that Matt had obviously chosen to sell these last few years—even though it was entirely none of his business.

He could actually feel the suspension on the

low-slung sports car suffering due to the amount of different feed he'd just purchased from a supplier.

And he was mad about how remarkably attractive the vet nurse was. Her dark red hair had been windswept and strewn about her face, her uniform dirty, and his first reaction wasn't entirely gracious as she'd walked in with the dirty puppy. But it seemed that she was unfazed by his bad temper.

It suddenly struck him that he hadn't even asked her what her name was and he groaned at his pure bad manners. That sent off another wave of annoyance in his head at how disappointed in him his father would have been.

Truth be told, the second that Elijah Ferguson had even glimpsed the familiar countryside every part of him had been on edge.

There wasn't even a reasonable explanation for it. And he knew it. It wasn't as if he'd had an unhappy childhood or been abused in any way. His mother and father had both loved him. But his father had been obsessed with his job. He'd always been working long hours, tending to horses or sheep on farms at three in the morning, missing Eli's football matches because of an unexpected emergency. Falling asleep at school assemblies because he'd been up all night. Everyone had loved David Ferguson, including Eli.

It was just hard to tell anyone how it felt to literally have an absent father. Always feeling second best to a job. Joining his dad as a young kid at the practice on a Saturday had been the only way to get a part of his attention.

Even as an adult he hadn't really been able to articulate it. So it just hung above his head, as words always unspoken, feelings never really being acknowledged, and a part of himself feeling resentful and stupid. He'd had a good life. His father had been delighted by his career choice. He'd been so proud of Elijah being top of his class.

And all of that had just made Eli want to run further and further away.

Today, as soon as he'd set foot in the place, he'd been jittery in a way it was impossible to describe. Again, he felt foolish. His father had been dead for six years now. But memories of him were all over the place. The photos. The colour of the walls. The layout of the practice. Matt hadn't changed a single part of it.

As he turned back towards the large country practice, he finally paid attention to the little blue car parked in front. It was covered in mud. Clearly the nurse had gone off the road to recover the puppy. He remembered the fierce look in her eyes as she'd demanded to know his credentials, as she'd clutched the puppy to her chest.

He liked that. He admired that. And the thoughts caused a gut punch to his stomach. Last time he'd had his attention drawn by a member of staff he'd practically sold his business down the river. That was the last thing he'd ever do again. The last.

He pulled up alongside the car and walked back up the stairs to the entrance. It was later than he'd planned and as he opened the door he could hear her talking on the phone in a low, sympathetic voice. 'I'm so sorry,' she was saying.

He frowned. What was going on?

Something made his footsteps slow, and he heard other parts of the conversation. Test results. A cancer diagnosis. A poor prognosis. Alarm bells started going off in his head.

Who on earth was this woman, and what on earth was she doing?

'Who are you talking to?' he demanded as he walked inside the room.

She started, and the puppy, which was on her lap, gave a little jump.

'Just one of our clients,' she said. 'They were waiting for some results from tests that Matt took last week.'

Her green eyes were wide and he'd clearly surprised her.

'And you think it's your job to do that?'

He could see her bristle. She turned her head

away from him and continued her conversation on the phone. 'Mr Sannox, our new vet has just arrived. I know this is really upsetting for you. Why don't I drop by later and I can tell you everything you need to know?'

'You won't,' snapped Eli. It was all he could do not to pull the phone from her hand. She was really overstepping. And what was more, he hadn't even asked her name so he could actually demand that she stop right now.

'Finish that call.' His hands were on his hips right now. This shouldn't be happening. Not in his practice. News like this should always be delivered by a vet. She had absolutely no right.

But whatever her name was, she completely ignored him, actually standing up and putting her back to him as she continued to talk. 'Yes, I'll see you about three o'clock. No problem at all.'

If he hadn't noticed the tiniest tremble of her hand he would be yelling right now.

She put down the phone and turned to face him, eyes blazing. 'I was right about you.'

It was the last thing he'd expected her to say. 'What?'

'I actually contemplated if I could rely on you to give results like those. And guess what? I thought not. And I was entirely right. How dare you interrupt me when I'm telling someone their pet is going to die? What's wrong with you?'

She was angry now. Her jaw was clenched.

'What's wrong with me? What's wrong with you? What gives you the right to think you should be giving results like that without them being checked by a vet first? Do you even understand the results? Do you know the treatment options? Are you qualified for any of this?'

Oh, no. A horrible thought crept over him. This woman had demanded to know his credentials earlier—he hadn't even thought to ask about hers.

Not only did he not know her name, he didn't know if she was qualified in anything.

His brain was going mad. The logical part screamed, *The lawyers told you the two vet nurses were qualified.* One of them he'd known for ever. This one…? Had she been here a year? Two? He couldn't remember.

She stepped right up under his chin. 'Let's get things straight right now, Elijah Ferguson,' she said, an unexpected accent appearing in her tone. 'You don't ever talk to me like that again.' The words were hissed. 'You left here, after appearing this morning, not even telling me where you were going, when you'd be back, or even if you were going to be working here in future. As far as I know, *I'm* the only qualified person on shift today.' She pressed her hand against her chest. 'I know these people. I know exactly how much Rudy means to Mr Sannox, and I know exactly what's happened in his life these past few years. I have a duty of care to him, and to his pet.' She flung her hand to the ceiling. 'So, you go off and worry about pet food, while I deal with the patients and tell them the news they don't want to hear.'

Her accent, which had started as a mere hint, was now pure Liverpudlian. The anger which had also started as a hint was now emanating from every pore of her body.

'Jack Sannox?' he said, his skin growing cold.

She blinked in surprise and nodded. 'Yes.'

Lead was settling in his stomach. 'I know him,' he said automatically. 'This is his dog?'

'His border collie.' Her words were careful. 'He lost his wife a few years ago. He's become quite solitary. Something happening to Rudy will kill him.' The words were dramatic. But it seemed that Aurora had learned rapidly about farmers, their livestock and their pets.

'So, you've told him,' Eli repeated.

She looked at him carefully with those calculating green eyes. 'I've told him,' she said, holding his gaze. 'Because from what little I saw of you this morning, didn't give me confidence you would treat the case with the compassion it deserves.'

Wow. She wasn't messing about. Could he really work with this woman—even if it was for only a few weeks? He was instantly annoyed and offended. But should he be?

He straightened his own back and shoulders and held out his hand towards her. 'Elijah Ferguson,' he said. 'But call me Eli. Qualified eight years ago. I might not appear a very good human, but I can assure you that I'm an excellent vet.' He let out a long stream of air from his lips. 'And I know Jack Sannox. I went to his wife Bessie's funeral.'

His hand was still hovering in midair. She hadn't moved yet.

She'd changed since he was out, and her tunic was now a pale green, complementing her eyes. Her previously scruffy hair had also been combed and pulled back into a neat bun at the nape of her neck. She looked much more professional, and what was more, she had an extremely professional air. It was something that most people couldn't quite put their finger on. But she had it.

And though he was reluctant to say it, the fierce protection he'd now witnessed for both animals and owners was actually what he looked for in a colleague.

She still hadn't shaken his hand. There was tension in the air. They certainly hadn't started on the right foot. He wasn't even sure if this situation could be retrieved.

He brazened it out. 'I'll be working here for the near future. In the meantime, we're trying to recruit a new vet. If I have to take someone newly qualified I will, then hopefully mentor them for a short while to get them up to speed until Matt is well enough to come back and work alongside them. So, in effect, for a short period I'll be your new boss.'

Her shoulders tensed at those last words. He could see a million things flash in her eyes. And he was pretty sure one of them was her resignation. Considering this practice was currently losing staff like a dandelion shedding seeds in the wind, it wasn't what he wanted to hear.

Finally, she stepped forward and shook his hand with a firm grip. 'Aurora Hendricks,' she said, her accent vanishing once more. 'I've been here eighteen months, and it's always been a team approach. I'm not much for hierarchy. And yes, I am fully qualified. I have a BSc in Veterinary Nursing, and I know exactly what those test results mean.'

Aurora. An unusual name. But it suited her. There was something else though. Something strangely familiar about her that he couldn't quite place. Had they met somewhere before?

A little quiver of something ran through him. With her dark red hair, pale skin and green eyes, she was certainly attractive. He was sure if he'd met her before she would have made an impression. So, what was it about her that was familiar?

She took a deep breath, letting the words she'd said settle before she continued. 'And I don't just mean the science of the results. What I mean is, I'll likely be going up to Jack Sannox's farm for the next year to keep an eye on him.'

And that was when he knew.

That was when he knew that he had to find a way to work with this woman.

He needed her beside him, not against him.

He nodded. 'Aurora. It's an unusual name.'

She looked surprised that this was where the conversation was going. 'Well, "call me Eli",' she said, as quick as a flash, 'Elijah isn't so normal either.' She glanced out of the window. 'My father named me. After the actual Aurora Borealis. Aurora means dawn.'

He gave her a rueful smile. 'Well, my dad named me too. And he wasn't religious, but he remembered the name Elijah from Sunday School as a kid, and just liked it. I'm probably lucky he didn't name me after his favourite breed of cow.'

'Angus or Galloway?' she quipped.

He rolled his eyes. 'More than likely something neither of us have ever heard of.' He took a careful breath. 'If you don't mind, I'd like to familiarise myself with Rudy's case, then I'd like to go with you later today to speak to Jack. He will need extra support, because it's likely there will be no treatment that will actually make a difference.'

He turned his attention to the puppy in her arms. The little guy hadn't even squirmed during their exchange, just watched everything with his big brown eyes. He leaned forward and smiled. 'What are we going to do with this guy?'

'This is Bert,' she said determinedly.

'Where did that name come from?'

She shrugged. 'A reliable friend. I've posted a pic on our website. But since he's not tagged, I'm assuming he isn't actually owned by anyone. We might need to see if the local shelter can arrange someone to foster or adopt.'

'What about any of our clients?'

'What do you mean?'

'Is there anyone that might be looking for another dog? A companion for another dog?'

Aurora looked thoughtful and then wrinkled her nose. 'We've had a few older clients die in the last few months, and myself and Anne have managed to place their pets with other clients.'

She sighed. 'I think we might have used up our supply of local, willing pet fosterers.'

He reached over and took Bert in his arms. 'He looks about eight weeks. Puppies take a lot of work. Maybe he already had an owner who just wasn't ready for the work involved.'

It only took a few moments to make a decision. 'Let's give it a few days on the website and see what happens. I'll vaccinate him, and in the meantime he can stay here with me. There were kennels outside at one point, I'll go and have a look and see what state they're in.'

'You're staying here?' She seemed surprised.

He shrugged. 'I told you earlier, I could move into the house but it doesn't seem worthwhile. I want to use it as an incentive for the new vet. I'll just sleep upstairs. There's three bedrooms, a living room and a bathroom. There's even been a new kitchen put in.'

'You do know that if we take a patient overnight, either myself or Anne usually stay in one of the other rooms?'

He tucked Bert under his arm. 'You do?'

She nodded.

'It's okay.' He shrugged. 'I'm sure we can make it work. It'll only be for a few months. And I don't snore,' he added.

She arched her eyebrow. 'But I do.'

And there it was. Another challenge. It seemed

that Aurora Hendricks was someone who was going to keep him on his toes.

He leaned down and nuzzled into Bert. 'Let's go find some earplugs, kid. We've got to plan ahead.'

CHAPTER TWO

THE RAIN WAS pelting down as Aurora arrived the next morning, and the normally paved area in front of the practice was swimming in mud. She turned and frowned at the nearby hillside. There had been some slippage in the past—was it going to happen again?

She shucked off her wellies at the front door, knowing she had some flat shoes in her locker—and promptly stepped in a pool of puppy pee.

'Ew,' she said before smiling. It wasn't the first time, and wouldn't be the last.

'Sorry,' came a voice from the doorway. Eli had Bert tucked under his arm. 'We tried the kennels last night after I'd fixed them up but—' he looked down at Bert '—it seems that Bert is actually a house dog.'

Aurora couldn't help but smile. She peeled off her wet socks and walked across the tiled floor, rubbing Bert's head. 'Are you just showing him who's boss?' Bert licked her hand. 'Guess you'd

better get started with the toilet training then,'
she said.

He looked down at her painted toenails. 'How
about I get you a pair of socks first?'

She nodded gratefully, and was pulling the
thick woollen socks onto her feet as Anne came
through the door.

'Typical Scottish summer,' said Anne, shaking
off her umbrella, and then stopping short. 'Eli?'
she said in wonder, before crossing the room in
long strides and enveloping him in a giant hug.

Aurora's gaze flicked from one to the other.
Anne only worked here three days a week now.
But she'd been here from the time that Eli's dad
had run the practice, so it was obvious that they
would know each other.

Eli, surprisingly, returned the hug with a relieved expression on his face. Had he been worried that Anne wouldn't be happy to see him?

'Who is this?' she asked, rubbing Bert's head.

'A stray, we think,' he said, glancing over at
Aurora. 'This is Bert. I'll keep him for the next
few days to see if anyone comes forward.'

'Sure you will,' said Anne, still smiling. She'd
released him now but tucked her hand into his
arm. 'Let's just go and have a cup of tea and
catch up a bit. You can manage, can't you, Aurora?'

Aurora gave a nod. Eli looked a cross between

still being relieved along with a mad dash of panic. 'Can you put Jack Sannox in the diary for later today, since he wasn't up to it yesterday?'

Aurora gave a nod as Anne swiftly moved Eli through to the kitchen, talking the whole time.

She checked through the patients for the day. She noticed that Eli had put a few notes next to some, mainly questions on getting some more information from owners or looking at medications or treatment plans. She took her time to read them all. He was thorough. He'd also left some notes and instructions about the surgical list for tomorrow, asking her to call all the owners to remind them of the instructions for their pets, prior to any procedure.

Aurora always did that automatically, but he wasn't to know that so she tried not to let it annoy her and just left it for now.

She sighed as she looked at a few of the notes he'd left regarding Rudy and Mr Sannox. Jack had called back and asked them to change their visit until today. He'd said something about needing a little time.

In all honesty, she would have preferred to see Jack yesterday, if anything, just so she could give him a hug. Aurora finished what she was doing and tried not to be curious about the conversation that was clearly going on in the kitchen.

She'd have loved a cup of tea but didn't want to intrude.

She'd always enjoyed working with Anne, who came equipped with a million stories and a world of expertise. She lived in the nearby village and had never even considered working somewhere else. Aurora could remember a few times when Anne had casually mentioned that it was a shame that Elijah hadn't taken over from his father, but had always backed the words with something like 'children should always spread their wings'.

An unexpected arrival—a cat with fleas, brought by a horrified owner who asked a myriad questions about her designer wardrobe and furniture—kept her attention away from the conversation in the kitchen. Aurora spent a considerable amount of time concentrating on treating the cat and emphasising how important it was to continue treatment, before covering the basics about vacuuming the home, washing all bedding and soft furnishings and spraying everything with flea spray.

After that, there were some routine appointments. Anne and Aurora shared the vet nurse appointments, accompanying Eli when required and keeping an eye on Bert.

Anne opened the store cupboard and blinked at the newly stocked food. She leaned over and checked the side label before giving an approving nod. 'This one is hypoallergenic. It will actually suit a lot of our patients with more sensitive tummies.'

Aurora smiled. She hadn't even looked that closely. 'So, what do you think of our new vet?' she asked, trying to sound innocent.

She could tell that Anne was bursting to talk. Anne had lots of skills but keeping secrets wasn't her best—although she could, when necessary, be discreet.

'I'm so happy to see Eli again,' she said with a smile. 'He's grown up to be the picture of his father.'

'Has he?' Aurora had seen the photo on the wall earlier, but didn't think they were so alike.

'Oh, yes,' said Anne with authority. 'Same height and build. Eli has his mother's colouring, but his mannerisms are identical to his father's.' She gave a soft smile. 'It brings back lots of memories.'

Aurora wondered how many questions she would get away with. 'His father and Matt were partners, weren't they?'

Anne nodded. 'Right up until David retired. He worked on much longer than he should have. But by then Sarah, his wife, was dead and Eli was away working someplace else. He didn't want to leave Matt on his own.'

Aurora looked out over the Scottish country-side. Right now, it was difficult to get a good view, with the sheeting rain and small mudslide from the hills nearby. But usually this view was a wild array of green, a dash of some heather and a few spots of white sheep.

'Why on earth is it so hard to recruit around here?'

Anne gave a sorrowful shrug. 'I'm not sure. I think for a while David was too picky, and Eli seems to have inherited his father's traits. When the practice passed to him, he constantly didn't think any of the applicants were good enough.' She gave Aurora a knowing glance. 'You know the thing—he didn't want to work here, but no one else was good enough?'

Aurora frowned as she tried to make some sense of her new workmate. 'Interesting.' She paused, looking in the direction of the kitchen to make sure the coast was clear, and then asked the ultimate question. 'So, why did Eli never come back to work with his dad, or take over?'

Anne wrinkled her nose. 'He'd opened his own practice for a while on the outskirts of London. Not sure what happened there. I guess right now it's just about timing. Matt's sick and Frankie's left. What other option did he have?'

And that answer left Aurora with an uncomfortable feeling. Anne was going to retire soon.

But Aurora had another twenty years or more to work. If they couldn't recruit another vet, this practice might fold. She didn't want to end up out of work. She loved her cottage and where she lived. She didn't want to have to move. But if Eli was only there on a temporary basis, she might need to consider other options.

Anne nodded towards the car park as another car pulled in. 'Recognise them?' she asked.

Aurora shook her head, 'No idea.'

Eli met her at the front door. As soon as he stood next to her, she got a waft of his aftershave. Fresh but woody, it made her breathe in even deeper. Darn it. The last thing she needed was to be attracted to someone she worked with. Particularly when he could be occasionally snarky. Mixing work and pleasure was never a good idea. It didn't help that he glanced sideways at her and gave her a half smile.

A couple in their twenties entered the practice with a cat carrier. Although they didn't have an appointment, there was a short gap where they could be seen. Eli showed them through to one of the examination rooms. Aurora instantly had a weird feeling. She watched the interaction between the couple as they removed their cat from the carrier and placed him on the examination table.

Eli asked them some details as he examined

the cat, which was called Arthur. Again, as she watched him, she appreciated how thorough he was. But something about the couple seemed off. It was that niggling feeling right between her shoulder blades that she really couldn't explain to anyone. Aurora had had this before—it sometimes caught her by surprise.

The man seemed to continually talk over his partner. He also kept glancing towards Aurora, even though she was not speaking to him directly. She was merely making notes on the computer as Eli examined the patient. His continued glances made her nervous and uncomfortable; he even hinted at a smile a few times towards her when he knew his partner was looking elsewhere. There was just something creepy about him.

She could sense that Eli caught something in the air. He gave her a curious look but continued with his examination, and after a few careful questions Aurora knew exactly where this diagnosis was going. Eli looked at them. 'I think I can say with some confidence that Arthur has diabetes. All the symptoms you've described— the weight loss, the excessive drinking and excessive eating—all point in that direction. I only need to run a few minor tests to be able to confirm it.'

The women looked pale. 'Is this serious?' she asked.

Eli nodded. 'It can be. But diabetes in cats is not uncommon and it's a condition we can treat.'

'Will he need injections?' asked the guy. 'My gran has diabetes and she requires injections.'

Eli nodded again. 'That's very likely. Why don't you leave Arthur with us for a few hours, and when you come back we can confirm the diagnosis and make a treatment plan?'

The guy shot another few glances in Aurora's direction and she shifted uncomfortably in her seat. She hadn't spoken a word to him during the consultation, so knew that she had done nothing to attract his attention.

'Is everything all right?' asked Eli as soon as they left.

Aurora gave her shoulders a little shake. 'Just something about that guy. He made me uncomfortable.'

She didn't want to go into any details. Being assaulted, and then being stalked, had a huge influence on her life. The outcome of these had affected both how she lived her life and her decision-making. It had been built into her TV contract that she would be covered for any consequences from being in the TV series. She knew that essentially had been around any possible accidents or injuries but, thankfully, her assault had also been covered—and not for a short period of time. Now, all these years later, she still attended counselling sessions when she needed them. They'd started intensely but now happened as and when Aurora ever decided she needed them. She had that odd prickly feeling that she'd be making contact with her counsellor some time soon.

She stood up and walked over and picked up Arthur. 'How about I get started on those tests for Arthur and you can prescribe his insulin?'

Eli gave a nod and started taking more notes. Aurora half hoped that only the woman would come back. She would need to spend some time with Arthur's owners to explain his new diet plan, and how to do his injections. They'd already left insurance details, so she knew Arthur would be covered, and it would likely take another few visits to get his condition stabilised.

It had been a strange start to the day. Eli had been nervous about seeing Anne again and wondered how she might act. But Anne had been warm, friendly and professional. He just had a sense, deep down, of a slight feeling of disappointment that emanated from her. It could all be in his head—maybe it was just old feelings being rehashed?

Anne had been well aware of the underlying

hostility that lay between Eli and his father. But she showed no hard feelings towards Eli, and seemed happy to see him.

He still wasn't entirely sure about Aurora. She'd seemed a little off in the earlier consultation, but maybe he was just misinterpreting things.

He was still trying to get to grips with how the practice was run. It seemed that Anne and Aurora shared the variety of roles, and he wondered if that was the best use of their time. Aurora had mentioned the practice being a team approach. It was hard to get a sense of that when he was the only vet. And he wasn't sure how much time and energy to invest in finding out, when he would only be here a short space of time.

But Aurora intrigued him. He could sense something from her earlier when she'd been uncomfortable in the consulting room. He'd almost felt a shift in the air. He was slightly annoyed that he hadn't picked up on anything, but would pay better attention in the future. He still wanted to find out a little bit more about her and her experience. His eyes were continually drawn to her, no matter how hard he tried for them not to be. His brain was constantly wondering about her. And it was odd, but he could sometimes swear there was a buzz in the air between them. But maybe he was just imagining it.

He wondered if he would get that opportunity to find out a bit more about her when they visited Jack in a few hours' time. But in the meantime, he had other things to concentrate on.

Bert was showing no interest in toilet training. It had been so long since Eli had looked after a puppy that he'd forgotten how hard it was. He cleaned up a variety of puddles and took Bert back outside with some treats to try and encourage him to toilet outside and reward that behaviour. No matter where Bert eventually ended up, he would likely need to be toilet trained, so it was worth the extra time and effort. More people were likely to adopt a puppy if they knew the toilet training routine had started.

Anne shouted them all through to the kitchen, where they all prepared lunch. She looked at the visits for the day. 'What is going on at the Fletchers' farm?' she asked.

Eli looked up. 'What do you mean?'

Anne put her hand to her chin and looked thoughtful. 'It's in the book for today but there's no notes next to it. I'm sure that Matt has already been there a few times. I think some of the cattle have been poorly—but I don't think there was anything specific.'

'I have no problem going back up there,' said Eli. 'Has Don Fletcher phoned down again?'

Anne shook her head. 'The writing in the

book is definitely Matt's. He must've put a note on here a few weeks ago that he wanted to go back.'

Eli was thoughtful for a minute. 'Put it forward a few days, please. I want us to spend a bit of time with Jack Sannox this afternoon.'

Anne nodded and changed the diary. Lunch was quick, and Eli spent a bit of time checking off everything he would need for the few surgical procedures that were scheduled for the next day. One lesion to be biopsied. One cat, and one dog to be neutered.

Aurora's answers were swift to each query. 'Done, done, and done.'

He got the hint that she was getting annoyed with him. But this was basic stuff. He didn't know Aurora, and had no idea what her capabilities were. Last thing he wanted was for an animal to present tomorrow who hadn't been properly prepared for surgery. Then it would require cancellation and would be a waste of time for all concerned. He was only ensuring every box was ticked. It was what any good vet would do. If Aurora didn't like it? Too bad.

The afternoon passed quickly and soon it was time to do the home visits. For farms, it went without saying that the vet had to visit. For domestic animals, home visits were much fewer. Occasionally when an animal had reached the end of their life span, and was clearly in pain or desperately unwell, some owners would ask for them to be put to sleep at home, rather than in the practice. Eli knew that Matt and his father always respected the client's wishes in these cases, and he would do the same. He pointed at a name on the list that had been scored out. 'What's happening with this one?'

Aurora took a deep breath. 'Mrs Adams wants another day. She says she's not quite ready.'

He took a quick glance at the notes. An elderly cat, signs of dementia, untreatable cancer, now being incontinent, and its back legs weren't functioning. 'Are you sure she can cope?' When an animal reached this stage it was like being a full-time carer. It could take a lot out of owners.

Aurora pressed her lips together and gave a tight nod. 'She'll cope. She'll phone us back when she's sure she's ready.'

'Does she have pain relief for her cat?'

'Of course, we would never leave any animal in pain.' There was a tiny bit of defensiveness to her words.

'Okay then, ready?' he asked as they made their way outside to head to Jack Sannox's farm.

'We can't go in that.' She smiled, pointing at the low-slung sports car. 'Have you seen the farm roads?'

He pointed to the garage. 'Don't you know

my dad was a bit of a car fiend? He's got another three in there. There's an old eighties Land Rover. It's built like a tank and it's fit for any farm road. He used it for most of his visits while he worked here.'

The car wasn't modern enough to have a key fob press-button lock, so Eli had to do the old-fashioned way of opening the doors with the key.

Aurora climbed in. Part of him wanted to get to know her a little better. He couldn't deny how attractive she was. And she didn't wear a ring. But that meant nothing these days. After his previous experience, the last thing Eli wanted to do was have any kind of relationship with a member of staff. So why was he even having these thoughts? He couldn't deny how attractive she was, but she was prickly at times.

As the thought entered his head, he almost laughed out loud. Prickly? So was he. More than prickly. But he couldn't help it. Being back at the family home and practice was conjuring up a whole host of past feelings—ones that he really hadn't wanted to deal with. And now? When, if he didn't recruit another vet, the whole place would be under threat didn't seem like the best time to deal with things.

As she sat in the Land Rover next to him, the scent of her perfume drifted towards him. Hints of amber and musk. Quite distinctive. Her hair, which had been tied up earlier, was now down around her shoulders. The long, dark red bob suited her, and looked more sculpted that he would have expected.

'What?' she asked unexpectedly.

His stare had clearly been noticed. He decided to play things out. 'How long have you been here?'

'Eighteen months,' she answered easily.

'And what brought you to Scotland? Was it family? Or did you get married?'

She gave him a distinct side-eye. 'I'm not married. No partner. This practice brought me to Scotland.'

So, the fact he'd been asking if she had a partner had not been lost on her, and he pretended not to be secretly relieved.

'You came here for the job?'

'Of course I did.'

'Where did you train?'

'Hawkshead.' The Royal Veterinary College. The most prestigious place to carry out vet training, or vet nurse training.

'Outside of Edinburgh is a long way to travel.'

She shrugged. 'I don't have family ties, and I'd worked already in outer London, I wanted to move to a place where there was a chance to work with both domestic and farm animals.'

He gave a smile as they continued along the

winding country road. 'Not a lot of people want to work with both types of animal.'

She waved a hand at the clothes she'd changed into. Big green wellies and a large, dark waterproof coat. 'I don't like to be caught unawares. We're going to talk to Jack about Rudy, but if there's another farm issue he wants us to look at, I like to be prepared.'

Eli couldn't help but be a little impressed. He'd stashed his own stuff earlier in the back of the Land Rover. It was nice to know that Aurora was prepared too.

'What about your accent?' he asked. 'I've noticed it tends to come and go.'

For a moment there was silence, and he wondered if he'd stepped over a line he shouldn't have.

'My accent?'

He swallowed. He'd started the conversation. He couldn't back out now. And, for some reason, he wanted to know. His head flooded with thoughts about his past experience. Could Aurora be pretending to be someone she wasn't? Was there a reason she changed her accent at times? He needed to be able to trust those he worked with.

But as she brushed a length of her hair behind her ear, and he caught a glimpse of her pale skin, his stomach clenched. She was anxious. Anxious he found out something she was trying to hide?

'Yes,' he said firmly. 'Most of the time you don't seem to have an accent at all. But occasionally the odd twang seems to slip in.'

'The odd twang?' she repeated. This time he could see her eyebrows raised. She looked as if she were about to roast him.

'Yip,' he said with a smile in his voice as he turned onto the road towards Jack's farm.

'My accent does come and go,' she said carefully. 'I grew up in Liverpool. But when I worked in London some of the clients appeared to have an issue with my accent, so I tried to tone it down.'

It was an odd kind of explanation. London was one of the most diverse populations in the UK, with a multitude of accents. But he did concede that certain parts of London had old-fashioned clients who might be a bit haughty towards a Liverpudlian accent.

'No excuse for behaviour like that,' he said promptly. 'I've worked all over the world. I get that my Scottish accent can be quite broad, and I've had to repeat myself on numerous occasions, but I wouldn't try and hide my accent.' He shot her a glance. 'If I'm in another country, I usually get mistaken for Irish instead of Scottish. But I can live with that.'

They pulled up outside Jack Sannox's cottage. The word cottage was a bit of a stretch. The farmhouse was much more impressive as it had been extended over the years, but the original parts of the cottage were still there. He obviously took pride in his home.

Eli took a breath. 'Wow… Haven't seen this place in years. He's extended—it looks great.'

Aurora climbed out of the Land Rover. 'I've only been here once before, when there was an issue with the pigs. Matt said the work had just finished and Jack gave us a full tour. He was very proud.'

'So he should be.'

They moved to the front door and Jack opened it with a solemn expression on his face. He led them through to his sitting room, where Rudy was lying on a rug on the sofa. Jack sat down next to him.

'How's he been?' asked Eli, bending down so his face was next to Rudy's and stroking his head.

'He was up last night whimpering. I don't think the painkillers are working.'

'I can increase them,' said Eli instantly. 'But it may make Rudy drowsy.'

'He's so used to being by my side, walking the fields with me, riding the tractor,' said Jack, a definite waver in his voice. 'He's just not going to be able to do that.'

'No, he's not,' said Eli reluctantly. He wanted to give Jack a realistic expectation for what happened next.

Jack sighed and stared out of the window, one hand on Rudy.

Aurora moved and sat beside him, taking his other hand in hers. 'It's not fair. And we know that. None of us deserve the dogs that we have— they're all just too good. I know this time of year is difficult. I know it's around the same time that your wife died.'

Jack's eyes widened in surprise; he turned to look at her. 'But you never got to meet Bessie.'

'I know, and I'm sorry about that. But you're the one I need to worry about.'

Jack blinked and Eli could see the wetness in his eyes. 'No one left to worry about me,' he whispered, and Aurora leaned over and gave him a hug.

'That's not true.' She looked over at Eli. 'I'm sure we can make Rudy comfortable, and give him another few months.'

Part of Eli wanted to be annoyed. But the way she was looking at him with those green eyes was almost sending him a secret message. He had written in Rudy's notes that he thought he could make the dog comfortable for the next few months. Maybe she was just letting him know that she was following his lead?

Jack turned to him. 'I don't want my dog in pain. Are you sure there isn't anything else that can be done?'

Eli spoke in a low, serious tone. 'His cancer has spread. Some of the organs that are affected could give him other symptoms. But most of these we can control. I can certainly control his pain. There's another medication we can try—a cancer medication that can also shrink some of his tumours and give him a better quality of life.'

Jack gave a sniff. 'A few months, you say?'

Eli nodded. 'I'll talk you through the medications. I brought them with me.' He moved back over and kneeled in front of Rudy again. 'I think you'll do okay as a house dog, Rudy.'

Rudy looked at him with his big brown eyes, and Eli remembered why he was a vet. For this. To take care of animals that had brought joy to families and give them a comfortable end to their life.

He looked at Aurora, who still had one hand in Jack's, her other arm around his shoulder. She was squeezing it. It struck Eli that he didn't know who might have hugged Jack since his wife had died a few years ago. This could be his first hug since then.

He also wasn't sure how Aurora had found

out about when his wife had died. Maybe Matt had told her? But however, she'd found out, she'd taken the information into consideration when here. He liked the fact that she'd thought about the whole situation, and not just the immediate circumstances.

They left Jack nearly an hour later. They were quiet. It was always sad when discussing plans for a terminal pet.

Aurora leaned her head against the window. 'I'm not sure if Rudy will want to be a house dog.'

'I'm not sure either,' admitted Eli. 'But we'll just have to play it by ear, and give Jack the support he needs.'

She turned her head towards him and locked her eyes on his. 'This,' she said quietly. 'This is part of the reason I wanted to move. You get to know these patients. You get to know what matters to them. In the city, it was just a constant stream of French bulldogs, dachshunds, cockapoos, cavapoos and chihuahuas. Most of the time we never saw them on a regular basis. We didn't get to form any kind of relationship with people. The turnover was incredible.'

'And you decided that wasn't for you?'

She gave a nod. 'Or maybe I just like cows,' she said with a smile.

There was something in that smile. Something

that made him know that she was being entirely honest.

But as soon as he had that thought, something else flashed into his head. But was he really a good judge of character? After all, he'd thought his last practice manager, Iona, was honest. He'd been sucked in by everything she'd said. They'd even started dating. Then the bills had started to arrive. It seemed that money from the practice had been funnelled off into places it shouldn't go—mainly Iona's bank account.

She'd offered to take over the wages system, the banking, the accounts. In other practices, it was a fundamental part of the practice manager's role. She'd come with excellent references—which he'd later found out had been faked—and he'd been thankful for the assistance.

It wasn't until another vet in the practice had taken him aside about an unpaid bill, that he'd found one day when he came in early, that Eli had any understanding at all that something was amiss.

And as the world had come crashing down around him, and his staff had been forced to find other jobs, and Iona had disappeared just as quickly as she'd appeared, Eli Ferguson had been left feeling like a complete and utter fool.

It seemed that fraud was harder to prove than he'd first thought, particularly when it seemed that it was his signature on some of the accounts. He'd had to dig into what little of his savings he still had to engage experts to confirm that he hadn't signed for certain things. Loans and credit cards had been the most popular. But that was the reason for his earlier visit to his accountant and solicitor. He'd had no option but to file for bankruptcy.

He wouldn't be able to be a real financial partner in his father's practice for a number of years. Instead, he would have to be an employee. And if he was embarrassed about that it was just too bad.

So maybe his judgement couldn't be relied upon at all. Not when it came to business or financial matters.

And any thoughts of how attractive Aurora Hendricks was, how cute her smile, the shine of her hair, or the fact she was feisty, with a warm heart, he had to put clean out of his head.

He was only here on a temporary basis. And he would do well to remember that.

CHAPTER THREE

AURORA STILL HADN'T quite got a handle on her new boss. She didn't want to admit she found him a little intriguing. He was handsome, there was no denying it, with his tall frame, his tousled light brown hair and his blue eyes. That darn designer stubble made her palms itch to touch it. If she'd met him at a bar somewhere she would definitely be interested. But their initial meeting had been a bit unusual.

In a way, she was glad that he'd caught the sharp side of her tongue and how protective she was of her work space, and any animal in it. That was important to her.

Then there was the fact she'd been uncomfortable around that cat owner the other day. He didn't need to know why. But her spider-sense never tingled without good reason. She'd learned to trust her instincts. It had been part of the reason she hadn't really panicked at their own first meeting. Eli might be a bit untouchable, but he wasn't intimidating or threatening.

She was still unsure about her job security though. Whilst vets might be hard to recruit in this part of the country, it seemed that the population around Edinburgh had veterinary nurse as a first career choice. Jobs were usually sought after. She'd been lucky when she'd interviewed for here. Both Anne and Matt had been in the middle of an emergency surgery—a dog who had developed a blockage in their bowel. It was a surgery she'd been involved in before and she'd offered to roll up her sleeves and assist so to speak. They'd hired her shortly afterwards and she'd been happy here.

The outskirts of Edinburgh was also a good place to hide. But hiding? Was that what she was actually doing?

Half of her hoped that no one remembered her fifteen minutes of fame. But, like any TV series, the show had ended up streaming on some of the satellite services and gained new fans. Every now and then she saw a social media post about *Where are they now?*

No one had ever got her location right. But there had been a few sightings—particularly when she'd qualified as a veterinary nurse and started working just outside London.

She wanted a private life. She didn't want to be dragged back into the #MeToo debate. She'd stood up for herself at the time, and now wanted to just get on with the rest of her life. She no longer had an agent. She'd drifted away from the fellow cast members on the series, and most of the crew. She'd changed her mobile number, and since her Equity card was under her acting pseudonym she'd felt relatively safe.

Of course, there was the inevitable person she'd gone to school with who occasionally commented on her disappearance from the TV screens, but most people thought she'd headed to find fame and fortune in the States, and failed. She was actually happy for that rumour to continue. It meant that life was safe, in this little part of the world.

The world didn't really understand the damage she'd suffered. The assault had left her feeling vulnerable and frail. The stalking had left her feeling unsafe. She'd had to build herself back up, take advice, attend regular counselling. Self-defence classes with regular refreshers helped too. But, most of all, she trusted her instincts. She would make sure she was never alone with that new client on any occasion. It didn't matter what reason she gave to Anne or Eli—she might even just tell them the truth. She'd learned to believe in herself, and that was what she'd do.

Today was going to be a bit different. She'd told Eli that she was interested in working with farm animals, and today they were doing several visits to farms.

'Are you really ready for this?' asked Eli as he climbed into the old Land Rover.

'Are you?' she asked, glancing at their list. She wrinkled her nose. 'Have you met all these farm owners before?'

He shook his head. 'I only know one out of three. I've been on two of the farms before, but one of them has changed hands.'

She gave him an amused glance. 'I've checked the notes. We have mysterious cows at the Fletchers' farm, temperamental pigs at the Sawyers' and a possible lame horse at Jen Cooper's riding school.' She gave an approving nod. 'It's going to be a good day.'

He gave her an amused sideways glance. Maybe he hadn't quite believed she did love farm work. Well, he would soon find out.

They ended up going to the Sawyers' farm first as it was closest. Shaun Sawyer took them to his pigsty, where two of the pigs had been separated out from the others.

It was clear that neither of these pigs were happy. They were grinding their teeth, were listless, with lots of abdominal kicking.

'Any vomiting?' asked Eli, as he prepared to go into the sty.

Shaun shook his head. 'Only minimal. And not for the last few hours.'

Aurora prepared herself too, and Eli gave her a sideways glance. 'I don't suppose they've escaped at all?' she asked as she swung her leg over the fence. The field around the pigsty had some straw but also a decent amount of mud. Aurora wasn't bothered at all.

Shaun pulled a face. 'They did a few days ago. Five of them did. But we managed to get them back relatively quickly.'

She jumped down, just as Eli did, and moved over to the nearest pig. She followed his lead and they both checked for any obvious bloating or signs of intestinal blockage. 'This one is a bit tachycardic,' she said.

'Mine too,' said Eli. They both checked the pigs' temperature, and Eli walked back over to Shaun. 'My gut feeling is this is colic. You've got an automatic feeder in action to stop gorging, plenty of water and plenty of space for the pigs to move around. There's no sign of obstruction at present—but you know that can be rapid. It could be they've eaten something that doesn't agree with them when they escaped. There is always a higher risk of twisted gut as we come into the summer and temperature fluctuates. But I don't think that applies right now. If we think there's an obstruction we might need to X-ray or ultrasound them.'

Shaun frowned and shook his head. 'Can I watch them a bit longer?'

Eli nodded. 'You can call me if you have any concerns. I'll give you some non-steroidal anti-inflammatories for them both.'

'Where did they go when they escaped?' asked Aurora.

Shaun inclined his head. 'Over the field and into the school playground.'

'Ah,' she said with a smile. 'Any chance they raided the school bins and overdosed on some sweet treats?'

Shaun pulled a face. 'My pigs? More than likely.'

They stayed a bit longer, observing the pigs for any signs of something more serious, before finally getting ready to leave. As Aurora went to swing her leg over the fence, there was a loud squelch and her foot came over, leaving her welly boot stuck fast.

The momentum carried her, and she landed on the other side of the fence with a laugh.

Eli shot a careful glance at Shaun and then they both burst into laughter too. Eli was still in the pen, so made his way over to her boot. He had to grab with both hands to finally free it, and nearly landed in the mud himself.

By the time they'd rinsed their wellies and got back into the car they were still laughing.

'What's next?' asked Aurora.

'You choose,' he said. 'Horse or cows?'

'Cows are my favourite farm animal,' declared Aurora. 'So let's leave them to last and go and see the horse first.'

The journey was only fifteen minutes and as the countryside sped past Aurora settled a little more comfortably into her seat.

'Where did you work before?' she asked.

As soon as the words were out of her mouth she realised it might not have been a good idea. He bristled. He actually bristled. Then he took a breath and said quickly, 'I've worked all over. I worked in Madrid for a while, then in Brittany in France, three months in Italy, then in the US in Florida and Maine, and in Lincolnshire in the UK.'

'Wow!' said Aurora, feeling part admiration and part envy. 'That's a huge range of countries.'

'I went for the experience with the animals.' He gave a smile and raised one eyebrow, as if he was just admitting something. 'In Madrid I worked in a practice that specialised in horses. Brittany was mainly farms. Florida—'

'Tell me it was alligators!' she interrupted.

He laughed. 'I did encounter one on a golf course, but not through work.'

'Darn it,' she muttered, then frowned. 'So, what was it in Florida then?'

He gave her a sideways glance. 'Turtle rehab.'

Her eyes widened. 'You're joking, aren't you?'

He shook his head. 'Are you telling me you don't think turtles should have care too?'

She stuttered for a moment. 'Oh…of course I don't think that. It's just such a change.'

'Working with sea life was such a great opportunity. I jumped at the chance. When I moved to Maine it was a real mix again. I was part of a practice with forty vets. I saw domestic animals and dairy and beef cattle, equine and poultry.'

Aurora couldn't take her eyes off him. 'It's like you stuck one finger in an atlas to decide which country to go to, and one finger in Pasquini to decide what animals to look after.'

He waggled a finger. 'Not all animals are in Pasquini.'

'True,' she admitted. Then she gave him a sideways glance. He seemed much more relaxed around her now. Less defensive. She wondered why he'd bristled at first. 'That must have been a lot of exams.' She knew that vets had to sit country specific exams to get the licence to practice.

He groaned. 'You have no idea. Thankfully, exams have never really bothered me.'

'Just as well,' she said as they turned into the riding school and pulled up outside the stables.

Jen Cooper stuck her head from one of the
stalls and walked quickly over to meet them,
getting straight to business. 'Thanks for coming.
It's Bess. I noticed this morning her gait was different. It's her right leg. She was fine yesterday,
and there's been no accident.'

'No problem,' said Eli as he held out his hand.
'Eli Ferguson. I've got a bit of experience with
horses, so let me have a look.'

'Where did you get your experience?' said Jen
casually as she opened the stall door.

'Jerez,' he said simply.

Aurora stopped walking—as did Jen. 'Jerez?'
they both said in unison.

The school was renowned for the world-fa-
mous Andalusian horses that danced in shows.

Both heads turned towards him, and Eli held
up one hand. 'What I'll say is that those horses
are kept in pristine conditions, have the best veterinary care and some of the best facilities I've
ever had the pleasure to work in.'

Aurora hid her smile. She knew exactly why
he might think they would comment. Some people didn't like animals used in a show, or sport
for that matter, and queried the conditions and
attention.

Somehow, she knew every word he said was
true. She might have only known him a few days

but she already had a real sense of the man and his values.

'What about the bulls?' asked Jen, her gaze narrowing.

Eli shook his head. 'I had no involvement with any of the bulls in the vicinity. My sole area was the horses. The equestrian school was very clear to make sure all who dealt with them knew they had no part in any of the bullfights or any of the bull runs that happen.'

Jen gave him a careful look. 'Okay, let's go and have a look at Bess then.'

Eli worked steadily, using the scale that some veterinary surgeons used to grade lameness in horses. He wasn't afraid to get up close and personal and once he was sure that Bess was steady and not upset he waved them over as he examined one of her hooves, picking it out with a hoof pick, checking for foreign objects, sharp stones or nails. 'Tell me a bit more about this morning,' he said to Jen.

'No problem. Out in the paddock as normal. Then out for a gallop late morning. She was fine until lunchtime yesterday.'

'Hard ground or soft ground?' His head was still dipped over Bess's hoof, his blue eyes peering carefully at her as he gently examined her.

'There's a very slight purplish-red spot,' he

said. 'I think this might be a stone bruise. Do you have any pads you can use while this heals?'

Jen gave a swift nod and headed towards a large box in the stables. 'It goes without saying Bess will need to rest, and I'm happy to come back and take another look in a few days.'

Aurora looked over at Jen, who she hadn't met before. 'Do you know what to look for? Inflammation, formation of a haematoma or an abscess?'

Jen gave her a serious nod. 'I'll get our farrier to come over and balance the hoof and remove the shoe for now.'

They talked for a few minutes more as Aurora stood on the sidelines. It was interesting to watch how Eli worked. It was true, he did have a good deal of knowledge about horses, and for a few moments she wondered if Jen and he were testing each other.

But then she quickly realised he was just trying to get a feel for how experienced Jen was, and what kind of treatments he could recommend to her, knowing she could carry them out safely.

The batting back and forward between the two was interesting, and Aurora started to have a good sense about his experience. At first, it had seemed all flash, sitting so many exams, working in so many countries, with such a range of animals; he'd seemed a bit like a child in a sweetie shop who couldn't decide which to try first.

But now she wondered if it was just a genuine thirst for knowledge. And what made it even more irritating was that she admired him for it. Why did this guy have to be so darn attractive?

By the time he was finished he gave her a nod and they headed back to the Land Rover.

They were certainly starting to get more relaxed around each other. Aurora took some notes from her bag. 'I checked through the computer and the diary next to Matt's desk to see if I could find out any info about the Fletchers' farm.'

She turned her head towards Eli, who was looking at her curiously. He wrinkled his nose. 'We haven't met before, have we? Because I think I would remember.'

Aurora's skin prickled. 'No,' she said as easily as she could manage.

He shook his head. 'You just seem a bit familiar.'

'I can't think how. I'm sure our paths haven't crossed.'

She could tell him. She could ask him if he'd ever watched the show. Most vets she'd come across since she'd changed profession usually said they'd tuned in to see what the show had got wrong. That didn't really surprise her. She had some friends who were nurses or medics who regularly watched some of the medical TV series to see if anything was remotely familiar.

But somehow she just couldn't get the words out. Was she embarrassed by her previous job? No. She wasn't. But it was all the repercussions from being in that show that played on her mind. It still sometimes gave her sleepless nights. The assault. The stalking.

She just didn't want to talk about all that any more. She'd put it behind her for a reason.

'Do you have a brother or sister that I might have come across?'

Darn, he was persistent.

'Only child,' she said, pasting a smile on her lips. 'I must just have one of those faces.'

She took a breath, and started on the notes again. 'I have to be honest. Matt isn't a great diary keeper.'

She held up her hand as Eli looked at her in surprise. 'Let me finish. What I mean is, the diary on his computer he didn't actually use as a diary. I think he might have started, but then he used it to just take notes, or write lists for himself. So it was almost impossible jumbling through to find out what he'd written about the Fletchers' farm.'

'Did you find anything?'

She gave a small shrug. 'Some scribbles about

further tests…phoning Dave, but I have no idea who that is. And checking symptoms.'

'Symptoms of what?'

She pulled a face. 'That's just it. He didn't write that part. It must have been all in his head.'

Eli gazed out onto the road ahead of them and pulled out. 'I just don't think I can phone Matt to ask him about this right now. I'll just have to go to the Fletchers' farm and get a feel for the place. Matt's wife texted me last night to say that his veins weren't standing up to the chemo drugs and they were putting a central line in today.'

Aurora inhaled sharply. 'So it's definitely not the time to call about work.'

'No,' he agreed, giving her a smile. 'It absolutely isn't.'

Aurora pointed to the road ahead. 'Just up on the left. This is the family that you know?'

Eli nodded. 'Well, I did when I was a kid. I mean I would have recognised them in the nearest village, but we didn't hang around together. I knew Dad was their vet, and every conversation was to do with the animals on the farm.'

'So, any clue what it might be?' she asked as he turned onto the farm road.

'Not a clue until I get there' he admitted, and she actually quite liked that about him.

When they approached, the farm seemed strangely quiet. Eli had already made his way to the nearest cow pen, but Aurora knocked on the cottage door. There were some farm vehicles around, but no actual car.

The door opened to a pink-cheeked woman. Aurora put her hand to her chest. 'I'm Aurora, the vet nurse. I'm here with Eli, our new vet. We're looking for Don Fletcher.'

The woman shook her head. 'Barb,' she said, putting her hand on her chest. 'It's taken me two weeks to persuade him to go the doctor, and his appointment is in ten minutes.' She lifted one finger to Aurora, 'Don't dare call his mobile and give him an excuse to come back.'

Aurora lifted both hands. 'I wouldn't dare. Would you mind coming and speaking to Eli?'

Barb shook her head and lifted a thick jacket from a peg near the door. She was already wearing boots so led Aurora back to where the cows were.

Eli was already checking over one cow. It was slightly scrawny-looking and in the space of time it took them to reach him he'd checked the eyes, ears and listened to the chest.

Barb held out her arms. 'Hi, Eli,' she said. 'Long time no see.' Like many farmers, she moved onto business. 'They're just generally sickly. Nothing too specific. Matt came about a month ago and said he'd come back. They're eating and drinking—maybe not as much as before. And we've been careful. It's just one herd that's affected.'

Eli stood up. 'How many herds?'

'We have beef and dairy. Three separate herds.'

'All kept in separate places?'

She nodded. 'Mainly, except for a few escape artists.'

Eli looked thoughtful and gave her a nod. 'Let's take a walk around,' he said.

They were at the farm for more than two hours. Eli looked at the layout of the fields, the dairy sheds, the pens, the hay/straw store and so much more. He examined seven different cows, all with a variety of symptoms. There were a range of coughs, some minor, some more severe, some cows were more tired than usual, and some had lost their appetite. After a long conversation, Barb agreed to keep the cows separated who were showing any symptoms, while Eli consulted about tests.

'It's a bit of a mystery,' he said as they climbed back into the Land Rover. 'None of these cows are really sick.'

'But there are enough symptoms for you to ask her to isolate?'

He nodded. 'You just never know. Lots of animals are similar to humans. Things spread. I'd like to do a bit of research and get back to the farm for more testing.' He frowned as he drove. 'I'd also like to get a chance to see Matt's note-books to see if I can make any sense of them.'

Aurora was instantly offended. 'You mean when I couldn't?'

'If I meant that I would say it,' said Eli promptly. He continued, not giving her a chance to break in. 'I do similar things to Matt. I doo-dle, I write when people talk to me. And I don't always do it on the same page. If I'm writing animal notes, that's entirely different. But if I'm on the phone, and scribbling while listening, I doubt anyone would make much sense of what I've written. But it makes sense to me.'

He heaved a huge sigh, as if he knew she was still trying to make out whether to be offended or not. 'Believe me, I've driven fellow vets and nurses to despair in the past. My clinical notes are clear. But my own? Never.'

Aurora kept her mouth closed. It would be easy to pick a fight right now, but it wouldn't re-ally serve any purpose. Today had been interest-ing. She'd got to see Eli Ferguson in a variety of settings, talking with a whole host of owners. He was new to most of them too, and it was fasci-nating watching them all try to get the measure of him, and decide if they trusted him or not.

Would she trust him with a pet? Likely. But as a person? She was still unsure.

She was certain there were sides of Eli she hadn't seen yet. He could be snappy at times—as she knew could she. His good looks were distracting. But Aurora had never been the kind of person to rely on looks alone. She always looked much deeper. And Eli's depths were still clearly hidden.

As were her own. At some point she would tell him she'd been in a TV series. It should make absolutely no difference to their working relationship, or how he saw her. But she'd sometimes felt that her previous vet colleagues had looked down on actors. Even though they shouldn't. Some of the smartest people she'd ever worked with were actors.

And whilst she could feel herself occasionally warming to Eli, she wasn't ready to reveal that part of herself. It would lead to questions, and uncomfortable memories.

And he didn't need to know that. Not yet anyway.

CHAPTER FOUR

THINGS IN THE practice settled down over the next few days. It was almost as if they fell into an easy routine, with Bert easily being the star of the show.

Aurora and Anne hadn't tried that hard to find somewhere to place him as yet. There was no urgency about the request, and he and Eli seemed suited to each other. Granted, there were occasional puddles in the hall, and even something else one day, but a vet's practice was used to animals having accidents and they all took it in their stride. It probably helped that they all frequently took Bert outside to try and imbed some toilet training rules with him.

So Aurora was surprised when Eli appeared in the doorway with a car harness for Bert. 'Will you come in the car with me? I have a potential home for Bert.'

She felt a little jolt of sadness but leaned over to grab her jacket. 'Okay, but who is it? Is it someone we'll know?'

Anne looked up from her desk. Aurora couldn't quite read the expression on her face. 'You'll know if it's the right place,' she said, looking steadily at Eli. She waited until he met her gaze, then gave him a nod. She picked up a piece of paper beside her. 'There's a message for you, Aurora. A…' she wrinkled her nose '… Fraser wants you to call him back about his cat, Arthur. The cat was recently diagnosed with diabetes. Quite insistent, actually. I did offer to speak to him, but he only wanted to speak to you.'

Aurora had an instant chill. 'They're not actually registered as our patients. And I'm sure it's the woman's name we had, not his. We saw them as an emergency.' She was silently praying that Eli would tell her not to call back.

But he was too busy with Bert. 'You can call later,' he said, not really paying attention.

Aurora gave a wave of her hand. 'Just leave it for me. I'll get to it later.' She pressed her lips together. A telephone call she could manage, but if the owner wanted to come in she would have to mention things to Anne or Eli.

As she went out to the car with Eli, she expertly manoeuvred Bert into his car harness, clipped him in, then climbed in the back seat next to him.

'What is this?' said Eli as he sat in the driver's seat.

'Last time in a car was traumatic,' said Aurora. 'I'm going to keep him company.' As Eli started the car, she continued. 'Or we're just going to sit in the back and plot against you.'

'That sounds more like it,' agreed Eli as they pulled out onto the road.

Aurora softly stroked Bert. 'So, no one has contacted the website about the picture we put up. How come you think you've found him a home?'

Eli turned his head to glance at her. 'This is just a meet and greet. I met a family the other day who said they wanted another dog. I told them we'd found a collie mix puppy who seemed healthy and they said they were interested.'

'Do you know these people? Where did you meet them? Are they patients of ours? What kind of dog do they have?'

'Whoa!' Eli laughed as he lifted one hand from the steering wheel. 'This feels like the third degree.'

'Actually, it's the fourth. I'll be telling Anne about this. If you think I'm bad…' She let her voice drift off and shook her head. 'You have absolutely no idea.'

She could see his face in the rear-view mirror. He was watching the road ahead but frowning. 'That's right. She used to give Dad a real hard time about rehoming pets.'

'And you know why that is?'

She saw the spark as the thought landed in his head. 'A dog should never be rehomed more than once.' They said it in unison and both laughed out loud.

He groaned. 'I'd forgotten about that. That's why I got the Anne stare before we left.'

'It sure is.' Aurora was smiling now as they turned into one of the nearby villages on the outskirts of Edinburgh. 'Where do they live?'

'Here, in Stockbridge. I met them at the farmers' market, and that's where they'll be today.'

Aurora sat a little straighter. 'You're not even seeing their home? We're going to the farmers' market?' She groaned. 'Give me your whole vet background again, please. Because I'm having trouble believing any of this.'

The village was already busy and it was clear the farmers' market had already started. He pulled into a car park and turned around to look at her. She'd moved Bert onto her lap and was holding him protectively.

'Do you honestly think I haven't done due diligence? I went to their house a few days ago. I met their teenage son, and their other dog. They work every day at the farmers' market, and I suggested we meet here in case the dogs aren't sure of each other. I'd hate for the other dog to be snappy because another dog came into their home.'

Aurora narrowed her gaze. She couldn't keep the ironic tone from her voice. 'You have concerns.'

Eli sighed and took a breath. 'They want a puppy to help socialise their other dog.'

'No,' said Aurora, pulling Bert closer. She was only partly joking.

'Their other dog was fine,' he said, and she was sure he was trying to sound reassuring.

'But?' she asked.

He took a breath. 'But they bought their dog at the beginning of Covid and didn't have much chance to socialise it. It's definitely a people person dog. I'm just not sure it's another dog dog.'

Aurora nodded. 'So we take Bert along, and see how the meet goes?'

The expression on his face tightened slightly. 'It's just… I won't be here for long. I don't want Bert to think he's found a home, and for me not to give him a chance of another. I like the little guy. But I will move on soon. It's selfish of me not to try when an opportunity came up.'

Aurora licked her lips. She knew it was inevitable Eli would move on. He'd said so right from the start. 'We don't seem to have any vets beating down the door.'

It was probably out of order. But she knew he'd put another advert out.

A dark look crossed his eyes but he didn't respond, just turned back around and opened the door. Aurora climbed out, clipping a lead onto Bert's collar.

The sun was rising high in the sky. Scottish summers could be unusual. It wasn't strange to have a few perfect weeks in June and then four weeks of rain for the whole of July—just when the schools closed. But today was just perfect.

She slipped her jacket off and tied it around her waist. 'It's going to be a scorcher,' she said, and turned abruptly when Eli burst out laughing.

'What?'

He shook his head. 'Your accent. It's like you have a gift for them. You sounded as though you came from Glasgow then.'

Aurora felt her cheeks flush. Accents had always been her speciality. Even though she'd stripped her own right back, with certain phrases and words, her brain seemed to automatically mimic the way she'd initially heard them used. She hadn't even thought as she'd spoken out loud.

He clearly noticed that he'd embarrassed her and pointed along the footpath. 'This way to the market. Let's have a stroll around before we go to meet the Kings.'

Aurora was grateful for the distraction and encouraged Bert as he walked well beside her. The market was busy and after a few moments' hesitation Eli bent down to pick Bert up. 'He might get overwhelmed by all the feet, and the food smells,' he said.

Aurora nodded in agreement. 'Let's go over here.'

They moved over to a large array of flowers and plants and Aurora picked some orange gerberas. 'These have always been my favourite. My gran had these in her garden when I was a child.' The seller wrapped them in some paper for her, and they moved on.

Next, they sampled some cheese. But Eli pulled a face when the one with chilli clearly hit the wrong spot. He started coughing and Aurora couldn't help but laugh, before she pulled a bottle of water from her bag. 'Stop coughing around my dog,' she murmured as he took a sip.

His eyes were watering now, and the stall-holder was laughing appreciatively. 'Always one that gets caught out,' he said with a broad smile.

They moved onto some craft stalls, bakery, bread and fish. Aurora paused for a moment. 'I wonder if I should get some for dinner.'

Eli looked at her, then licked his lips. For a second she wondered if he was nervous. 'Why don't you just let me buy you a big lunch once we've met the Kings? You might not even want a dinner.'

She looked again at the fish, wondering if she even had the ingredients in her house to make the sauce she'd want alongside. 'Okay, then. Deal,' she said.

They moved to a fruit and veg stall, where a couple in their fifties were serving and a brown cockapoo was hiding under the table.

She noticed that Eli kept Bert in his arms. 'Hi,' he greeted them, tucking Bert under one arm as he shook both their hands. 'This is Bert, the dog I told you about.'

Mrs King came out from behind the stall and started talking to Bert. 'Aren't you a wee beauty,' she said, giving his ears a rub.

Mr King came out too, and they both fussed over Bert, who seemed nonplussed by the whole event.

Mrs King eventually went to bring out their cockapoo, who was obviously shy. 'Tyler, come and meet Bert.'

Eli put Bert on the ground near Tyler, staying close. Aurora watched carefully. She'd met lots of anxious puppies and dogs. It was far more common than most people realised. Tyler was clearly one of those dogs.

There was sniffing. Bert, being a pup, was more boisterous and Tyler retreated under the table. But Mrs King persisted kindly, trying to encourage the dogs to interact. Mr King still had a few customers to serve but he was keen too, and Aurora quickly realised they were a kind couple, and true dog-lovers. She could see why Eli had considered them.

After nearly fifteen minutes, when Tyler had come out a few times, and retreated on each occasion, they finally agreed the first meeting was over. Eli shook both their hands again and picked up Bert, threading through the busy market with Aurora following.

'I know a place,' he said over his shoulder, leading her away from the main market towards a pub with multiple tables outside in the garden. There was also a little fenced-in section that was called a puppy play park, and they were right next to it.

'This place does quite a lot of fish options. Thought you might like to try, after wistfully gazing at the salmon,' he teased.

She reached over to swat his arm. 'I was not wistfully gazing at the salmon,' she said in mock horror.

'You were,' he teased, nodding at Bert. 'Wasn't she?'

It was almost as if Bert nodded too.

'Traitor,' she muttered, unable to keep the smile out of her voice. The waitress appeared, handing them menus and taking a drinks order. There were no other dogs currently in the puppy play park.

'I'll let him have a runabout,' he said as he filled up one of the water bowls. 'Let me know if anyone else appears.'

Bert was happy to play and when the waitress came back to take their food order he was jumping in and out of a stationary tyre in the play park.

She gave Eli a stare as she ordered. 'I'll have the sea bream, please.'

He raised his eyebrows as he handed his menu back to the waitress. 'I'll have the Cajun salmon,' he said sheepishly, and they both laughed as the waitress laughed.

The sun was beating down, although their table was a little shaded by a parasol. Aurora automatically took some sunscreen out of her bag and put some on her arms, before handing it over to Eli. 'Danger of being a redhead,' she said with a smile. 'Always have sunscreen.'

Eli nodded gratefully as he slid some on too. 'What did you think of the meet?' he asked.

'I think it's a no,' she said simply, holding up her diet Coke towards him. 'Tyler isn't ready for another dog in the house. He's too shy, and I think there might be a good chance he'll retreat further into himself.'

Eli tipped his head to one side and looked at her curiously. After a second he lifted his soda and blackcurrant too. 'I completely agree.'

'What will you tell the Kings?' she asked curiously.

He looked thoughtful for a moment. 'They adore Tyler,' he said. 'I think they'll know themselves. They would never do anything to upset him.'

'Here's hoping,' she said, glancing over at Bert. 'Oh, look, he's got the zoomies.'

They laughed as they watched Bert run around in circles at a hundred miles an hour.

'Do you have any other visits today?' she asked.

He shook his head. 'I'm going to do some more reading about cows,' he said with a sigh. 'Something is definitely bothering me.'

'It'll come to you,' said Aurora with a smile as her sea bream was put down in front of her. 'Usually in the middle of the night, and completely out of nowhere.'

Eli looked a bit surprised. 'Is that when things come to you?'

'Always,' she said as she sampled her fish. 'Like, if I've met someone that day but can't place them. And it annoys me all day. Then, in the middle of the night, I'll remember it was Sally from school's Auntie Jean. Or it was a patient from Hawkshead who has moved miles away, and because I'm not there any more I couldn't place them.'

'Do you ever sleep?' he asked with a smile on his face.

A memory flitted across her brain, and she pushed it to one side. Sleep at one time had evaded her for months.

She gave him a smile. 'I sleep like a log. It's the one reason I've got a cat and not a dog.'

Eli looked momentarily confused. She waved one hand. 'Because at the beginning you have to get up with a puppy in the middle of the night. Them waking because they need the toilet would generally wake a person. But...' she sighed '... I have slept through an alarm in the middle of the night before. Cats can use a litter tray. Not useful if you're trying to toilet train a puppy.'

'Where were you going that you needed an alarm in the middle of the night?'

It was a natural question, but it made her stall. She'd been going to catch a flight at Heathrow for filming in South Africa. She'd ended up with a taxi driver hammering on her door to wake her. But she just didn't want to get those words out. 'I was going to a festival,' were the words that came out. From nowhere, from absolutely nowhere, and she was cringing before she'd finished the sentence.

'Do you like festivals?' Eli asked, his eyes brightening. 'Where have you been? I love festivals. Used to do them all when I was a bit younger.' He gave her a broad grin. 'Remember the famous year at Glastonbury when it turned into a mud bath? That was me.'

Her brain was now on overdrive and it was entirely her own doing. 'Isle of Man,' she said as a little bit of her died inside at the continuation of her work of fiction.

His brow furrowed for a second. 'What one was that?'

'Can't remember,' she said quickly. 'I just realised sleeping in a tent was not for me.'

'Not a camper?'

She shook her head. At least this was true. 'Not a chance. I like comfort. I like electricity. I like heating. I want a comfy bed. A kettle. And the last thing I want to do in this world is have to squat in a forest to pee.'

He started laughing again, and Aurora started to relax. 'You're a five-star hotel girl, then?'

She held up her glass to him again. 'Without a shadow of a doubt.'

Part of her was a little sorry. If she'd been honest about her previous job, she could have told him about the wonderful lodges she'd stayed in while they were filming the vet series in South Africa. The lodges were in the middle of the

Kruger National Park and were amazing. She could have been honest about the animals and wonderful vets. But again, it would lead to memories of the not good parts. The assault. The stalking. She'd worked so hard to put all that behind her. The spider-sense feeling had led her to have another online session with her counsellor the other day, and she was taking comfort from some of the outputs of the session. There was no quick fix. Not for what she'd gone through.

She just didn't want to let those memories in, not on a gorgeous sunny day like this. Not when she was currently watching Bert jump around a dog play park having the time of his life.

It hadn't gone the way he'd wanted. But, then again, Eli wasn't entirely sure how he'd wanted it to go. He'd meant it entirely when he'd said he wanted to give Bert the chance of a good and permanent home. But it had felt too easy to say that the Kings wouldn't be a good fit.

He could feel himself becoming even more curious about Aurora. There was that familiar feeling around her. Anne had mentioned casually that there was no other half in her life. The more he spent time with her, the more the walls he'd built up around himself seemed to relax a little. Or maybe it was the setting. Being back at his father's practice hadn't been quite as bad as he'd thought it might. The work was interesting.

But he still worried about trusting those around him. It was ridiculous. He wasn't responsible for the accounts at the practice. That was still Matt's domain. But whilst he was off sick Matt had given him access to the practice credit cards, and told him that 'one of the girls' would likely handle the salaries.

It made him naturally jumpy. He wasn't sure how things normally worked around here. Last thing he wanted to do was interfere with the normal. But didn't he also have a responsibility to keep an eye on things? He couldn't deny he still had trust issues when it came to money— and especially for the business. He'd already let one business go to the wall; he couldn't let it happen to another. He pushed the money aspect from his head.

Because Aurora had hit a nerve earlier. He'd only had one enquiry so far about joining the practice—and it was from someone who wouldn't qualify for another six months. Eli spent his nights scouring the internet for other vet jobs— so why would he imagine anyone else wouldn't do the same? Did the outskirts of Edinburgh compare to the heat of San Diego, or the learning curve of working in the bush in Australia?

Bert gave a short yap—not quite a bark yet—and Eli turned his attention back to their puppy.

The thought stopped him hard. *Their* puppy? The practice's puppy, of course. He gave a little shudder.

'Cold?' asked Aurora innocently. Her dark red hair had fanned around her shoulders, and he could see her attracting glances. He was trying so hard not to notice just how attractive she was, or how the casual drift of her perfume instantly caught his attention.

Had he learned nothing from his last experience?

He set down his knife and fork. 'Not at all,' he said quickly. 'Want another drink?'

Aurora shook her head and nodded behind him. 'I think there's another dog about to come in.'

Eli caught sight of the black Labrador entering the pub grounds with her owners. He picked up Bert from the play park and slipped him back on the lead next to them. 'I'll just settle the bill,' he said, signalling to the waitress. 'Is there anywhere else you'd like to go?'

Aurora leaned back a little, stretching out her back and looking thoughtful. 'There was a bookshop along the street. It had stacked tables outside. I wouldn't mind having a look.'

'Sure,' said Eli, scanning his card to the machine the waitress brought over. 'It's a bit less busy down there. Let's see how Bert does.'

They walked casually down the picturesque street. There was no traffic as this part of the road was cobbled. All the shops had old-fashioned frontages, painted in a variety of colours. Some had window boxes on the upper floors filled with colourful flowers.

'This place is like a picture postcard,' murmured Aurora as she walked alongside him.

'It's a lovely town,' said Eli, stopping and looking through the glass of the butcher's shop.

After a few moments Aurora bent closer, her hair brushing against his face as she joked, 'Eli Ferguson, are you wistfully gazing at a steak?'

He burst out laughing and shook his head as he walked away. Two minutes later, Aurora stopped walking as she stared in the front window of a clothing shop.

She held up one hand as he opened his mouth. 'Yes, Eli Ferguson, I'm wistfully gazing at a pink shirt.' Her hand went to her back. 'In fact, give me two minutes.'

Eli watched in amazement as she ducked inside, had a conversation with the woman behind the till, who crossed to the other side of the shop and looked through a few hanging shirts before pulling out a pink one and carrying it back to the counter. Aurora leaned over to look at the tag and nodded in agreement as she pulled out her purse.

Literally, two minutes later, she was back by his side, bag in hand.

'You just bought that.'

'I did.' Her smile reached right across her face. It was the first time he'd noticed her eyes sparkle. She clicked her fingers. 'This is the way I shop. I see something, I like it. I check my size and I buy it.' She shrugged and laughed. 'Boyfriends in the past have loved it, but my girlfriends all hate it. They like to spend hours in shops.'

'You don't need to try things on?'

She wrinkled her brow. 'I know what size I am. Unless the shop is unusual and runs bigger or smaller than normal, it's never an issue. And the people behind the counter know that about their clothes. They do generally let me know.' She smiled and held up her shirt. 'Fastest female shopper ever?'

He gave a short laugh. 'I'm sure there must be some kind of medal for that.'

She rolled her eyes. 'Guess what? That medal is made of either books or chocolate.'

In a lightning move, Aurora ducked into the next shop, a bakers, and came out carrying a white box. 'Don't ask—' she smiled '—it's a surprise for the journey home.'

They moved to the next shop, which was stacked up with books on the tables outside. People were browsing casually. 'Why don't you go in?' said Eli. 'Bert and I will wait outside.'

She shook her head. 'Oh, no. I love to rummage. The best and most obscure stuff is likely to be out here.' She started sifting through the stacks and Eli joined her. It only took a second for him to see something that interested him. He pulled out a dog-eared hardback with a faded blue cover.

She moved closer. 'What is it?'

He flicked it open. 'Just a book about an old shipwreck.' He gave a rueful smile. 'This is my weakness.'

She looked at him with a broad smile. 'Not old musty vet books?'

He had the tiniest inkling of something again. But he pushed it away. 'Oh, no, that was my father's weakness. I spent my life surrounded by them, and inherited most of them.' He held up the book. 'Shipwrecks is my go-to non-fiction.'

'Egypt is mine,' she countered, and he couldn't help but be intrigued.

'Really? Why?'

'So much history, so much unexplained, so many interesting people. And how did they build those pyramids?'

He smiled. 'You don't go for the conspiracy theories?'

Her eyebrows raised. 'Oh, I love those. I half believe that thirty-year-old film about gates made of stars that said the aliens brought the pyramids down and they are secretly spaceships.'

'That would be kind of cool.' He held her green gaze. She studied him in return, and for a few seconds he was frozen. Stuck in that place that made the sounds and colours fade around them, and for Aurora to become his only focus. She was captivating. Her perfume aroma drifted near to him on the breeze, sparking his senses. For a moment there was nothing else. Just her, and him. He could already imagine her in that pink shirt she'd just bought, and how it would bring out the red in her hair even more vividly.

And then a little body nudged against his leg and broke him out of his momentary spell.

He blinked and shook his head, licking his lips. 'Think there's any Egypt in amongst this lot?' He nodded to the stacks of books.

'Give me a minute,' she said, and he watched as she took a few steps, her eyes scanning up and down the books like a true shopping professional, moving a few stacks before stepping back with a sigh. 'Nope, no Egypt.'

'You did that in under a minute.'

'Told you. I don't waste time.'

'Want to go inside?'

She glanced down at Bert, who had tucked himself under the table. 'Let me go and grab a thriller. I need something to read tonight. I'll pay for yours too.'

She went to add something, but Eli held up one hand, laughing, 'You'll only be a minute.'

True to form, she came back out holding a new release. 'Set on a cruise ship,' she said with a grin. 'A woman wakes up and everyone else is gone.'

'That does sound good,' said Eli. 'I might borrow it when you're done.' He held up the book she'd bought him. 'Tell me how much I owe you.'

'Don't be silly,' she said. 'You bought lunch.'

'Then thank you.' He looked down at Bert. 'Come on, little guy, that's enough walking for today.'

Bert seemed quite happy to continue, but the heat was building and Eli didn't want to walk him on the pavements any longer than necessary. He bent down and picked him up, tucking him under one arm.

Aurora leaned over and stroked Bert's head. 'We're going to find someone for you, little guy, don't worry.'

'Have you ever had a dog before?' He was curious.

She nodded. 'Yes, and no. My parents bought a red Labrador when I was a kid, but couldn't handle it. My gran ended up taking Max and since I went there after school every day I was always with him.'

'So, it worked out well?'

'It did. He was a great dog, and my gran was just too old to handle a puppy again when he finally passed away. It leaves such a gap in your life—you know, when you lose an animal.'

He looked at her carefully as they reached the car. 'So, if you could bring your dog to work every day, would you think about it?'

Her steps slowed. 'What do you mean?'

He opened one door to strap Bert in. 'I mean, I've fixed up the kennels outside now. Bert is quite happy running around in the enclosure during the day.'

'You want me to take Bert?'

He was trying to find a delicate way to put this, but was clearly failing. 'Well, maybe.'

'But what about in winter? There's no way I'd leave a dog outside in the snow we get.' She climbed into the car, but kept talking. 'And what about when you leave and there's a new partner? They might not take kindly to staff bringing their pets to work.'

'Or they might love the idea.'

She pulled a face. 'Not when we have to go

into emergency surgery and might be stuck in there for hours.'

Eli sighed and nodded. 'Okay, so you've got me there. But if that happens in the next few weeks, Bert will need to go in the kennels out back. At least I know he's safe there. It was just a thought,' he said as he started the car.

He pulled out into the traffic and Aurora opened the white box. 'Iced raspberry dough-nuts,' she said, offering him one.

'These match your new shirt,' he said as he took a bite.

'So they do.' She smiled as she took a bite of her own. 'I didn't even think of that.'

As they pulled out of the village and onto the country road he shot her a glance again. 'At least tell me you'll think about it.'

She gave him a hard stare. 'About Bert?'

He nodded.

'What if you decide you want to keep him yourself and take him wherever you decide to go?'

Eli shot a glance in his rear-view mirror at the puppy sleeping on the back seat. 'It would get too complicated,' he said. 'Particularly if I de-cide to go abroad again.'

'You're not done running away yet?' she asked.

The words prickled, and his hands tensed on the wheel. 'I'm not running.'

'Okay,' she said simply as he shot her a sideways glance. But the expression on her face made it clear she didn't believe him. 'But why would your next job be far away again?'

He swallowed. He could tell her the truth. He could say he'd opened up a practice for the last few years in England, and ended up going bankrupt because he'd been conned. But somehow, telling that story didn't have a huge amount of appeal.

'You could always just stay a bit longer at your dad's old practice,' she said, as if it were the easiest thing in the world. 'Or stay for good.'

It was like throwing a bucket of water over him. 'I won't be staying,' he said firmly.

Aurora opened her mouth again. It was clear she had a million arguments around this. But she must have caught sight of the expression on his face because, instead of speaking, she gave half an eye-roll and took another bite of her doughnut.

He glanced at his own expression in the mirror. It wasn't pretty. His jaw was clenched tight, just like his hands on the wheel, and his own doughnut was currently languishing in his lap.

He took a breath and let his shoulders relax. This had been a good day. Probably the first he'd had in a long time.

He wasn't going to let anything spoil it.

'Just promise you'll think about it,' he said again.

A hint of a smile appeared on her lips. 'You're going to get my new boss to sack me, aren't you?'

He winked. 'Don't worry, we'll write it into your contract that you can bring your pets to work.'

Aurora sighed and leaned back in her seat, 'Okay, I'll think about it.' She wagged her finger at him. 'But that's all. *Think* about it.'

And as the countryside sped past, Eli smiled too.

CHAPTER FIVE

AURORA WASN'T TOO sure how to feel about anything.

Her afternoon with Eli Ferguson had whipped up a whole host of strange feelings. She hadn't expected to enjoy herself so much. She liked sparring with Eli. She liked finding out more about him.

And she couldn't pretend she wasn't a little disappointed when he'd said, categorically, that he wouldn't be staying at his father's practice. There had been a definite edge to his tone. One that made her understand there was likely a whole host of things she didn't know about.

Anne hadn't been too free with information. It was obvious she had a deep loyalty to David Ferguson and, in turn, to his son.

As for Bert? She'd love a dog. But, due to the nature of her job, it just wasn't practical. If Eli had actually meant what he'd said…

The phone rang and she answered automatically. 'Ferguson and Green veterinary practice.'

'Can I speak to Aurora, please?'

There was something about the voice. It instantly made her defensive.

She was hesitant with her reply. 'Who is calling, please?'

'It's Fraser, Fraser Dobbs. She was supposed to phone me back about our cat, Arthur.'

Aurora straightened up at the implication. 'You were called back, Mr Dobbs. A message was left for you yesterday at four-twenty p.m.' She could remember precisely when she'd called because she'd been relieved to get an answer machine.

There was a humph noise at the end of the line. Another thing that pressed her dislike buttons.

'Well, I want to speak to her now.'

'You are speaking to her, Mr Dobbs.'

He went into an immediate tirade about the cat, and how essential it was for him to come and see Aurora, and when could he get an appointment. She tried not to let her past experiences affect her. Maybe this gentleman was just concerned about his animal, and wasn't coping with the long-term condition.

She asked some questions, explaining things as best as she could. But everything always came back to the same thing—he wanted to bring Arthur in, and see her.

It made Aurora distinctly uncomfortable.

It wasn't entirely uncommon for some patients to prefer to see the same individual in a vet practice. It helped with continuity of care, and with maintaining therapeutic relationships. Occasionally, some pet owners became a little possessive over staff members, but this was usually when a pet was severely ill.

Aurora looked at the appointment calendar. Her spider-sense was tingling again, and while she wouldn't refuse to see a patient, she would make certain she wasn't going to be in the practice alone.

She asked a few questions around his partner, to see if she would be attending too, letting him know it was best to see them together, in case his partner had any questions of her own. He made some brush-off excuse to let her know that he would be attending alone, and that his partner didn't really understand anything about it.

After another few minutes they agreed on an appointment the following week, when Aurora knew that Eli would be around. She would talk to him about this later.

She replaced the handset, wondering what on earth she would say to him about this. As an employee, she should let him know that the individual made her uncomfortable. But, on the other hand, she didn't want him to think that she was unwilling to work with difficult clients, or when a pet owner had anxiety over their condition.

Bert trotted around the corner towards her, and she bent automatically to rub him behind the ears.

'Naughty, naughty,' came the sigh from the corridor.

'What?' Aurora looked up, amused, and surprised, with her eyes wide.

Eli had a cloth in his hand as he rounded the corner. He almost fell over them.

'Oops,' he said. Then his face coloured.

'Bert,' he said quickly, 'I was talking to Bert.'

Aurora glanced down the corridor, where a small puddle glinted in the sunlight. 'Really?' she teased. 'Because I'm not sure you're allowed to talk to employees that way.'

She picked up Bert and stood up, walking into the nearby consulting room.

'And doesn't our good vet know that our dogs don't get into trouble when they pee indoors? We just take them outside and clean it up without a fuss.'

'Well, this will be non-fuss number four this morning,' said Eli as he grabbed the mop and bucket from the corner.

She looked at Bert. 'Come on, son. Let's go outside for a bit.'

She left Eli mopping as she took Bert out to

the run next to the kennels and set him down. Almost immediately, he did another pee. 'Good boy,' she said as she gave him a tiny treat.

'He does it to play me,' sighed Eli behind her. 'He pees inside, I bring him out. He pees outside, I praise him, take him back outside and he looks me in the eye, and does another.'

'Have you forgotten how hard the puppy stage is?' She smiled.

'Oh, I think you could say that.'

'When was the last time you had one?'

He shook his head. 'Honestly? Years ago. I've adopted or rescued mainly.'

'The old boys and girls?'

He nodded. It was common practice that vets or shelters were frequently left elderly pets, particularly when costs became more difficult for owners. Older dogs and cats in shelters were often overlooked when people came to find a new pet.

'There's something nice about giving an old dog or cat a great last few years,' said Eli, a wistful look on his face. 'Sometimes it's only a few months, but just devoting yourself to their care and attention for that period of time, letting them know they're settled and loved, is worth it.'

Aurora straightened in surprise. 'Eli Ferguson. You almost sound as if you have a big melting heart.'

'With animals?' he said. 'Every. Single. Time.'

'And with people?' She couldn't help herself, and as he turned to look at her she had a wide smile on her face.

He wrinkled his brow and looked a bit sorry about life. 'When you're concentrating on your animals there isn't much time for people,' was how he answered the question.

But Aurora wasn't going to let him get away with that. 'Come on, you mean to tell me that in all the time you stayed in—' she swiped her hand '—Florida, Spain, France and Maine, you never dated?'

He raised his eyebrows and the edges of his mouth tilted up in amusement, 'Good memory.'

'I'm a stickler for details. You'll learn that.'

He was still amused. 'Will I?'

'Only if you answer the question.'

It was like a standoff, but Eli was too quick. 'I will if you will.'

She tilted her head and put her hands on her hips. 'What?'

'Your other half? Or exes? You haven't mentioned anyone.'

There were a few seconds of silence.

'You first,' said Aurora.

Eli licked his lips. 'I dated a few people casually in each of the places you mentioned.' He took a slow breath, and then said rather slowly,

'I've kind of learned I shouldn't mix my personal and professional life.'

Wow. That was saying something. It was like a slap on the face. And though her first thought was to be offended—particularly when this had definitely seemed a bit flirtatious—she kind of got the impression there was more to this. Eli Ferguson actually looked a bit hurt, and a bit wary.

And he would never realise this, but his words actually resonated with her.

'I dated someone at work once, and it didn't work out particularly well.'

'Really?'

She wrinkled her nose. 'I was a bit younger, and it was just kind of awkward, when you split up and still have to work together.'

He let out a long, slow breath, along with a kind of ironic laugh. 'You have no idea,' he said.

She stared at him, curious. 'Well, that's kind of cryptic.'

He paused for a moment, as if he was actually going to give her more information—fill in some of the blanks that she was conscious were still there. But he just put his hands on his hips and stretched his back. 'That's for another time, and likely a lot of beer.'

She blinked and pressed her lips together, because she hated where her head had automatically gone. Straight back to the pub they'd had lunch in, but there at night, on an actual date. Her brain did that in a few milliseconds, and she was cursing it.

She didn't want to think about Eli Ferguson like that. One, he was her temporary boss. Two, he wasn't staying. Three, there were still some things he wasn't sharing. And four, she hadn't been honest with him about herself. None of these things could add up to a healthy fling or relationship.

She gave an amused smile.

'What is it?' he asked.

She shook her head. 'Daft memories. Mainly around a very bad date and falling into a table full of beer that, unfortunately, was all in pint glasses instead of bottles.'

He shuddered. 'Messy.' Then one eyebrow arched. 'But was it you that fell on it, or your date?'

'Oh, it was my date. He was a friend of a friend, and had gone to the pub early as he was nervous and drank himself blind drunk. When I arrived, he got up to buy me a drink and went straight back down again.' She bit her bottom lip to stop herself from smiling too hard.

'Poor guy probably never recovered.'

'Oh, he did. I danced at his wedding last year. You know the mutual friend? They got married.'

'She set you up when she liked him herself?'

Aurora smiled. '*He* set me up. One of the best weddings I've ever been to, and the part about the almost date made it into the wedding speech.'

Bert had finished his toileting and made a beeline for them both, catapulting himself at Eli, who had to reach out his hands to catch him. 'Whoa, little guy.' He held him up to his face. 'How can someone so small jump so high?'

The phone started ringing inside and Aurora darted in to answer it. Eli followed her in, carrying Bert. She gave him a careful look as she spoke on the phone. 'Hey, Marianne, how is Matt? He is? Okay…' She paused. 'Yes, I'm here with Eli now.' She mouthed the word to him. *Visit?*

He immediately nodded.

'Yes, we'd love to. Today?'

Eli nodded again.

'No problem, we'll see you in an hour.' And then she paused for a moment. 'Is there anything you need? Anything you want us to bring?'

Marianne started to immediately say no, then there was a small noise at the end of the phone, and Aurora knew she was crying.

'Marianne, ask me for anything. It's absolutely no bother and we're happy to do it.' There were a few more sniffles and something about not wanting to be a bother. 'You're not a bother. Send me a wee text, and we'll pick up whatever you need on the way there.'

'Everything okay?' asked Eli as she replaced the receiver.

Aurora shook her head. 'She phoned because Matt's concerned he didn't get to do a proper handover and wants to see you.' She gave a sad smile. 'He's conscious that not all his notes are up-to-date.'

Eli pulled a face. 'His notebook—I haven't even had a chance to look at that yet. Where is it?'

'In your desk drawer,' she said, not taking pleasure in the fact he hadn't looked yet. She'd begun to actually wonder if she might have missed something he could spot.

He opened his drawer, pulled out an A5 green-covered notebook and started flicking. His smile was broad. 'Matt is exactly the same scrawler and doodler as I am.'

Aurora watched him as her phone sounded with a text message notification. 'Marianne said that he's sleeping loads right now while he's mid-treatment, so might not be awake for too long.' She gave a soft smile. 'She's also given me a list of girl's things that she needs. She's clearly been running about for Matt and forgot about herself.'

She looked out of the window as Eli kept flicking, writing a few random notes himself. 'I wonder...' Her voice tailed off.

'You wonder what?' His blue eyes met hers.

She pulled a face. 'It's just that on the way there we'll pass their favourite restaurant. I've been there with them a few times. I know what they like.' She glanced at her watch. 'It's nearly five o'clock. How do you feel about us getting them some takeout dinner?'

'Sounds like a great idea.' He glanced down again and his hand froze over a word. 'Oh, no!' He let out a sharp expression.

'What?' Aurora was genuinely startled. She moved behind him to bend over his shoulder and see the word that had stopped him.

Badger. With a question mark next to it.

It was on the bottom corner of one page. The corner had creased upwards so it was almost hidden. But the top of the page held information about the Fletchers' farm.

Eli closed his eyes for a second. 'Don't suppose we know the last time the Fletchers' cattle had their TB tests?'

Aurora instantly felt her mouth go dry. Bovine TB was serious. Herds could be wiped out. Farms could be ruined. Badgers were a protected species, but could also have TB and carry it, and secrete it in their urine, faeces or any wounds. If cattle had direct contact with infected badgers, or if cattle feed or water was contaminated by badger excretions, then TB could pass between the species.

'Is that what Matt suspected?'

Eli flicked another few pages. 'It could be. It's not clear. The symptoms could match, but it could also be a host of other things. Darn it.'

'Maybe that's what Matt wants to talk to you about?'

He nodded solemnly. 'Could be.' He looked up again. 'Do you want to get changed before we go visiting? And, apart from the restaurant, where do we need to stop off?'

'A supermarket,' she said quickly. 'And yes, I will get changed. Is it okay to use the shower upstairs?'

'Of course,' he said, settling back down at the computer to keep checking some files.

By the time Aurora came down the stairs she'd changed into the pink shirt she'd bought the other day and jeans, and her hair was combed loose. Eli had made a few notes with questions to ask Matt, but he was also conscious his father's old partner might not be up to it. He'd dashed upstairs to change his shirt and brush his hair and was ready to go. He hadn't been sure of what Matt's relationship had been like with the newest member of staff, because there hadn't been an opportunity to have that conversation, but from

Aurora's expression on the phone today it was clear she was close to both Matt and Marianne.

Her suggestion of buying them dinner from their favourite restaurant was thoughtful and a nice touch.

The drive was just over half an hour, and whilst thoughts of TB were flitting around his head he tried to push them away.

'Didn't take you long to wear your new shirt,' he said.

Aurora looked down at herself and brushed the shirt. 'This is actually the second time. It's soft and really comfortable. I might go back and try and get it in another colour.'

He smiled, doing his best not to notice how good it looked on her. Her dark red hair was stunning against the pastel pink of the shirt, and it seemed to complement and enhance the green of her eyes. His eyes couldn't help but linger on her lips. Her make-up was always light, but she'd clearly put on some extra lipstick when getting ready. That, with her long lashes, made her look like some kind of film star.

He had a weird jolt again. Just like he'd had before around her. The wave of strange familiarity that he just couldn't put his finger on.

They chatted easily about books, films and a few of the farms along the way. Eli started telling her about cases Matt and his father had dealt

with when he was a boy. It was odd how easily
the memories flowed. But these ones weren't
dimmed by feelings of neglect. When anything
had been happening in the practice, his father
had welcomed any interest or assistance.

'The stoat ended up where?' laughed Aurora,
tears streaming down her face.

'In our pipes. First under the floorboards in
the staff kitchen. Then inside the wall upstairs.
He was like a magical Houdini. It took seven
days to finally catch him again.'

'What did his owner say?'

'Oh—' Eli waved his hand '—that was old
Gus Bryant. He just laughed and said to bring
him back when we found him.'

They pulled up outside the supermarket and
Eli joined Aurora inside. She hovered near the
tower of baskets, then changed her mind and
grabbed a trolley. 'You know what. I'm just
going to buy them some things. Food, house-
hold stuff, toiletries.'

'I'll grab some crime books,' said Eli. 'Matt
always loved those.'

Aurora didn't scrimp. She bought chicken,
fish, steaks, some fresh fruit and vegetables,
alongside milk, cheese, crusty bread, and a whole
array of women's toiletries. As they neared the
checkout she stopped at the chocolate aisle and
ran her eye along it. 'There!' she said happily.

'Marianne's favourites.' They packed the food into the boot of his car and she directed him to the local restaurant.

Eli couldn't help but look at the menu as Aurora ordered Matt and Marianne's favourites. He put his hand on her arm. 'Once we've seen Matt, we'll come back and eat here. We might as well. No point driving back and making food at home.'

For a second she didn't say anything, and he realised his hand was still on her arm and she was staring at it.

'Sorry,' he said instantly, pulling his hand away.

'It's fine,' she said briskly, but he noticed her rub the spot with her other hand.

It only took five minutes for the kitchen to put the meals together, and Aurora carried them in covered plates. As they pulled up outside Matt's house, Eli felt a wave of nerves. He had spoken to Matt on numerous occasions, but he hadn't actually seen him in person since his father's funeral.

Everything about the house was familiar, from the six grey steps leading up to the pale blue door to the front window that spilled out warm light. He got the shopping from the boot as Aurora climbed the steps, balancing the plates and ringing the bell.

The familiar ringtone of the ancient bell made

his face break into a smile. A few seconds later, Marianne opened the door and ushered them both inside. Her eyes filled with tears when Aurora explained what they'd brought.

'You're an angel,' she said, sweeping Aurora into a careful hug, then taking the plates from her. 'Let me put them in the oven to stay warm. Matt's just taken his anti-sickness meds, and we need to give them time to work.'

'He's not keeping things down?' asked Eli, concern lacing his voice.

The small, grey-haired woman met his gaze. It was almost as if she hadn't heard what he'd said. 'So like your father,' she said with a smile, before holding him in a long hug.

His awkwardness vanished in an instant, with the familiar smells of the house, and warmth from Marianne. 'I've missed you both,' he said quietly. She would know. She would know exactly what he meant, and how he felt, because Marianne had been witness to it all. She was too kind to ever say a bad word about her friend— his father—but that didn't mean she'd been blind to his shortcomings.

They padded quietly through to the sitting room. Even though it was a warm summer evening, the fire was lit and Matt was covered in a dark red blanket. His treatment was obviously making him feel the cold.

His skin was translucent, and he'd lost a lot of weight since the last time Eli had seen him. He was shocked by Matt's appearance. But Aurora didn't miss a beat, she crossed the room in a few steps and dropped a kiss on Matt's cheek.

'It's so good to see you. We're missing you so much.' She quickly mentioned a list of patients who'd enquired after him and wanted him to come back soon.

Warmth spread through Eli's chest. This was the benefit of being a long-term vet somewhere. The patients and people knew you. They noticed when you weren't there. Had anyone noticed when Eli had left any of his previous posts?

He hoped so, but it wouldn't be the same as this. He moved quickly, first shaking Matt's hand, then kissing his cheek too, and automatically sitting on the little footstool at the bottom of the chair.

Matt bent forward and cupped his cheek. 'It's so good to see you again.'

Eli's hand covered Matt's. He had so many good memories of this couple. So many times he'd stayed at their house, or had their support for school or sports events.

'You too,' he said slowly, hoping his voice wouldn't break.

There was a chance he wasn't going to have Matt much longer. He didn't need to ask questions. He didn't need to focus on scans or treatment plans. One look at Matt, plus the expression on Marianne's face at the door, told him everything he needed to know.

They didn't have children of their own. Marianne had nieces and nephews, but Eli had been the one to whom they'd shown undying support.

He settled on the stool as Matt started talking about the practice. It was clear he wanted to get things in order. As Eli pulled Matt's notebook from his back pocket he wished this didn't need to happen. But he had to respect Matt's wishes.

Aurora caught his eye and nodded towards the kitchen. 'I'm going to help Marianne unpack,' she said.

Matt quickly went through some patients, including a planned complicated surgery that Eli would have the skills to take over.

'What about the Fletchers' farm?' he asked cautiously.

But Matt was still sharp as a tack. 'Cows still sick?'

Eli nodded. 'I found some of your notes, but they weren't exactly in order.'

'It's the badgers,' said Matt without hesitation. 'Check the badgers.' Then, as if he could read Eli's mind, 'The bovine TB testing is due next month.'

Eli's heart dropped like a stone. He'd half

hoped it had recently been scheduled and bovine TB could have been ruled out. But not now. 'I'll deal with it,' he said quietly.

Matt looked as if he wanted to say a whole lot more, but sagged back against the cushions on his armchair. 'Okay,' he replied simply.

He glanced to the door and back to Eli. 'So, you've put all that stuff behind you?'

Eli knew exactly what he was referring to. He sighed. 'It's resulted in bankruptcy. Iona will face criminal charges if she's ever found, but the practice property was repossessed and I was left with a whole pile of debts.'

'The staff?'

'I used my savings to pay their salaries. I did that as soon as I realised what had happened, and knew there was much more to come. So, I prioritised their salaries and notice periods, gave them all references, and closed the practice doors while the fallout happened.'

'You could have come to me!'

'For my stupidity? For trusting someone who took my livelihood? She got enough from me. I would never have come to you for something like that. It was my mess. I had to sort it.'

'I would have helped you,' Matt said shakily, and Eli's heart squeezed inside his chest.

'I know you would have. But I can start again. I just need to sort things out with yours and

Dad's place, and then I'll take myself off somewhere else, and decide what comes next.'

'You have a practice. You have staff. You have a community where some people have known you since you were a boy.'

Eli couldn't get a reply out. He wouldn't hurt this man for the world. He couldn't explain how the practice brought back memories he found hard to push away. He just gave a shake of his head. 'I just can't do it. Not now.'

Matt tilted his head a little as laughter could be heard from the kitchen. 'What do you think of Aurora?'

Eli gave an embarrassed laugh. 'We've exchanged a few words, but she seems to be a good vet nurse.'

'She is. Smart as a whip. I'm worried someone will try to steal her. When she started I had a few emails from another vet who had met her down at Hawkshead. They were impressed by her. I think a few had given her alternative offers, but...' he smiled broadly '...she chose us.'

Eli was curious about that. 'She's young to move up here by herself. Does she have family around here?'

Matt shook his head. 'She's from Liverpool. No family up here. As far as I'm aware, her mum and dad are still in Liverpool.'

Liverpool. He was getting used to hearing the remnants of the accent when it emerged.

'No husband?' Eli queried.

Matt leaned forward. He had a grin on his face, and a sparkle in his eyes. This. This was the way he'd always remembered Matt. 'And why would you be asking that? Has Aurora Hendricks caught your eye, Elijah?'

Eli gave a fake shudder. 'Don't. You only call me Elijah when things are serious.'

'And they are. She's a beautiful girl, with a big heart and...' he narrowed his gaze on Eli '...possibly too good for you,' he finished with undisguised relish.

Eli laughed. Matt had always teased him like this. All good-heartedly.

He glanced at the open doorway again. 'She's...nice,' he said. 'Thoughtful. And passionate about the animals.'

There was a noise and they both looked up. Marianne was carrying in the steaming hot plates of food on a tray. The smell was delicious. 'Look what Aurora and Eli brought us from Eldershaw's restaurant. Our favourite.'

Eli stood up, pulling over the nearby table so Matt's food could be close to him. He leaned over again and kissed Matt on the cheek. 'It was lovely to see you—enjoy your dinner and we'll catch up in a few days.'

Matt's frail hand caught his and squeezed it hard. 'Love you, Eli,' he said with a glimmer of a tear in his eye.

'You too,' was as much as Eli could manage, before hugging and kissing Marianne too, then heading to the door.

When they got outside, they both stood on the top step for a few moments. He could hear Aurora's shaky breaths; his own weren't much better.

'Okay?' he asked.

'I could really use dinner about now,' she answered.

He was grateful. Neither of them wanted to admit how sick Matt was. There was time for that later.

They climbed down the steps, into the car and drove back to the restaurant, where they were seated at a table at a window looking out over the back terrace and gardens. The sun was just beginning to dim, sending streaks of orange and red across the darkening sky.

'Do you want me to drive back?' she asked as they looked at their menus.

'Why would you ask that?'

Her eyes shone with sympathy. 'Because you've known Matt all your life. I saw the shock register on your face when you saw him. I just figured you might like to sit here and have a beer with your dinner.'

He was struck by how considerate she was being. 'I've driven the car before on visits to farms, so I know I'm covered on the insurance,' she added.

He hadn't even thought of that. Thank goodness she had. 'You know, I'd really appreciate that,' he said.

Eli's head was all over the place. The swamping memories, being back at his dad's practice. The mixed emotions of the love he still felt for his father, added to the adult perspective now, where he could see he'd been neglected in some ways. The anger that still simmered on a daily basis at being conned so thoroughly, and so well, that his only option had been to use his savings to pay the staff wages before declaring bankruptcy. That deep down regret that he'd lost the ability to trust people, and it now affected his everyday life.

And yet he looked at Aurora and felt…something.

He didn't want to, and he shouldn't. But he couldn't help it. Something just seemed to radiate between them, to spark. Whether it was the too-long glances or the occasional flirtatious chat, he wasn't imagining this. He just wasn't.

The waiter came and took their order. 'Is there some kind of irony that I'm ordering the same

things we got for Matt and Marianne?' he asked
as he sampled the beer.

'It's one of the best things on the menu,' she
said simply. 'And I'm getting the other.'

There was a quiet ambience around them.
People at the tables chatted in low voices. There
were no loud boisterous parties and Eli was
grateful.

'What do you normally do on a Friday night?'
he asked her.

She was thoughtful for a few moments. 'Watch
TV, allow my cat to make a fool of me, or read
a book.'

'What about parties, or nightclubs?'

'I did that when I was a bit younger. I'm past
that. I don't mind the occasional wine bar. Or I
went to one of the observatories at night, on a
tour where you can see all the stars and realise
just how small this planet is. I liked that.'

'I did that Night at the Museum thing when
I was younger—when you sleep next to the dinosaur bones in a museum.'

'Oh, wow,' she said enviously. 'That must have
been great.'

'It was. But my friend snored, and another
friend had an accident. Kind of spoiled the
mood.'

She leaned back. 'I would have so loved that.'

'The snoring, or the peeing?' he teased.

'Don't be silly. Just the experience. Lying there, looking up at the dinosaur bones and wondering what life would have been like if we'd lived at the same time as the dinosaurs.'

'Only a mere sixty-five million years in between.'

She took a bite of her salmon. 'You're nit-picking now.' She tilted her head. 'But you're a bit like that, aren't you?'

He put a hand to his chest, feigning mortal offence. 'You wound me. Just because I pay attention to the details doesn't mean I'm a nit-picker.'

She looked up from under her thick lashes. 'That's exactly what it means.'

The conversation flowed easily. The food was delicious, and as two hours slipped away, Eli finally started to find some peace.

As they walked out to the car, he turned to her. 'I guess I need to face the fact that Matt isn't likely to get to work to train a new vet any time soon.'

She held his gaze as she opened the driver's door. 'So where does that leave us?'

Us. That was what she said. And he knew she meant the practice. But it didn't stop a good percentage of his skin from prickling. Would he ever be ready for another *us*?

The roads were quiet. Aurora turned on the radio and selected a channel that played soul music as they made their way back to the vet practice, where her own car was.

Eli contemplated all the things he could do next. None of the options made him happy—at least he didn't think they did.

'I hadn't planned on staying, but if I want the practice to successfully continue, I'd need to stay for at least a year after I recruit a new vet—maybe even longer.'

'You make it sound like a prison sentence,' she said simply.

The words made him cringe. 'I just have mixed-up memories about this place. After my mum died, my dad was juggling things. I know that he loved me but, to be honest, I think he loved the practice more. He missed out on a lot of things that are important to a kid.'

She shot him a glance while she drove. 'Did he have any help?'

'Matt and Marianne. He and Matt shared the workload but—' he shook his head '—it seemed like whenever there was something important for me: a football final, a school concert, a big exam—' Eli sighed '—there just always seemed to be an excuse for him not to be there. Always an emergency, or a planned surgery, or he'd forgotten to put it in the calendar. And the thing is, I know Matt and Marianne reminded him. I know Matt always offered to do whatever the vet thing was at that point.' He closed his eyes tight for a second and scrunched up his face. 'I can even remember a conversation I wasn't supposed to hear, when he asked Matt to swap with him, so he didn't *need* to come.'

'Oh, Eli,' she said softly.

He opened his eyes again and gave another soft shake of his head. 'So, Matt and Marianne would come. I'd stay there if he was called out in the middle of the night. And they were great. I think, in truth, they were as frustrated with him as I was.'

'Do you think you reminded him too much of your mum?'

He turned to look at her, watching how the final remnants of purple light cast a glow across her skin and hair. 'I wondered that at one point, but I don't really resemble Mum at all, I have much more of my dad's features.'

'Maybe you have your mum's mannerisms, or habits. Apparently, I've inherited some of my gran's traits, and even sometimes, when something comes out of my mouth, I cringe, because I can almost hear her voice in my head saying it too.'

'I guess I might have. I just still have a deep-down feeling that I had a dad who loved his work and the animals more than his family.'

'Do you ever wonder if you might get like that?'

He leaned his head against the window. 'Don't miss anything with those punches, Aurora,' he said, a light tone still in his voice.

She shot him a worried glance. 'Sorry, I really should think before I speak.'

'One of your gran's traits?'

She gave him a grateful smile. 'Absolutely.'

They pulled up outside the practice and both climbed out of the car. Eli walked around the bonnet and met her halfway.

Now, she was lit up from the back, streaks of silver, purple and deep navy behind her. She sensed it, and glanced over her shoulder and laughed.

'I guess someone thought we needed good lighting,' she said easily.

They locked gazes, and Eli took a step forward. It seemed entirely natural.

'Thank you,' he said in a low voice. 'For this afternoon, and tonight.'

She stepped forward too. Now, they were only inches apart. She lifted her hand and put it on his arm. 'It's fine. I was glad to be there. I don't think you should have gone alone.'

He focused on the hand on his arm. And all the sensations that were shooting along his nerve-endings. His eyes moved slowly from her hand, up her body and to her face.

Their gazes locked again. Green eyes. Big green eyes with dark lashes. Dark? She must be wearing mascara.

As they stood in silence, Aurora licked her lips. This time she took a mini step forward. Eli's hand lifted and rested on her hip, just as her own palm tightened on his arm, almost as if she was willing him even closer.

They moved in unison, lips brushing for the briefest of seconds before they locked entirely. Her hands wrapped around his neck, the length of her body pressed up against his.

He didn't want this kiss to stop. He refused to let any memories of the last person he'd kissed invade his mind at this moment. He refused to let himself be swayed by the fact Aurora was a workmate.

He was wise enough to recognise the different circumstances. There were no similarities here. He could concentrate on this.

The feel of her lips against his. The pressing of her hands around his neck and back. His lips moved to her face, her ear and her neck and she let out the tiniest groan. He could taste her perfume on his lips, feel it with every inhale.

She let out a breath and stepped back, nervous laughter filling the air between them. Her pupils were dilated, the green of her eyes nearly invisible.

'Whoa,' he said, trying to catch his breath.

'Whoa,' she repeated, a broad smile across her face.

She blinked for a second, obviously letting the cool night air clear her head. 'Not how I expected the evening to end,' she said.

He wasn't sure about her tone. Was it regretful? Was she questioning herself? Did she have doubts about their kiss?

'Me neither,' he said. He couldn't be untruthful. 'But I'm not sorry.'

She licked her lips again, and he wondered if he should invite her in. But Aurora was too quick for him.

'I have a cat to get home to, and you have a puppy to attend to.' She let her shoulders relax, and she swung her bag over her head. 'I'll see you Monday?' she said.

'Sure,' was all he could reply. Was she dying to get away from him?

She gave a wave of her hand as she headed over to her own car. ''Night,' she called as she climbed in and drove away.

''Night,' the reply came on his lips. But he stayed where he was and watched as her car headlights finally faded into the distance.

What on earth would Monday bring now?

CHAPTER SIX

ANNE WAS MANNING the phone with an annoyed look on her face. Aurora was immediately on edge. Did Anne know that she and Eli had kissed the other night?

She immediately stuck her bag in her locker and came through to the main reception. 'Want me to take over?'

Aurora had learned that although all tasks were supposed to be shared, there were some things that Anne just didn't enjoy doing. She had a pad and a calculator and a spreadsheet open on the computer. Aurora recognised the software immediately. Wages? Was there an issue?

The wages software was usually easy. Hours entered. Checked by the accountant, salaries paid.

'I think I made a mistake. Matt should still be getting paid sick leave. Eli is on the payroll now, you and I have our hours inputted, but Frankie called to say he hadn't been paid for his final week's notice. He had holidays owed, so he should still have been paid. But I can't find the glitch in the system.'

Aurora nodded. 'That's right, I remember us having that conversation. Do you want to swap? I've got Mrs Pringle coming in to get some information on getting her cat spayed. Do you want to have the chat, and I'll have a look at this?'

'Perfect,' said Anne, out of the chair like a shot.

Aurora smiled. She really didn't mind. She was sure she would figure things out.

Half an hour later, Bert sniffed his way around the corner towards her. 'Hey, little guy,' she said, picking him up and setting him on her lap.

She was still petting him as Eli came around the corner. 'Hey,' he said easily.

'Hey,' she replied, unable to help the smile on her face. She hadn't slept a wink the other night. Too many what-ifs had floated through her mind.

It had been spending the afternoon and evening with him that had just drawn her to Eli, stronger than ever. She'd seen him vulnerable at Matt and Marianne's, the love they all had for each other very apparent. The meal had been delicious, but the conversation in the car?

It had felt as if she was finally getting to know Elijah Ferguson for real. There were some real mixed-up feelings about his dad. She could tell he was doing a lot of unpicking himself. But he'd been honest with her. Now, whilst she might not really understand the resentment he felt deep down, at least she could empathise. Coming back here was tough for him. And the realisation on the same evening that he would likely have to stay here for at least the next year—was that what had done it for her? Knowing this flirtation and attraction might have a chance of lasting more than a few weeks?

It had certainly helped. She'd never been the kind of girl to look for very short-term. She liked a chance to get to know someone and be part of their life on a regular basis.

And the kiss? The kiss had taken her breath away. Literally.

She'd wanted to get in her car and drive away? Absolutely not. Had it been the right thing to do, for him and for her? Absolutely yes.

She'd needed that space. She needed to work out how things would be at work between them. Some people couldn't handle a relationship with a workmate, but she certainly hoped that she and Eli were adult enough to work this through, because she actually wanted to see where it might go.

It honestly felt like something was sparkling inside her. She hadn't really wanted to attempt any kind of real relationship in the last few years, since her assault on set, and the stalking fiasco afterwards. The long-term counselling had given her the rational grounding that she needed. She'd learned to forgive herself, and respect that she wasn't responsible for either incident. She'd learned to apportion blame appropriately. She'd started to trust herself again. She'd been so cautious ever since both incidents—probably to the point that she recognised she pushed people away, and likely hadn't given anyone much of a chance in the last few years. But she was getting there.

And this was the first time she'd *wanted* to give someone a chance. She'd felt the buzz, the connection, that she hadn't felt in years. But this time she was older, more confident, and surer of where she was in life, to take it and grab it with both hands.

But would Eli grab it with her?

'Are you up for going back to the Fletchers' farm today?'

'Of course,' she said as he moved over, closer to her.

'I know you were planning on talking to Matt about it. Did you get a chance?'

His face was serious. 'Yes, he's definitely thinking it could be a risk of TB due to the badgers. He said the farm was due to do their bovine TB testing next month. We need to get up there, find out as much as we can, and see what we can do next.'

'Want me to get changed?'

He nodded then glanced down at the screen. His gaze narrowed. 'What are you doing?'

She was a tiny bit surprised at the edge in his tone. 'Wages, swapped with Anne. She said there was a flaw somewhere, and Frankie hadn't been paid for his last week. I've just checked, amended it, and forwarded it on to the accountant to check.'

He blinked, nodded and said in a low voice, 'Okay, go and get changed and I'll meet you back down here.'

Was that slightly awkward? She wasn't sure, because her head was so full of the potential consequences of finding bovine TB on one of the farms they served. It was massive and would involve a huge team of professionals to work through the issues.

'I've phoned Don Fletcher to let him know that Matt suspected there potentially could be an issue with the water or food supply transferred by badgers. He's devastated at the potential threat to his herd, but happy to do everything he can.'

'We'll need to check the cows, isolate them, contact the authorities and arrange testing.'

He nodded. 'It's going to be a long day. Let's go.'

If she'd expected some lightness today, Aurora knew she wasn't going to get it. A flirtation at work was nothing. This was someone's livelihood and herd. She had to be completely focused on work, and play her part to gather as much information as possible.

It was late evening by the time they got back to the practice. They'd spent hours at the farm, talking to Don, checking the cattle, making sure they were sufficiently isolated. It did look as though the food supply could have been compromised. Some badgers were either ingenious or sneaky, and potentially could have infected the food or water supply. Since there was more than one herd, there had been long discussions about making sure there was no crossover of usage of areas. Plus, ensuring that no cattle, equipment or milk could leave the farm. In amongst all this were the huge array of phone calls to Defra, the government agencies and departments who dealt with potential bovine TB, Public and Environmental Health and the Animal and Plant Health Agency. It was exhausting.

They'd followed all the personal cleansing and disinfection rules on entering and leaving the farm as a precaution, and the testing was arranged for the next day, along with one of the specialist vets. But both of them still felt grubby. Aurora was pulling at her tunic top and jacket.

'Want to grab a shower?' Then he looked at her again. 'How far away is your place? Do you want to just stay here, rather than drive home tonight, since we need to be back at the farm early?'

She hesitated, but only for a second, because it did make sense and she was already feeling too tired to drive.

'Okay, thanks.'

Aurora was familiar with the layout of the rooms. The place had previously been some kind of small family estate, the downstairs mainly converted to house the practice, with upstairs occasionally used by visitors or staff.

She understood Eli had been staying there rather than use the vet's house next door, which he hoped would attract someone to the new job, but she hadn't really seen much of how he was living.

By the time she came out of the shower, she could smell something cooking in the upstairs kitchen. She knew this one was rarely used and, as such, was immaculate, or at least it had been until Eli arrived.

He had white flour on the tip of his nose. Bert was in the corner of the kitchen, drinking from his water bowl then making short work of his food.

'Making pizza,' he said, clearly a bit frazzled.

She changed into new scrubs, which she always kept at the practice. This pair were older and well worn, so more comfortable than usual. 'From scratch? You didn't have anything frozen?'

He gave a shrug. 'I lived in Italy. I know how to make real pizza.'

'You know how to make a mess,' she joked.

He looked around the kitchen and nodded in agreement. 'I certainly do. Let's hope it's worth it.' He opened the fridge and pulled out a bottle of white wine. 'Want some?'

'After today? Abso-blooming-lutely.'

He poured two glasses and kept peering into the oven, checking on the pizzas. After a few more minutes he pulled them out and put them on wooden boards. Instead of sitting at the small table in the kitchen, he gestured with his head. 'Want to go through to the sitting room?'

'Sure.'

The sitting room window was wide open, letting the warm summer evening air filter into the room. Eli set the boards and pizza cutter down on the low table in front of the grey sofa, then flicked on the TV. 'Football, football or football?' he asked in a jokey manner.

Aurora glanced at the clock. 'One of the history or mystery channels, please. I'd like to hear about Machu Picchu, the Pyramids, the Rosslyn Chapel or the Titanic, please.' She gave him a quick wink. 'I'll even watch something about an old shipwreck if you can find it.'

He walked swiftly through to the kitchen, grabbed their wine glasses and sank down beside her. 'Do you know how long I've wanted to hear those words from someone else?'

'I guess I'm just permanently nosey and curious,' she said. 'I'd love to work on one of those shows.'

It was a throwaway comment. And she had considered working in the background of TV, rather than as an actor or presenter. But for a second she froze, wondering if she'd just revealed too much.

But Eli clearly didn't take too much from the comment. 'Me too,' he said with a spark in his eyes. 'Can you imagine how much more doesn't reach the screens? It must be fascinating.'

He grabbed a slice of pizza and took a bite and she did the same.

'Wow,' she said as the flavour hit her tongue. 'That's amazing.' She stared at the pizza base suspiciously. 'It's got a bit of bite to it.'

He nodded. 'The tomato base sauce has a hint

of chilli—more like an Arrabbiata sauce? I think it makes it tastier.'

She nodded in agreement, her brain swirling. This was the time. This was the time to mention her previous job, and why he might think that he recognised her. She could just do it casually, ask him if he'd ever considered a different career before training as a vet. But now she knew the answer to that would be no. It wouldn't be an easy subject to introduce that way.

There was a noise from the corner, and they both turned their heads. Bert had snuggled down in his basket and was comfortably snoring. They started laughing at the same time.

'A snoring puppy?'

'Lucky me,' said Eli. 'I'll sound his chest tomorrow, but I think it's just how he's lying with his little head tucked in.'

He took another breath. 'There's two extra bedrooms across the hall. You can pick whatever one you like to sleep in.' The words came out so quickly that they almost ran together. Was he nervous?

She picked up her wine and took a sip. 'Perfect, thank you. I'm just glad I didn't need to do that drive home. I might have fallen asleep.'

'What about your cat?'

'Miss Trixie will be fine. I already texted my neighbour to feed her and go and check on her.'

'You called your cat Miss Trixie?' There was scepticism in his tone.

'She's a rescue, she came with the name. But I have to say, The Queen would probably suit her better. She thinks the rest of the world is there to do her bidding, and I swear she looks at me with disdain most of the time.'

'The world of cats,' he sighed. 'One day, scientists will be able to understand a cat's thoughts, and I genuinely think we will all be horrified by how badly they think of us all.'

She laughed. 'Oh, I can almost guarantee it.'

He reached out and touched her arm and she flinched. She hadn't even had a chance to have a single thought. It was just slightly unexpected, and it was her body's automatic response.

Eli's face changed instantly. 'Aurora, I'm sorry.'

She reached for the spot on her arm and shook her head. He'd shared so much about himself in the car. Wasn't it at least time she shared a little bit in return?

'It's me,' she said. 'I had an experience when I was younger that came as a shock.'

He was sitting very still on the sofa next to her.

'It makes me nervy. I feel as if I have a spider-sense that tingles sometimes.'

'With me?' he asked, looking horrified.

She gave him a soft smile. 'No, not with you, Eli. But if anyone touches me and I'm not expecting it, my body just reacts.'

He closed his eyes for a second and just breathed. 'I am so sorry,' he said. 'That should never have happened.'

'No,' she said calmly, 'it shouldn't. But sexual assault happens to women all over the world. And I was, like most, shocked at the time, blamed myself, and didn't want to report or complain.'

'So, what happened?'

'I finally admitted things to a much older member of our team, who had much more direct methods. He reported him, and when others heard, other women stepped forward to say he'd grabbed them, or cornered them too.'

She gave a sigh. 'Actually, just knowing that made me feel a whole lot better. It wasn't just me. He'd been the same with other women, and I absolutely wasn't to blame.'

Eli gave a careful nod. She could tell he was treading warily, but she'd noticed he'd stuffed a clenched fist under his leg on the sofa.

'Did he get sacked?'

'Yes, and no reference.'

'Did the police do anything?'

She'd been in South Africa at the time. But police forces the world over weren't much different.

'An alleged sexual assault is difficult to prove. Unless a grab has been particularly forceful it sometimes won't leave a mark. I didn't want to put myself through a trial, where some might have doubted me, or thought that I deserved it.'

'That's awful.'

'It was. But I survived it.'

And a lot more too, she thought.

'I had no idea,' he said earnestly. 'I'm sorry I alarmed you.'

The screen flickered in front of them and the titles for a documentary on the *Marie Celeste* appeared. Aurora felt partly relieved.

'Do you know what I could do with?' she asked.

'What?'

'A hug,' she said simply. 'Refill my wine glass, let me slump on the sofa next to you, watch some interesting TV and not worry too much about what tomorrow will likely bring. I need a few hours of nothingness.'

'I can do that.' He picked up their glasses, walked to the kitchen to refill them, and when he got back to the sofa he relaxed down as Aurora leaned against his side. His arm went easily around her shoulders and she just rested against him.

'Perfect,' she murmured.

* * *

Eli's head was spinning, as his body would quite like to react in a normal way to having a woman he was extremely attracted to this close. But he concentrated hard to try and dampen all his desires.

The documentary passed the hour easily. They sipped their wine, and he enjoyed the heat and feel of her next to him. The curves of her body against his. The clean scent emanating from her hair and body.

As the credits started to roll, she looked up at him with those too green eyes. She didn't even speak, just lifted her mouth to his.

He was tentative. He was wary. Because now he was in new territory. Now, he was conscious of his every move and not wanting to give her any reason to feel nervous. So he let Aurora lead the way entirely.

And she did. As their kisses deepened, and hands brushed against each other's skin, it was Aurora who made the move to swing her leg over and sit astride him, letting him run his hands up her back and touch her smooth skin.

It was Aurora who tilted her head back to give his mouth access to the delicate skin on her neck.

And it was Aurora who positioned herself where she could clearly know the effect she was having on him.

'How about I don't sleep in one of the spare rooms?' she asked.

He tried not to let out a groan. 'You want to steal my bed now too?' he joked.

Her eyebrows lifted. 'I want to steal your bed with you in it,' she replied.

He thought they might take things slow, but she stripped off her clothes on the way to the bedroom and turned to face him as he entered.

'Always so slow?' she teased as she climbed into bed.

Eli had never shed clothes so quickly in his life as he joined her on the bed.

'You sure about this?' He had to ask. He had to make sure they were both on the same page.

'Absolutely,' she replied with a big smile on her face as she pulled him towards her.

CHAPTER SEVEN

TESTING A HERD of nearly one thousand seven hundred would have been a nightmare. But, thankfully, the Fletchers kept their herd segregated, and it was only two hundred cows that could have been exposed.

The seven who were considered symptomatic were tested first, with their tuberculin skin tests to be read in seventy-two hours. In the meantime, Don Fletcher wasn't looking too good himself.

'Don,' said Eli, already knowing what the answer might be, 'do you drink unpasteurised milk on the farm?'

'Every day,' he admitted. 'Public health are sending someone out to test me later today. Me, and Jake, the herd boy. He has breakfast here every morning and we both drink unpasteurised milk.'

'Any symptoms?'

'GP already asked me a few questions days ago. He's ordered a chest X-ray, but the public health person said they will need to look at that and the TB test together to consider a diagnosis. Chest X-ray is booked for tomorrow.'

'What about Jake?'

Don frowned and shook his head. 'Not sure who his doctor is.'

'I'll let the team at public health know and they'll arrange a chest X-ray for him too.'

Don sighed. 'We've reinforced around all the stores and water supply, but it's really too late now. Once bovine TB is in the herd, the cow-to-cow transmission can be high.'

'Let's just wait and see what the tests show.'

Don nodded as Eli finished up all the things he needed to do on the farm that day.

It had been a strange morning. Nice to wake up with Aurora in his arms. Reassuring to notice how comfortable she felt beside him. Unusual to discover how in synch they were in the kitchen in the morning, where both of them had refused to even function before they had coffee.

There had been a serious atmosphere this morning. Because they knew the day ahead was going to be tough. To her credit, as soon as they'd arrived at the farm and after taking one look at Don, who was pale and thin, Aurora had gone with the vet from the Animal and Plant Health Agency, along with one of the farm hands to get things started.

Eli had assisted where he could, then gone back to chat with Don in the farmhouse for a while. Don could already have tuberculosis, which was impacting on his health. But Eli was also conscious of the immense amount of stress and pressure an event like this would cause to a farmer. The health and wellbeing of the farming community was always at the forefront of his mind.

'I'm surprised you're still here,' said Don, in between coughs.

'You are?'

Don nodded. 'I thought you'd cut and run as soon as you could.'

Eli decided to be honest. 'I wanted to, but Matt is sick. I'm not sure if he'll be well enough to come back, and I'm still advertising for another vet. Until all that happens, I have to stay.'

'Do you think you'll get someone?'

Eli raised both hands. 'It's difficult. I might be able to attract someone newly qualified, but even then I'd need to stay and oversee them for at least a year. So, my plans have had to change.'

Don looked at him for a few moments. 'I'm glad to hear that.'

'You are?'

'Of course I am,' he replied. 'If you close, the nearest vet practice is twenty-five miles away. And I don't know those people. Your practice—

Matt's? I've known you both for years. I trust you both. If Matt hadn't been sick, this would all have happened probably some time last week. But I'm grateful that as soon as you both had that conversation you picked up the phone to let me know what you were thinking, and what would happen next.'

'It's what every vet should do.'

'But not all do. I've heard tales from other people that other agencies have just turned up at their farm after the vet has left.'

'I'd never do that to you, Don.'

'I know, son.' He reached out and placed his hand over Eli's. The gesture was small, but meant so much for an old guy like this.

Eli's eyes fixed on their hands. This. This was part of why he was here. He'd never want to let the farming community down. This was part of why he loved his job so much. Working in all parts of the world was great. Learning and getting experience with other kinds of animals was also great. But farming was the backbone of so much in Britain.

He'd always known his father had completely loved it. And that, in turn, had made him want to invest his time and energy in different ways, and in different places. But the reality was that he, Elijah Ferguson, loved working on the Scottish farms. And for some reason it seemed as if he was only truly realising that now.

Aurora appeared at the doorway. 'Everything okay?'

Don pulled his hand back and gave her a nod. Aurora walked over to the stove in the kitchen and turned the hob on. 'Barb phoned with strict instructions I was to make sure that you ate, Don. She's left this pot of soup, and said it was big enough for us all.'

Eli moved over to join her, cutting bread from a thick loaf. 'He is looking thin, and pale.' He glanced at Aurora, who was pulling out bowls and had found a soup ladle. 'I'm glad Barb phoned you.'

They exchanged a small smile. He liked how resilient she was, and how she wasn't afraid to jump in and help. One of the farm hands went to round up all the others and plates of lentil and ham soup, along with thick farmhouse bread, were served to all.

'I need to get the recipe for this,' Aurora whispered in Eli's ear. 'I am absolutely rubbish at making soup.'

He smiled in surprise. 'The first thing you're not good at. I learn something every day.'

'The second thing might be pizza,' she freely admitted. 'I've never made pizza from scratch before. Some might say that last night you were just showing off.' There was a glint in her eyes.

'What part?' he immediately joked and laughed as colour seemed to spread up her cheeks. But no one else in the room had noticed. It was as if they were in their own private bubble.

When everyone was done, Eli loaded the dishwasher as Aurora made Don a coffee and cut him a slab of gingerbread that Barb had left.

Something was dancing around in his brain. He liked her. He liked her a lot. But he'd been down this road with a colleague before. Someone who had pulled the wool over his eyes.

Yesterday, he'd noticed that Aurora had been in the practice's accounts. Granted, it was a small place, and everyone might do more than their role. But neither his solicitor nor accountant had mentioned that the wages were done by the staff themselves. Matt had mentioned it. But to Eli, with his naturally suspicious mind, it all seemed a bit strange.

It wasn't as if Aurora had tried to hide it. She'd been upfront and said Anne had been struggling, the last employee hadn't been paid and she was helping. Was it really normal for a vet nurse to do the wages?

Maybe it was because he'd been working in other countries. Most other practices had been much bigger than this one at home, and there had been finance offices to deal with all the wages. He couldn't remember what had happened in the past. He'd been too young to care and then, as a teenager, he'd only been interested in the animals, not the running of the practice. This could be entirely normal.

But he'd need to check.

He hated he felt like that. But he couldn't push it away. It was just too important. If he was going to be around for the best part of a year or more, he really needed to get a better handle on the day-to-day running of the practice. He should have done it before now.

'What's wrong?' Aurora asked.

'Nothing,' he said quickly.

'Are we ready to go then?'

He nodded and they followed all the cleansing and disinfectant rules before they left the farm. As they drove along the road Aurora gazed at the scenery.

'You know, I was thinking. You could make some improvements to the practice.'

'What do you mean?' He wasn't sure why he was instantly alarmed.

'It's just that, last night, I noticed upstairs has clearly been renovated in the last few years. Downstairs, the practice looks a bit tired by comparison.'

'You think?' He hadn't really thought about it

at all. He'd worked in some state-of-the-art practices, and some middle of the road. His father and Matt's practice had never really entered his thoughts at all.

'It's just, as you're advertising and looking for someone new, if you brightened the place up a bit, got some new equipment, it might attract some new candidates.'

Okay, what she said made sense.

'And you've already made a start on the kennels out back.'

He nodded. She was right. The kennels at the back had been used during the good weather to sometimes monitor pets or keep them until their owners returned to collect them. They'd been pristine in years gone by, but had obviously been less of a priority in recent times. It had taken some blood, sweat, tears and some timber to resurrect Bert's playpen, but he could take some time to do the rest, particularly when it was nice weather.

'I could do the rest of the kennels,' he said slowly.

'Then we could think about the two treatment rooms. The doors could do with replacing, and maybe a new sink in one. The floors in both could be replaced and they could do with a coat of paint each too.'

'Are you turning into one of those house

shows on TV, where they throw you out for a couple of days, then the owners come back and find they've turned a library into a disco?'

She gave a small laugh. 'Not quite. I just think it might help things. And I'm happy to help. I can put a few things through the accounts.'

It was like a chill going through his veins. He tried to be rational. But being a victim of a crime, and realising how many tiny tells there had been that he'd missed, had imprinted on his brain.

Last night had been the best night he could remember. Aurora's lips on his, her skin against his, and that feeling of connection that he'd always been seeking but had never found before. All of that was currently skewing his rational thoughts.

Aurora must have noticed the way his hands had tightened on the steering wheel because she gave him a strange look. 'Forget it, don't worry. It was just a suggestion. Why don't you wait another few weeks and see if you get any applicants?'

His heart ached. She was trying to help him. And if this was genuine she might think him ungrateful. But if this was something else— something cold and calculating that he'd missed before—then there was still a chance to stop things.

As he drove along the last mile to the practice his mouth was bone-dry. He couldn't pick up the phone to Matt. It wasn't fair. He couldn't ask him the questions he wanted to ask. Like how well he knew Aurora. If he'd checked her references and qualifications.

Then, cutting clean through those thoughts, was something else. Was this it for him? Was this how he was going to spend the rest of his life? Second-guessing. Never trusting, always questioning what anyone told him.

He wanted to believe not. Maybe it was just timing. Maybe it was just because this was the first time he'd really let someone close since Iona. It could be that he would always have been like this next time around—and Aurora was just caught in the emotional crossfire.

He hated the way that sounded. He hated more the way it felt.

'I'll think about it,' he said, knowing his words might sound a bit abrupt. 'I'm still thinking about a lot of things with Don Fletcher's farm. Let's deal with that first.' He looked sideways. 'And, there's some other things to pick up. Jack Sannox and Rudy for one.'

She turned to face him. 'Do you trust me to do that?' There was an edge to the question.

'Of course I do,' he replied.

'Then I'll go tomorrow if we're not back at the Fletchers' farm all day.'

He licked his lips, trying to be rational and calm. He was a vet. There were a number of crises right now for his clients. Some huge in volume, and some smaller—but with equal emotional value.

'I would really appreciate that,' he said steadily. And he realised he meant it. Jack Sannox and his wellbeing mattered to him. From everything he'd seen of Aurora in her professional capacity, he had absolutely no reason not to trust her. If she was worried about Jack, she would let him know.

Aurora's phone buzzed and she pulled it out of her pocket as they reached the practice. She frowned. 'It's Anne, saying that patient with the diabetic cat is insistent on talking to me again.'

Eli's head shot around. 'Are you worried?'

He watched as she took a deep breath and focused on the practice building instead of him.

'Let's just say that my spider-sense tingles around him.'

'Then we don't see him. I'll ask Anne to tell him that our books are full, and to divert him to another practice.'

He could see the wave of relief wash over her, not just from the visible welcome slump of her body. This had been hard for her—hard for her to admit. If they hadn't connected last night, might she not have told him?

That was the last thing he wanted for staff that worked for him.

'Thank you,' she said, her voice a little shaky.

He reached over and took her hand. 'Any and every time,' he said firmly. They sat for a few minutes while she collected herself, then she gave a big sigh and fixed a smile on her face.

'Let's go back inside.'

They were met by Bert at the door, who looked as if he'd been up to mischief. Anne simply raised her hand from the desk. 'Don't ask,' she said.

Eli smiled and walked over to her. 'The man you texted Aurora about, the one that's been insistent about dealing with her?'

Anne nodded.

'Can you phone him back and say unfortunately our books are full, and refer him on to another vet practice, please?'

Anne met his gaze. She was one of those characters that didn't need things spelled out to her. 'No problem, I'll do it now,' she said, picking up the mobile handset and moving into another room.

'What have we got this afternoon?' asked Eli, as Aurora walked back through to Reception.

'Two dogs. Both are being considered for

breeding. Eye checks done. DNA tests completed with no concerns, but both need to be sedated to get their hip and knee X-rays completed for grading.'

'What kind of dogs?' Eli asked. This was routine work for this practice. Not every practice had the qualifications or skill to do these kinds of tests, but it was something both Matt and his father had insisted on continuing. Mainly because it helped keep up the quality of dogs being bred, and it was profitable.

'One Labrador, and one dachshund,' said Aurora.

He gave a nod. 'No problem. I'm going to spend some time writing up the notes from the Fletchers' farm, then I have a video call with some of the other agencies at five o'clock tonight. Give me a nudge, will you? I might forget.'

'We'll be finished the X-rays long before then, and I'm happy to stay later if either of the dogs takes some time to come out of their sedation.'

'Thank you,' he said, meaning it. She really was an excellent staff member.

Anne came through once he was settled at the computer. 'Anything you want to tell me?' she asked.

Eli felt heat rush into his cheeks. How on earth could Anne already know that something was going on between him and Aurora? His father had always said not to underestimate how astute she was, but that was usually in relation to owners who didn't quite tell the whole story about something.

'Er...' he started, stuttering over his words. 'I might have started dating someone,' he said.

It was like being a fourteen-year-old again. Anne had just started at the practice then, and used to leave him tongue-tied. But he was a fully grown adult now. Should he really tell her this stuff? She didn't have any right to know.

She'd just blindsided him.

A smile appeared around her lips. 'Anyone I know?'

He took a breath. 'Maybe,' was his response as he straightened himself up and got ready to explain that this really wasn't something to discuss.

But Anne rested a hand on his shoulder, the smile disappearing from her face. 'I was talking about Matt,' she said sadly. 'Marianne said you visited last night.'

His face fell, and he inwardly cringed. Of course she'd meant Matt.

'But I welcome the other news,' said Anne, in a way that only she could.

He moved his hand and put it on hers, looking up. 'He wasn't great, Anne. Much sicker than I realised. His colour was almost translucent, and he's lost so much weight he hardly looks like

Matt any more.' He sighed and looked down for a second, before he had a moment of realisation. 'But you knew that, didn't you?'

She gave a slow nod. 'I would never have said anything to you, until I knew you'd been to visit.' She paused for a moment, her face the most serious he'd ever seen it. 'You have to think carefully about the future, about what makes you happy, Elijah.'

'I know,' he admitted. 'And I still don't know what that is.' He put his hand on his chest. 'I still don't know if I have the heart to be here.'

Anne stayed silent for a few moments. 'Only you can answer that question.'

'I know,' he sighed. 'But there's so much going on right now, and so much to think about.'

'You're right. There is. But at some point you have to take some time to stop and think. Just promise me that.'

He gave a nod and Anne slipped her hand from his and disappeared back through to one of the treatment rooms.

Aurora was feeling odd about things. One part of her was fizzing with excitement. She'd only ever experienced telling one potential partner in the past about her sexual assault. The reaction had been confused, with a real reluctance to try and reach out to her. She got that. It scared some people. But Eli's reaction last night had been different.

He'd accepted what she'd said. He'd been angry—even though he hadn't said anything. He'd been sorry she'd had that experience but had been supportive. Then he'd still reacted to her touch. With caution, maybe. But his touch had been just what she'd needed.

It had revitalised her. It made her feel real again. Parts of herself that she'd kept hidden had been unleashed. She'd also felt good about revealing a part of her history with Eli. He'd taken it well, and she knew she still had to tell him about her past career.

She was just worried that he would think less of her. The reactions of colleagues at university and in placements had made her so glad that she'd worked as an actress under another name. Even those colleagues who'd said they admired the TV show had still treated her as a bit less. It was actually shocking how the world seemed to assume that anyone who was an actor wasn't clever. She hated that.

She could already tell that Eli was beginning to trust her professional judgement and competence. She didn't want that to be compromised.

Then there was the stalking. It was another horrible dark hole in her mind, and if she really wanted to have a relationship with someone it would have to be revealed.

She didn't want to think about any of that right now. She wanted to live in the moment. Let the electricity continue to spark between them. See where things led. For a few moments today she'd wondered if something was off. But then again, when was the last time she'd been in a relationship? Maybe she was just rusty. Maybe she should make more of an effort?

They worked closely together the rest of the afternoon. Both dogs were sedated and X-rayed without any concerns. The little dachshund took a bit longer to recover completely and Aurora was happy to stay with him until he was wide awake and his owner came to pick him up.

Once she handed him over, she walked back through to one of the offices, where Eli was still working on the computer.

'Ready to finish?' she asked.

He looked up. 'Nearly—why, is something wrong?'

She shook her head. 'I just wondered if you want to do something.'

He must have got a hint she had something planned. 'Like what?'

'Well,' she said slowly, not trying to hide her smile, 'I know it's summer. But there are two options. We could head to Portobello Beach for chips and ice cream, or we could head into the city and catch one of the last tours of the graveyards and the dungeons. It should be dark enough by then.'

He leaned back in his chair and folded his arms. 'Wow. Two great suggestions.' He looked out of the window. 'What time is the last tour?'

'About eleven,' she said, 'and they last about an hour. We could grab dinner some place first.'

He closed his eyes for a second. 'Or we could take Bert with us and go for a walk on the beach. It's years since I've been to Portobello Beach,' he said with a smile.

'How long?' she queried.

'Maybe eighteen or nineteen years. I wonder how much the place has changed.'

'Chips and ice cream it is, then?'

He nodded. He seemed genuinely happy. 'Let me go and get changed. Do you want to get changed too?'

She nodded but said, 'My house is on the way. Can we stop there and I'll run in and grab some clothes, and check on Miss Trixie?'

'No probs,' he said. 'Give me fifteen minutes. I'll finish this, jump in the shower and grab Bert.'

Bert could clearly sense something was going on as he started to get excited. Aurora wrestled him into his harness for the car journey, and Eli appeared a few minutes later in jeans, a white T-shirt and brown leather jacket.

All it did was remind her just how handsome he was. He looked like something from an aftershave ad.

This time the car that Eli pulled from his dad's garage was an old-style silver Aston Martin.

'You have to be joking,' she said.

He shook his head. 'Perfect for a wee drive to the beach.' He laid a blanket over the back seat and secured Bert in place. 'Let's go.'

She had to give him directions to her house. It was slightly odd for her. After her stalking experience, she'd been careful about what name she used, and how many people actually knew where she lived. She'd kept it to a minimum. She directed Eli through her village and to her cottage. She loved her home, was proud of it. Her garden was immaculate. And although the house had new windows and shutters, it had a traditional wooden red front door.

'Your place is lovely,' said Eli as he pulled into the driveway.

'Thank you,' she replied with a smile. 'Do you want to come in while I get changed?'

He gave a nod, then glanced at Bert and changed his mind. 'I'll just take Bert for a walk around the garden first.'

Aurora nodded and got out of the car, leaving

her front door open behind her and dropping her bag on the table near the entranceway. She ran up the stairs, took the quickest shower in history and grabbed some clean clothes out of her bedroom, while Miss Trixie watched her with apparent indifference from the top of the bed.

The temperature was still warm, so she grabbed a pair of white capri pants, flat shoes and a white-and-green-striped T-shirt. As she went back along the corridor she noticed Bert and Eli still outside. Her eyes caught sight of a pile of mail from the day before that she hadn't even looked at. But the thing that caught her attention was her stage name—Star Kingfisher—on one of the envelopes. Not only that, it was addressed to her stage name, with the actual house address. It hadn't come via her agent like most mail did.

Her skin chilled. Had someone tracked her down? She swallowed hard. Her stalker had gone to jail but had been released less than a year later. She hadn't heard anything from him in years. Could he have tracked her down again?

She felt sick.

'Ready?' came Eli's voice from outside.

She stuffed the letters into her bag. She'd look at them later. Eli was outside, as Bert sniffed around the garden.

'Didn't you come in?' she asked.

'We got as far as the sitting room,' he said. 'Like your purple sofa, by the way. But Bert was sniffing around too much. I was too scared he'd relieve himself on your nice purple rug.'

She smiled, because she couldn't quite laugh yet.

He held up one hand as she stepped outside. He hesitated a second then gave a little shrug of his shoulders. 'Just wondered if you wanted to bring anything for tomorrow.'

Now, her smile broadened. 'Are you asking me to stay overnight?' she teased.

'Only if you want to.'

She stood for a few moments, letting him think she was considering things, before turning and going back in, putting tomorrow's food out for Miss Trixie. She grabbed another few things, flung them in another bag then went back out to lock her door.

As she turned around, something about the car flashed through her head. 'Has that car been in a film?'

Eli gave a bashful smile. 'One nearly the same was in one of the James Bond films. I'm not sure how or where my father ever got an Aston Martin from, but he only took it out on special occasions.'

'So, is that what I am,' she asked as she climbed in, 'a special occasion?'

He laughed as he started the car. 'Of course.'

The drive down to Portobello Beach was beautiful. The sand was a dark yellow and the tide was currently coming in with blue waves and white peaks as they found somewhere to park.

'Will the car be okay here?' asked Aurora, feeling a little worried.

'It's a car,' said Eli easily. 'And—' he spun around, holding his hands out '—the people here are good. They're not going to make off with a James Bond car. Remember what happens to any villain that tries.'

She frowned for a moment, trying to remember what did happen to people in those films, but her mind was a blank. And she was secretly pleased that he liked her home, even though he hadn't got to see much of it.

They moved along the street, which was filled with locals and holidaymakers. She could hear an array of different accents and even though it was late in the evening there were still some children down on the beach, playing on the sand.

Eli lifted Bert up into his arms. 'Right, little guy, let's see what you make of the sand, and the sea.'

They made their way down onto the beach. As the tide was part way in, they didn't have to walk too far. Bert loved it. There was no other way to describe it. He looked at the sand between his paws for a few moments then had a dig, sending sand flying. Next, he rolled in it. Then, when they moved closer to the sea, he didn't hesitate to run straight into the waves.

'He loves it!' declared Aurora as he splashed her again and again. She took off her flat shoes and walked through the waves with him, grabbing the lead from Eli. 'This is freezing though,' she yelled over her shoulder as Eli crossed his arms and stood laughing at them both.

A crowd of twenty-somethings walked past, with one nudging the other and then all turning to look at them. Were they looking at him? Or her? Nope, they were definitely looking at Aurora, with her dark red hair flying madly about and her laughter as she interacted with Bert.

'Your feet will take an hour to heat up,' he said, shaking his head as they both made their way back to him.

'They won't. These shoes, they're actually made from a kind of recycled material. They can be washed and are waterproof.' She gave him a wink. 'What's more, I have them in twenty different styles and colours.'

He groaned. 'I knew there had to be a flaw somewhere beneath that perfect smile.'

She moved closer, cutting out the wind between them that was blowing briskly. 'You think I've got a perfect smile?' she said.

She was trying to pretend to be cool, but the man in front of her was one of the most handsome guys she'd ever seen. A few other women had glanced in their direction. With his blue eyes, scruffy styled hair and designer stubble, he was attracting lots of admiring looks. She almost wanted to make sure everyone knew he was with her.

He put his arms at either side of her hips as she moved closer. 'I think your smile is pretty great,' he said. Her hair, which was whipping around her face, was caught by him, with a strand tucked behind one of her ears. 'And I think the colour of your hair is stunning.'

'You do?' They were chest to chest now. She decided it was time to tease him again. 'So, last time you were at Portobello Beach, did you kiss a girl?'

He threw back his head and laughed. 'I wish. But I'm doing it this time,' he added, before putting his lips on hers.

And for the first time in a long time Aurora thought she might get a chance at happy ever after.

CHAPTER EIGHT

THE FIRST LETTER seemed almost like a mistake. A fan apologising for sending a letter to her address, which was more of a query to ask if Star Kingfisher would be returning to the vet series. The second letter asked why she was living her life under another name, and if she was trying to keep her identity a secret.

Aurora tried to phone the police officer who'd dealt with her stalking case—but he'd moved on, and no one else could really help.

She was left jittery and unnerved.

In the meantime, work was getting busier by the day. Bovine tuberculosis had been confirmed in some of the Fletchers' herd, which sent a huge chain reaction of next steps. All the other cattle were tested, with no milk or beef allowed to be sold or moved from the farm.

The impact on Don Fletcher's farm was huge, along with the repercussions for his workers. He himself had been diagnosed with TB, as had his younger farmhand. The system was designed to recompense farms affected by bovine TB. However, all things took time.

In the meantime, all the surrounding farms had concerns, and testing was arranged for them too. Aurora and Eli spent huge amounts of time on virtual meetings, coordinating with all the agencies involved.

Eli himself was clearly stretched. He was doing the work of two vets. There had been contact from a French vet who was interested in coming to Scotland, and there had been a few enquiries by those due to qualify. Two had arranged to come and see the practice, but Aurora was already convinced that working alongside one vet wouldn't appeal to a new graduate. They usually wanted to find their feet in larger practices with bigger support networks.

With all this happening around them, it seemed as if there wouldn't be any time for Aurora and Eli. But, strangely, this wasn't quite true.

There was a consistent and ongoing connection between them. When a pet had required overnight care after surgery, Aurora had volunteered to stay over. It happened on rare occasions, when animals had a slower recovery from their anaesthetic, or their owner wasn't quite equipped to take care of them.

Eli had waved his hand. 'I can do it. I'm here anyway.'

'But you have a million other things on, and you need to get some sleep,' she'd insisted. 'I can set the alarm and get up a few times in the night to check. It's fine.'

And she did. Of course, she hadn't minded at all that they'd decided to take the little cat upstairs and held it on her lap as they watched TV on the sofa, his arm around her shoulders and her head on his neck.

It was such a comfort. She was just trying to get her head around the fact she could actually have something real. Seven years ago, she'd been the apple of a number of guys' eyes—but it was hard to separate who was interested in her, Aurora, as opposed to who was interested in tabloid fodder and headlines about the latest popular actress.

She didn't have to worry about that with Eli. He only knew her.

The next week passed easily. They continued to work together, supporting the members of the farming community around them, learning how to create a new team. Anne watched with the permanent hint of a smile on her face. She said very little about it, but occasionally remarked on how the practice was beginning to run smoothly again.

They were making plans to head into Edinburgh for the evening when the doors of the practice burst open and a teenage girl ran in, clutching something in her arms.

'I can't believe it. I am so sorry. I never even saw him.'

Aurora and Eli were on their feet in seconds, Aurora wrapping her arm around the girl's shoulders as Eli eased the little animal from her arms.

It was a dog—a puppy, and almost a carbon copy of Bert. One of its legs was clearly broken and the only sound it made was whimpers.

Aurora steered the girl to a chair. 'Tell me what happened.'

'It just ran in front of me.' She crumpled and put her hands on her face. 'I hit it with my car. I've only had my licence for six months. I didn't have time to stop.'

'Where on the road were you?' she asked gently. She was trying to be patient, but knew she had to assist Eli urgently.

The girl explained. It was near the spot that Aurora had climbed through the woods to find Bert.

'Phone your mum or dad,' she said. 'Ask them to come and get you, and let us take care of the puppy.'

She hated to do it, but she had to leave the girl in the waiting room to go and look after the puppy. She dialled Anne on her mobile as she took the few steps into the treatment room. It was likely they would be busy for the next few hours and the practice would be left uncovered. Anne answered immediately, and said she would be there in ten minutes.

Eli's head was bent over the puppy as she entered the room, washing her hands and grabbing a trolley with IV supplies.

He spoke gently. 'He's so scrawny,' he said, then pressed his lips together.

Her heart ached. 'She knocked him down near where I picked up Bert. Do you think they could be from the same litter?'

'Highly likely. Can't imagine how this one has managed to keep going.'

The little dog's ribs were clearly visible. Eli had his stethoscope out and was listening to the puppy's abdomen. 'Sounds okay.' His eyes flickered to the back leg. 'It's badly broken.'

She knew what he was going to say. The little puppy was so scrawny and thin; he had to contemplate if it could withstand an anaesthetic.

They worked together, shaving the hair on one of his front legs, inserting an IV to give fluids for the puppy's too fast heart rate and low blood pressure. Aurora put some oxygen on, and drew up some pain relief for Eli to insert.

'What do you think?'

The little guy's whimpers started to die down. Eli took the opportunity to draw some blood and handed it to Aurora. She knew automatically what to check for. This was another way to ensure the puppy would be fit for anaesthetic.

The practice had been able to screen their own bloods for a number of years and it saved time on the more regular tests. Complicated blood tests still needed to be sent to more specialised labs, but in times like this the ability to check for themselves was crucial.

'He's a little bit dehydrated,' Aurora said, showing him the blood results.

He nodded. 'I'd like to weigh him,' said Eli. 'I need to know how much anaesthetic he could tolerate. This could be touch and go.'

'Let's give the opioids another minute to kick in,' said Aurora. 'I'll need to lift him onto the scales.'

Eli was gently stroking the little dog's back. 'There, there,' he said. He met her gaze. 'Operating might not be a good idea. There's a chance he won't tolerate the anaesthetic. And we already know he doesn't have an owner. Not when he looks like this.'

Aurora gave a nod, but pulled the scanner from the nearby drawer to check for a microchip. Of course, there was none.

Eli looked her steadily in the eye. 'We'd need

to look after this guy ourselves in the rehab period before we hand him over to a rescue centre.'

'We can do that,' she said steadily. 'I think we have to give him a chance.' Their gazes remained locked. 'Why have one Bert, when we can have two?' she said with a smile.

Eli had been upfront to begin with about not wanting to stay. But since their visit together to Matt's, it was as if all parameters had changed. They both knew he'd have to stay for at least a year. Recruitment was still open. Another vet had yet to materialise.

Before that visit, he'd asked her to consider adopting Bert. But nothing had been mentioned since. Maybe she was jumping to a whole host of conclusions here. Maybe the fact they were in a relationship was clouding her judgement. But she didn't think so. He'd revealed part of himself to her. She understood why he struggled with the memories of his past here. And he, in turn, had been a good personal support about her assault. It gave her faith that she could continue to move past that and form a meaningful relationship.

There was a noise as the front door opened and Anne bustled in. She was her usual reliable self, her eyes catching sight of the young girl in the waiting room and their own situation in the treatment room.

She gave them a wave of her hand. 'Go and do what you need to do,' she said.

They disappeared into the theatre. The little dog was anaesthetised, his leg area prepped and draped, with the theatre lights adjusted to give Eli the best possible view.

Before cutting the skin, he took an X-ray to see what he was dealing with.

'It's broken in two separate places. I'll need to plate and pin.'

Aurora knew that would take a few hours. They worked together steadily, her assisting where required and monitoring the little dog's breathing and vital signs. There were a few scary moments, when the little dog had a burst of tachycardia during the procedure. But things settled down.

Eli kept a close eye on the puppy's blood pressure, ensuring adequate IV fluids were given, since he was already a little dehydrated. 'Thank goodness there's not much blood loss. I'm not sure his body could take it.'

He leaned back, arching himself to stretch out his spine. As he finished his delicate work he looked at Aurora. 'Do you think there's any chance there are more of them?'

'Don't say that.' She shuddered. 'It's bad enough I missed one. I'd hate it if there were others.' She licked her lips under her mask. 'Do you think we should go and check later?'

He paused for a second, then looked down again. 'Let's wait and see how this little guy does first. We need to get him through this before we worry about anything else.'

After a while, Anne stuck her head through the door. 'The young girl was picked up by her mum and dad. I've to give them a call to let them know how the puppy is.'

As Aurora gave her a nod, Anne paused for a second. Even from the other side of the theatre, Aurora could see the flash of concern in her eyes. 'There's another query about the wages that I can't answer.'

Aurora didn't hesitate. 'That's fine, leave it for me. I'll sort it later.'

Eli gave her a fleeting gaze, and for the briefest of seconds she thought she saw something strange in his eyes. But, next second, the alarm sounded and they both turned their attention back to the puppy.

'We should give this guy a name. We can't keep calling him dog, or puppy.'

'Why don't you pick the name, since I picked Bert?'

'You picked Bert because you said it was someone good that you worked with?'

She nodded.

'Okay, in that case, this guy can be Hank.'

Aurora couldn't help but smile. 'Hank?'

'Yes, when I worked in Maine, I worked with a vet called Hank. He was one of the good ones. Great accent. Great values. I really admired him.'

Aurora looked down and stroked the little one's head. 'Okay, Hank. Here's hoping you can wake up soon and we can introduce you to your brother, Bert.'

Finally, the surgery was finished and the wound stitched. Anne came into the room. 'I'd made scones at home, so just brought some when you phoned. I knew you'd be here a while. Go and have something to eat and I'll monitor him while he recovers.'

'Hank,' said Aurora. 'We've called him Hank, and think he could be Bert's brother. The accident was in the same kind of area.'

'Oh, dear,' said Anne, stroking his head. 'He does have the same distinctive white flash on his head.' She gave a little nod. 'Off you two go.'

They walked back through to the kitchen, where the plate of scones sat, along with the kettle boiling. Eli pulled off his cap and sighed as he sat down. 'We'll just need to wait and see how things go.'

Aurora went to sit down, then changed her mind. She walked through to the back kennels and shouted Bert in, picking him up and cuddling him while she sat at the table.

'You okay?' Eli asked, pouring the tea.

'Yeah,' she sighed. 'Just wishing that the day I found Bert, I found Hank too, and all of this never happened. That little guy has been foraging for himself for nearly a month. It doesn't bear thinking about.'

Eli carried the tea over and reached across, rubbing Bert's head. 'You can't think like that. At least you found Bert. He's doing great, aren't you, guy?'

Bert lifted his head into the air and sniffed. 'Is that the scones you smell, or is it your brother?' asked Aurora, giving him another cuddle.

Eli split the scones and spread them with butter and jam, putting them on two plates, and she continued to hug Bert.

'What will we do with Hank over the next few days?'

'I can ask Anne to do some extra hours. I'm sure she'll be happy to.'

'Okay then.'

'Because...' he met her gaze with a smile '...we will need some time off.'

'We will? What for?' she asked with a smile, warmth flooding through her like a comfort blanket.

'I've booked us onto something.'

'That sounds mysterious.'

'There's a graveyard tour in Edinburgh, by bus. Does the underground stuff too. But also some drinks and snacks as we do the tour. Thought we might give it a try.'

'That sounds like fun. You thinking about the Scottish weather again?'

He gave a shrug. 'You know what it's like. The graveyard and vault tour are probably best in October and November. This seemed like a fun added extra, and it doesn't leave until eleven at night.'

'Why do I have a feeling there's something you're not telling me?'

He gave a wide grin. 'It might be billed as a horror comedy tour.'

She laughed. 'Is the horror the actual comedy?'

'I guess we'll find out.'

'When are we going?'

He pulled a face. 'I'd booked for two nights' time. That was before Hank though. I'll check with Anne, to see if she can cover or not. If not, we can change it.'

Aurora nodded and, as she ate her scone, lifted the pile of notes that Anne had written this afternoon while manning the desk and answering the phone. Most were for repeat prescriptions. Anne had already printed them, and was just waiting for Eli to sign. She and Aurora would dispense and phone the owners back to let them know to collect the medications. There was another with some follow-up details Aurora had asked about a dog's diet. One query about a sick parrot. And a final one that made her stop cold.

Caller on the answering machine asking to speak to Star Kingfisher? Quite insistent. Must be wrong number.

A chill swept over her entire body. *No, not here too.*

She closed her eyes for a second and tried not to throw up. Could this be her stalker again? The kidnap attempt hadn't been a physical kidnap attempt, but the police had got wind of it, and foiled it. There was clear evidence of the stalking. Aurora had texts to her phone—even though she'd changed her number a few times. Letters sent to her house. And emails to her agent, and to her own private email account. All of them bombarding her to continue in her role, when it had been announced she was leaving the series.

She hadn't actually had to appear in court with her stalker. She'd been protected from that. And she'd never seen him in person. Just his police mugshot, and a picture of him entering court seven years ago. Would she even recognise him if she saw him now?

That actually scared her more than she wanted to admit.

She had to tell Eli. She had to tell Anne. It made her insides curl. Not only would she be letting them know she'd had a past career she'd kept from them, but now she was potentially bringing trouble to their door. What on earth would they think of her?

'Aurora? You okay?'

She opened her eyes and took a quick gulp of tea to soothe her bone-dry mouth.

She tried to be rational. Matt knew about her past career. When she'd applied for the job—although she hadn't written it on her submitted CV—she did tell him what she'd done in her late teenage years. He'd brushed it off easily, asked a few questions about the animals she'd interacted with on set, and what she'd learned about them. But once she'd answered his questions she'd said she was just trying to have a new life, and he'd said he respected that, and wouldn't mention it again.

So she hadn't been totally dishonest.

She took a deep breath. 'Yeah, there was just something I was going to mention—'

But she got cut off. Anne appeared in the door way. 'Eli, I need you.'

They were both on their feet in an instant. Animals could crash after anaesthesia. The most common signs were tachycardia, low blood pressure—both of which had been borderline for Hank—and hypothermia, which he was exhibiting now. Anne had wrapped a silver blanket around him.

'I'll give something else to reverse the anaesthetic again. Can you increase the rate on his IV fluids please, Anne?' asked Eli, checking the wound, then taking out his stethoscope to listen to Hank's chest again. They were all silent for a moment, before he pulled the stethoscope from his ears. 'No fluid in his lungs. No heart murmur, just a consistent tachycardia.' He touched Hank's head tenderly. 'Just a little guy who might not have the pull to get through the other side of surgery. Maybe we shouldn't have done it. Maybe this was cruel?'

It was the first time she'd ever heard Eli doubt anything he'd done as a vet. No practitioner was infallible. There were always times they had to weigh the odds and hope they worked in their favour. Had she pushed him to do this?

She put her hand over his. 'This wasn't cruel. This was us doing our best and trying to give Hank a chance.'

Anne gave a slow nod. 'There's the human side too. If I had to tell that teenage girl that we'd had to put the puppy down, I doubt she'd get over it. Hank had a chance, and he still does.'

Eli gave a slow nod and sighed. 'I just hate these parts of the job. He's just so scrawny. I've used minuscule amounts of drugs on him, as I have to be so careful about what his body can tolerate.'

'I have an idea,' said Aurora. 'Give me a minute.'

She ran through to the kitchen and picked Bert out of his basket, holding him firmly in her hands as she walked back through to the recovery area.

Bert made a little noise, as if he picked up the scent as soon as he came in the room. He started to scrabble a bit, but Aurora held him firm. 'No, honey. Hold still, let me take you over to him.'

Hank murmured too, coming around a little more from the anaesthetic now the drugs were kicking in, and sniffing the air.

Eli and Anne smiled as Aurora brought Bert nearer, talking quietly in his ear the whole time. She held Bert close enough to rub his head next to Hank's. Bert desperately wanted to get closer, but she didn't want him to knock Hank's leg, so she manoeuvred around, allowing them to see each other, to lick each other's face, and to touch with their paws.

'It's probably a million times better than any drug,' said Eli, giving her a smile that warmed her heart.

It struck her just how much she wanted this to work. She'd never met anyone like him before. And although she needed to tell him about her alternate identity, she was still glad that he just knew *her*. And liked her.

What had started out as rocky had blossomed very quickly into something special. And as she watched him lean over Hank, stroke his head and talk to him, she realised she loved this man. She actually loved him.

His too long, scruffy hair that she could run her fingers through. The stubble on his face that would scrape her cheek. The feel of his muscles flexing under the palm of her hand. That look from those blue eyes that made her insides want to melt.

She could do this. She could stay here. She loved this place already, but had never really considered it for ever. But now? With Eli? It could be.

But could she be his for ever too?

Trust for her had been so hard since her past experiences. But trust with Eli had always seemed unquestionable—even when she hadn't liked him those first few hours, she'd never felt unsafe. She'd never been worried.

But there still seemed to be an edge to Eli. Something that lay deep down beneath the surface. She wondered sometimes if she really knew everything about him.

But then, he didn't know everything about her.

That would have to change.

But as she watched him take care of Hank, while still holding Bert close to her chest, she knew there was a time and place for everything. And this wasn't it.

CHAPTER NINE

'I THINK I might fall asleep,' said Eli, as they climbed onto the decorated bus.

'Me too,' Aurora whispered as they were led to a table on the bus where a skeleton was in one of the seats.

'Guess this guy won't mind,' joked Eli, as he slid in next to the skeleton and slung an arm around its shoulders.

'Maybe that's what we all look like when we get off the bus,' joked Aurora, as one of the attendants approached with a tray of cocktails, all smoking and bubbling.

Eli picked something green and Aurora something peach-coloured and they both took a sip. 'Ouch,' laughed Eli, his cheeks drawing together. 'Well, that one is a bit strong.'

Aurora's eyes started to water. 'Mine too.' She gave a little choke. 'One of these will definitely be enough.

The last few nights had been tiring. Hank hadn't settled well. They had no idea where he'd been sleeping in the woods, or how long Bert and he had been separated from their mother, but he was difficult to get to sleep.

Both of them wished Bert could be in beside him. But Bert still had jumpy puppy traits that meant he could unwittingly hurt his brother, so they were waiting until he'd healed a bit better. They'd also spent a whole afternoon tramping around the woods to ensure there were no further puppies abandoned, but had found nothing. It had been a relief.

As the other passengers loaded and the guide gave an overview of what would happen, Eli studied Aurora.

He didn't mean to. He just did it every opportunity that he got.

She was beautiful, with her skin slightly tanned and a few freckles across her nose, her dark red hair and bright green eyes, he actually couldn't believe he'd got this lucky.

More than that, she had a good heart. She was feisty. She didn't put up with any nonsense. She had a real understanding of the farming community that actually put him to shame.

He'd underestimated her in the first few seconds of meeting her—but he'd never been that foolish again since.

Every day he spent around her, he learned more about himself, and more about her. Part of him felt as if coming here had been cathartic. Part of him felt as if seeing Matt had been a wakeup call, to be grateful for life, and all that was in it.

But meeting Aurora had been the icing on the cake.

He'd never experienced a spark like this. He'd thought he had. But now, with hindsight, he realised he'd been fooled. Every time he looked at her, he had a fresh wave of emotion. She affected every part of him. His senses seemed to go into overdrive around her. Just one whiff of her perfume was enough to send goosebumps across his skin and blood rushing to other parts of his body.

It was time to talk. Time to feel his way to seeing if he could make this more permanent. He still had questions. He still had trust issues. He wasn't sure they would ever go away. But those were his issues, not hers.

Aurora hadn't given him reason not to trust her.

He wondered if things had just moved too quickly between them. How he felt certainly had. He loved her. He was sure of it. He wanted to work next to her every day. He wanted to take her for a drive in every car in his father's garage. He wanted to replace some of the photographs in the hallway with some newer ones—one of them together, one of them with their dogs. But how would she feel about that?

The bus pulled out. The journey would take a few hours, with some pitstops along the way. They'd go on a visit to Greyfriars Kirkyard and walk to the statue of Greyfriars Bobby. They'd pass Holyrood Palace and go along Grassmarket and close to Edinburgh Castle. They'd go back down the Royal Mile, learning ghastly and ghostly history wherever they went, and finally finish with a visit to the underground vaults.

He leaned back into his skeleton friend as they listened to the comedian. The mood on the bus was light, jovial and the drinks seemed to be going down well.

He took a breath. 'About the practice,' he said.

'Yes?' She looked up straight away.

'You've probably guessed this because you were with me when we visited Matt and Marianne, but I'm going to stay.'

'For good?' There was an edge of hope in her voice. And he cringed inside. His answer should be yes, but he still couldn't honestly say that.

He swallowed. 'I'm going to stay for at least a year, then take it from there.'

'A year?' Was that disappointment in her voice?

'At least. One of the potential applicants looks like a good candidate. You met her—Cheryl

Wood? She, her husband and children are keen to move here. Her husband's a school teacher and they know there are plenty of jobs in the area. She's had some maternity leave during her studies, so qualifies in September.'

'The school term here starts in August. Won't that be too late for her husband?'

'He can work on the teaching bank. Apparently, there are lots of hours, and it will give him a chance to get to know the area, and where he might want to work permanently.'

'Only a year?'

He blinked and put his hand on his chest. 'I'm still not completely sure if I want to take over Dad's practice. Working here has been better than I thought. I'll always be known as David Ferguson's son, but I'm beginning to feel as if I can put my own stamp on the place.'

'Does that mean you'll let me decorate?' She'd already shown him some plans and given him some costs to update parts of the practice.

'I showed them to Matt, and he likes the idea.'

'You did?'

'I did.'

'But you still can only say you'll stay for a year?' Her voice had softened slightly.

'Aurora,' he said softly, 'I don't want to make false promises. I think this could work out. I think I might like to stay. But, until I know for sure, I only want to promise that I'll stay for the next year.'

She looked at him steadily and he continued.

'You have to know that a big part of why I want to stay is you.'

She sucked in a breath. 'Me?'

He gave her a smile. 'Absolutely.'

The bus jolted and both their drinks slid across the table, Eli barely catching them with one arm.

She let out a laugh, then leaned forward, her face serious as she reached out and touched his hand with her fingers. 'I'm glad you want to stay because of me, but you have to want to stay because of you too.'

'And that's the part that's getting there. You just have to give me a little more time. There are a few other complicating factors that mean I can't take over the practice completely. I have to let Matt and Marianne look after my dad's share for now.'

'But Matt's...' She let her voice tail off and pressed her lips together.

His other hand met hers. 'And I'll cross that bridge if I need to. For now, I don't.' He took another breath. 'And if I do decide I don't want to stay, I'll talk to you about it first.'

Her brow creased. 'So you can say goodbye?'

'No, so I can ask you if you want to come with me.'

She stayed very still. 'That sounds serious.'

'I am serious.'

'We've only known each other for a short time.'

He gave her a level look. 'I know that, but I know how I feel.' His insides were doing somersaults. It struck him that having this conversation on a bus, where both of them were essentially trapped for the next few hours, meant things potentially could go horribly wrong.

'How do you feel?' she asked, her fingers clenching under his.

He kept his voice steady. 'I feel like I've met someone that I can picture myself spending a lot of time with.'

Her voice was equally steady. It was almost as if she was challenging him. 'Spending a lot of time with, as in a fling? Or spending a lot of time with, as in something else?'

The question was close to the bone.

He didn't hesitate. 'Definitely something else.'

A slow smile started to spread across her face, and she leaned over and rescued her peach cocktail. 'Is that something we should drink to?'

'I think it is,' he said, picking up his green cocktail and clinking it against hers.

The two of them were smiling, and Eli had to untangle himself from the skeleton to lean across the table and put a kiss on her lips. Her lips were cold and sweet from the cocktail, and he instantly wished there wasn't a table between them.

'When can we get off this bus?' he groaned.

Her eyes gleamed as she pulled her lips from his. 'I have to see Greyfriars Bobby. I have to do the unthinkable thing of touching his nose.'

'I don't think we're allowed to,' he whispered. The act of touching Greyfriars Bobby's nose by visitors was frowned upon, and had caused the paint to have to be restored on numerous occasions.

'You can distract everyone else,' she said.

He shook his head in mock horror. 'I'm a Scotsman. I don't think I can do that. It goes against the grain.'

She rolled her eyes and signalled to the waiter on board for another drink. 'It's just your luck—' he grinned as the waiter plonked a blue glass down in front of her, again with smoke pouring from it —to end up with a patriotic Scotsman.'

She raised her eyebrows at him in disdain, then looked warily at the cocktail. 'I have no idea how they do this, but I like it. Okay, if you're going to fail me at Greyfriars Bobby, then we need to talk about our dogs.'

It was that little word. *Our.* It struck him straight in the gut and he liked it more than any other word on the planet.

'What about our dogs?'

'They're brothers. I don't think we should separate them. They've been through enough trauma.'

'Ah.' He lifted his own glass, which was looking remarkably empty. 'You're going to play the trauma card, are you?'

She smiled. 'To be honest, I don't think I need to, do I?'

He shook his head and smiled. 'What kind of vet would I be if I didn't have a rescue dog?'

'And what kind of vet nurse would I be if I didn't encourage you to have two?'

He raised his glass to her anyway. 'To Hank and Bert?'

She clinked his glass and lifted the still smoking blue liquid to her lips. 'To our boys.'

CHAPTER TEN

THEY COULDN'T HAVE timed things better. Aurora had called the pet hydrotherapy pool this morning and there was a cancellation. Things were quiet today, so they'd left Anne at the practice with Bert, and she and Eli had brought Hank to the treatment centre.

Hank was improving slowly. His wound had healed perfectly but he was walking with a slight limp. Eli had X-rayed him again to check the position of the plate and it was perfect. But a visit by a pet physio had told them that his back leg muscles were imbalanced and needed building up and the best way to do that was in a pool with hydrotherapy.

Since their colleague knew they were professionals, she'd agreed to set the programme and teach them how to assist Hank, with only a few check-in sessions with herself. The one thing she had been clear about was that the first time they immersed the little guy in water they both went in with him.

Neither of them had objected to this, and Aurora had changed quickly into her red one-piece swimsuit and tied her hair up in a pony-tail, before emerging and meeting Eli, in his dark swimming shorts, at the door.

'Shouldn't we be in Ibiza, dressed like this?' he joked.

'If only,' she sighed. 'But then I would need a shedload of sunscreen, so I can live with this.'

Hank was sniffing the air, obviously smell-ing the chlorine.

'Does this count as a date?' She smiled as she took her first few steps into the small pool.

The treatment centre was perfectly equipped. There was a small pool that could be used for any pet that needed immersion or swimming therapy. Then there were smaller set-ups with treadmills underwater to allow the dogs to ex-ercise without the full weight on their legs.

'This would have to be one of the weirdest dates in history,' said Eli as he stepped into the water, let his shoulders go under and then held out his arms for Hank.

He whispered in his ear as he took Hank from her. 'Check out the beginners. All the others have wetsuits on.'

Aurora looked around and pulled a face, re-alising they were the only people with actual swimsuits on. 'Well, we're new to this. And, let's face it, we'll do anything to help our boy build up his muscles. If I have to come here every week and put on my swimsuit, I will.'

Hank's front legs were paddling in the water. He seemed to be a natural.

'Hey,' she said, 'did I ever tell you about my red Lab, Max?'

"You mentioned him."

She raised her eyebrows. 'Well, one day, Max and I went for a walk around the boating pond back home. I took him regularly along a river walk and he would bound in and out of the edges of the water, actually skipping, but he'd never really swum. Then one day we walked around the boating pond, and I swear he took a look and then just soared.' She made a motion with her arm. 'He actually soared through the air and landed straight in the middle of the boating pond.'

Eli looked at her. 'I take it he swam?'

'Oh, no.' Aurora shook her head. 'He sank like a stone.'

'But all Labradors can swim.'

'No one told Max that.'

Eli started to laugh. 'What did you do?'

'What do you think I did? I jumped in to save him. Pulled him up, and my boy, he hadn't jumped in at the edge of the boating pond where there were reeds and sand. No, he'd jumped in at the end where there was a concrete wall. I had to push him up over it, then try and haul myself up.'

Eli started to laugh. 'That must have been fun.'

She gave him a hard stare. 'I was like a giant squid. It's safe to say it was not the most elegant moment of my life.'

Eli couldn't stop laughing and Hank looked up in surprise. 'Don't worry, little guy,' he said. 'You look like you can definitely swim.'

They both watched Hank, who seemed to like the water and didn't seem fazed by it at all. Aurora gave him a kiss on the head. 'Who's a good boy then?'

They stayed in the pool for another ten minutes, making sure Hank was fine, before moving over to one of the standalone set-ups that had an underwater treadmill. One of the treatment centre staff came over and set things up for them, following the plan that had been laid out to strengthen Hank's muscles and improve his range of movement.

Once the tank was full, the treadmill started gently and he walked along with a bewildered expression on his face, licking the dog peanut butter at the front of the tank that was there to keep him focused.

'We'll never get out of here.' Eli smiled. 'If

peanut butter is the standard treat, he'll never want to leave.'

'As long as his leg gets better, that's fine,' said Aurora. She was looking around at all the facilities available. 'I've never been in this place before. It's such a great set-up.'

Eli nodded in agreement. 'I've referred clients to similar places before, but I'm glad we've had the chance to come along and try this out for ourselves.'

They spent the next half hour in the treatment centre, then took turns getting changed, dried Hank off, then moved outside to the attached coffee shop.

Hank was happy to lie at their feet while they sipped their coffee.

'Matt's looking a bit better,' said Aurora. 'He had some more colour yesterday when I dropped off some things for Marianne.'

'He messaged me,' said Eli. 'Said he felt as though the treatment might actually help him rather than kill him now.'

'Chemo is just horrid,' said Aurora. 'I've a few friends that have gone through it. Things are always better when they come out the other side.'

'He has another few rounds still to go.'

'I know. Is there anything else we can do to help them?'

Eli looked at her. He took a breath and reached

out and took her hand. 'And that's what I love about you.'

She blinked. 'What?'

'That you think about other people. And you genuinely mean it. You thought about them right from the beginning, to get Marianne's shopping, and both of them dinner.'

Aurora gave a little shrug. 'Don't think I don't know about you helping them set up new smoke alarms the other day.'

He shrugged too. 'But you know how big a part they played in my life when I was a boy. You've only worked at the practice for the last eighteen months.'

She gave a smile. 'But that doesn't matter. When you meet people—inherently good people—you just know it. And the length of time you know them doesn't come into it. What's important is that you know if you needed help they would give it. And it's why you're happy to step up and do things for them.' She gave a smile. 'Anne bakes for them every week. I don't have that skill set, so I'm happy to do other things.'

Her mind flashed back to first meeting Matt. She smiled. 'You know, when I came for my interview, they were both in the middle of an emergency surgery. I offered to scrub in and help.'

'You did?' Eli's eyes widened. 'Matt never told me that.'

Her brain was currently spinning. He'd used the word *love* a few moments ago, and her heart rate had instantly started racing. A few nights ago, he'd told her he'd stay at least a year, and would ask her to go with him if he left. All the barriers that had been in place in her head were now simply falling away.

Was Eli Ferguson going to be the guy she could take a chance on, and hope for a happy ever after?

Her brain flashed to the interview with Matt afterwards, when she'd told him about her past career, and he hadn't been judgemental at all. He'd actually just wanted to know about the animals and her experience. Maybe Eli would be exactly the same.

She opened her mouth to tell him just as Hank decided to wake up and nudge her leg.

'Oh—' Eli smiled '—that's the toilet training nudge. We'd better go outside.'

She nodded and smiled too. It could wait. It wasn't urgent. It had waited this long after all.

And as they strode out into the Scottish sunshine he slipped his hand into hers and a warm glow flowed through her. Perfect—everything was just perfect.

CHAPTER ELEVEN

IT WAS BUSY. He had to go to Don Fletcher's farm today, as some of the cattle were going to be destroyed and he knew that Don was upset. Public health had also decided to screen the other farm workers who weren't currently displaying any symptoms as a precautionary measure, and Don was upset about that too, thinking he'd put his workers at risk.

Eli checked on Bert and Hank. Bert was running up and down the run, and Hank was nestled in some bedding, catching a little sun. Hank was healing slowly, but well. He was eating and drinking and gradually gaining a bit of weight—his muscles a little stronger every day.

He waved to Aurora, who was on the phone to someone, to let her know he was going, and grabbed the mail on the way out. Matt had warned him the practice insurance was due to be renewed and he wanted to keep on top of it.

As he reached the farm his four-by-four slid a little on a slight build-up of mud. It was a typical Scottish summer with occasional flashes of monsoon type rain. As his car drew to a halt, the mail landed in the footwell.

He groaned and leaned over to pick it up, noticing for the first time that one of the letters was in fact a credit card statement. He frowned, not remembering using the credit card, and tore it open. The total amount made him stop. Four thousand pounds? What? He scanned quickly, not really recognising the names of any of the places where money had been spent.

His mind jammed with a million thoughts—all of them panicking, none of them good. He glanced at the farm, knowing he had a job to do.

This would have to wait.

No matter how much he didn't want it to.

Aurora hadn't gone to the farm today. She was catching up on filing some notes and going through the plans for the updates, making sure she had ordered everything she needed. Two of the deliveries were arriving today and she wanted to make sure she was here to receive them—living out in the middle of nowhere meant having a failed delivery was always an issue.

The practice officially had shorter hours today, with the afternoon off for staff training. But Anne had gone out to see Jack Sannox and

Rudy this afternoon, and Aurora was still keeping an eye on Hank.

The front door jangled, meaning someone had opened it. Her delivery? Maybe. She walked through to find the owner of Arthur standing in the hallway.

'I'm sorry. We don't have any appointments this afternoon. Is something wrong with Arthur?' She looked around him, expecting to see his partner walking up the steps behind him. But they were empty.

And so was the practice. She was alone right now, with the exception of Hank and Bert, and a small rabbit in the back who was recovering from surgery.

Her spider-sense didn't tingle, it yelled.

The man gave her a strange smile. 'Yes, I just need you to go over some of the principles of diabetes again. We're struggling with Arthur.'

'Didn't our vet say we were oversubscribed right now? Didn't you manage to find another vet?'

She was trying her best not to panic.

'We couldn't find another vet locally. Our cat is sick. He needs treatment. He's very lethargic.'

Now, that could be truthful and could happen with newly diagnosed animals.

She gave a small smile, a good vet nurse wouldn't turn a sick pet away. 'I thought you said your gran was diabetic, and you understood things?'

Was that cheeky? Maybe.

'I understand the injections, but that's about all.' There was something about his facial expression, as if it was fixed in place and he was playing a part.

'Would you like to make an appointment to come back and see the vet?'

'He isn't here?' It was a pleasant enough question, but it made Aurora feel as if a million caterpillars were currently trampling over her skin.

'He's out back,' she said automatically.

'I didn't see his car.' The man kept smiling. What was his name again—Fraser?

'He has a lot of cars. His father was a collector.'

There was a long silence as the man kept looking at Aurora. His eyes swept up and down her body, making her feel even more uncomfortable, then fixed on her face.

'I can give you some reading material about diabetes in cats. It's probably best you start there.'

She moved to the computer at the reception desk, searched in the files and started printing things off.

'I think I'd prefer a chat,' he said smoothly. 'I have lots of questions.'

Aurora might not have been in any bad movies, but she'd seen her fair share. This was like one of those, where the creepy guy cornered the heroine.

This was not happening to her. She'd taken self-defence classes a number of years ago, on the recommendation of the policewoman in charge of her stalking case. But right now, all those moves seemed to have vanished from her brain.

'I'll start,' he said easily. He moved his hand and clamped it on top of hers, which was on the reception desk. 'Like, why did you change your name?'

Every cell in her body screamed. Her instincts were telling her to pull her hand away and get out of there. But she actually froze. It was as if something icy chilled her entire body and stopped her from moving.

'I mean, Aurora is nice too. But it's not like Star. And what about the TV series? Nothing has been good since you left. The ratings have tanked. You have to go back. I've even thought up a whole scenario for your character, Tara, so she can get back in the thick of things. And don't you think it's time Tara was the main character, instead of a supporting one?'

Her mouth was dry. She could barely speak.

'I want you to leave,' she said. The words came out strangely. Not like her voice at all.

'That's not very friendly.' He didn't even blink an eye.

Everything she'd hoped for. Everything she'd thought she could finally have. And he was here. Spoiling it.

'Your name isn't Fraser, is it?'

He smiled, pleased to have some recognition. 'Anyone can change their name after a few years. I like Fraser. I think it suits me.'

'You are supposed to stay away from me. There's a restraining order against you.'

He shrugged. 'Different country, different laws.'

'I'm done asking, now I'm telling you to leave.' Her voice had got just as icy as her body felt. But she was angry. She was angry at him for invading her private life and ruining her chance of happiness. She'd run away from this guy once. Now she'd have to run away again. Leave the job that she loved. The home that she was happy in. And the man that she'd told herself it was safe to love now.

He looked around. 'But Star, we've finally got a chance to chat. Let's take it.' He went to move around behind the reception desk, and she reached out and grabbed what was nearest. That was the thing about working in a vet practice—

constant cleaning—and the nearest thing was a mop and bucket.

She swung around with the wet mop and directly hit him in the face with it, grabbing the length of the broom like a weapon across her chest and pushing him square in the chest. He was already staggering backwards, caught off-guard by her movement, as Eli came rushing through the door.

'What the...?' he said as he took one look at the situation and put a foot on the guy's chest to keep him on the floor.

She'd never been so glad to see him.

'Eli, this is Brandon Rivers. He was convicted of stalking me a number of years ago and has decided to come and pay me a visit, even though there is a restraining order against him.'

Eli looked down at the floor. He squinted. 'I thought this guy's name was Fraser.'

'Apparently he's changed it.'

'You didn't recognise him?'

'We never came face to face in the past. And I was protected from seeing him in court. This is the first time we've met in the flesh.'

Eli reached down and grabbed the guy by the scruff of the neck. 'Call the police,' he said.

Brandon turned his head and started yelling at Aurora. 'But Star, you've got to come back to the *Into the Wild* series! They need you. We need you. Tara needs to be reunited with Owen!'

Eli looked completely bewildered as Aurora called the police. She explained the situation in a few short sentences, and they promised to send someone immediately.

Eli had taken Brandon into another room and closed the door, so he couldn't see or shout at Aurora. She had no idea what was being said in there. But even though Eli was here, she still didn't feel safe with Brandon in the same building as her.

Had he followed her home some time? Was that how he knew her address?

It was all so overwhelming, but she was determined not to crumple. Not to sink into the corner like she really wanted to and cry her heart out.

The beautiful life that she'd made for herself was over.

Eli's head was on a perpetual spin cycle. He'd been mad driving back to the vet practice. Mad about the amount of money put on the practice credit cards, which he wasn't entirely sure had been discussed and agreed.

For all he knew, she could have added a million personal things into the purchases and he wouldn't be unable to unpick it. This wasn't how a successful business was run, and he knew that better than anyone.

But when he'd walked in the door to see Aurora fighting off some man, all thoughts had gone out of the window. His instinct to keep her safe had gone into overdrive. Now, he was stuck in a room with a man who didn't seem rational or reasonable, who kept calling Aurora by another name, and she said she already had a restraining order against him. Was this the man who had sexually assaulted her?

It was all he could do to keep his hands to himself. Brandon had made a few shouts about wrongful imprisonment, but Eli couldn't care less. He'd attacked a member of the practice, apparently had history for it, and the police had been phoned.

They could sort it out, and take this piece of trash with them when they did.

He desperately wanted to go into the other room to check Aurora was okay. But that wouldn't be wise right now. He could tell from the look on her face that she wanted to be as far away as possible from Brandon or Fraser, or whatever this guy's name was. Who changed their name?

There was a sharp knock at the door, and a uniformed officer walked in, assessing the situation. 'We can take this from here, sir,' he said to

Eli. 'My colleague outside would like to speak to you.'

The rest of the afternoon passed in a daze. There were conversations about Scottish and English law. A large purple bruise had started to appear on Aurora's hand. She'd been looked after by a female police officer, who'd been sympathetic and ruthlessly efficient. Both he and Aurora had been asked to go to the police station the next day to make formal statements, but for now Brandon Rivers was taken away in the back of a police van.

Eli ran his fingers through his hair as he walked back through to the practice kitchen, where Aurora was sitting, a cup of tea—which looked cold—between her hands.

'Want to tell me what just happened in here?' he asked.

She sat very quietly for a moment.

'Do you at least want to tell me what your real name is?'

He could see the hurt in her eyes. But he had to know the truth. The woman he loved hadn't been truthful with him. In more ways than one. He just couldn't believe he was in a situation like this again.

'My real name,' she said, her jaw tight, 'is Aurora Hendricks.' She was glaring at him now. 'My acting name was Star Kingfisher. I was in a show about vets, ironically. It was called *Into the Wild* and filmed in South Africa.'

As she said the words his mouth fell open. Pieces of the jigsaw puzzle were falling into place. He didn't watch many TV dramas but he had seen snippets of the show—mainly to see them dealing with lions, tigers and giraffes.

'That's why you looked familiar,' he said, not quite believing this.

She kept talking. 'It was the show I was sexually assaulted on, by one of the grips. I left shortly after, but as soon as I came back to England I started to be stalked. It happened over the course of a few months. The police became involved as they uncovered a kidnapping plot, and Brandon Rivers was arrested, convicted and jailed. Part of his bail conditions were that he knew I had a restraining order against him. In the meantime, I wanted a new career. I retrained as a vet nurse and haven't looked back. At least not until today.'

Her voice was quite flat. It was almost as if she was scared to let any emotion out because she was trying to hold things together.

'Are you okay?' he ventured. He had to ask—no matter what else was going on in his head—because it was the right thing to do.

'I don't think I'll ever be okay again,' she said simply. 'I thought I'd put all this behind me. I thought I could forget about it all. But it seems like I'm never going to shake him off.'

Eli sat very still. He had questions. He had multiple questions. Most of all he felt betrayed by the fact she hadn't trusted him enough to tell him who she was. This was the woman he loved. This was the woman he'd planned to spend the next year with—and maybe even more. But after his previous experience, trust was everything to him. How could he even imagine a life for them without it?

'Why didn't you tell me who you were?'

'What did it matter?' she shot back angrily.

'Because trust matters to me. A lot.' He left it there and she sighed, running her hand through her hair.

'You don't get it. At university, some people recognised me from the outset. They treated me as if I was stupid, not clever enough to pass the exams, and they certainly didn't take me seriously. As time went on, I managed to shake off Star—partly because I went back to my natural hair colour. I found out that if someone realised later I'd been on the 'vet TV show' as everyone called it, their opinion of me seemed to fall. It's a thing about being an actress. For reasons that are totally invalid, people seem to think an actress can't be serious about having another career.'

Eli let his head hang down as he tried to take

all this in. He understood that Aurora had been targeted and attacked today. That had to be terrifying. What he wanted to do was give her a big hug and tell her that everything would be okay. But for reasons he couldn't quite explain, the vibe between them had changed.

He took a breath. 'Can I ask you something else?'

'What?'

'The accounts. The credit cards. I got a bill today I wasn't expecting.'

She screwed up her face. 'Wh…what?' It was as if the question had totally thrown her.

'It's thousands. I wasn't sure what had happened.'

She shook her head. 'What's happened is the plans you looked at, and agreed to—the plans that I billed out for you, I've ordered all the supplies. The paint. The new sink. The plumbing. The worktops. The facing. The supplies. It all arrives in the next few days then we can sit down and plan where to start.' Her voice had become quieter as she continued. 'Or at least I thought we would.'

Eli blinked. 'I looked at the plans. I showed them to Matt and told you he liked them. But I hadn't okayed them yet.'

'You had.' She was clearly annoyed now.

He shook his head. 'I wanted his overall approval before starting the work. Then my plan was to get into the details specifically. It wasn't a signal to go ahead.'

The furrow in her brow increased. 'But it was. I have receipts for everything I've ordered. The lists were detailed already. I haven't gone away from them.'

'But you used the practice credit card without talking to me first.' He was trying not to sound angry. He was trying to keep it locked down inside.

'But I thought you'd said yes. I thought you'd know.'

He took a long slow breath as he watched the last part of the life he'd thought he was getting finally crumble around him.

'My last practice went bankrupt. It went bankrupt because the practice manager—who I was dating—ran up tens of thousands of debt, and also took out loans against the practice. I had no idea she was doing it. And I found out too late to save the practice.'

There. He'd said the words out loud.

'But… I haven't done anything like that,' Aurora said. 'I've ordered supplies to update the practice. There's no loan.'

He closed his eyes. So much was whirling around inside his head. He wanted to find the right words. But for now, he actually didn't know what they were.

'This is why trust is essential to me, Aurora.'

She stared back at him. 'What I left out was minor. A small part of my past. I told you about the sexual assault.'

'You think someone being jailed for stalking you is minor?' he asked incredulously.

'No, of course I don't!' she shouted back. 'But you can't judge me, you can't judge us, on your past relationship. A relationship that *you* kept hidden. I'm not her—whoever she is.' She took a breath, and then added, 'And having a practice that went bankrupt? That's a big deal, Eli. That's something you should have been honest about. You know the arrangements here are simple. Anne or I do the wages, send things to the accountant. If you'd said there had been issues in the past, and you wanted to oversee that stuff yourself, we would have understood. At the very least, I could have copied you into every email that was sent so you had a record.' Her voice was shaking, along with her whole body. 'It seems we've both not managed to be entirely truthful with each other.'

There was silence. They both stared at each other, then Aurora stood, the chair scraping on the floor behind her.

'I can't stay anyway. Now that he's found me.

I'll never have peace. I can't be here any more. I have to start over.' Her voice still trembled. 'I thought I'd found something here. Something that gave me a chance of a whole new world.'

He couldn't help but speak too. 'I thought I'd found something too. But trust is the most important thing to me, Aurora. I'll always wonder if there's something else you haven't told me. I don't want to doubt you. I don't want to doubt this relationship. But when you've been in the position that I have, this makes things almost impossible.'

He should stop her. He should try and convince her to stay. But right now, he just couldn't. His brain was still telling him to stop and think. He had to take time to discover how he felt about all this. If he could ever trust her again.

She reached the door and stopped, her hand on the doorframe. 'I'm sorry, Eli,' she said.

He looked at her. 'I'm sorry too.'

It was true. He was. For this. For her. For them. And for this whole situation that neither of them had asked for, or wanted.

And then he let her walk away.

CHAPTER TWELVE

AURORA STARED AROUND her house. She loved this place. She'd made her mark on it. Decorated with plain staples with lots of splashes of colour. She loved her garden. The neighbours. Even the drive to work.

And now? Because Brandon Rivers had this address she would never feel safe again.

But that wasn't the thing that was making her sick to her stomach. Not at all.

It had been the expression on Eli Ferguson's face when he'd been asking her questions. He hadn't cared about her past life as an actress. That hadn't made him think any less of her at all—her fears had been completely unfounded.

But the simple fact that she hadn't told him had been her undoing.

She'd always known there were more layers to Eli. She'd thought—a bit like herself—they had time to strip them back, bit by bit, at a pace they'd both be comfortable with.

She hadn't expected everything to come crashing down around them.

But then the money questions. She'd spent last night tossing and turning, trying to remember the exact conversations. She'd honestly thought the conversation on the bus had been the signal to go forward. But the more and more she took things apart, she realised that she might have got things wrong.

She was horrified when Eli had revealed what had happened to him in the past. But she was even more hurt by the fact he had obviously considered that it might be happening again.

Aurora had always been meticulous about money. It was why she'd been able to buy herself a house outright, when some of her previous co-stars had spent thousands on designer clothes and pricey wines.

The very fact he might have thought… It just made her cry even harder.

She tried to be reasonable. She tried to remember that he felt as though she'd broken his trust. And then he'd found a credit card bill, with items he felt he hadn't authorised.

She'd blown it. She'd blown everything. The best thing she could do right now was get her house on the market and try and find another job.

And while it was easy to consider the job, and

acknowledge the mistake she might have made there, what wasn't easy was the ache in her heart. Eli Ferguson's face would appear in her head for a long, long time. She loved him. She hadn't told him but she did. He was the first man in a long time she'd had faith in, and she'd thought he would keep her heart safe. She'd even started to imagine a future together, no matter where that might be.

She brushed the tears from her face and stood up, looking around her house and realising she would have to get it ready to start viewings.

It didn't matter how painful it was. It was time to move on.

It had been a long night. Matt had been rushed into hospital with sepsis due to an infection in his central line, and Marianne had made a call to Eli.

But things had turned during the night. He'd started to respond to the antibiotics, and his heart rate and breathing had settled back down. Eli had taken Marianne home, made her tea and toast and sent her to bed. It was easy to see exactly how much of a strain this was all putting on her.

He went back to the hospital to check on Matt again and was pleased when the consultant arrived at the same time as he did. The consultant stayed for a while, talking about the fact that the central line had been the route of the infection, and suggesting its removal and another method of delivering the chemo. He'd clearly got the impression that Eli was Matt's son, and neither of them stopped to correct him.

Once he left, Eli sat down and took Matt's hand.

'You should know,' said Matt, 'that I named you as my other next of kin. In case it all got a bit much for Marianne.'

Eli squeezed his hand. 'I'm honoured to be named as your next of kin, and I promise to keep an eye on Marianne.'

Matt leaned back against his pillows. 'You look terrible.'

Eli laughed. 'Thanks. Someone kept me up all night.'

But Matt shook his head. 'It's not that. What is it?'

Eli sighed. There was no point in lying, and if he didn't tell Matt the truth he would then just worry about what might be wrong. So, as succinctly as possible, he told him the truth.

Matt gave him a soft smile. 'It's just a mix-up. A misunderstanding. You're adults. You can talk about that. And hurry up and give the place a facelift. Just be glad Marianne wasn't in charge, she would likely have spent five times as much.'

Eli opened his mouth to object but Matt held up one hand. 'I get to do the talking today.' His face was serious. 'Tell me honestly—how have you felt about being back at the practice?'

Eli took a few seconds to answer. He put his hand on his heart. 'I've enjoyed it in a way I never thought I was capable of.'

Matt smiled, and that meant more to Eli than anything. 'And what's helped you enjoy it?'

Eli threw up his hands and sat back in his chair. There was no point in answering. They both knew the answer.

'Then you have to fight for it.'

Eli shook his head. 'I can't. She wants to leave. She needs to move to get away from this guy.'

'Then find a reason to make her stay. Get a lawyer. I'll give you my friend's number. He's a criminal lawyer and he'll be able to help her. Find a way to keep the woman you love safe, Eli. Because there's nothing else so important.'

His skin prickled. 'I never told you I love her.'

'You didn't have to. I could see it.'

Matt took his hand again. 'Don't make your life just about work, Eli. That's how you'll end up. There's more of your father in you than you like to think. Reach out and fight for the person you love.' He smiled wryly. 'I don't even have to tell you this. You already know. Aurora is a gorgeous girl. Full of fire. Just what you need.'

He lay back against the pillows, clearly pleased with himself.

He waved a hand. 'Now, hurry up. And be sure to tell Marianne I told you off. She likes to be good cop; I'm supposed to be bad.'

Eli stood up and smiled, kissing Matt on the side of the face. 'You'll never be bad cop,' he said.

CHAPTER THIRTEEN

HIS HEART SANK like a stone when he saw the estate agent board in the garden. She'd been serious. She was leaving.

He sat outside the cottage for a few moments, telling himself to stop planning everything. He'd spent all of the drive over thinking of all the ways he could say he was sorry, and ask her to stay.

He had the number for Matt's solicitor and had stopped to pick up a few other things before he'd got here. But he wasn't sure that any of them would work.

She opened the door on the second knock, and he blinked. Her normally immaculate hair was tousled and she had her pyjamas on.

She sighed. 'What do you want, Eli?'

'To talk to you.'

'I'm not sure there's anything left to say.'

'Can I come in?'

'Are you a viewer? Are you offering to buy my cottage?' Her words were sharp.

She licked her lips and paused for a second,

so he took a chance and pointed to the car. 'And can I bring our boys in?'

Her bottom lip quivered. 'Hurry up,' she said, before turning and walking back inside.

He collected Hank and Bert from the car, putting them on their leashes, but carrying Hank instead of letting him walk.

When he went inside the house and closed the door, he could see Aurora through the patio doors that led out to the sheltered garden. Toilet training was still a work in progress for the puppies and she knew that. He walked through towards her, and she held out her hands for Hank. He nestled in her lap while she patted him and looked him over.

'I've missed you,' she whispered to him, as Eli let Bert off the leash to run around the garden while he settled in the chair next to her.

'I've missed you,' he said.

She looked at him. He handed her the phone number. 'Matt asked me to give you the name of his friend, a criminal lawyer who will help you.'

She reached out and took the paper. He could actually sense a little relief from her. 'Thank Matt for me.'

He nodded. 'He also told me off.'

'He did?'

'Said our argument was a misunderstanding. And he's right.'

'The money part?'

He nodded.

'I've gone over and over that in my head. I honestly thought you'd told me to go ahead.' She shook her head. 'But that's not the part that bothers me. It's the fact you thought I could be like your ex.'

He winced because he knew she was entirely right. He put his hands up. 'You're right, and the truth is I know you're nothing like my ex. But the experience jaded me so much that I had trouble seeing past it. I was duped. And I have felt such a fool ever since. For the last year I've had trouble with any new friendship because I always wonder if someone's aim is to con me.'

Aurora looked at him with pity. 'That's no way to live a life. You were unlucky.'

He looked her in the eye. 'But me being unlucky affects the life I can lead for the next few years. I can't take over the practice, I can't be a partner. I can only be an employee.'

'And why's that bad?'

'It's not. But being bankrupt is a stain that will hang over my head for years. I won't be able to get a mortgage in the next few years.'

'I don't need a mortgage. I own this place outright,' she said easily.

'I'm just trying to be honest with you,' he admitted as Bert came up and nuzzled at his knee.

'Not only am I a crap boyfriend, I'm also not a very good catch.'

There was the hint of a smile around her lips. 'You're not the only one who let the past affect them.'

His gaze met hers. She took a deep breath. 'I hated that when I told vet colleagues in the past about being an actress—or even if they found out on their own—they just seemed to think less of me. I hated that. I was serious about my job, and didn't want every question about when I was going back to South Africa.' She shook her head. 'Then there was the other stuff. I guess I was trying to forget all about it, to distance myself from it. It was reported in the press at the time, but two weeks later it was all forgotten about.'

She leaned her head on her hand. 'Except by me.' She looked truly sad. 'When the police told me about the kidnap threat I was terrified. You have no idea the thoughts that went through my brain.' She gave him a sad smile and shrugged. 'I'm an actress. I have a vivid imagination.'

'I can't imagine,' he said, a wave of sympathy flooding over him. She must have been terrified. How on earth could he even understand that?

'So when he appeared again...' She swallowed, and he could sense she was struggling. 'I felt like a fool—because I'd never seen him in person, and then he'd already been in the practice, and was that deliberate or am I just the unluckiest person in the world that he turned up where I was working?' A tear slid down her cheek, and he reached over and took her hand.

'If you hadn't appeared...' She shook her head. 'I don't know what I would have done.'

'Aurora Hendricks, you were doing a *spectacular* job,' he said. 'You were like some kind of kung fu fighter. I don't think the guy knew what had hit him.'

'It was pure adrenaline,' she admitted. 'I vomited later, and slept for hours.'

'Well, I'm glad I did appear. You don't deserve that. No one should treat you like that. You deserve, and are entitled, to feel safe.'

She sagged a bit further into her chair. 'But where does that leave me?'

'It leaves you with a sorry excuse of a boyfriend who made a mess of things, but loves you very much and wants you to stay.'

Her bottom lip started to tremble again.

'I will do anything I can to keep you safe.'

'But you don't want to stay,' she said in a cracking voice.

'What I want is to be where you want to be,' he said without a moment's hesitation. He leaned towards her. 'I started to love this place again,' he admitted. 'But a big part of that was you. If you want to stay then I want to stay. If you want to start afresh somewhere else then I'm happy to do that with you.'

'But you would be leaving behind your father's practice.'

'And I'd find a way to make my peace with that. My priority is you.' There was a nip at his ankle and he bent down and picked up Bert, who licked his cheek.

'I am the man who was so shameless that he brought our children with him to help him plead his case. That's how desperate I was.'

Aurora looked down to where Hank was still on her lap. She kept stroking him. 'If I honestly can't feel safe once I've spoken to the lawyer, you'd be willing to move somewhere else with me?'

'Absolutely. I love you, Aurora. Your happiness is what counts.'

'What about our boys?'

'If we need to get them passports, we can.'

She smiled. 'I love you too. And if can, I want to stay. I love working here. I love the community. I love the job.'

He moved in front of her, kneeling and resting his forehead against hers. 'It's you, me and our boys against the world. How does that feel?'

'That feels like for ever,' she said as her lips brushed against his, and he kissed her and didn't let go.

EPILOGUE

THE GUESTS LET out gasps of surprise and gave a round of applause as Hank and Bert trotted proudly down the aisle towards the groom. If dogs could smile, they were currently smiling.

'I can't believe you trust your dogs better than me with those rings,' Eli's childhood friend and best man whispered in his ear.

Eli kept his gaze on his dogs as he spoke out of the corner of his mouth. 'You lost your front door keys seven times in school. How many times have you had to replace your driving licence? And tell me right now where your car keys are.'

John looked momentarily panicked then shrugged his shoulders as he gave a casual smile. 'Oh, go on then, trust the dogs.'

Eli bent down to pat each of his beloved dogs on the head as they arrived at the top of the aisle, each with a bow around their neck, with a ring attached.

They looked very pleased with themselves, and sat eagerly at Eli's feet, waiting for treats.

The music changed and Eli stood up, watching as his bride emerged at the bottom of the aisle. Her dark red hair was pinned at the sides but cascaded down her shoulders. He took a breath, trying to remember to keep going as Aurora moved down the aisle towards him, her father beaming proudly.

Her dress was stunning. Cream, and off the shoulder—Bardot-style was what she'd told him—with a fitted waist and stunning satin figure-hugging skirt. Although she wore a veil, it didn't cover her face, but instead framed it, letting him know just how lucky he was.

But he already knew that.

Their wedding was a little unconventional. All pets had been invited to the outside ceremony. The Scottish weather was behaving today and blessing the guests with some bright sunshine. Jack Sannox was there with his new rescue dog that Aurora and Eli had found for him. After the sad loss of Rudy, they'd kept a careful eye on him for a number of months, and when a mixed breed rescue had been dropped at the practice it hadn't taken them long to know where to match her. Isla was on her best behaviour, sitting next to her owner.

Matt and Marianne were guests of honour in

the front seats. Aurora and Eli considered them family. One year on, Matt was on the road to recovery, and was back working two days a week in the practice. Their newly qualified vet, Cheryl, had shaped up better than anyone could have hoped for, and she and her family loved their move to Scotland.

The Liverpudlian half of the outside ceremony seemed to be in competition around who could wear the most spectacular hat. Aurora's mother was winning, her bright pink and navy hat obscuring some people's view of the ceremony.

Eli met the green gaze of his soon-to-be wife and mouthed one word. *Gorgeous.* Her face lit up. She glowed. He'd heard people say those words about brides before, but now he could see it with his own eyes.

As she moved alongside him he slid his arm around her waist and kissed her cheek. He just couldn't help it. They'd been through so much this year. The court case had taken its toll. Aurora had continued her counselling, and Eli had joined her when appropriate.

Even though Brandon Rivers had been convicted again, and given a much sterner sentence, there was still a sense of disquiet around them. It had led them to their latest decision to return to one of Eli's previous roles with the horses in Jerez in Spain for the next year. Hank and Bert were ready to go with them. They all needed a break—a chance for some space to let Aurora heal fully, and for their relationship to blossom into the beautiful marriage it was about to become. It was likely they would return to Scotland the following year to take over from Matt when he would finally retire.

The ceremony started and, as planned, at one point Aurora bent to pull the satin ribbon around Bert's neck that held Eli's ring, and he did the same move with Hank, to reveal her ring.

She'd never looked so bright. She'd never looked so radiant.

And as they said their vows and slipped on each other's rings Eli knew he was the luckiest man on earth.

He pulled her close to him for their kiss. 'Love you, Mrs Ferguson,' he whispered as his lips touched hers.

She wrapped her hands around his neck. 'Love you, Mr Ferguson,' she responded. Then, with a glint in her eye, she leaned back.

'I might have some news to share.'

His eyebrows raised. 'You've adopted another puppy?'

She beamed as she whispered in his ear. 'Not another puppy. But let's just say our family of four is expanding.'

Eli picked up his bride and whirled her around

as his puppies barked in excitement and the wedding guests applauded.

And it truly was a perfect day.

* * * * *

MEDICAL

Life and love in the world
of modern medicine.